Praise for *Pretty Face*

"Lucy Parker's dialogue is top-notch, and the London theatre world is still a terrific place to set contemporary romance. So many of the things I loved in *Act Like It* are present in this novel—the dramatic (literally) world they live in, the challenges of managing their public lives and private lives, and the crackling sharp dialogue."
—*Smart Bitches Trashy Books*

"*Pretty Face* hooked me from the start and did not let go. It was a pleasure to wallow in the pages and it was exactly the escape from the real world I needed."
—*Dear Author*

"*Pretty Face* is a terrific read and one I'm recommending wholeheartedly. Along with the funny, the romantic and the sexy, the author also makes some great points about sexism and celebrity culture, and writes moments of true poignancy that will have you reaching for the Kleenex. *Act Like It* put Lucy Parker on my auto-read list; *Pretty Face* has put her damn near the top of it, and I'm eager for more."
—*All About Romance*

"When you find yourself laughing out loud, wiping away tears, and rereading passages you just read, you know that you've found a real gem among a sea of contemporary romances. [Y]ou'll be left with a smile on your face and wanting to read more about this world the author has created—a testament to her skill in crafting a romance worthy of a standing ovation."
—*Harlequin Junkie*

Also available from Lucy Parker and Carina Press

Act Like It

Also watch for the next book in the London Celebrities series, coming soon from Carina Press!

pretty
face

LUCY PARKER

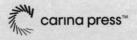

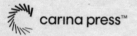

ISBN-13: 978-1-335-01326-2

Pretty Face

Recycling programs
for this product may
not exist in your area.

This edition published by arrangement with Harlequin Books S.A.

® and TM are trademarks of the publisher. Trademarks indicated with
® are registered in the United States Patent and Trademark Office, the
Canadian Intellectual Property Office and in other countries.

www.CarinaPress.com

Printed in U.S.A.

In memory of Pat, George and Ray,
my grandparents. Still missed. Always loved.

pretty
face

Chapter One

Excerpt from *London Celebrity*:

Final Curtain Call for London's Golden Couple

Two months after she called time on her relationship with director Luc Savage, Margo Roy has eloped with Italian tenor Alberto Ferreti. No details have been released as to where the happy event took place, but the couple are believed to be honeymooning in Capri.

Meanwhile, it's rumoured that everyone's least favourite TV flapper, *Knightsbridge* star Lily Lamprey, is considering swapping cocktails, sequins and seduction for a role in Savage's opening run at the Queen Anne Theatre. His usual line-up draws heavily on veterans of the Royal Shakespeare Company, so it would be a shot-in-the-dark casting, but Lamprey obviously has hidden depths—or perhaps talents of a more obvious variety…

At the time of their split, both Roy and Savage claimed no third-party involvement. We'll take their word for it.

It was the last straw when she seduced the vicar.

In the space of nine painful minutes, the asthmatic

blonde had stolen a cheap reproduction of a Gainsborough, mistakenly spiked a martini with arsenic instead of a sedative, and accidentally ploughed a Hispano-Suiza into a Cabinet Minister. In between acts of homicidal lunacy, she fluttered improbably black eyelashes and danced an enthusiastic Charleston.

Luc wasn't surprised she was continually short of breath. He was pretty bloody speechless himself. He froze the clip on an artistic shot of a suspender belt catapulting towards a crumpled, abandoned cassock, and didn't waste words. "No fucking way."

His stage manager tore his gaze from the screen with obvious disappointment. "Not *exactly* what I was expecting," David Benton admitted. "*Knightsbridge* seems to pull a decent cast, in general. My wife's obsessed with the show. Never misses an episode." He wiggled his eyebrows. "Might do my husbandly duty and keep her company on the couch now. I've obviously been missing out." With a return to seriousness, he added, "Although, as much as I appreciate the young lady's dexterity with feathers, I really don't think…"

No. Neither did Luc. And nor would any paying punter with functional ears and a brain working somewhere above the trouser line.

It had taken two months and an extortionate increase in salary to coax Amelia Lee away from the casting department of the Majestic and onto his own staff. If Luc had realised she was in the midst of some sort of psychiatric episode, he would have added a few weeks' holiday to the incentive package.

Seeing his expression, Amelia put down her coffee mug. "I'm assuming you haven't actually watched the audition reel I forwarded. Three days ago." She looked dismissively at the large screen where he'd cut short the debauchery of the dog collar. "Obviously you can't make a judgement on the basis of that performance. The script is pants. And that character is a generic, two-dimensional male fantasy. Bat your lashes, girls, hitch up your skirts, get your tits out and the ratings up. Meryl Streep would be stuck paddling in the shallows, given that material to work with."

Luc glanced down at the headshot he held. In static black-and-white, the blonde's face was cast into clever shadows that carved out a few interesting hollows and angles, rescuing the end result from vacuous beauty. Her eyes were dark, and this time appeared to contain at least one thought. He turned it over, looking for the photographer's credit. He or she might be worth culti- vating, if they could coax that from what he'd seen on the screen.

Then he tossed the image onto a growing pile of unsatisfactory faces. "I believe the whole point of—" he checked her résumé without much interest "—Lily Lamprey's inclusion as a possible was her role on *Knightsbridge*. What was your helpful contribution, Eric?" He didn't wait for a reply from his marketing manager, who had reached out to rescue Lily from the slush pile and was staring fatuously at her photograph. "Hottest show on TV? She might attract the younger demographic?" He flicked the headshot out of Eric's hand. "I see we can add the middle-aged, overworked and easily impressed to the list."

"Says the man who keeps clutching her photo." Ame- lia grinned at him. He'd known her for fifteen years and he could see the gibe coming before it left her mouth. "You might be middle-aged and overworked, but I'd never have called you easily impressed. If I'd realised you were that susceptible, I'd have sent you Lily's latest magazine spread and considered the matter settled."

Nothing like working with friends. Everyone appreciated a hint that the Grim Reaper was breathing down their neck the moment they turned forty.

"Remind me again why I wanted you on board."

"My wit? My charm? My compromising photos of you from *The Importance of Being Earnest* opening night gala?"

Luc shook his head, reluctantly and only slightly amused. A headache was beginning to form behind his left eye, although his vision was clear so hopefully it wouldn't turn into a migraine. He'd been woken at six o'clock by a call from his contractor, cheerfully informing him that the delivery of Italian tiles for the theatre foyer was short by about three hundred, which followed the cue of everything else that had gone wrong this month.

He was more concerned about the flesh-and-blood problem than the bricks-and-mortar one. If they didn't recast this role in the next couple of days, there weren't going to be any people in the theatre to *require* a tiled foyer.

Eight tedious days of workshop auditions, sitting through scene after scene of botched Stoppard and stilted Shakespeare, sifting through talent, looking for potential. He could usually tell within five minutes if an actor was suitable for the part they wanted, and which people had the right connection to form a company. Chemistry wasn't rehearsed; it sparked into life at first contact or not at all. But nobody was infallible, and this casting was vital.

And at this point, he might as well have walked into Piccadilly Circus at rush hour and randomly contracted the first dozen people to cross his path. He'd already lost his first choice for the role of Mary, thanks to Margo acting like an infatuated teenager, and now his Elizabeth had fallen off a stepladder while painting her bedroom ceiling. She'd broken both ankles and would be immobile for at least six weeks. He'd sent flowers from the company, calmly accepted her regretful resignation, and mentally throttled her.

They were starting rehearsals in less than a fortnight. For a number of reasons, the main one being expense, changing the schedule was not an option. His second-choice Mary was already costing a fucking fortune and would happily seize any opportunity to indulge in temperamental bullshit. Luc had no intention of giving her legitimate reason to complain. Next week he was taking the entire cast away for a long weekend in the country. Enforced bonding and a lot of alcohol usually cut several corners in turning a roomful of individual egos into a working ensemble.

It also usually kick-started at least one co-star romance, but sex was an inevitable complication in every production. He seemed to have the unwanted knack of putting together lovesick idiots who laboured under the delusion they were the next Burton and Taylor. It almost always ended in tears, and occasionally meant recasting one of the roles before the end of the run.

In this case he hadn't even got to the start of rehearsals before he had to recast. Five business days to pick a new Elizabeth I from the reserve list. Which did not include Flapper Barbie, despite the best efforts of the board to convince him otherwise. He had no problem, *in theory*, using the celebrity pull of a screen actor, providing they were right for the part and could make the transition to the stage, but this was one of the key roles in the play. There was only so far he was willing to compromise artistic integrity for profit.

He hadn't invested this much time and money into restoring the Queen Anne only to see it founder on the rocks of an opening-night flop.

For the second time, he tossed Lily Lamprey's photograph aside. "No."

"If you'd actually looked at—" Amelia was interrupted by a quiet knock on the door.

A catering assistant came in with a trolley of sandwiches, pastries and the makings of tea and coffee. Ibuprofen and a pint of lager would have been more welcome.

"Should I serve, sir?" the young man asked, impeccably polite. He was slightly built, freckle-faced, and Luc couldn't tell if he was actually fifteen years old or if he himself had just become so fucking old that every person under the age of twenty-five looked as if they ought to be at home playing with blocks.

"Thanks," he said, keeping his increasing irritation out of his voice. He wasn't going to vent on a kid earning minimum wage and obviously battling a severe case of nerves. "First day?"

Another quick glance. "Just temping, Mr. Savage."

When the tea things had been transferred to the conference table, David reached for an eclair and took a large bite. Wiping cream from his mouth, he said, "Where are we, then?"

"Lily Lamprey." Amelia raised a pointed eyebrow at Luc. "Yea or nay? And *nay* is an unacceptable answer until you've watched the reel, dropped the attitude and given her proper consideration."

"*Yay* was certainly my reaction." Eric was drooling on the headshot again. For the love of God. The guy needed to get out more.

The pressure in Luc's eye socket was spreading to his temple. "On your recommendation, I sat through almost ten minutes of jazz hands and the corruption of the clergy—"

"Actually," Amelia said, "you watched ten minutes of one previous body of work, with your nose in the air and your mind on construction bills, and wrote her off after the first simpering thirty seconds."

Luc took another brief look at the headshot. Lily Lamprey was exceptionally pretty—and, from what he'd seen so far, nothing more. "She has limited stage experience. Her only major role to date is on the worst show on CTV, in a part that could be understudied by a blow-up doll, and vocally she sounds as if she should be charging by the minute. Either she runs up eight flights of stairs between takes or she's taking the piss out of a character pulled straight from C-grade film noir, in which case I privately applaud the sentiment, but it's not exactly a professional approach to—"

There was a clattering sound near the door. The catering kid ducked his head and fiddled with an empty cup. It seemed to be taking an unnecessarily long time to rearrange and remove the trolley.

Pressing his thumb and forefinger against his eyes, Luc let out a short, hard breath. "I do not need a breathy Marilyn Monroe impersonator to add a bit of sex appeal in case the critics get bored. I'm not sure where you got the impression that I'm restoring the Queen Anne as a day-care training scheme for overly ambitious teenagers, or that I would be interested in an escapee from utter shit like *Knightsbridge*, but—"

"She's twenty-six years old, Luc, and you're not a misogynistic prick. You're a businessman. From a marketing perspective, Lily Lamprey would be a cash cow. *Knightsbridge* was the second-highest rated show in the country last week—"

"Then in the interests of the viewing public, I truly hope she's the worst actor on it."

Amelia continued as if he hadn't spoken. "Her character is…divisive. A lot of fans would like to throw her under a bus, but it's made her a household name. She's constant tabloid bait. She'll fill seats." She skewered him with a look. "You've got an eagle eye for potential. And you know full well I wouldn't put my reputation on the line by backing a dud prospect. She has something." She checked her watch. "You've been here since seven. Go home, take this—" she pushed an iPad at him "—take something for your headache, and a few deep breaths, and watch the fucking reel. If you still think she's not worth bringing in, I'll tell the board it's a no-go and we'll make the final call from the shortlist." Her lips thinned. "Although I'm not sure why you're paying me such a lovely lot of money if you have no faith in my judgement. If you're just going to veto me again and cast another overpriced troublemaker like Bridget Barclay…"

"When Bridget slips on the skin of a character, it's seamless. When this show opens, she'll *be* Mary."

Bridget was an exceptional actress. She had to be. Offstage, she was a total bloody nightmare.

"We should have cast Margo," Amelia said, for the five-thousandth time.

"And I would have," he agreed. For the five-thousandth time. "If Margo wasn't on her honeymoon and otherwise engaged." In shagging an Italian tenor. For three straight months, which seemed almost unbelievably out of character for his ex-girlfriend, who usually couldn't be prised away from the stage or a film set for more than a few hours at a time.

The gossip columnists still had whiplash over that elopement. People were naturally having a field day speculating over whether he'd been cheated on, which he hadn't, and whether he was heartbroken, which he wasn't. He was happy *she* was happy with her new husband. He even liked Alberto Ferreti, although he could have done without the other man's tendency to hug anyone who came within arm's reach, be it friend, stranger or his wife's ex.

He'd just be a lot *happier* if she'd capped the honeymoon at a perfectly reasonable two weeks and not skipped the country at this particular moment. Because he fully agreed with Amelia. Margo would have been the better choice as lead, as he'd informed her more than once, running up against the brick wall of her husband's fucking cuddles every time. She was turning down what could be the defining role of her stage career to drift about the Italian coast having sex in a houseboat. Clearly true love, but bad timing.

"So long as you're prepared to reel Bridget in when the claws and fangs come out," David put in bluntly. "I told you I wouldn't work with her again. I still come out in an anxiety rash every time someone mentions *Amadeus*."

"If she acts like that anywhere near my stage again, she's out. And she's aware that doors will immediately close in every other theatre worth mentioning. She'll behave."

Amelia suddenly snorted, regaining a scrap of humour. "I'm amazed she had the spine or the stupidity to go full-on diva around you in the first place. If you'd pop round mine every night and use your death stare on my kids, I'd be a well-rested, even-tempered angel of a woman. Do it for the team."

Luc laughed for the first time all day. "How are the boys?"

"Fine," said their mother gloomily. "Jay says they're either going to end up in parliament or prison." She jabbed the iPad at him again. "Hudson Warner's pushing for Lily in a big way, and you know what he's like when he gets a fixed idea." Luc did know. It was remarkably similar to when Amelia got a fixed idea, and bringing up his chief shareholder wasn't going to help her case. He was one budget meeting away from pinning Warner's photo to a dartboard. "I'm telling you, it's not the most out-there suggestion. There *is* an actress under all that second-rate burlesque bullshit. Obviously she's not as vacant as she plays in *Knightsbridge*."

"If she was as vacant as she looks on screen, she wouldn't be able to tie her own shoes." Luc gathered up the rest of the paperwork. "We'll meet back here tomorrow at eight-thirty to make a final decision."

He had three other prospects in mind. None of whom sounded like a bloody helium addict. Lily Lamprey was the type of actor who could be found in triplicate in every casting agency in the city, and they didn't have time for this.

Given his week so far, it seemed par for the course when he almost fell over the tea trolley on his way out the door. The catering kid flushed a blotchy red under the freckles and determinedly avoided Luc's gaze.

Luc had no intention of going home at four o'clock in the afternoon, but took part of Amelia's advice and hunted out a few painkillers in his office. The benefits were destroyed by yet another call from his contractor, with yet another construction issue.

There was a time when the Queen Anne had been the most iconic theatre in the West End. Seven generations of Savages had run it successfully until his grandfather had inherited, and it had become synonymous with third-rate melodrama and sordid cabaret. For the past twenty-five years, it had been so run-down it had been taped off as a hazard zone.

Luc had spent twenty of those years producing hits for other people's theatres. He'd moonlighted in Hollywood, directing bullshit blockbusters that paid considerably better than films with decent actors and scripts that made sense, and taken a lot of prospective investors out for lunch. He'd put up with the interference of Hudson Warner for months. He hadn't slept properly for weeks. But the restoration was finally taking shape.

Another call, this one from his solicitor, was interrupted when Lana Cho banged open his office door. The casting assistant didn't bother to wait until he'd ended one conversation before she launched into her own rant. Apparently Bridget Barclay was refusing to join the meet-and-greet the following weekend because she had a sore throat and obviously fancied a pre-emptive case of can't-be-arsed-itis.

It was half past seven by the time Luc got off the phone with Bridget, having informed her that unless she could present a medical certificate confirming she'd contracted leprosy, the plague or dragon pox, her presence was contractually required. He also suggested that it was a little early to piss off everyone involved in the production, and that her throat might heal more quickly if she just contemplated her grievances silently instead of shrieking them at the top of her lungs.

He tossed the phone aside and swore.

Margo probably wouldn't appreciate it if he flew to Italy and forcibly towed her love boat back to the Thames.

He looked at the tablet on his desk. He had a dinner reservation at eight-thirty. It was likely to be his last date in some time if Amelia removed a body part of her choice tomorrow, so he sat down with a sigh and located Lily Lamprey's audition reel.

At the first line, he winced.

Oh Christ, that was her actual voice.

He'd given her the benefit of the doubt and assumed she'd adopted the phone-sex panting for the *Knightsbridge* role. She obviously did play it up; her natural voice registered a few degrees lower in tone. It was still off-pitch and it was weak. She'd be hoarse by intermission and lip-synching by the curtain call. She was far better suited for television work, and had probably already landed the only role she'd have the range to play.

He almost killed the screen there and then, but Amelia's accusation of prejudice echoed in his ears and he kept watching. He remained expressionless throughout the taped performance, but at the midway point, he leaned in.

When the clip ended, he sat back and narrowed his eyes.

Well.

It *was* there. The glimmer of possibility Amelia had picked up on. Even with the gangster's moll doll-face, and the godawful "Happy Birthday, Mr. President" candyfloss voice, it was—amazingly—there, that ability to take the essence of a character into herself, to let it crawl over her skin, and show in her eyes, and direct the movements of her body.

Under the soap-opera shit, an actor.

It took her too long to hook her audience. She ought to be able to transform at a finger-snap. The voice was problematic. Potentially disastrous. She would need outside training, additional effort and expense.

But there *was* something about her. Something that gelled, that reached out and tugged suggestively at his conception of this version of Elizabeth.

She could—possibly—do it.

So could the other three actors on his personal shortlist.

And if she failed to live up to that spark of possibility, she would undermine the entire production. The critics would shred both of them.

She wasn't worth the gamble.

He was in the car park, reaching for his keys, when his phone rang. Amelia's name flashed onto the screen. He answered, and heard the sounds of outraged hollering as one of the demon children resisted being hauled off to bed.

"Did you watch the reel?" she asked over the racket, getting straight to it, and Luc returned the serve.

"Watched it, point taken, still no."

"Damn." The angry roaring in the background dulled. He assumed she'd either escaped to a different room or slipped the little bugger a quick sedative. "I was hoping we could take the easy route for once. For someone who claims to be cool-tempered, you have a real habit of steering us into Drama Town."

He opened the car door and tossed various files and electronics onto the passenger seat. "Very long day, Amelia. If you could translate that into English in the next ten seconds—"

"I've had Warner on the phone, ruining the buzz of an expensive bottle of red. Does nobody around here understand the basic concept of a Friday night?"

"What does the old bastard want now?"

"He's pulling rank. He wants Lily Lamprey in this show and he's not backing down."

Luc snorted. "Warner doesn't have rank to pull. This is my production. My theatre. The board has no say over casting."

"Technically, no. But he *can* pull his backing, in which case your mortgage increases by millions of pounds, and I'm thinking that's not a financial hit you can afford until the theatre is up and running."

"Is that what he's threatening?"

"That was the underlying suggestion, yes."

"It wouldn't be as financially catastrophic as a bad opening run." He slid behind the wheel. "And it's a bluff. Even Warner isn't so thick that he'd jeopardise his investment over what I assume is an elderly infatuation. Or is she a blood relative?"

"Luc Savage, die-hard romantic." Grudgingly, Amelia admitted, "He's her godfather. Lily Lamprey's mother is Vanessa Cray, the Irish singer. You know—schmaltzy, jazz stuff. Not really my thing. Warner was allegedly one of her boyfriends back in the day, a revelation that forced me to imagine him in a sexual context. My brain attempted to self-destruct and I had to Google pictures of kittens to recover." There was a burst of static. "Are you still there?"

"Unfortunately, yes."

"Lily's father is a peer. Don't bother making a snarky comment. You live in fucking Kensington, rich boy. The Savages' Cockney roots are so well buried by now you'd need a map and a deep-sea drill to find them."

Luc switched the phone to the wireless system and pulled out into the Southbank traffic. "A peer. Not Jack Lamprey? The penny-dreadful sex kitten is Jacko Clubs's daughter?"

"Jacko Clubs?" she repeated disbelievingly. "Chummy with his Lordship, are we?"

"I've met him once or twice. He was a friend of my father's a long time ago, until they fell out over my mother. Or he heckled Dad at Drury Lane. I can't remember which was the proverbial last straw."

"By the look of his London house, he must be one of the few genuinely wealthy peers. Or mortgaged to the hilt and reduced to letting the public fondle his antiques for twenty quid a pop."

"Lamprey's a mainstay of the rich list. And the family black sheep. Took centuries of old money—made the respectable way through war-mongering, tenant-exploitation and tax evasion—and tripled it by founding and investing in a good percentage of London's nightclubs. Mostly the dodgy ones. I suspect he'd pick your pocket for fun, without blinking an eye."

Not that his family could talk. His grandfather's approach to business would have made Lamprey seem more like a gambolling lamb than a black sheep.

"Maybe don't share that opinion with Lily when you contract her."

Raindrops began to patter against the windscreen and Luc flicked on the wipers. "Jesus, Amelia. Did Warner catch you burying a body, or are you on the Lampreys' payroll?"

Amelia made the sound that usually preceded her loss of temper. "Look. I have to deal with enough pissy little boy tantrums at home. Warner's being a real dick about this and I don't think it's worth the aggravation. You can bring her up to scratch."

Luc groaned.

"Take Warner out of the equation and consider on the basis that she came to you through the usual channels."

Apparently he was going to hit every red light in the city. "She wouldn't have got beyond a conversation between her agent and a junior receptionist. Most of the talent on our books have performed in at least *one* production," he added sarcastically.

"She's done stage work."

"What, am-dram and student Shakespeare at the Institute?"

"Luc." Frustrated vibes were rolling through the phone. "You've always acted on your instincts and it almost always pays off. What happened to the born gambler?"

"He took a header out the window when I signed a multimillion-pound mortgage."

"I've got a feeling about this."

It would be easy to mock that statement, but he was paying Amelia her "lovely lot of money" for her own instincts, which were usually sound and occasionally genius.

"Hell," he said after a moment, with feeling.

"See, I knew the real Luc was lurking somewhere beneath that boring-as-eff exterior. When the theatre is up and running, and the press gets off your back, you might even dig up your sense of humour." Amelia hummed with satisfaction. "I'll call her agent and get her in for a meeting ASAP."

"No promises."

"Look on the bright side. Bridget Barclay hates your guts and is going to be an absolute shit to direct, even *if* her performance is worth it. This'll be a nice contrast for you. If you cast Lily Lamprey, she'll be so grateful for the break that she'll think you're an absolute god."

Luc Savage was a pompous prick, with a head the size of the O2, and—if there was any justice left in the world—most likely a penis the size of a grape.

Lily's thighs squeezed tight. The man between them stopped midway through a fake orgasmic moan and grunted. She grimaced down at him in apology; he pulled a horrific face in return.

The active camera angle was fortunately aimed at her back.

From the corner of her eye, she could see the studio clock. Still plenty of time, but she couldn't afford too many more takes. Closing her eyes, Lily deepened her breathing and cried out.

That was uncannily like the sound her first car had made when the engine died on the M3. She was slaying it vocally today.

"Cut." Of the three directors working on *Knightsbridge*, Steve Warren was the one who least enjoyed filming the many, *many* sex scenes. He had a yen for

the dodgy political storylines and occasional backstreet violence. There were only so many ways people could writhe around in the buff, squeaking and panting.

Lily shared the general air of over-it. Even the newest assistant was yawning and secretly texting. A month ago, he'd been permanently red-cheeked and unable to look directly at the fake action.

Her own phone was back in her dressing room, cuddled up against an almost empty packet of Jammie Dodgers. She'd stress-eaten seven biscuits, way too early in the morning, pushing the limits of even her tolerance for sugar. She still felt sick and perversely blamed Savage for that too.

"…wailing like a spooked bat," Steve said crossly. She tuned back in to the criticism. "This should be old hat by now. You seem to spend most of the week getting your kit off."

Yes. Once again, she *had* spent most of the season tossing her suspender belt and sequins across the room and leaping astride one cast member or other. How kind of someone to notice. Pity that Steve didn't think to drop a word in the writers' ears, to change the repetitive movements of their fingers.

When Lily had originally read the pilot script and locked herself into a four-year contract, it hadn't been immediately clear that the characterisation of Gloria was sexist as hell and about as deep as a puddle. The writers had started off softly. Gloria hadn't become truly vile until halfway through the first series.

As a newbie with a point to prove, it had seemed important to secure *any* acting role to get her foot in the door. And at that sweetly naive age, she had told herself that Gloria would evolve for the better over time, become more complex and subtle. There had finally been a few tantalising glimpses of hope this year, a hint at meatier material than batting her lashes and shimmying onto another lap.

Instead, Gloria had settled for systematically nicking the duke's prized paintings and fitting a third married lover into her busy scheme-and-shag schedule.

Lily was fed up to the back teeth with faking orgasms, not a skill she'd ever felt the need to perfect in her personal life, and it was obviously starting to show in her performance.

She did take her work seriously, even when it was complete bullshit.

"I know." She was still perched on Ash's stomach, concealing his discreetly bound-up groin, and he was politely looking to the side, to avoid eye-to-nipple-shield contact. And people said working in television wasn't really that glamorous. "I'll pitch it lower."

"Let's just go for soundless bliss, shall we?"

"Does that go for me as well?" Ash tried to insert a fingertip between Lily's big and second toes. He'd discovered she was insanely ticklish there after the series two writers had gone off on a toe-sucking tangent. Not a high point for any of them. She brought her heel back and whacked it against his thigh.

"As you don't sound like a hyperventilating mouse—" Steve reached to hand a clipboard to one of his hovering assistants "—no. It does not."

For a supposedly closed set, they seemed to be approaching Tesco-on-Christmas Eve numbers of people. Both she and Ash had requested core crew only. As usual, totally ignored.

"I think I preferred last week's 'constipated camel,'

thanks." She tried to get back into position without kneeing Ash in the kidney or accidentally shuffling into willy territory. It was a close call when he decided to do a full-body stretch. "It had more of a ring to it."

She took another paranoid look at the clock, and Steve caught the anxious time-check.

"Do you have somewhere else to be?" he asked with heavy and totally false concern.

"No."

She had handed in her resignation over a month ago, about five minutes after her contract had expired, but she had no intention of telling her bosses she was hoping to do a career U-turn into theatre. It was highly probable that Luc Savage was going to send her packing at the first opportunity. Considering the first impression she'd apparently made on him, she had no idea why his people had called her agent to request a face-to-face, but she would hold on to this chance tooth and nail.

The West End had been her ultimate goal for ten years. Savage was one of the best directors in the business and this production was going to be a sell-out. She wanted to be a part of it.

She tried to keep her attention focused on Steve's continued mutterings, and on Ash, who was rubbing his thumbs over her knees in a way that had nothing to do with sex, scripted or otherwise, and everything to do with a good friend and the tense rigidity of her body. She kept her eyes away from the clock.

She never rushed scenes, but today—

Places to go, auditions to nail, self-important arse-bags to convince.

She didn't want to end up in a panicked rush. One thing her father had taught her was that a player didn't cede advantage to the enemy before the game had even begun.

"Right." Steve raised a hand. "Let's get this in the bag. Think sexy. Think *silent*."

They wrapped the scene in a record fourteen minutes, with one brief hiccup near the end when Ash tried his hand at improvisation and attempted to scoop his shoulders under her legs. They both went flying off the edge of the desk, which broke Lily's tension so effectively that she cry-laughed her way to a reapplication of mascara.

At least Steve was gratified. "Nice one," he said, with considerably more enthusiasm than he'd shown for their actual performance. "Gag reel gold."

Lily was still grinning when she left the set, tying the sash on her robe, and followed a limping Ash back to the dressing rooms. Several doors were open and Ben Farley's new hoverboard had left a trail of destruction. Daily deliveries from the post room usually involved cool freebies for the teenage cast and reminders from the in-house legal team for everyone else.

Ash pointedly rubbed his knee.

"Well, I'm sorry, but give me a bit of warning next time you decide to go all Cirque du Soleil. Preferably about six months in advance, so we have time to stretch first." Shivering, she unlocked her door. The studio heating was aimed at those wearing four layers of wool, not thin polyester and a flesh-coloured thong. "I suggest a few yoga classes before you try that recreationally."

Ash flicked water from his bottle at her. He followed her into her dressing room for his usual post-shoot routine of lounging and eating her crisps. After arranging the folds of his dressing gown with exaggerated care, he poked nosily through a stack of her fan mail—which was now vetted by an unfortunate intern. She got a lot of hate mail about Gloria's antics, and had the honour of receiving the most dick pics in CTV history.

Lily flung off her own robe and did a mad, chilly dash for her clothes. She pulled up her black jeans with one hand, via a few jerky hip movements that turned into an impromptu foxtrot when she lost her balance, and scooped up her phone to thumb the home button. There were two missed calls, one from her agent.

"Please don't cancel," she said aloud as she dialled her voicemail, and Ash looked up at once.

"Hey, hey. Who's got herself a new man, then?" He put about fourteen crisps in his mouth and didn't bother to chew or swallow before he continued, "Which poor sod is it this time? Tell Uncle Ash."

Lily listened to the message from Peter. Thank God. Just confirming the time and place. Two o'clock at Savage Productions in Southbank. "Luc Savage."

She flicked a soggy crumb from her sleeve when Ash almost succumbed to death by crisp explosion.

"Luc Savage?" Ash repeated, still coughing. He swiped at his mouth and chin. "*You're* shagging *Luc Savage*?"

She wasn't sure whether she or Savage was the one who ought to take offense.

"Not if he was the last man on the planet." Lily shrugged into her jacket and gave up the idea of finding two matching socks as laughable. The room looked like several dozen people had physically exploded their clothes from their bodies.

Ash hooked an arm over the back of the couch, turning to face her fully. "Have you scored a West End audition, you clever girl? How the hell did you wrangle that?"

Not flattering, but valid.

"You assume that I wasn't headhunted for my sheer overwhelming talent." She perched on the edge of the couch to do an inventory of her handbag. Wallet, throat lozenges, breath mints. All necessary. Condoms, which she emphatically wouldn't need today, but which she wasn't leaving in her dressing room again, after the balloon animal incident. There were several hazards to working with teenage boys and man-children.

"From *this* role? By Luc Savage? Not unless he's having a midlife crisis and putting on a musical production of *Gentlemen Prefer Blondes*. *We* know you can act, and that you're a life-winning, joy-spreading delight, but—and don't take this the wrong way—less privileged folk might be under the impression that you're a complete twit."

"Savage's summary was slightly more colourful, but that was the gist, yes."

"Have you already auditioned? One of the brutal ones, was it? You should have told me. I've got a tried-and-tested remedy. Involves a stamp in your passport and a lot of Spanish booze."

"I'm sure I'd enjoy having my stomach pumped in Barcelona as much as the next person, but it wasn't a direct mauling. I got the character assassination secondhand."

"Explain, *por favor.*"

"Jamie in catering has been temping over at Savage Productions. He served the Lord and Commander his tea and biscuits the other afternoon." Lily wrapped the chain of her necklace around her finger. "During a casting meeting. Apparently I look like I'd need direction to put my shoes on."

"Fuckwit." Ash scowled and ran a hand through his tousled hair. That was some serious bed-head. Or desk-head, to be accurate. Their characters tended to have quickie sex on the sly. Usually in the study. Occasionally in a car. Once in a baptismal font. "Do I need to storm down there and throw some punches?"

"I appreciate the gesture, but I don't think watching you get beaten to a pulp would cheer me up enough to make it worthwhile."

"I beg your pardon." Ash made a lazy fist and waved it about. "I lift a tenth of my own body weight with these bad boys."

"In what, shopping bags at Harrods?" She dodged the dive he made for the sensitive spot on her ribs.

"Hey." Ash caught her hand. "Lily. Forget whatever Savage said. The man obviously doesn't know a thing about you. What's the sum total? A few clips of Gloria giggling and gyrating? He hasn't even spoken to you yet."

"That's partly what worries me."

Ash considered that. "Well, it could be worse," he offered feebly. "You could have a really strong accent to iron out. You could be *mute*. Some people can't speak at all. There are people who'd *love* to have a porn voice."

"I'm going to need my crisps back now."

Chapter Two

Luc Savage looked like Gregory Peck, circa some dapper time between *Roman Holiday* and *To Kill A Mockingbird*. There was more bulk in the shoulders, silver in the hair and darkness in the soul; otherwise, the resemblance was uncanny. Lily had seen him once before, at an opening night for another director's play. The theatre had been full of famous faces that night, and the production distractingly bad, and she hadn't paid him any particular attention. Her mental image of him had been formed more closely and recently by Jamie's faithfully repeated insults, so she'd been expecting something more along the lines of an orc.

Any resemblance to Old Hollywood charm ended at his bone structure.

He stood in the doorway to his office, surveying her. When she'd arrived, his secretary had also done a head-to-toe sweep, and then shaken her head in apparent disbelief, which hadn't built Lily's confidence.

She stared back at him, directly into his unimpressed grey eyes. She had put a stranglehold on her nerves during the long wait, dialling back from jiggling knees to a bit of subtle nail-picking.

Yet all of a sudden, she wasn't nervous at all.

This was Luc Savage. Award-winning, career-making, ego-curdling Luc Savage. Get-in-my-way-and-I'll-crush-you-like-a-bug Luc Savage. And her driving instinct was to touch the tips of her boots to his—and then stand her ground until he stepped back first.

Her spine prickled.

After a long pause that was too charged to be awkward, he stepped forward and extended a hand. "Luc Savage."

She glanced down at his fingers wrapped around hers. "Lily Lamprey."

They released each other's hands; their eyes met again.

Game on.

Savage's eyebrow rose, just a little. He tilted his sleek dark head in the direction of the open door. "Take a seat."

With one simple gesture, he managed to suggest that it wasn't strictly *necessary* to curtsey, but feel free. Sadly, she was far too ambitious to do a Queen's Guard salute, outside of her sarcastic imagination.

She had an inkling their opinion of one another was not going to improve much over the next painful minutes.

Inside his office, she sat down gingerly on one of the guest chairs. The room had probably been decorated by an expensive firm; the colour scheme was an inoffensive grey and cream, and the furnishings were impersonal. Generic landscapes on the walls where she might have expected framed playbills and signed photographs. If there had been a sentimental framed shot of Margo Roy on his desk until recently, it had obviously been confined to a bin, but she somehow doubted it. He didn't exactly exude romance. And he was well-versed in the icy "No comment" when it came to public speculation about his private life.

As someone who had been accused of sleeping with most of her male co-stars, all of whom were married or in committed relationships, Lily had no issue with giving the metaphorical finger to prying paparazzi. But there was a way to do it without coming across like a dick and attracting rebound bad press. Case in point: Margo, who seemed to have supplied all of their charisma as a couple and who actually smiled occasionally. Savage obviously subscribed to the Victoria Beckham school of posing. Margo was probably well rid.

There were still shock waves over that split. They'd been the West End power couple. The modern-day Burton and Taylor. Minus all the heavy drinking and extracurricular sex. She assumed.

Lily released a deep breath and leaned back, and almost had a heart attack when the ergodynamic chair unexpectedly reclined. She flailed her way back to an upright position. If she'd ever deluded herself that she was an elegant, graceful woman, this day would have been a sad wake-up call. Her cheeks burned.

Savage managed to sit down like a normal person. "You all right there?" he asked blandly, and he was just an odious, odious man.

His fingertips came down to rest on her resumé, and she nodded at it. *Don't blush.* "You'll notice gymnastic and acrobatic training listed under special skills. As you can see, I'm a tragic loss to the circus profession, but I just couldn't get past the clown phobia."

The corner of his mouth flickered. She couldn't tell if it was amusement or derision. She could guess, however.

"I see athletic training," he agreed, glancing down the list of mostly true skills. The archery was a bit of a stretch, and consisted of an episode of *Knightsbridge* when Gloria had got drunk, crashed the duchess's birthday party, and shot a flaming arrow into the pile of presents. Ash had eventually snatched the bow from Lily in exasperation and completed the shot so they could break for lunch. It seemed unlikely that Elizabeth I was going to be pinging arrows into the audience, however, so she couldn't see that particular lie being exposed.

"I also see screen experience. Several film roles. Voice training." His own voice turned slightly ironic on that one and he slanted a look at her, but surprisingly refrained from pointing out the obvious.

She couldn't exactly deny the problem. If she wasn't paying attention, her speaking voice tried to slip into a register somewhere between film noir and a chipmunk. Teenagers in the street, checkout operators at the supermarket, men on the Tube—half the strangers she met thought she was trying to be sexy, which either weirded people out or resulted in unwelcome offers. The other half thought she had a brain the size of a Tic Tac. Years of voice lessons had widened her range, but it still wasn't ideal.

"What I'm not seeing is stage experience," he finished coolly. "If this is up-to-date, you haven't set foot on a stage since you finished at the London Institute, apart from one stint in a celebrity panto. I don't think I need to point out the difference between performing in the West End and doing a bit of look-out-he's-behind-you for charity."

She studied him thoughtfully. "It's a lost art, condescension. Most workplaces are so PC these days that you just don't get patronised in quite the same way."

This time, both of his eyebrows came up. If he wasn't careful, he was going to have an actual expression soon.

"This would be my first major stage role, yes. And I assume the only reason you're even considering me is because I come with a TV following." Most people despised her character, who had a solid track record of inserting herself between popular couples on the show. Sometimes literally. But *Knightsbridge* itself was a money-spinner, and she was at least…memorable, apparently. "I'm not deluding myself that I'd have got through your front door if you couldn't exploit my name for ticket sales."

"Exploit?"

"Make sound economic use of?" she suggested helpfully, and his face retreated further into the Ice Age.

"I don't recall that many past difficulties in filling seats."

Oops. Three minutes into the meeting and she'd already trodden on his ego. At this rate, she wouldn't even get to read the first line of her monologue. After the short-notice call, she'd stayed up until one in the morning re-memorising it, in case she needed a prepared piece. Fortunately, she'd had minimal lines to learn for the show today. *Faster, harder, Oh God, yes*, and *Of course I love you, darling, but he needs me* didn't require a lot of mental effort.

"In spite of not having trolled the soap opera sets for staff before."

She was beginning to see why there had been a recent spate of tabloid articles about his abrasive management style. Instead of looking down his nose at the vocally challenged, maybe he ought to direct his energy into his people skills.

"It's not a soap opera," she felt obliged to point out on behalf of her pay cheque.

It was unquestionably a soap opera.

"It's a period drama."

It was *Dynasty* with feather boas and Charlestons instead of shoulder pads and hairspray.

The abruptness with which he changed the subject spoke volumes. "Would you rather stand or stay sitting to read?" He picked up the sheaf of typed script that she'd been trying not to make sneak glances at.

She'd already had to sign confidentiality papers stating that she wouldn't discuss any content from the play, should the audition be unsuccessful. The playwright, Benjamin Starkey, had won the Methven Prize eight times, six more times than anyone else in the UK, and *1553* was his first new play in four years. It was going straight to the West End, it was attached to Savage Productions, and it was reopening the Queen Anne. They were taking secrecy to an extreme to keep up the promotional momentum; this was the first time Lily had seen any of the dialogue she was reading for.

"I'm fine like this." Considering the balance issues she'd had so far today, completing such difficult tasks as dressing herself and planting her arse on a chair, she wouldn't tempt fate by walking around. Out of habit from table reads at CTV, she reached down to unzip her boots and pulled up her socked feet to sit cross-legged.

Savage handed her the script excerpt, about five pages of dialogue. "This is from the penultimate scene, the first and only time that Jane, Mary and Elizabeth are alone together. The play is a character study, not a historical narrative. The individual journey of each woman is key. Elizabeth has fewer scenes than her sister and cousin, but she has to hold her own against two very strong personalities. The weight of expectation is on her. In 1553, she was a pawn in the game. Eventually, she'll take the throne. This is the future Virgin Queen, a master tactician—and a young woman in a very precarious position. The actor who takes this role needs to find the heart of Elizabeth, latch on to and hold the audience's sympathy. If we do this right, every core character will have the loyalty and empathy of the room, torn three ways."

He opened a small cupboard that turned out to be a mini-fridge—and God, he kept chocolate cake in his office, like a relatable person with a shit diet.

Fortunately, he didn't offer her any cake, as she probably would have taken it. He pulled out two bottles of water, tossed one to her and cracked the seal on the other. "I'll give you a minute to skim through the scene."

She read with the script propped on her lap, absently clutching the water bottle to her chest and picking at the label. She was hyperaware of him for about thirty seconds, listening to the sounds as he drained his bottle of water. She could hear him breathing. Then she became lost in the writing. She read it through once and reached into her bag to snag a pen. Belatedly, after she'd already scrawled a few words, she looked up at him. "Sorry, do you mind if I jot down some notes?"

He was watching her closely, his expression unreadable. "Do what you need to do."

After a moment, she clicked off the pen and looked up. "Right."

"I'll read for Jane and Mary." He nodded at the nearby tripod. "All auditions are recorded, so you're aware. No one outside the management team will see the footage."

If there was one thing she was used to, it was reading lines in front of a camera, but never in front of someone who could blackball her theatrical career with one phone call.

How bad do you want this? Ash had asked before she'd left the studio.

Savage turned on the camera. "Ready?"

Bad. She wanted it bad.

He kicked off the scene, reading in a flat monotone. He was purposely emotionless, giving her absolutely nothing to work with and bounce off. She was forced to rely completely on her own interpretation. She glanced up at him every few seconds, but it was like trying to get a smile out of Picasso's *Portrait of Gertrude Stein*. A stony mask.

Her voice cracked halfway through, but she continued without a stumble. When she closed Elizabeth's impassioned monologue, there was a long silence. She stared down at the paper.

"Again," Savage said, and she flipped back to page one.

They read the scene four times before he closed his copy and set it back on the desk. He went straight to the crux of the problem, and didn't bother to sandwich the criticism between token compliments. "Your voice is a real issue. We have a very good speech therapist on contract. She could work with you on a vocal hygiene programme, but realistically, you need to be hitting a much higher level on your delivery and you would need to get there quickly. Rehearsals begin in less than two weeks. Part of it is laziness."

She was so caught on his first statements, the tummy-jump of hope followed by the let-down, that it took her a second to react to that last remark. "Laziness?" she repeated. It fucking was not. She turned up on time. She learned her lines. She put in the groundwork. She was lazy on Sundays, when she got up, walked to the café around the corner from her flat to collect her pancake order, and then returned to pyjamas and bed. She wasn't lazy when it came to her work ethic.

"You're babying your voice. Literally," he said drily. "Helium Barbie has to go."

A long time ago, Lily had owned a Ken Doll. She'd once discovered that putting her thumbs on his neck and applying the exact right amount of pressure beneath his plastic ears caused his head to pop off. It probably wouldn't work with Savage.

He leaned against the edge of his desk, arms folded, as he continued his impersonal assessment. "It's frustrating as fuck to listen to. If I played the recording back on mute and we focused entirely on your physical performance, totally different story. You're defaulting to the easiest level on your vocal delivery, and the way you're breathing and swallowing is never going to give you the long-haul projection to make it through one performance, let alone six a week. I don't usually advise an actor to come in and lower the tone, but in this instance…"

"That *was* a lower tone," she said glumly. She was well aware that voiceover and narration gigs were never going on her resumé. The female Benedict Cumberbatch, she was not.

"God help us all." Turning off the camera, he glanced down at her abandoned boots. "I'd like to see you on the stage." For another heart-stopping moment, she thought that was a job offer, but he continued, "We'll move through to the amphitheatre. Shoes optional."

Savage Productions had a no-frills theatre that was used for teen outreach programmes. Lily had been to their charity production of *Romeo and Juliet* last year. Fun acting. Great cause. Not her favourite play. Self-indulgent teenage stupidity at its finest. Most likely, if they'd survived their mistakes, middle-aged Romeo and Juliet would have looked back on the whole debacle and wondered what they'd made such a fuss about. It was one of the great literary examples of unhealthy co-dependency.

It might be a bit hypocritical to label Savage an un-romantic.

The boots went back on. She wasn't walking around his building in her mismatched socks.

As they walked through the corridors, they passed members of staff who glanced up and greeted their boss with friendly smiles. Despite the tabloid mud-flinging, he'd obviously earned a lot of professional respect.

She personally had nothing but respect for him on a professional plane. As a director, he was one of the greats.

However, he'd rated her longest-running performance as being on par with a blow-up doll and just called her Helium Barbie to her face. As a human being, he was a total dickhead.

A youngish, cocky-looking guy in a sharp suit came out of the lift, stopped in his tracks and actually wolf-whistled at her in his workplace.

He then caught sight of Savage, and Lily witnessed the interesting phenomenon of every ounce of colour leaching out of a man's face in about three-quarters of a second.

"Mitchell." She'd thought Savage's tone was cold when he spoke to her. This was arctic by comparison. "Since you obviously have time on your hands, you can demonstrate cold-calling for the student interns. General office, second floor. And I'll see you in my office at five o'clock."

She *almost* felt sorry for Mitchell, whose spiritual home was clearly a roadside construction site. He looked so mortified and *shrivelled* as he stammered an apology.

"You need to direct that apology about two feet to the left," Savage cut in. "I'm not the one you just publicly embarrassed and disrespected. This is Lily Lamprey. You seem to be under the impression that she's an inanimate object brought into the building for your amusement."

Wow. If she hadn't been privy to the load of sexist crap that had come out of his own mouth, she'd be quite impressed by that. It wasn't that much better to say something just because the breathy Marilyn Monroe impersonator in question couldn't hear it.

"Sorry," Mitchell managed, throwing the word in her direction. The colour returned to his cheeks with a vengeance as he scuttled off. Until the past minute of his life, he'd probably thought pretty well of himself.

Savage held open the door to the amphitheatre for her. "I'm sorry. That was totally unacceptable."

She hesitated and then lifted one shoulder in an awkward, hunched shrug. "It's like you said," she said carefully. "In this business, people can forget you're a real person. Or they think you're public property. They think they know who you are." She looked back at him. "Based on a fictional character or their own assumptions."

And by "their" assumptions, possible boss, sir, let's all read "your."

Savage was still striving desperately for a facial expression, but she thought she saw a wry flicker in his eyes.

"Bring that fuck-you attitude to your performance and we're another step up the ladder" was all he said in return, mildly.

It was like no audition she'd ever been to, and she'd racked up quite a list. She stood on the wooden stage, reading lines with as much depth and volume as she could manage, to empty seats and one lounging man in the farthest row.

"As loud as you can without losing expression or falling off the cliff and shouting," he interrupted, and annoyingly she could hear his resonant tones perfectly, despite the fact that he was visually a dark blur.

Anyone with a speaking part would have a concealed microphone pack to help with projection in the towering, multi-level Queen Anne, but she got it. Her voice had to be strong.

"Lower, slower, and breathe where you would naturally pause."

She started again—

"I can't hear you."

And again—

"Not *that* slow. You're not being paid by the minute."

And again—

"You're regal. Stately. You rule this room. You have

no fucks to give. And, underneath it all, you're frightened."

And—

"*Frightened*, not full-on panic attack! If you need some sort of inhaler, raise your left hand. Otherwise, breathe between sentences, not *through* words!"

Let's face it, she wasn't getting this role.

When she'd finished butchering Starkey's brainchild, and Savage had probably pulled out most of his hair, he lifted a hand—universal director-speak for "put a sock in it." He stood and came back up the aisle, his footsteps a dull echo on the paisley carpet. She sat down on the edge of the stage, leaving her feet and life goals dangling.

He took a seat in the front row, opposite her, leaning forward to rest his forearms on his thighs. A lock of black hair touched with grey fell across his brow.

If he asked her how *she* thought she'd done, the way therapists pulled the intensely irritating "why do *you* think that is?", her mood was officially going to plummet through the floor.

His question, when it came, surprised her. "How do you feel?"

Tired, depressed and fully capable of cleansing your fridge of cake.

"Frustrated," she said honestly. "I feel like I've got the instructions, I know what I'm doing, I *like* what I'm doing, but I'm just—not there."

He rotated his thumbs, ropey tendons moving under the skin of his hands. His eyes were shrewd. "You have…a certain look. Have you struggled to get roles in the past because of your appearance and your voice?"

"Yes," she said after a moment, uncomfortably. He

must know that she had; he'd been extremely reluctant himself to even meet her in person.

"Your physical appearance is irrelevant in this case," he said bluntly. "There's a distance in live theatre that you don't have in TV and film, and skilled makeup artists can produce an illusion of good looks and youth in any face, regardless of the base material they have to work with. Being beautiful is not going to help you here."

He'd called her beautiful. Not vapid, not vacuous, not even pretty. Beautiful. In a calm, disinterested way, like it was just a fact. The sky is blue, the grass is green, you're beautiful. She suddenly flushed.

She twisted her fingers together as he went on, "It's also not a detriment, which I can see might be the case in some instances." He frowned. "The vocals, though—"

"Are a problem."

"Are a disaster," he corrected, and she winced. "You managed to halve Elizabeth's IQ in one paragraph." It had been a short-lived warm glow. Nice while it lasted. "And you're starting to annoy me now." *Well, pot, meet fucking kettle.*

"There's only so much you can achieve without professional intervention, but you're still not pulling your weight. Your performance is falling well short of your capability."

She blew out an exasperated breath—probably in the wrong place to optimise her *feelings* in this scene—but was saved a repetition of "But—but—but…" when his phone rang.

He pulled it from his pocket, glanced at the screen, and turned all thunderous. "Sorry," he said, scowling.

Wow, visibly pissed off. It must be bad. Seemed like someone would have to burn down his house or kidnap his grandma or something to provoke that sort of reaction. "I'll have to take this. Two minutes."

Maybe an irate employee was suing him.

"How the hell can they be the wrong design? We approved the sample. So now we're short *six* hundred tiles?"

A renovation fail. That was barely worth the eavesdropping.

She jumped when her own phone vibrated in her pocket. At least she'd remembered to put it on silent. Savage's call didn't look like it was ending anytime soon, so she snuck a peek at the screen. It was Trix. Her best friend was due back from a gala performance in Paris, and Lily had forgotten to tell her she would be locked down in an audition. She probably ought to send it to voicemail, but Savage was heading for the back of the theatre with long, hacked-off strides and her alternative was to sit here in uncomfortable silence.

She swiped to answer. "Hey, are you at the airport?"

"I'm in the flat. Got an earlier flight. Thanks for taking me back in, by the way," Trix added cheerfully. "The landlord at my new place says I should be able to move in after New Year's Day."

"Happy to have you."

"Are you at the studio now?"

"No, I'm at my audition with Luc Savage. For *1553*."

There was a brief, startled pause. "Shit. Did I interrupt? Sorry! What the hell are you talking to me for?"

Lily glanced over to make sure Savage was still occupied. "It's all right. We're on an unofficial break at the moment. I think he's talking to his contractor."

"Right, well, how's it going?"

"The word *disaster* has been thrown around."

"Don't do your perfectionist thing, where you obsess over everything you did wrong and ignore everything you rocked."

"I'm trying not to. It's hard." Steadying herself with her free hand, she jumped down to the floor. She needed to pace. "I don't know. I think my voice issues are going to be a deal-breaker."

"Did he say that?"

"He said it was a huge problem. Apparently he's got a top speech therapist on speed-dial, but he's doubtful it would be enough, with the limited timeframe before the play opens."

"I told you that woman you've been going to in Hammersmith isn't good enough. You should ask him for the person's number regardless, if this is going to be an ongoing issue. And don't write yourself off. If Savage wasn't interested, he would have ushered you out of the building in five minutes flat. He wouldn't be talking about voice specialists."

Ash had said something similar, and now that she'd met Savage, she had to agree. He didn't beat politely around the bush. He also didn't hold back with the criticism, so she had no idea which way the judgment call was going to swing.

"And no matter what happens, you got a personal audition with Luc Savage. Give yourself some credit. He gets top billing for a reason."

"Tell that to the tabloids. I see there's another article painting him as the villain who drove off Margo Roy and bullied multiple employees into submission," Lily muttered, purely out of frustration. She wasn't Savage's biggest fan, but she knew a smear campaign when she saw it. *London Celebrity* had had a controversial change of editor recently, after the previous incumbent had slept with the married Minister of Education and ironically been exposed by his own newspaper. Their already low standard of reporting had now dropped to below sewer level.

"Yeah. Conveniently full of vague, anonymous sources. Did Savage hit a staffer at *London Celebrity* with his car or something? Someone over there really hates him. Bet it's pissing him off too. His reputation's been solid until recently. So totally work-focused that he never got any press, unless it was tagged on to something about Margo." Curiously, Trix asked, "How are you finding him?"

Contradictory.

"'You'll have to speak up,'" Lily said quietly, in her best bossy man-tones. "'I can't hear you over the sound of the half-arsing. Are you a woman or are you one of Cinderella's mice? Was that a laugh or an asthma attack? Louder. Lower. Less. More. *You're shouting!*'"

Trix snorted. "I hope he's not right behind you."

Lily turned around as she spoke. "No, he's—"

Literally right behind her.

"Um," she said into the phone, meeting Savage's even gaze. She was pretty sure her heart was now lodged somewhere around her tonsils. That black eyebrow rose again, sardonically. "I'll call you back later."

Trix was desperately trying not to laugh. "Oh my God, he's right there, isn't he? Sorry, but you might be right after all. It's definitely going to be the vocals that swing it."

Savage leaned back against the stage and crossed one ankle over the other, exuding infinite patience.

Lily gritted her teeth. "I'll see you at home."

"I'll have pizza and vodka waiting at the door."

Ending the call, she slipped her phone back into her pocket. Plan A was to immediately dissolve into the carpet. When she remained corporeal and the silence stretched, she was at a loss.

"There's really no way to recover, is there?"

"Perfect illustration of my point," he said unexpectedly.

She didn't know what that meant, but suspected it was leading into another of his personal insults—and okay, fair cop on this one. She'd been pretty opinionated about *his* unprofessionalism behind *her* back.

"As you've now ably demonstrated," Savage went on, with forgivable irony, "you *are* capable of lowering the register of your voice when you want to. Ergo: lazy."

And ergo: unemployed, shortly.

After imitating him with deadly accuracy and zero spatial awareness, Lily was now impersonating a beetroot. However, when she was pissed off and whinging to her friends, her voice transformed. She *could* do depth, when she could be arsed, and with strength, not pseudo-sexiness. She had smashed most of his preconceptions in the first five minutes, and wasn't tapping into half of her potential. She was becoming a dangerously appealing prospect. He'd always enjoyed surprising an audience and seeing an actor develop beyond their self-imposed boundaries.

Although he strongly suspected that she would be

an even bigger pain in the arse than Bridget, in very different ways.

She kept rubbing her nose, which he'd noticed was her go-to fidget when she felt unsure of herself. He looked at his watch and took pity on both of them. He had enough footage to review with David. "I think I've seen enough."

"Yeah, I can imagine," she said with a grimace, and pulled on the end of her nose. She could add confidence issues to her mental worksheet. The best actors he oversaw had a strong core of arrogance, ideally balanced out with a sense of humour so they weren't a complete and utter shit to work with. The ones who needed constant validation eventually broke under the pressure. A West End run was brutal, competitive and exhausting.

"Someone will be in touch in the next twenty-four hours. We're doing a full cast and crew meet-and-greet this weekend, so we aren't mucking around with this."

"Okay." She picked up her bag and reached out her hand. "Thanks."

Automatically, he closed his fingers around hers again. Her skin was calloused. She'd listed guitar on her resumé, so it was possible that wasn't a lie. Like her circus acrobatics. He almost grinned.

She started to turn away, and then paused and turned. Reaching into her bag, she pulled out a small notepad and pen and scribbled something down.

She tore off the sheet and held it out to him. "I couldn't help overhearing that you're having tile problems. This is the importer my father uses for his businesses. They're top quality and reliable. Might be worth a call."

He didn't think his expression had changed, but he

must have given her a look she'd seen before when her father came up in conversation, because she narrowed her eyes. "It's completely legit."

Yeah, well, he *had* been wondering. Jack Lamprey's profit margins were in the upper strata of wealth, and not many straight and narrow paths led there.

He glanced down at her scrawled handwriting. "Thanks."

She passed David on her way out the door. His stage manager smiled politely into her face, and then turned around to blatantly watch the rear view. The sudden annoyance that rose in Luc's chest reminded him he had to deal with Mitchell before he went home. He was running a company full of sexist fuckwits. Himself included, apparently.

"Don't drool on the cast," he said when the other man reached him. "It's not a good look."

David looked at him. "We're caving into Hudson Warner's blackmail, then, are we? Marilyn's on board?"

"Don't—" He stopped and blew out a heavy breath.

What, it pisses you off that you were a prick about her because it turns out she possesses multiple brain cells and might make you a lot of money? Otherwise, it's open season and totally fine for the Boys' Club to make dick remarks about pretty blondes?

Stress, sleep deprivation, a few more missing tiles, and he ended up with Amelia's voice in his head, offering irritating home truths.

"I don't give a fuck about Warner. The audition went a lot better than I expected. We'd definitely need to bring in Jocasta—" or rather, they'd have to go *to* Jocasta in Oxford, because the speech therapist didn't leave home for a client sight-unseen and voice-unheard "—but I'm leaning towards Lamprey over Clarke."

They reviewed the footage in his office, David watching with folded arms and rampant scepticism. Several times, they stopped the recording, backtracked, commented.

"You're right," David said at last. "In the connection she's made to the material, she's far and away the best. I'm worried that she won't be able to hold up vocally for the long haul, though. There are very good actors who just aren't suited for theatre."

"Agreed. Maybe not the case here."

David studied the screen, where Lily was frozen midway through the monologue. There was a look of such agonised decision on her face, knowledge tinged with regret, the princess caught between two opposing forces.

"Maybe not," he conceded. "But it's a hell of a backfire if you're wrong."

Luc kicked a chastened marketing assistant out of his office at three minutes past five, and then phoned Jack Lamprey's tile importer to request samples.

Maria, his head of PR, stopped him on his way out the front doors at seven. She had an iPad in her hand and her lips were compressed.

He rolled his eyes and held out his hand for the device. Through the glass doors, a camera flashed as their fingers touched. Maria had probably just propelled herself into his bed, in the mind of anyone who believed the gossip blogs. His stock had gone up with the paparazzi since the breakup. They were rabidly looking for Margo's ex's rebound fling, and, according to one particular tabloid, anyone he'd bullied into a nervous breakdown. "Let me guess. Zach Byrne at *London Celebrity*. What crock of shite has he printed now?"

"He's got hold of Damian Cost, who claims he had to work fourteen-hour days and crawled from his death-bed with campylobacter because you wouldn't let him take the day off. And that he's still owed money." Maria looked disgusted. She'd had to run around after Cost with a metaphorical tin of whitewash when they'd all worked together on *The Velvet Room*, trying to cover his meth-fuelled mistakes and outbursts before they leaked to the press.

"He's still owed something." Luc flicked through the article and found about two statements that were halfway factual.

"Byrne's also suggesting that you have violent ten-dencies and got into a physical altercation with Richard Troy at the Theatre Awards."

"I do have violent tendencies when it comes to Rich-ard Troy. I had a long-running fantasy of folding him into human origami and launching him into the stalls. But it would have stuffed my no-claims bonus on the cast insurance."

"Besides which," Maria said, "Richard was at the Awards for about forty-five seconds this year. He waited until Lainie got her award, went all smug-husband and then hustled her out of the building before his own cat-egory was called. The creepy, invasive *West Enders* blog says they had sex in a limo."

He might have to try Amelia's doubtful method of brain-cleansing and run a Google search on cats. "Thanks for that. The day really wasn't bad enough."

"This is getting a little out of control. We could take it to court."

Even more expense and unwelcome publicity. He had no desire to participate in Byrne's one-sided feud. He'd tried to mend fences with the Byrne family in the past; it had achieved nothing. "So far, most of the vitriol is coming from one source only, it's over the top, circumstantial, and interest will die down once people get over the situation with Margo or remember they have lives of their own. Whichever comes first."

"What's with the personal vendetta? Did you steal Zach Byrne's Tonka truck when you were kids or something?"

"Zach Byrne is sixty-five years old, so thank you for *that*." Luc handed back the tablet. "A very long time ago, Byrne's father made the extremely ill-advised decision to go into business with my grandfather. He lost everything, Byrne grew up in poverty, and he's now got a forum to express his feelings about that."

Maria frowned. "Well, it's hardly your fault. Your grandfather's been dead for—"

"Years. Correct. My father tried to make financial compensation when he could; so did I. Byrne adamantly refused our 'blood' money, which apparently we've inherited from a rotting heap of corruption."

They'd actually inherited nothing from Johnny except the falling-down theatre, a problem Luc's father had happily passed into Luc's hands. The money he'd put into it, he'd earned himself. And despite what was written in Byrne's editorials, he'd done it without fiddling his taxes, taking food from babies' mouths, or conning vulnerable pensioners.

"I see. That would be why—"

"—my name has appeared in *London Celebrity* at least twice a day since he took over as editor, with allusions to dodgy business practice and multiple fascist dictators? Yes." Luc shook his head. "Just keep an eye on it for now. If Byrne's named sources are limited to Damian Cost, who burps gin fumes and sits at a forty-five-degree tilt during interviews, I'm not overly concerned at this point. If it gets out of hand, we'll intercede."

"You're the boss."

"That would explain why my name is on all the bills."

It was pitch-black outside when he drove to his parents' place in Shepherd's Bush via Harrods, which was lit up like a cruise ship in port, the rectangular dimensions outlined in bulbs like an architectural sketch. Manic Christmas shoppers were out in force. He picked up flowers and the Egyptian chocolates his mother liked, and walked five blocks back to where he'd found a lucky park.

He was freezing and exhausted by the time he let himself into their house and followed the sounds of anguished groans and enthusiastic shouts to the living room.

"Where's the ref?" his mother asked indignantly as he opened the door. She was curled up in an armchair with her bare feet tucked beneath her, much the way Lily Lamprey had sat during her audition.

He looked at the TV. "I didn't realise *The Great British Bake-Off* was a contact sport. Happy anniversary. Why did I think you were married in September?"

"He *spat out* a perfectly good scone," Célie said indignantly, her French accent still strong after almost fifty years of living in London. Her voice, both speaking and singing, had barely altered since she'd first made her name in opera. He couldn't help appreciating the dulcet tones more than usual. "We did get married in September. The fourth." She smiled at her husband. Cameron Savage was sprawled full-length on the couch, looking amused. "It's forty-seven years today since your *papa* said he loved me."

"I see."

"Also since we first made love."

He paused in the act of handing over the gifts.

His older brother grinned at him from the most comfortable armchair. Alex indicated the coffee table, where an orchid sat in a gift-wrapped pot. "Welcome to the club of feeling like a complete pervert for bringing celebratory flowers."

No kidding.

Luc surveyed Alex. "You look better." The last time he'd seen his brother, Alex's divorce had just been finalised. There had been a lot of bitterness and ridiculous hunger-striking.

Alex had been the only person surprised by the failure of his brief marriage. Even the woman who'd baked the wedding cake had seen that estrangement on the horizon. Luc's ex-sister-in-law was a nice enough girl. She was intelligent and ambitious. She was also nineteen. His brother was forty-six and a moron. A considerably out-of-pocket, depressed moron.

"Yeah, well." Alex looked distinctly shifty. He should probably start putting more cash aside for spousal support. Luc could hear the distant sound of inappropriate wedding bells, take two. "I sort of met someone."

"That's great." Luc took the free armchair and stretched out his legs. "How old is she?"

"Fuck off," Alex returned without rancour. "She's thirty-two."

Well, it was an improvement. By the time he was hobbling around a retirement village, his brother might actually hook up with someone his own age.

"Don't curse," said their mother severely, the woman who had been known to out-swear case-hardened sailors in an Irish pub. She had a chocolate wedged into one cheek like a squirrel and was admiring the flowers. "What beautiful lilies. You usually buy me roses."

"How's the casting going?" his father asked. He had so far managed to restrain himself from interfering in the theatre renovations, but Luc suspected the grace period would soon be over.

"We're getting there."

"Are you still taking everyone to Aston Park this weekend?"

Both Elizabeth I and Mary I had stayed at Aston Park when it had been a private home, so it seemed like a thematic choice for the meet-and-greet, and the hotel owners were fairly hospitable.

"Unless the forecast is right and Shropshire gets a massive dumping of snow."

No way in hell was he risking getting snowbound with Bridget. How to lose every shred of sanity in one easy step.

Célie changed the channel during the ad break and landed on a chat show. A very familiar blonde was seated on a couch, fending off the determined prying of the comedian host. The man seemed to be incapable of pursuing a line of conversation without resorting to eyebrow aerobics and desperate humour. The show had obviously been pre-recorded, since Lily's hair was longer on the screen. Today, it had been a silky, shoulder-length tangle.

"So you don't believe in love?" the host asked, and managed to turn a completely vapid question into something offensive.

"I don't believe that you're somehow *completed* by romantic love. You aren't born half a person, doomed to drift through life unfulfilled until you find someone who can validate you. You're a whole person with a whole life, that you might choose to share with another person. Or you might not. Your body and mind are your own. Your happiness is your responsibility and your right." A strange, fleeting expression touched her face.

"Hear, hear," Célie said, and ate another chocolate. "Fucking men. It always has to be about them in some way, doesn't it?"

Cameron raised his wineglass to her. "Happy love anniversary to you too, darling." He looked at Luc. "You were saying? About casting?"

Luc nodded at the screen, where the host was trying—and failing—to worm a controversial sound bite out of Lily about her soap character's sex life.

"Our Elizabeth I."

Chapter Three

A car was coming for Lily in ten minutes and she was cutting it fine with her packing. For the past couple of days, since the casting director at Savage Productions had called her agent with an official offer, she'd been existing in a surreal bubble. She kept bouncing back and forth between elation and terror. With a fair whack of incredulity. After Savage's charming critique and her own disrespectful fuck-up, she'd assumed he would chuck her headshots in the bin.

"I say this as someone who would probably rescue her books first if the flat burnt down and then come back for you, but you may not need eight books for one weekend," Trix said from the doorway. "I fear a meet-and-greet *might* involve social interaction with nonfictional people." She had four sets of tangled fairy lights slung around her neck. They'd found *Elf* on TV last night and she'd come down with rapid-onset Christmas spirit. Lily had come home this afternoon to a wreath on the door and a bald tree in the living room. Judging by the state of the lights, Trix would still be standing here unwinding them when she got back next week.

Lily slapped a hand down on a teetering pile of books

before it collapsed. "This is the third edit. I've already weeded it down from fifteen."

It wasn't an option, being away from home without her favourite books. Her Kindle was great for down-time between scenes at the studio, but when things went tits up, she needed her favourite characters physically *in* her hands. She was actually looking forward to the weekend—the hotel looked gorgeous on the website, she hadn't been out of London in months, and there were several actors in the cast she wanted to meet—but so far, her interactions with Luc Savage had proved somewhat stressful.

She added a worn copy of *Jane Eyre* to the stack.

She wasn't sure what kind of clothes she was sup-posed to take. It was fine if it was just cosy fireside chats with the rest of the cast and crew, but going away en masse did smack horrifyingly of corporate team-building. If she ended up climbing rope ladders in the snow or playing the trust game with Bridget Barclay, falling back and expecting to land safely in the lead-ing lady's arms, she was going to need really grippy trainers in the first instance and probably a first-aid kit in the second.

She was also packing for a night in Oxford, as ap-parently the country's best speech therapist could be found haunting the Bodleian, and Savage was wasting no time. They were going straight there on Monday.

"What are your plans for the weekend?" She tried to close a bulging zip. "Are you going out with Aiden again?"

Trix was literally wrapped up in her fairy light ca-tastrophe. "No," she said, twisting and turning, and shedding plastic bulb covers at an alarming rate. "We went out for dinner on Tuesday, and over dessert he suddenly asked if I didn't think I was a bit old for pink hair. Apparently I'd be quite pretty with dark hair." Lily twisted to look at her. "Yeah. Then Prince Charming made some kind of comment about how it's so refreshing that I don't wear any makeup offstage, because a lot of girls try to hide their freckles. Implying that I ought to go home and pack on the concealer immediately. I *was* wearing makeup, by the way. Just not a full face of greasepaint."

Trix had a permanent role in *The Festival of Masks* cirque burlesque show and was usually heavily made-up to look like a broken porcelain doll. She went through two jars of cleanser a month, scrubbing off the thick paint each night.

"Not that it would be his business if I chose to go out wearing just my face." The words came out sharply before Trix made an obvious effort to relax. "Then he made fun of cos-play." She gestured at her pale pink bob and the trail of little stars tattooed up her neck. "Do I look like someone who thinks dressing up is lame? I do it for a living, for God's sake." She crossed to the wardrobe and stretched up to feel around the shelf where Lily had stored all the miscellaneous decorations last Christmas. "Anyway, it was getting a bit serious."

"You've been seeing him for three weeks."

"Exactly." Trix pulled down a garland of tinsel and plucked at it thoughtfully. "Practically a relationship."

Her eyes were shadowed.

Lily's stomach tightened, but before she could speak, the doorbell rang.

Trix looked at the partially zipped cases. "You get the door. I'll try to tame the beasts."

"Thanks." Lily got to her feet but hesitated. "Trix—"

The bell rang again, at impatient length. "Better answer that before they give up and leave, and you're stuck fondling vicars for the next ten years." Trix handed Lily the hideous, winking plastic Santa her dad had sent her in one of his more whimsical moods. "Put this on the mantel on your way past, would you?"

Lily hid it behind a pile of towels in the linen cupboard before she went to the front door. She pasted on a polite expression as she opened it. She was expecting a hired driver who wouldn't be looking forward to a six-hour round trip in this weather.

Luc Savage's quizzical eyes met hers, then dropped to her wavering smile.

"Hello," he said, when it became clear she was too startled to speak first.

"Um, hi." She came to with a slight jerk and shifted aside to let him in.

He was dressed more casually than he'd been at his offices, but still impeccably. His wool jumper looked soft and touchable, and he'd thrust his hands casually into the pockets of well-pressed dark trousers. His shoes were shined, his hair neatly combed and his jaw clean-shaven.

If she saw a black-and-white photo of him, she really would think he was an actor from the forties or fifties.

Which reminded her that he'd thought the same about her, and his comparison hadn't been a compliment.

He looked grim, and her stomach gave a sharp churn. God, he wasn't revoking the contract, was he?

Savage cleared his throat. He seemed annoyed with life in general. "Unfortunately, there's been a mix-up at the hire car company and we're short several drivers. You're with me, if you don't object."

His tone suggested that if she objected, she could renew her acquaintance with the evening train service.

What she meant to say was something along the lines of "Thanks for the lift."

What came out of her mouth was "What, all the way to Shropshire?"

Trix, appearing in the doorway to the bedroom, coughed into her fist.

"No." Savage nodded politely at Trix. "I thought I'd do a wild detour to the Forest of Dean and leave you there with a compass and a Swiss Army Knife. Consider it the final audition phase. If you can make it to Aston Park alive by the end of the weekend, I'll stick an extra fiver in your pay packet."

Sarcasm, insults and a nasty habit of appearing without warning. She was going to be sharing a car for three hours with the Demon King from panto. She wanted to be annoyed, but couldn't hold back a small smile.

Trix brought the suitcases from the bedroom, towing one in each hand. She was five foot nothing and tiny, and could probably have fit *in* the luggage without having to bend her head. Lily hurried to take them from her and collided with Savage, who was apparently on the same errand. There was an awkward moment in which they stumbled, accidentally hugged and burst apart in silent horror.

Trix blinked.

Lily felt her cheeks burning again. What the actual fuck. It was as if the part of her brain responsible for normal foot and hand movements went under general anaesthesia every time they were in the same room.

"This is Beatrix Lane." Now her voice was wooden as well as breathy. Fantastic. "Trix, this is Luc Savage."

"Nice to meet you, Mr. Savage."

Savage shook Trix's hand. "It's Luc." His eyes returned to Lily. "To cast members as well."

She tested that out in her mind. She was on first-name terms with all the production and direction team at CTV, but it had taken a long time to get used to greeting some of them informally. Oddly, with Savage—with *Luc*—it seemed natural.

Probably her self-conscious being contrary and not wanting to put the perpetrator of the blow-up doll comment on a pedestal.

"Well," Trix said to Lily. "Enjoy your jaunt to the country while the rest of us are slaving away under the house lights."

"Trix's playing Pierrette in *The Festival of Masks*," Lily found herself explaining, even though she couldn't imagine that the man whose name was synonymous with high-brow drama had much time for the musical spectaculars.

He surprised her. "Impressive. I've seen the show. It's excellent."

Trix looked so happy at that moment that Lily felt a rush of gratitude towards him.

"Thanks," Trix said, almost shyly. "A lot of people at the Old Wellington have worked with you. They all raved about the experience."

Luc's response was wry. "After the tabloid memoirs of other former team members, that's good to hear." His phone beeped and he flipped open the case. "I'm sorry to rush Lily away, but it's a reasonably long drive and we still have someone else to collect on the way." He glanced down at the suitcases. "Is this everything?"

Lily grabbed her handbag and snack bag from the coffee table. "That's all."

She hoped he had plenty of space in his car. She didn't want to leave one of the bags behind. Besides dragging along half the contents of her bookshelves, she always felt it was better to come back with unworn clothes than to run short on knickers.

She didn't need to worry. His vehicle seemed to be suffering an identity crisis, unsure if it was a car or a freight truck. It was black with semi-tinted windows and looked like it ought to be part of a presidential cavalcade. The tyres were almost taller than Trix.

Luc opened the boot to stow her bags and Lily saw snow chains. It was, as her snarky weather app said, "so freaking cold—are you sure you didn't enter this location through the back of a wardrobe?", but the forecast had improved to a lot of rain and very minor flurries, so hopefully not enough to affect the roads or strand them in the countryside.

She hugged Trix goodbye, which elicited a protest when she squeezed too tight in her lingering concern, and still didn't look at Luc when he held the door open for her.

He didn't mention who the second passenger was, and they drove in silence until he drew up outside a townhouse in Pimlico. There was a bright pink Lamborghini parked outside. As cars went, it was pretty fucking amazing. Unfortunately, thanks to the paparazzi, Lily knew who it belonged to. She was frankly blown away that Bridget Barclay hadn't insisted on a commute by private helicopter.

Luc sat for a moment in silence, his wrists resting on the wheel.

She cleared her throat. "You all right there?"

"Just mentally preparing. And despising the car company with every fibre of my being."

"Did they cancel all the cars at the last minute?"

"Just two, but not until everybody else had left, so it was this or stick you both on the train, alone and at night."

Yeah, she'd figured the artistic director and company CEO didn't usually moonlight as a chauffeur.

Reluctantly, he opened his door and got out, and she glanced over her shoulder.

"Should I move into the backseat?" She had a feeling Bridget was going to expect top billing in every respect.

Luc stuck his head back into the car to fix her with an even stare. "Leave that seat free and I will literally cut your salary in half."

Hey, she was the lesser of two evils. She'd have to watch that these heady compliments didn't go to her head.

He took the steps to the front door in one stride, rang the bell and disappeared into the house. Eight rounds of her Sudoku app later, he came out with two Louis Vuitton weekender bags, a dog bed and a cartoon storm cloud over his head. She could feel the aggravation all the way from the tank.

While he was putting the luggage in the back and letting in a lot of bitingly cold air, Bridget made her entrance in a Burberry coat and rose-gold sunglasses. Her black hair was swept into perfect waves, just touched with silver that probably wasn't natural. All she was missing was a silk scarf tied over it, Grace Kelly–style.

She was clutching a massive pillow under one arm and cradling a bichon frise in the other.

Lily had seen her from a distance at the TV Awards this year, when Bridget had been a guest presenter, but a phalanx of black-suited minders had informed everyone in sight that Mrs. Barclay didn't wish to be disturbed, as if they'd all been planning to latch on to her like spider monkeys and screech for an autograph.

Bridget stood on the pavement, waiting glamorously. When Luc went to open the rear door, she nodded at the front passenger seat where Lily sat.

He said something sharply to her, which Lily couldn't hear through the thickness of the glass, and looked slightly incredulous when she responded.

His shoulders rose in a visible search for patience, before he took the puppy from her and opened Lily's door. "Bridget is graciously extending you the privilege of holding Penny Sweets for the next three hours. Since she's tweaked a tendon in her knee and requires the full length of the backseat in order to recover in time for rehearsals."

The screaming subtext of *"bullshit"* hung in the air between them. Lily pressed her lips together to hide her smile. Spreading her coat across her knees, she reached for the puppy.

Luc continued to hold it, ignoring the indignant squirming. "Do you actually like dogs?" He didn't trouble to speak quietly. "Because otherwise she can sit on the lap of the person who supposedly can't exist without her for two days."

Bridget huffed, and Lily tore her eyes from Luc's penetrating gaze. Private amusement lurked in the grey depths. "It's fine." She took the ball of fluff for a cuddle.

A tiny wet nose touched her palm. She could feel the rapid fluttering of a little heart. "She's gorgeous. And she's not exactly a Great Dane, is she? I'm sure we'll cope for a few hours."

Penny Sweets took exception to the comment on her size and immediately let loose with a series of high-pitched yips.

Luc pinched the bridge of his nose. "I know it's tempting to look for an off switch, but Bridget swears it's a real-life dog."

He opened the rear door, and Bridget settled herself on the spacious backseat with some energetic pillow-fluffing.

Lily greeted her cheerfully, trying not to sneeze at the heavy musk-based perfume. Bridget looked her up and down, frowned and put in her earbuds.

Okay, then.

By the time Luc returned to the driver's seat, the puppy had curled into a quiet ball and was chewing on Lily's thumb.

She rubbed the little fuzzy head. "I take it you're not a dog person."

Luc negotiated the turn into the busy traffic flow before he replied. "Oh, I'm a *dog* person. I'm pretty sure that what you're cuddling is the inside of a cushion. Although it sounds like a car alarm, which I admit adds to the confusion."

They slowed to a stop at an intersection. He glanced over at her and then down at her lap. Briefly, the corner of his mouth curving, he lifted his hand from the wheel to offer a fingertip for the puppy to nip. His fingers grazed Lily's as he returned his attention to the road, and he frowned—just a flicker of discomposure.

Absently, she rubbed the back of her hand against her lap as they drove.

"Do you have a copy of the full script I could look at?" she asked when they reached the outer boroughs and got onto the motorway.

Luc opened a bottle of water with one hand. "Do you get carsick?"

"Well…"

"Then no." His Adam's apple moved as he drank. "There's a selection of audiobooks on the internal system. Dial on the left side. Choose whatever you like."

The cunning manoeuvre also known as *Don't talk to me*.

She was impressed with the extent of the car's book collection, which ranged from Ernest Hemingway to Lee Child. She homed in on the Ngaio Marsh murder mysteries.

"How about *Surfeit of Lampreys*?" Luc slanted a glance at her. "For some reason, that speaks to me tonight."

She rolled her eyes, but did go with her namesake. She'd always thought the eccentricities of the fictional Lamprey family had nothing on her flesh and blood.

He turned his head and caught her staring.

In response to his silent enquiry, she panicked and made shameless use of the puppy. "Um, I think Penny Sweets needs a wee. She's fidgeting."

He muttered that of course it would be on the fucking motorway, and indicated at the next exit.

Lily had almost forgotten Bridget was in the car, but when they stopped at a shopping centre, where Penny Sweets obligingly peed on the single strip of grass by the road, she woke up from her impromptu nap and began to live up to her reputation.

"Why have we stopped?" she demanded, emerging from the car. The streetlights cast a demonic red tint on her face.

"Blame your property's minuscule bladder." Luc was clearly having none of the impending strop.

"But it's cold!" Her voice hit a level that Lily thought even she would struggle to achieve.

No shit. It was December, and it was England.

"We might as well get some food while we're here," Luc said, totally ignoring her. "I'd rather not stop again in case the weather packs in."

Bridget looked with distaste at the three dining options: Starbucks, Pizza Express and Wagamama, but didn't insist that they produce a Michelin-starred restaurant on the spot. "I'll have a fruit salad and a green tea," she said grudgingly to Lily.

"Does she look like your maid?" Luc asked, before Lily had a chance to do more than blink. "Food expenses are included this weekend. Personal slaves are not. I will, however, mind the Furby while you're stretching your faulty tendon on the walk, since I value my upholstery."

Bridget opened her mouth, thought better of it, and speared him with a vicious look. Taking the twenty-pound note he extended, she stomped off towards the restaurants with nary a limp.

This was going to be a merry weekend. Lily assumed Bridget was a professional onstage, at least, or she wouldn't have been cast. Luc had directed her before, and it seemed like one-chance saloon. Cock up and don't expect to come back.

Luc watched her stalk away and muttered, barely comprehensibly, "Fucking Ferreti."

Lily flicked him a curious glance and he changed the subject. "Get whatever you like." He handed over another note. She obviously *was* the lesser irritant in this specific situation. She'd scored a fifty. And everything in her rebelled at taking it.

"I have money," she said stiffly. A gust of icy wind crept beneath her coat, which had a new stain on the front she hoped was melted Jaffa Cake and gloomily suspected was puppy poo. At least it was a cheapie from the Next sale. She folded her arms and shivered.

Luc had picked up Penny Sweets and tucked her into the opening of his own coat. It seemed to be instinctive when he stepped to the side, acting as a buffer between Lily and the rising wind, trying to keep her warm as well.

Well, that was…kind. And kind of unsettling.

"Of course you have money." His impatient tone was at odds with the chivalry. "You've been on a primetime salary for four years, and your father is Jack Lamprey. If you couldn't afford a few noodles, you'd need serious budgeting help."

Best never mention the Audi R8 she'd bought during her first year on the show, then, which had resulted in having to cut out takeaways for six months. Her first big endorsement cheque had temporarily gone to her head.

"This is a work weekend. I'm sorry if I'm trampling on your feminist principles," he went on sarcastically, rubbing the puppy's trembling back, "but it's company policy to cover expenses when we drag you away on location, not an assumption that you're a woman and therefore incapable of providing for yourself. And I'm fucking freezing, this dog is about to tunnel a hole through my chest, and would you just take the money already?"

Ten to one, she'd just knocked Bridget off the podium for biggest pain in the arse. She'd never had a reputation for being difficult to work with and didn't want to earn one. She wasn't going to lie down and let arsehat comments roll over her, but he was being totally reasonable at the moment. "Sorry." She took the money and wound the note around her finger. "Er, thanks for dinner?"

"On behalf of the company, no worries."

She suspected this was one of the worst evenings he'd had all year.

"I'm going to Pizza Express." Automatically, she reached out to soothe the puppy when it whimpered, but withdrew her hand at supersonic speed when she stroked Luc's knuckle. She hoped her cheeks were already red from windburn. "Um…what would you like?" She anticipated his exasperation. "I'm not being passive-aggressive and trying to earn my keep. There's no point all three of us going separately, playing pass-the-parcel with the dog. We'll be here all night."

He shrugged. "A slice of anything and a black coffee. Thanks. You might want to go all out on the cheese while you can, because once we get to Oxford and you're under Jocasta Moore's thumb, dairy's off the menu. Probably chocolate and caffeine too."

Her expression made him grin, properly, for the first time. He had cheek grooves, like dimples on steroids, and he looked momentarily *nice*. Like he had a personality with facets beyond frosty grump. Otherwise, he wasn't magically transformed, no years instantly dropping from his face. He still looked forty-odd, just disturbingly jolly.

When they were back on the road, Lily restarted the audiobook for a while, but it was difficult to follow the story with Bridget complaining about everything and anything that crossed her mind.

It became almost funny, waiting to see how far she could scrape the bottom of the barrel for a whinge—an evening jogger's reflective safety jacket made her eyes hurt—and watching Luc's struggle to keep his responses civil. If his production didn't depend on Bridget retaining her tongue to deliver her lines, Lily thought he would have yanked it out by force and strangled her with it.

About half an hour from Aston Park, Bridget's body took pity on them and returned her to a snuffling sleep. The countryside was so dark outside the window that Lily could only see reflections in the glass. She watched reflection-Luc check his leading lady in the rear-view mirror.

"God," he muttered. "I thought I'd gone deaf for a second."

She swallowed a yawn and turned in her seat. A question had been in her mind since he'd mentioned her father at the rest stop, but even if she'd been able to get a word in, she hadn't wanted to discuss her family while Bridget was conscious. "Do you know my father?"

He at least knew *of* her father. She hadn't missed the recoil in the amphitheatre, when she'd kindly attempted to assist him with his interior decorating dilemma. Like she was trying to foist mob connections on him or something. Start with a few tiles, end with a horse head in the bed.

Her father lived by the creed that the end justified the means. Like his MP wife, he'd devoted the past few decades to a cause. Business on his agenda, women's rights and equitable pay on hers. Politically, Lily had always admired the woman who couldn't stand to be in the same room as her. *Unlike* Lady Charlotte, Jack had no qualms in bending the truth and playing the system if it ultimately benefited his projects.

But he *tested* the law; as far as she was aware, he didn't break it.

"We've met a couple of times." Luc navigated the tricky country road; there were no street lights, but several potholes. He didn't sound massively thrilled with the topic. "It's my own father who knows him well. Knew him well. He and Jack were poker buddies back in the day."

She grimaced into the blackness. "Sounds about right." Few gamblers didn't live to regret sitting down at a card table with Jack. Even in his seventies, her father was still wringing tears and inheritances out of grown adults who ought to know better. He never played with anyone who was betting on their sole source of income, or was drunk beyond the ability to reason, but that was his sole concession. "You said 'knew' him well, past tense. Jack didn't—"

"Empty the family coffers?" Luc supplied readily. "No, he fell out with Dad when—" He came to an abrupt halt.

Lily eyed him. "I appreciate the hesitation, but if it was over a woman, you can say so without shattering my delicate illusions. My mother was a twenty-five-year-old aspiring lounge singer and Jack was a fifty-year-old married club mogul when I was born. Infer for yourself."

There was a sound from the backseat, but she could just see in the dim light that Bridget was still asleep with her mouth open.

It was so quiet in the car. She could hear Bridget's snuffling, Luc's deep, even breathing, and tiny puppy snores. It was relaxing, stroking the silky ears. "I'm his daughter and I love him unconditionally, but he's not a good husband and his wife shouldn't *have* to love him unconditionally. I don't know why she didn't file for divorce decades ago."

She forgot where she was and who she was talking to for a second. The dark stillness seemed to invite confidences and a sense of unreality, like a fifth shot of tequila. It probably ended similarly in oversharing and regret. She sensed his glance burning into her ear and decided to stop rambling while she was behind.

"Jack obviously has an eye, or an ear, for singers." Luc unexpectedly turned her embarrassing monologue into a dialogue. "He made a pass at my mother and Dad was understandably pissed off. According to Célie, your father was shot down in flames and took it 'charmingly.'" There was a note of amused affection in his voice when he spoke of his mother, the French classical soprano Célie Verne.

Why had she even begun this conversation? In no profession was it appropriate to air your family's ancient dirty laundry to the person paying your salary, even if there was something of a memory lane crossover.

He was her boss. She'd had a preview of his drill-instructor, slave-driver approach to direction and was going to be existing under it for weeks. And he thought she was a medical marvel: the amazing walking, unfortunately talking, brainless woman.

All things considered, she still had no idea why she was in his car and not back on the audition circuit. It only underlined the fact that she needed to concentrate on the role and nothing else.

She felt all odd and prickly again.

It was the most bizarre reaction she'd ever had to a man. Not quite antipathy, not just bog-standard physical attraction, definitely not intimidation. She couldn't define it, and she wasn't happy about it.

For the remainder of the trip, she kept her breaths shallow. Even as the car was crunching over a long gravel driveway, and polite people were coming out of the glowing facade of an impressive stately home, and she was walking in ghostly footsteps up stone steps where Elizabeth I had once tread, she told herself it was because Bridget's perfume had made her nauseated in the stuffy heat of the car.

Not because she could smell the warm, spicy undertones of male skin.

Luc folded his arm behind his head. It was two minutes past two.

There had been four more construction delays before he'd left the theatre. After an eleven-hour workday, followed by a road trip he could only assume was some kind of karmic punishment, he should have fallen asleep within minutes.

He had to be in the library at nine to make sure the cast played nice. The crew were usually fine. It was the actors who tended to behave like opposing parties in a parliamentary debate, until they found their rhythm as an ensemble and started working off one another.

Dylan Waitely was likely to be the biggest problem.

The twentysomething was aging down a decade to play Guildford Dudley, Jane Grey's husband, but he already had the arrogance and immaturity of a teenager. He was an extremely skilful actor, and unfortunately he had the worst possible temperament to ground that level of ability. He was energetic, hard-working and could put emotive power into any character. He was also entitled, impatient and a cocky little bastard with anyone he considered beneath him. He was going to kick hard against the restraints of a comparatively minor role in a female-dominated play.

Amelia was resident den mother for the company once the casting was final, and she would have her hands full. Of the female cast, Luc was most concerned about Lily, the unknown factor. Bridget's ego would never allow her to flub her part, and Freddy Carlton, their Jane Grey, was at nineteen already an eight-year veteran of the West End. She never seemed fazed by anything that was thrown at her. He cast her whenever possible; she missed brilliance by a hair's width, but she was popular with audiences and the safe bet to Lily's wild card.

Lily, whose voice had been strained with cynicism when she'd spoken of her parents. If Margo had ever revealed that hint of vulnerability, his mind would probably have gone to how she could use it in her performance—because he was that much of a bastard.

His reaction to Lily in that moment had been entirely different, totally inappropriate and a blow to the gut.

He could swear that he still smelled the elusive scent of her perfume.

In a rush of movement, he threw off the expensive coverlet and snapped on the light. It cast a golden glow over a suite that was opulent and luxurious but far too sensual for his current taste. Aston Park was a popular wedding and honeymoon venue, and he could see why. Everything from the California king-size bed to the cushioned bay window and sunken hot tub was set up for endless hours of sex and infatuated cuddling.

He pulled on his discarded trousers and a crumpled T-shirt, then quietly left his room and padded barefoot down the corridor. He'd left the set sketches and character mood boards in the library. If he couldn't sleep, he might as well kill time with unnecessary tweaking of minor details.

The hallways were peaceful until he passed Dylan Waitely's bedroom door, which was reverberating with moans and squawks. It sounded like half a dozen amorous parakeets had been let loose.

Luc shook his head. He couldn't care less what his cast did behind closed doors if that was where it stayed, but he was fairly sure Dylan had only been married for about six months. Partners weren't invited this weekend, so obviously those marriage vows had been given a swift heave out the window. Of course, this *was* the PR nightmare who'd once ranked his former sexual partners by body type and performance on live radio, so not a massive surprise.

He wasn't sure why anyone bothered to get married in this business. It wasn't so much "until death" as "until I don't feel like it." Fidelity was no guarantee of a lasting commitment, either. He and Margo shared an identical philosophy on cheating—wouldn't do it, wouldn't forgive it—but they'd still come unstuck. After their last-ditch attempt at making it work, Margo had claimed that he would always put work first, that she was the perpetual understudy in his life—and admitted it was the same for her.

She was right. There hadn't seemed anything left to say after that.

She'd developed stronger feelings for Alberto in one week than she'd had for Luc in eight years. He was human, he had an ego, and it stung. But it didn't gut him the way it should have, after that many years.

God, he was actually jealous. Not of Alberto. Of Margo, of his chronically devoted parents, of anyone who could inspire that level of feeling.

Caught up in conflicting emotions, he shoved open the library door with enough force that it banged against the frame—and scared the living shit out of Lily Lamprey, who instinctively retaliated by chucking a book at his head. He didn't duck in time and swore when it caught him full on the chin and thudded to the ground. The noises echoed in the silent house, carried along beautifully by centuries-old stone acoustics, and they both froze.

A few tense seconds ticked by, but no other doors opened within hearing range. Luc exhaled, then bent to pick up the book and glanced at the spine. Jane Austen. He inwardly groaned. In his experience, women didn't get up in the middle of the night and start reading *Pride and Prejudice* unless they were in a serious emotional funk. He was in a shitty enough mood himself that he had no patience for patting a histrionic actor on the head.

He also wasn't thrilled to encounter Lily at this particular moment. She…jarred with his recent thoughts.

He looked at her properly. She was curled up on a huge window seat, cushions propped behind her back.

She wore pyjama bottoms and an enormous fuzzy pink jumper that made her look like a Muppet. Her silvery-blond hair was spiking out in all directions, which he assumed was from being pressed against a pillow, not because she reacted like a puffer fish when startled.

"Holy shit." She lowered the hand she'd pressed against her chest. "I was this close to needing mouth-to-mouth."

It was another of those painful moments when unfortunate words seemed to crystallise in the air around them. Luc naturally glanced at her lips. Lily turned bright red and clashed with her jumper.

"Although," she added, grabbing hold of her nose for moral support, "it would be a little difficult to administer when I keep sticking my foot in there." She pushed a mess of hair back behind her ear. "Sorry about smacking you in the face with a book. It's my knee-jerk reaction when something scares the bejeezus out of me. I throw things. Spiders enter my flat at their own peril."

"Let's hope no one opens a door when you're ironing or bricklaying." His chin was still throbbing. He had no compunction about the sarcasm.

She made a humming noise. "Opens a door. Tries to wrench one off its hinges like The Incredible Hulk. Po-tay-to, po-tah-to."

Amelia would be disappointed to learn that his death stare wasn't infallible. Lily smiled blandly in return.

He tossed back Mr. Darcy and Co., who packed a solid punch for their age, and she caught the book neatly and laid it on her lap.

Despite his resolve to collect the mood boards and leave her to it, he heard himself asking, "Can't sleep?"

She shook her head. She was tracing patterns on the

book cover with her fingertips; he found it difficult to
look away. "First-night nerves a little early." She snorted
softly. "I don't know why I tell you these things. It's not
exactly going to instil confidence, is it?"

"I'd rather you were honest, so I know where we are."
He meant "you" in a widespread, all-members-of-the-
company context, but it came out completely singular
and personal.

Jerkily, he walked over to the desk where he'd left
the mood boards. He lifted the displays for the principal character costume designs and the first three scenes
of Act One.

"Oh." There was a rustling noise as Lily got up from
the window seat and padded over to him. "Is that—Can
I see, or is it confidential?"

Her hair was tickling his jaw. He moved away, but
tilted the boards where she could see them. "We'll be
presenting them for the cast and crew tomorrow." He
glanced at the grandfather clock by the fireplace. "Later
this morning."

Lily bent closer to examine the drawings for her costumes. Her hand came out, fingertips hovering an inch
away from the fabric samples.

"You can touch."

She looked up with a quick smile before she stroked
the royal blue velvet. "Beautiful." She studied the first-
scene mock-up. "That's weird. It's a completely different visual, so why does it remind me of the procession
scene you did for *The Armada*?"

He looked at her speculatively. "The basic layout is
almost identical. Well spotted. Even the design team
haven't realised that."

"Well, I did see *The Armada* about five times. Unapologetic theatre buff. Actually, I went so many times that the *Digital Mail* posted some crap story that I was having a fling with Adrian Blair." She straightened, and they ended up nose to nose. "I wasn't."

Her eyes were deep brown, almost black, and shadowed with fatigue.

She frowned a little.

His brain suggested that the natural course of action was to reach out and smooth it away, and what the everlasting fuck.

This wasn't him.

He wasn't his brother. He didn't make a dick of himself running after women half his age. He wasn't even attracted to younger women as a rule; they tended to be at such a different place in life that there was no connection.

Although most women he spoke to went all out with the gushing and lash-fluttering, in the hope he might be bowled over by their star quality and give their career a leg-up.

Lily usually looked as if she'd rather knee him in the balls.

Apparently he found that an attractive quality, since his mind was continuing down inappropriate channels, telling him that her monster jumper looked very touchable and he'd probably quite enjoy nuzzling her neck.

Her eyes skated away from his. "I should go back to bed."

Fuck, he hoped his face hadn't reflected his thoughts.

He nodded. "You'll have to keep a regular sleep schedule throughout the run or you'll burn out. Best to start now."

That equally applied to him, at least for pre-production and rehearsals, which she would obviously like to retort.

"Right," she said, with just a hint of meaning. "I'll keep that in mind."

They moved at the same time, and she collided with him for approximately the twentieth time since they'd met. They were like a couple of bloody magnets. He discovered for himself that her jumper *was* incredibly soft, and that his body control regressed about twenty-five years when her breast momentarily flattened against his ribs.

"Good night," she said in a strangled, warm rush of breath to his collarbone, and disappeared out of the room like she'd been propelled from a slingshot.

She's on your payroll. And she was probably watching the Muppets while you were blocking your first show. You fucking pervert.

Luc bent his head, shoved his fingers through his hair and swore.

Chapter Four

Lily crashed into a solid male torso and hit the ice with a thump. Suddenly, the cushioned bubble-butt leggings Freddy Carlton had insisted she borrow—not so embarrassing. This would have been the last time she could sit down for a week otherwise. The lively teen had turned up at her bedroom door after lunch with "arse-saving products" and was clearly a genius.

She could almost *feel* Luc's scowl from here. He had not been a happy bunny this morning when his casting director, Amelia, suggested they all try out the private skating rink on the grounds. A muttered conversation had devolved into a furious, whispered spat, with stray sentences thrown out of the kerfuffle: "…already lost one idiot to broken legs…" and "…such a killjoy, they'll be fine…"

Amelia had finally turned her back on him and announced with a smile, "There'll be a hot chocolate bar and outdoor fires. Try not to snap any limbs or die of hypothermia. Enjoy!"

A large hand appeared in front of Lily's face. She grabbed it and let Dylan Waitely haul her to her feet. As she should have expected, he refused to let go, so she was left wobbling on the spot, trying to shake him off like a stubborn piece of cling film.

"Still playing hard to get?" he asked, grinning, and she was glad she wasn't playing Jane Grey, because even standing next to him onstage was likely to be a trial of uninvited groping. Poor Freddy.

She had seen Dylan recently in *Singin' in the Rain*, her favourite musical, and he'd been so good that she'd been looking forward to meeting him. The reality was a let-down.

"Still married?" she returned, and managed to free her hand.

Dylan shook his head sadly. "And here I thought seducing other people's husbands was your forte, lovely."

"Yes, well, I'm not really a man-eating homewrecker and you're not really a puddle-dancing Gene Kelly. Life is full of these small disappointments."

Luc appeared at the fence nearby. There were snow-flakes caught in his hair, so that he appeared to have aged a few more years in the past half hour. When she'd woken after three hours of sleep and stumbled grog-gily to the lush velvet drapes, the countryside had been transformed into a glistening whiteout. This was, bar none, the nicest place she'd ever stayed. The grounds around her father's home in Chesham were beautiful too, but she rarely even visited there. As a young child, she'd followed her mother on tour; in her teens, she'd gone to a surprisingly fun city boarding school. When she'd spent holiday weekends with Jack, it had been at the London flat he kept for business guests.

She might have had a tiny Elizabeth-Bennet-at-Pemberley moment while walking down the grand staircase this morning.

"Have you hurt yourself?"

She liked the way he phrased that, just to emphasize that it was her own fault if she had. He sounded slightly concerned, but probably had thoughts of recasting for a third time, with an additional level of difficulty. *Two* Elizabeths down with shattered limbs would generate jinx rumours. She could imagine how impatient he'd be with theatre superstitions. He probably stalked around backstage bellowing "Macbeth" at the top of his lungs.

"No. Not at all." She almost mentioned her well-padded backside but caught herself in time. She had no verbal filter around him. Her instinct was to blurt out whatever came into her mind, which was not only out of character, because she'd been burned enough times in the media to be guarded around strangers, but unlikely to be appreciated. His picture was situated under "workaholic" in her mental dictionary. Right under her father's image, slightly above her mother's. If it wasn't directly related to the production, she doubted he wanted to know.

Anyway, it seemed like a bad idea all round to mention her arse in front of Dylan. He'd already tried to cop multiple feels of it while she was toasting marshmallows in the outdoor fire, and had almost added a skewered testicle to his never-ending store of anecdotes.

Luc narrowed his eyes.

"Really. Not even a bruise. I won't be limping around rehearsals."

"You could," Dylan said. "Bridget has her bad knee. There's room for all sorts of imaginary ailments."

She bit the end of her thumb to cover a smile. "I think I'll go back inside for a while, though. It's getting a bit chilly."

She wanted to check out the hotel gym. She wasn't good at running, but she tried to do it regularly. With her body type and diet, she was always going to lean toward softness, which would be less of a concern once she'd finished filming for *Knightsbridge* and nobody had to see her in high-definition, but she did need to keep relatively fit if she was going to manage the West End schedule. Short bursts of sprinting also seemed to relieve stress. She wobbled towards the gate to remove her skates.

Dylan perked up. "Want some company by the fire? We could read lines together."

They had about six lines of dialogue together. He was a trier. It would be endearing if it were directed at his wife.

Luc was even less enchanted by the offer than she was. "Fireside fraternising with anyone in the cast or crew is off-limits."

Dylan was unabashed by the scowl, which Lily was beginning to think of in capital letters. The Scowl. "I thought that was the whole point of this weekend."

"Not for you it's not. Why don't you FaceTime your wife?"

Dylan smiled at Lily. "But the scenery here is so difficult to ignore."

"Try." Luc's voice fit perfectly into their frosty surroundings.

Lily debated the precise level of rudeness in just walking off and leaving them to their manly banter, and then did.

The snow crunched under her boots as she returned her skates and headed back to the house. She swiped it from the leaves of a hedge.

"Hey!" Freddy caught up with her breathlessly at the side doors. Her corkscrew curls were sticking out from under a fleece hat. "How'd you go?"

"Fell three times. Not even a bruise. You're a life-saver." Lily smiled at her. So far, the other women in the cast had been distantly polite or openly hostile, so Freddy's enthusiasm was particularly welcome.

"Portable cushions in your pants, I'm telling you. I'm considering adapting them for daily life. I'm appreciating this booty thing I've got going on." Freddy twisted to admire her backside. Then she grinned back. "I saw Dylan gliding to the rescue. Such a prince he is. What do you think of him?"

"I think he's a knob," Lily said frankly. "And I hope his wife went into that marriage with her eyes open."

"She went on some reality show last year and fucked around on him while they were engaged, so somehow I don't think she's doing a Faithful Penelope, sitting at home doing handicrafts while he's off getting his jollies."

Lily shook her head. "I don't know why people bother."

"Right? I mean, I can't imagine being stuck with one person for life either, but I wouldn't sign up for it in the first place. I figure, you sign a contract, you keep to the terms."

"You hopeless romantic."

Freddy laughed. Her eyes were dancing. "I might change my mind about the long haul if the new makeup artist is single. Did you see him? Built like a tank? Beard? Tattoos? Man-bun? Skin like warm chocolate? I think my lady parts spontaneously combusted."

Lily had noticed the very sexy man in question, yes.

He could probably open stubborn jars with his pinkie finger, and apply flawless liquid eyeliner in one sweep, and she'd seen him picking up an elderly woman's knitting in the guest lounge this morning. If he was still single, there was something wrong with the population of London.

"He's probably in a relationship." Freddy sighed. "There's really no flirtable prospect on this show. Everyone's either married, a dickhead, married *and* a dickhead, or old."

"There's Luc Savage," Lily said, and regretted it.

"Yeah, like I said—old."

He was only about forty.

The thought was instinctive, and totally contradicted her running internal narrative, which centred around a refrain of "too old," "boss," "on the rebound," "not interested" and "too old."

He *was* too old. For…some people. He just wasn't *old*. Unless you were nineteen and thought anyone over thirty was one stumble away from a hip replacement.

Freddy wrinkled her nose. "And intimidating. I feel like midthrust he'd be thinking about what you did wrong in rehearsal. Or he'd critique your performance afterwards in that impersonal robot voice. I like cuddlers." She suddenly, hastily, glanced behind them. "Oh, thank God. Imagine if he'd heard that. *Die*."

"He does have a habit of appearing out of nowhere," Lily agreed with feeling.

"Don't get me wrong, I love working for him. He brings this performance out of you that you couldn't even have imagined. It's just like teachers at school, I guess. Hard to think of them having a social life. Although he lived with Margo Roy for *years*, so I guess they were in love. They weren't exactly all over each other backstage. More like neighbours bumping into each other at the supermarket. Polite conversation, minds elsewhere."

"This is me," Lily said thankfully as they reached the first-floor bedroom wing. She liked Freddy a lot, but she was intensely uncomfortable with this whole conversation, and had learned her lesson about discussing Luc behind his back.

"I'm going to stretch out for a while. Catch up on some TV while I can." Freddy bounced down the hallway with so much energy that she made Lily feel about ninety.

In her room, she hunted out workout gear, making a huge mess of her suitcases in the process. It was almost too warm inside after the biting chill outdoors, but she skipped over a pair of shorts and pulled out yoga tights. With a house full of image-conscious actors, she doubted if the gym would be empty and she could never shake a lingering self-consciousness about her legs. It was why she appreciated the hemlines of her *Knightsbridge* costumes. When the script allowed her to wear clothes. One of the first times she'd appeared in a magazine, they'd gleefully pointed out the cellulite on her thighs. It still happened all the time and her skin should thicken with every catty article, but she was shy about showing too much leg in public. Which was infuriating.

In fact, it was so infuriating that she was going to wear the damn shorts. She had cellulite. Fuck it.

The self-confidence lasted until she found the gym on the second floor and walked in on Luc Savage doing push-ups. Shirtless. He had the body of a swimmer, all shoulders and lean muscles.

She actually put one foot behind the other and tugged at the hem of her shorts, trying to hide herself. Fortunately, he was busy scowling at the floor and didn't see.

By the time he sat back on his heels, she was composed. Not feeling at all naked. Not feeling at all irrationally crabby. "How did you even get here this fast?"

He stood and gave her another of his patented looks. Pointedly, he turned his wrist and checked his watch. "How did I walk about two hundred metres and change my clothing in a mere twenty-five minutes?"

Okay, so it had taken longer than she'd thought to find her sports bra. At least she'd bothered to put *on* a top.

Keeping a dignified silence, she put her towel and water bottle on a bench and made a beeline for a treadmill. They each planted a trainer on it at the same time.

With exaggerated gallantry, he stepped back and offered it to her with a sweep of his arm.

"Thanks," she said awkwardly, and took refuge in her running playlist, plugging in her earbuds.

She was aware of him running at her side, and at one point it seemed a bit ridiculous. The two of them, jogging to nowhere like guinea pigs in a play wheel, in front of a screen that seemed to be permanently fixed on the cartoon network. They were working out to *Spongebob Squarepants*.

When she slowed down to a walk and finally gripped the sides to lift her feet from the belt, Luc was still going strong. The muscles in his back moved under smooth, warm-looking skin.

Are you going to stand here objectifying your boss, or are you going to stretch?

She bent her leg and pressed one heel to her butt cheek in a token attempt at cooling down.

The sexual component of whatever she was feeling around him was becoming difficult to deny, and it didn't sit well. He was a good-looking man, but recognising that fact and finding him *attractive* were very different things. She was often physically attracted to people, but usually they were people who treated her with respect from the get-go.

There were three instances when she wouldn't touch a man with a sixty-foot pole: if he was already in a relationship or had very recently exited one; if she worked with him—or far worse, *for* him; or if he was more than a few years older than her. This was hitting the triple.

As long as it wasn't mutual and she kept it to herself, it was fine. It wasn't something she would ever pursue, and even if the universe decided to complete her mortification and Luc realised she was...*looking* at him, he would ignore it. This wasn't a man who would let anything interfere with the dynamics of his company.

He swung off his treadmill and tugged out his own earbuds, draping them around his neck. "I saw you heading inside with Freddy. You seem to be getting on well."

"Yes, we are. She's been great."

Luc tossed his towel aside and turned his full attention on her. "Meaning other people haven't?"

Like she was going to run to him telling tales—the poor, sad TV actor everybody resented for skipping the queue, who'd most likely got the part via somebody's casting couch. She'd overheard two separate conversations on that subject this morning.

She shrugged. "It's like any new job. There's a learning curve and it takes a while to find your place." Although quite a few people would have no problem putting her in it.

"There are a lot of strong personalities in this cast," Luc said, fairly tactfully, all things considered. "And a certain amount of spark helps with onstage chemistry. However, we don't condone workplace bullying—" there was a weighted pause "—despite the shit the tabloids are writing, so if it's becoming a problem, tell me."

No way. "I'd rather fight my own battles." She tried to equal his tact. "I don't think it's going to garner a lot of respect if I run to teacher every time someone's mean to me in the playground."

The corner of his lips lifted in that half smile. "Not a bad analogy. Particularly if Bridget's involved."

She couldn't help smiling back, and his eyes moved to her mouth again. She wondered if she'd imagined that he stiffened.

"Anyway," he said abruptly, "I'm glad you're connecting with Freddy. She's an old hat at this, but she's always been one of the youngest cast members and she's sometimes a bit isolated because of that."

"Yeah," Lily said slowly. "Well. We've been getting along well, but we're not exactly contemporaries. I'm closer to my thirties than my teens."

She heard a distinct snort.

She'd thought he was starting to view her with a bit more respect, so that was irritating on an almost primal level. "Any other aged wisdom to share with the kids, there, Grandpa?" she asked, probably justifying his jab at her maturity.

He looked about as approachable as Darth Maul, but then, unexpectedly, he laughed. A proper, eye-crinkling laugh. And her pathetic, perverse, masochistic little heart went *oh—it's you*.

For the second time in less than twenty-four hours, she mumbled something nonsensical, snatched up her stuff and bolted.

She stood under the shower in her bathroom for so long that the hot-water system started to flag. While she was drying her hair, she looked at herself in the mirror. As usual, nothing of what she was feeling showed on her face. Unless she was in character and actively using her features, they settled into... Helium Barbie. What had a review in *The Sun* once said? "Look closely enough into her pupils and you can actually see the tumbleweed bouncing past"?

Right at this moment, she was inclined to agree with that assessment.

She was already in a dark mood when she headed down to the library, where the window seat and books were calling her name. It didn't help when she heard someone *speaking* her name and recognised Bridget's strident tones.

"...boyfriend got her the part, but she's probably fucking Luc as well. She hardly stopped staring at him during the meeting, and they were *well* cosy in the car last night."

Twice today she'd turned and walked away from a similar situation. This time, anger rose in her throat, and she deliberately went into the small drawing room where a group of women from the cast and crew were sitting giggling over cocktails.

The laughter ended the moment she came into sight. More than one face turned an interesting shade of pink.

Lily met Bridget's enquiring, amused glance. "You

might as well say it to my face," she said calmly. "I can take it, you know. Go ahead."

Someone cleared their throat and the discomfort in the room was palpable, but she didn't break eye contact with Bridget, who was idly stirring the swizzle stick in her martini.

"Well, it's hardly a secret, is it?" Bridget's small smile didn't falter. "You're a TV... I suppose we could say 'star,' with no stage experience. Everyone knows you only got the role because Hudson Warner threw a tizzy and threatened to pull his funding from the theatre if his pet lamb didn't get her big break. Although I know Luc, and I find it hard to believe he would cave into blackmail without additional...persuasion."

It was the last implication that had brought Lily into the room, full of outrage and an unsettling edge of defensiveness, but her brain came to a dead stop at the first accusation. Hudson...

Bullshit.

Even in her mind, she could hear the uncertainty in her denial.

This whole thing had seemed too good to be true from the beginning. And she knew her godfather.

Bone-deep humiliation was a cold feeling.

She turned around and left the room without another word. Behind her, someone called her name hesitantly, with clear embarrassment.

She stopped a passing staff member and was told that Mr. Savage was in the ground-floor study.

It was a small room next to the library, dominated by a beautiful tiled fireplace and a massive mahogany desk. Luc was seated on the edge of it, frowning as he flipped through a sheaf of documents. She went in without knocking.

He looked up, his face registering surprise and then concern. Tossing the papers down on the desk without stopping to mark his place, he stood and spoke sharply. "Lily? What's the matter?"

She stared at him in silence, studying, thinking. He came to stand in front of her, and it seemed to be an unconscious action when he rested his fingers lightly against her wrists.

The pressure increased when she asked, bluntly, "Is Hudson Warner a shareholder in the theatre, and did he threaten to pull his backing if you didn't give me this role?"

"Yes." Luc didn't seem bothered in the slightest by the accusation, although he did realise he was holding her and let go. He even rolled his eyes a little. "Someone's been running off at the mouth. Who was it—Bridget?"

She didn't bother to confirm that. She was too busy seething. Hud had a howler of a text message coming his way. She occasionally used personal connections to give others a helping hand, but there were *limits*, for God's sake. It would be one thing if he'd used his influence to get her name in front of the casting committee for possible *consideration* for an *audition*, but to actually blackmail people into giving her a role outright... Especially when a catastrophic performance on her part would act like a cannonball on the whole production.

Hudson. Fuck.

"Look," she said, after a bit of inner weeping. "You've been pretty—" *brutally* "—honest with me so far. If you don't really think I'm right for this role—"

"I said that Warner threatened to yank his funding if we didn't cast his little darling." Luc turned to pick up a cup from the desk. He offered her a plate of biscuits, and, feeling a bit surreal, she took a Jammie Dodger. Her stress carb of choice. "I didn't say that we gave a shit. Your godfather makes at least one unreasonable demand a week. I pick my battles, throw him the occasional bone and tune the rest out." He bit into a chocolate digestive. "Close, are you?" he thought to add.

If anyone was concerned, that sound they could hear was the wind rushing out of her self-righteous sails. "Close enough that I *was* going to buy him a decent Christmas present, but carry on. We've established that I don't tell tales."

"We already had a shortlist by the time your name even came up; if you've been trying to break into the lists before this, your agent isn't doing much to earn his Christmas bonus. Yes, if Warner hadn't chucked your reel at Amelia, it's doubtful you'd be standing here right now, but I wouldn't cast even a bit part because Warner stamps his foot and points a finger. Everything I said stands. You've got a hell of a lot of work to do, but if I didn't think you'll get there, I would have tossed you back to the soaps. Are we clear?"

Honestly, he was such a bastard, and she'd never felt more like giving someone a hug.

Which would have been fine, if she hadn't actually *done it*.

It was one of the most awkward moments of her life. One moment she was standing there like a sane professional woman; the next, her nose was buried in his chest and she was hugging a human ice lolly. He'd frozen into cadaverous horror, and she was really glad she couldn't see his face.

She couldn't seem to let go. She wasn't sure where to go from here. Step back, clear her throat, give his hand a brisk shake, and sprint back to her room to die quietly?

Seemed like a plan.

Before she could put it into action, she felt a tentative brush against her back. And then his touch settled there, his palm wide and reassuring. God, she was *trembling*. Slowly, she pulled back and looked up at him.

Lily was a perpetual onscreen love interest. She knew how this played out. Eyes met, breath hitched, minds said "no, no, we shouldn't," body language said "hell yes, we should." Heads tilt, lean in, lips meet, snog, return of sanity, regretful dash from room. She *knew* the whole bloody cliché. *Everyone* knew the cliché. It never ended well.

And no fleeting moment, no matter how romantic or sexual, was worth risking her career. Or his.

So why was her own hand sliding around his ribs to splay against his belly? Why was she feeling him breathe, feeling his warmth? Why was he slowly reaching out, his thumb coming to rest under her chin, nudging up, just a fraction? Why was she arching up on her tiptoes, and why was that palm on her back helping her?

They breathed with their lips millimetres apart, staring into each other's eyes. His, usually professional and distant, were hot and turbulent.

It was entirely her fault. She kissed him first. She pushed forward across a distance that was minuscule in reality and a minefield in the potential repercussions. His hand tightened almost painfully on her back, gripping her as he continued to stand still for an extended moment. Then his lips were parting, his other arm was sliding around her, lifting her, turning her, his tongue was rubbing against hers, nipping, licking, abrasive, soothing. She was down on the desk and his weight was heavy on top of her, hard between her legs.

This whole scenario was so much sexier without four cameras stuck in her face, and Ash blowing raspberries against her neck to ease the tension, and Steve barking commands about what to grab next. This was Luc, and it was private and intense and *real*, and in that instant, she wasn't thinking about *what* he was; it was all about *who* he was.

His hand barely skimmed the curve of her waist, sneaking under her jumper for the slightest stroke of her tummy, a touch that made her jump. He soothed the reaction with a murmuring nuzzle below her ear. He didn't go near her bra fastening or her buttons. His mouth returned to hers and she met it, kissing him back, stroke for stroke, little nibbles of kisses followed by deep, searching, engulfing ones.

They kept pulling back to look at one another; his hands were unsteady on her, and she saw the shock that she knew must be reflected in her eyes. She'd kissed a lot of men, onscreen and off, and she was now living the cliché of infatuation: she'd never felt like this before. She was so intensely aware of everything about him: his smell, his taste, his weight, the slightly rough texture of his skin where silvered black hair grew.

He bent to press his lips against hers again, and just stayed there for a moment. It was a full stop, a gesture that lingered, both comforting her and letting her store the memory. Then he tilted to touch his forehead to hers and stroked his thumbs down her cheeks, over the upper curves of her ears.

Lily ran her hands between them, over the planes of his chest, shaping his arms before she touched a single fingertip to the point of his chin.

There was a long silence, broken only by their ragged breathing.

"If Hud does take his money and run," she murmured at last, shakily, "I suggest you set up a side business to raise the extra cash. Snogging lessons with Luc Savage. Every other bloke in London, take note. I've had Long Island Iced Teas in backstreet bars that packed less of a punch."

The disturbed expression in his grey eyes was momentarily eclipsed by a reluctant laugh. "Christ, you're trouble."

"I don't do this," she said directly into his ear. "Never."

"No. I know you don't." Luc levered up with an ease and grace she was never going to replicate. Fortunately, he took her hand and pulled her back to her feet with minimal floundering.

"Should I apologise?" Lily asked when she was vertical again. "Should you apologise? Or should we just call this the National Day for Wildly Inappropriate Behaviour and move on?"

Luc released her and ran his hand through his hair, managing to smooth it back into immaculate order with one sweep. It was a good thing he had those metaphorical "Not for you" stamps all over him, because in an actual romantic prospect it would be insufferable, that ability to emerge from any stressful situation without a hair out of place. Like those women in disaster flicks who survived tidal waves without smearing their lipstick.

"With the exception of a long-term relationship that had already begun by the time we worked together, I've never been sexually involved with anyone I've worked with," he said emphatically. "There's a lot of absolutely reprehensible, disgusting shit that goes on in casting offices in this industry, and most of it is borderline criminal. So I *should* apologise for what just happened." He looked at her in silence. "I can't," he said at last. That look was back in his eyes, the one she couldn't quite decipher. "I kissed you—"

"I kissed you. Technically." Although he'd been a fairly active participant in the whole misguided, shivery shebang.

"It was—" He stopped, obviously intensely uncomfortable.

It was like coming home.

She couldn't say that. She wasn't this woman. She was not going to be, for the rest of her theatre career, the actress who got her first big stage break and slept with the director. Some of the less reputable papers had already implied as much, but there was made-up sex and scandal, and there was knowing and living the truth.

There was self-respect.

He was speaking stiffly now, back in his robotic comfort zone. "But I can assure you that it won't happen again, and it will have no impact whatsoever on your role in this production or any other."

"It's okay," she said quietly. "I know you wouldn't punish or reward anyone professionally for anything that happened outside of work. You're not that sort of man."

That sent a flush of colour into his face. He tucked a

stand of hair behind her ear. Apparently realising what he was doing, he swore and took a deliberate step back.

Lily lowered her hand from where she'd instinctively reached to hold on to his fingers. "Maybe we ought to keep some distance between us for a while."

"Until Monday, you mean, when we go to Oxford together, and then the next four weeks of intensive, occasionally one-on-one rehearsals?"

Well, if he was going to be rational about it.

"You could try being pleasant and malleable," she suggested. "I'd probably find it a complete turn-off. I didn't realise I had this penchant for militant men. It's giving me whole new insights into my personality."

"Militant?"

"I thought it sounded more polite than 'bossy.' No?"

"I'm not bossy."

He actually sounded like he believed that.

"Okay, Captain Von Trapp. Keep telling yourself that."

She'd broken the stern director facade again. He was grinning. "Are you sure you weren't fired from CTV? Because if you talk to Steve Warren like this, I'm surprised you didn't find yourself falling down an empty lift shaft in the second episode."

She would never dream of speaking to Steve, or any other director, like this. It was just hard to return to business as usual when she knew what his tongue felt like against the roof of her mouth.

"No, amazingly I left by choice." Although her character was about to get a fairly grisly comeuppance. She'd received her final *Knightsbridge* script before they'd left London yesterday. Gloria's death would set up a whodunit plot for the next season. She wasn't really looking forward to filming the scene in which she was strangled to death with her own garter belt and left facedown in a puddle of absinthe, but her money was on the vicar's wife as the murderer. Neil Forrester, their head writer, liked to be provocative. Homicidal ladies of the clergy were right up his street.

"When do you shoot your final scenes?" Luc seemed to be equally determined to get things back on a professional footing, and finding it as difficult. His eyes kept wandering over her lips and tousled hair.

"End of the week. Then I'm all yours." She closed her eyes and groaned. "It's like I'm reading from the script for *The Cliché Film*, the unresolved sexual tension scene, isn't it? Do you want to kiss again? I think that was our cue."

Luc covered his eyes with his hand, but a knock on the door prevented him from giving up on her in despair.

Amelia Lee and Maria Finch came in, looking pinched and stressed about the mouth.

Amelia did manage a smile for her, but Maria went straight to the point. She strode over to the desk where Luc still stood. "Your nemesis strikes again."

That sounded dramatic, and like none of her business. Lily edged towards the door. "I'll just—"

Luc looked up from the laptop where Maria was already typing. They were lucky they hadn't knocked the computer off the desk earlier, but their…moment had been more intense than the theatrical writhing she did for show. They'd been focused completely on one another. On camera, Ash usually threw around a few items of stationery just for fun.

"I suspect you might as well stay. I'm sure you could look it up for yourself in your room."

He fell abruptly silent as Maria arrived at whatever she was looking for. Lily took a step forward, wanting to…do something. Help. Comfort. God—*cuddle.* He looked so stricken. And then seriously pissed off. But her movement caught his attention, and the sight of her seemed to make everything exponentially worse.

"What's going on?" she asked Amelia, when Luc went into a furious, low-toned argument with Maria.

Amelia grimaced. "*London Celebrity* is now making allegations that Luc had a string of sexual affairs with women he cast in his productions during the time he was living with Margo. And they're making it very difficult to issue any kind of denial or to sue for libel. They seem to have gained an edge of subtlety. It's all just rumour and so-called blind items. It's blatantly obvious they're referring to Luc and Margo, but with no names mentioned outright, any kind of statement from our end just looks like confirmation."

"Why the smear campaign? I know there's been a lot of press about the breakup, but *London Celebrity* seems to be taking the poisonous commentary to an extreme."

"Family connection," Amelia said vaguely, explaining nothing at all.

A phone rang and they all automatically checked their screens. It was Luc's, and he looked resigned when he saw the name of the caller. "Margo. Hi."

This definitely seemed like the time for Lily to leave. She excused herself politely to Amelia and lifted a hand at Maria, who was still eyeing her with suspicion. As she left the room, she heard Luc say, "Thanks, I appreciate it…"

His eyes met Lily's; the connection was only broken when she quietly closed the door.

Lily went back to her suite, bypassing the room full of gossiping women who seemed to exist a million years in the past. So much had happened in the space of a few minutes that she felt like she'd gone into the study as the person she'd been for twenty-six years and come out a different woman.

One who's a lot more like your mother than you thought, said the destructive little she-devil in her head.

No. This was nothing and never would be anything like that.

The memory of Freddy's voice was trailing her as well, looping around in circles. She'd said that Luc and Margo had seemed like bare acquaintances when they spoke in public. Lily had put that down to innate professionalism. Margo Roy had been one of her biggest acting icons for years. And Luc was about the last man on earth to indulge in workplace PDA. Or anyplace PDA.

Before he'd opened his mouth over hers, she hadn't imagined him unbending enough to be affectionate with anyone.

Even just now, on the phone—that had been his very recent ex, who'd left their serious relationship to marry someone else within weeks. He could be forgiven for sounding a bit pissed off. Lily had made more emotive calls to order pizza.

But when his weight had been pressing her down into the desk, his forehead nuzzling hers, his body aroused between her legs, there had been acres and layers of feeling in his voice.

Letting herself into her room, she flopped backward onto the bed, shoved her hands through her already-destroyed hair, then pressed her palms over her eyes.

And refused to think anymore.

Chapter Five

The arches and spires of Oxford were blurring into the mist and rain when Luc tucked an impatient hand under Lily's elbow and hurried her along at a faster pace. She kept stopping to gawk. He got it. He always felt it as well. There was a quality about places like Oxford that he rarely experienced elsewhere; it was similar to the feeling that washed over him when he stood backstage in the Queen Anne. As if he could hear the footsteps and the collective buzz of all the voices and personalities, the ordinary loves and triumphs and tragedies, that had crossed those paths throughout centuries of history. Individual lives, hands reaching out to touch stones, idlers sitting to think and stare from steps and knolls, were literally worn into the fabric of their surroundings. It was a fount of inspiration.

It also wasn't going anywhere, unlike Jocasta Moore, who would wait about two seconds beyond their arranged meeting time before dismissing them from her mind and delving back into the annals of whatever obscure research project she was working on now. The morning had been harried enough at Aston Park, making sure that every hung-over member of the cast and crew was flung into a car, and that nobody was still passed out under an antique bench or buried under a snowdrift somewhere.

They passed under archways and alleys on their way to the Radcliffe Camera, a journey that always made Luc feel slightly like a condemned prisoner on his way to a block and an axe—it was the gloomy tunnels, spiked wrought iron and general atmosphere of intimidation. Even the statues seemed to look down their noses.

A kid nearby seemed to agree. He glanced up at the snootiest of the stone sneers and flipped it off. He'd probably end up going far. Luc's private amusement vanished when the boy caught sight of Lily and did a head-to-toe leer that ended up skittering between her face and her chest. Without even thinking about it, Luc angled his body against hers—as if she needed shielding from the lechery of some zit-faced, hormone-driven teen she could handle without blinking an eye.

"I'm channelling the wrong character," Lily said suddenly. She was still struggling to keep up with his unchivalrous pace, and wouldn't be having an issue if she'd worn more sensible footwear. The heels on her boots looked sharp and thin enough to perform keyhole surgery. As usual, she was dressed like a Bond villain. On a positive note, his ears were adjusting to the tones of her voice. He no longer had to restrain a visible wince. She unconsciously echoed his own thought. "I feel like Jane Grey now, on my way to the chop."

"Don't be fanciful," he said, just to irritate her.

"I saw you jump when that gate slammed shut."

For the past two days, he'd been trying to ignore the most unprofessional moment of his career. It was proving to be almost impossible. She just made him want to smile.

He grimaced at her instead, which made her laugh, which in turn provoked a rush of warmth in his belly.

They made it into the Radcliffe Camera without incident and stood on the ground floor of the Baroque rotunda, dripping rainwater.

"Holy crap. I've come home to the mother ship. The books. The arches. The stonework. This is gorgeous." Lily glanced around, unbuttoning her coat. "I'm intimidated."

"What do you mean, you're 'intimidated'? It's a reading room."

"Yeah, but it's Oxford." Unsurprisingly, she was wearing more black under her black coat. He wondered whether the colour preference extended down to— *Fuck.* "I've never actually spent much time here and I've always wanted to. Although most of my ideas of the city are based on old episodes of *Inspector Morse*, so I'm expecting really snooty undergrads with perms, a few clinically insane professors and at least one murder by teatime."

"We've got forty-five seconds to meet Jocasta before she disappears into the depths of the most obscure archive on campus. If I have to spend the rest of the afternoon searching for her, stinking of wet wool and old books, I'll happily provide you with the token homicide."

As he marched her to the second level, he heard muttering behind him. She really was going to have to work on her vocal range. If she wanted to make an impact when she called someone a "bossy prat," she needed to project.

They found the desk that Jocasta haunted on a daily basis. It was a chaos zone of open books and messy sheaves of scrawled notes. There was no sign of the elderly woman, but the steaming cup of tea suggested that she'd been there recently. He was pretty sure it would get them banned for life if it was spotted by a member of staff.

After transferring the tea to an empty desk some distance away, he returned to Lily and pulled out a chair for her. "We might as well wait. Looks like she's coming back."

Lily picked up one of Jocasta's abandoned books and glanced at the title. *"The ID: A Personal Account of the Rise and Fall of a Dictator."* She flipped it open. "I had no idea you'd written an autobiography. That's impressive, writing a whole book, with your work schedule."

Luc plucked the book out of her hands. "I suppose you think you're funny."

"I think I'm hilarious." Lily crossed one leg over the other, then immediately returned both feet to rest on the floor, with military precision. She folded her hands in her lap, gave a tight-lipped smile to a passing librarian, and pasted a strange look on her face.

"I'm almost afraid to ask," Luc said, "but what exactly are you doing?"

"I don't know. I think this is my Oxford persona. I can't seem to help myself. I'm physically trying to slouch here and my back just isn't listening. It's like they're judging me."

He glanced around. The librarian had departed with a furious exclamation over the cup of tea. There was no one around except one teenager, who appeared to be slowly decomposing into his book stack. Somebody needed a coffee break and a shower. "Who?"

"Oxford. It's like it *knows* I don't belong."

"You do realise I'm not and never have been a student, faculty, porter, or in any way associated with Oxford either, and neither have any of the hordes of tourists thundering through the grounds?"

"Oh, well, *you*," Lily said, and made it sound like a new twist on a swear word. "You'd fit in anywhere."

Did she actually think that? Concerning lack of judgment.

He eyed her dispassionately for a moment before enquiring, "Are the popped shirt buttons and visible bra an essential part of the Oxford persona? Because I think we've come close enough to being kicked out on our arses with Jocasta's tea. I'm fairly sure seminudity is—"

She squawked and shot back to a normal sitting position. Her hands flew to her buttons and discovered them all in place. "You unutterable git. I thought I had my tits out in an annex of the Bodleian."

"Hallelujah." Luc leaned back in his own chair. "Normality returns. Retire the character and act like a human being. And this is an undergrad haunt. You know at least *one* person has had their tits out in the stacks."

Lily looked scandalised.

Tongue in cheek, he handed her a slim, battered text from the pile next to him. "Why don't you try to relax with an improving book?"

She turned it over to see the title. *When Less is More: The Art of Silence and the Power of the Non-Verbal.* Without having read one page, she nailed the entire concept with her response.

"Vulgar hand gestures," he said piously, "are also frowned upon in the Bodleian."

When the overly intense student glared at them, she had to turn her laugh into a low cough.

The art of silence gradually became quite relaxing as they sat waiting for Jocasta. Luc stretched, easing the tight muscles in his back and neck, and Lily's gaze moved over the shelves and balustrades.

"My mother is an Oxford grad," she said after a while. "So is my father's wife." Her lips moved, but the expression couldn't remotely be described as a smile. "One of several things they have in common."

God, he wanted to touch her. "Do you have a relationship with Lady Charlotte?"

"We'll make brief eye contact if we meet in public. Sometimes she'll nod. You can't blame her. If my husband got another woman pregnant, particularly the year after I found out I couldn't have kids myself, I'd slowly extract his testicles with a pair of rusty nail clippers."

"I've been cheated on, myself. Can't say I went to criminal and quite impressively disgusting measures, but it's not a good situation. For anyone."

Lily hesitated. "Was that—" She cut herself off. "Sorry. Fuck. Don't answer that. None of my business. And probably a really raw wound."

For God's sake. Did *everyone* read the tabloids like mindless, gullible sheep?

He sighed. "Margo didn't cheat on me." Lily looked as if she wasn't sure whether to believe him or just humour him. He'd run the gamut of "I'm fine" to "no comment" to "fuck off" so many times over the past weeks that it felt odd to just talk about it. "Our relationship was a failing proposition for at least four years. We were just too busy to devote enough time to calling it quits."

Which was…pathetic. He hadn't realised *how* pathetic until he'd spoken it aloud.

If you lived with a person for eight years and you couldn't honestly say they were more important to you than bricks and bills and scripted words—It was a fairly damning indictment. On both the relationship and his own character.

"A 'failing proposition'?" Lily repeated quietly, and he couldn't read the intonation or her expression.

Pity?

An instant internal rebellion against that, from her, caused him to snap his response. "It was initial attraction, it was lust, it was a meeting of common ground. Then it was…habit."

"And PR magic." That edge of cynicism was back in Lily's voice, and he lifted an eyebrow.

"I don't think that was high on the list of priorities. I respect Margo. I admire her. I think she's one of the greatest stage actresses London has seen in centuries. But our personal relationship should have ended a long time ago. It wasn't—" He stopped. "I'm glad Margo has found something that's…enough."

After a brief hesitation, Lily's fingers closed over his, and the fact that she'd voluntarily reached out to comfort him made him wonder about the state of his face.

A new voice, crisp and perfectly articulated, acted like the proverbial bucket of cold water. "'Somebody's been sitting in my chair, growled the Papa bear.'"

Lily snatched her hand away so quickly he almost heard the snap.

"Luc Savage. Always the highlight of my work calendar." Jocasta Moore looked at him critically from under a droopy red felt hat. Wisps of grey hair stuck out and seemed to quiver, as if they had an independent energy source and were reaching for him like faded tentacles. Her protuberant, incredibly pale blue eyes swung to focus on Lily. She stuck out a hand, heavy with rings on her thumb and every finger. "And this must be my next victim. Jocasta Moore, vocal specialist. If I take you on, you're either going to kiss my feet in a few weeks' time or want to slit my throat."

He gave Lily credit for not looking as if she wanted to bolt for the door yet. Jocasta was an acquired taste, but she was good enough at her job that she could be as eccentric as she liked. Regardless, he found himself doing that ridiculous piece of sexist crap again, taking a step closer to Lily. To protect her from the tiny little old lady.

Lily returned the handshake. "Lily Lamprey. Thank you for agreeing to meet me."

Jocasta's thin grey brows shot up. "Oh dear." She turned her pale gaze on Luc. "I'll take her." As if she were selecting a cut of meat at the butcher's counter. "I do enjoy a challenge." To Lily, she said, "I hope you're a hard worker."

Lily looked resigned, but her chin lifted. "I am." Her voice was firm. Still better suited to the adult film industry than the West End stage, but determined.

"Good-oh." Jocasta stood by the desk and tumbled her books and papers into an untidy pile. "Did I leave a cup of tea here?"

"It was confiscated," Luc said. "Hot drinks and open cups are probably grounds for hanging, drawing and quartering."

"What a bother," Jocasta said crossly. She turned to make shooing motions at them. "Well, let's go. No time to waste."

"Are we having a lesson right now?" Lily sounded taken aback. "What about your things?"

"Darling, nobody would *dream* of moving them." Jocasta said it with a sense of uncaring entitlement that Holly Golightly would have envied. From under the desk, she produced a red umbrella that probably ought to have been left downstairs as well. She gave Lily a gentle prod with it. "And of course we're having a lesson now. Have you *heard* yourself, my petal? The play opens in how many weeks? Five? Four? Good Lord. I can see I'm going to have to relocate to the bowels of hell."

"Could you not poke her like she's stray cattle, thanks?" Luc said mildly. "And do I need to remind you exactly how much I'm paying you for an all-expenses stay in London? You'll have enough money to vegetate here for most of next year, doing research into dead dictators and terrifying viral diseases, and God knows what else."

Jocasta's response was just as placid. "For *all* of next year, I think you'll find, my dove. You didn't *quite* mention the extent of the problem. My fee just went up considerably. And don't swear. It's the Bodleian."

Lily, despite her obvious embarrassment at Jocasta's brutal analysis, gave him an I-told-you-so look at that last admonishment. He grinned.

Jocasta's ramshackle little home was within walking distance of the campus, but the rain was coming down in sheets now, so they took a taxi. The streets were decked out for Christmas, but were currently a wet blur.

Jocasta lived in a semi-detached brick cottage that looked perfectly normal on the outside and like something out of Charles Dickens inside. Dust and books predominated. Lily was visibly fascinated. She'd folded her arms, so he assumed she was restraining the urge to touch things. He could have told her that Jocasta wouldn't mind if she examined every knickknack in the house. The elderly woman had no conception of personal space and privacy, as Lily would shortly discover.

Jocasta glanced at one of the many clocks. There were at least seven in the living room alone, and the out-of-sync ticking would have driven him demented. He wasn't tidy either, but there was mess and there was living in the decor of a backstreet junk shop.

"No time for tea. I assume you'll be back to London tomorrow? I'm surprised you could tear yourself away from the theatre overnight. Are you intending to take this one back with you?" She was still referring to Lily as if she were a possession.

"*This one*," Luc said, "probably has a horrific death scene to film at the CTV studios, so I won't be abandoning her to your tender care, no. I'll need you in London by Thursday."

Jocasta looked annoyed but didn't argue—wisely, given the rise in salary she'd just granted herself. Carelessly, she kicked aside a number of objects, clearing a space in the centre of an Arabian rug, where she paced around Lily in a circle, her eyes shrewd and focused.

"Put one hand on your throat," she said without ceremony, "and the other on your belly."

Luc sat on an overstuffed armchair and settled down to observe. Usually he would have his phone in hand and be halfway through clearing his inbox by now. He trusted Jocasta to do her job. The fact that he was more interested in what was happening in the room than in what was happening back in London spoke of things he was determined to ignore.

Lily did as instructed, and continued to follow Jocasta's barking orders for the next hour and a half without complaint, not making a lot of audible progress but obviously trying. Jocasta took her through body and vocal warm-ups, teaching her flow phonation, doing breathing exercises that transferred from voiceless to voiced fricatives on single breaths.

"What's going to be most important is taking out that breathy quality. You need to move the focus of sound forward. Say 'Monday.'"

"Monday." Lily had been slightly self-conscious at first, but now seemed to have forgotten Luc was in the room.

"Low effort in the throat and larynx, and high effort in the stomach and front part of the face. Mmm-mmmmonday."

"Mmmmmmonday," Lily repeated dutifully, and they could all hear the difference in tone.

Jocasta smiled for the first time. "Good," she said simply. "We'll get there yet. We'll have another session on Thursday, and then I want to meet with you for at least an hour every day during the rehearsal period. You're going to have to work your backside off."

Lily looked at Luc at last, including him in her emphatic reply. "I will."

Jocasta was eyeing Lily with approval now. It was the same look of affection that she bestowed on her pet rabbits. Luc tended to receive a very different stare. More like the one he'd seen her direct at the small boys next door who liked to lurk around corners with Nerf guns.

"When I tell you to breathe into your abdomen, you move your hand closer to your stomach." Without turning, Jocasta addressed Luc. "Come and stand here for a moment. I need distance to observe."

He raised his eyebrows at the tone, which reminded him strongly of an old headmaster he'd had, but got up and came to stand in front of Lily. He could smell the vanilla scent of her perfume again.

"Put your hand, palm out, about an inch from her belly."

He hesitated, and Jocasta shot him an impatient frown.

Slowly, he pushed up his sleeves and reached out, holding his palm close to Lily's body.

"Lily, repeat the last two sentences of the monologue, and breathe deeply enough into your stomach that you press against his hand. Don't move an inch," Jocasta snapped at Luc. She retreated to the edge of the rug, watching with critical eyes.

Uncomfortably, Lily began to recite the lines.

"Deeper," Jocasta warned.

Softness touched and then pressed into Luc's palm, retreated and returned. He could feel the warmth of her beneath the silky wool of her jumper. On the fourth inhalation, his fingers moved involuntarily, just a stroking inch, closing slightly against her middle. Lily shivered and stuttered. Luc dropped his hand abruptly and moved away.

"Hmm," Jocasta said drily. "You're obviously not an ideal assistant."

As if nothing odd had occurred, she waved her finger at Lily. "I'm putting you on a course of vocal hygiene.

I know you're not a smoker, but no alcohol either, of any kind. No spicy food, dairy, caffeine or chocolate, or anything that could cause reflux." Lily had looked appalled when Luc had warned her of that imminent ban, but now seemed too flustered to care. "And take care of your voice. Between periods of active practise, *rest*. For several hours a day, starting with the rest of today, don't speak above a whisper or don't speak at all." Jocasta shot Luc a darkling glance. "No matter how provoking he can be, I'm afraid you're going to have to master the talent of winning an argument without raising your voice."

She then added without warning, "And if you're very vocal during sex, you'll have to tone that down too. I'm not having all of my hard work undone because Savage is an unlikely provider of multiple orgasms. Although, in my extensive experience, the handsome ones are usually duds. Too preoccupied with admiring their own bits and pieces to worry about yours." She looked between them. "Interesting. An absolutely identical expression of horror. I know they say couples start to look alike, but this seems exceedingly quick. You can't have been together that long. Last time I saw you," she said to Luc, who was struggling to find adequate words, "you were still cohabiting with Margo. Very unsuitable match. Excellent voice, though."

It was Lily who found speech first and even had the strength of mind to follow her new regime. "Luc is my boss," she whispered. Her cheeks were on fire. "We're not involved that way. Although I'm sure he's not a dud," she unfortunately felt compelled to reply in his defence.

"If you say so." Jocasta checked her clocks again.

"Time to feed the rabbits and myself." She ignored Lily's continuing embarrassment and Luc's dangerous silence. "We're all having greens. I don't think I have enough for two extra."

Luc closed his eyes and summoned all reserves of patience. "We have reservations at the hotel for dinner. Thank you anyway." Once more, he felt no remorse about the sarcasm.

Jocasta didn't bother with protracted, polite good-byes. She managed to fling them out on her doorstep in about ten seconds, warning Lily to wrap her scarf about her throat before she closed the front door on them.

It seemed wise to follow Jocasta's cue and ignore the past few minutes. "You did well." That was terser than he'd intended. "She's right. There was minor improvement at the end, and I think you're going to make progress fairly rapidly once you get into the routine."

Lily's cheeks were still pink. "I hope so," she said in that very soft tone that was entirely different from her usual breathiness, and which was having an interesting effect on certain "bits and pieces" of his body. "I want this."

There was a quality in the words that echoed his own sentiments about the Queen Anne. He understood that kind of desire and ambition, and he nodded.

"And I don't want to be the weak link in the production."

His gaze turned level. "There's *never* a weak link in my productions."

That wasn't supposed to make her smile.

The hotel Luc had booked them into was very old-world and beautiful. Lily left her things in a comfortable bedroom before joining him in the restaurant. They made it through three courses with no eye contact and very little conversation.

Her gaze fixed on the central Christmas tree. It was at least ten feet tall and ablaze with fairy lights and glistening baubles. The pianist at the baby grand in the corner was playing an instrumental arrangement of "Silver Bells," it was all very mellow, and Lily had never felt less relaxed in her life.

She was stuck in a continuous replay of the session with Jocasta. Her head was full of techniques and critique. Breathing exercises. Muscle release. Luc's prowess in the bedroom.

A dud. She somehow didn't think so.

A small group of people approached their table, startling her out of her preoccupation.

"Excuse me." One of the young women cleared her throat. "Are you Lily Lamprey? From *Knightsbridge*?"

Lily glanced at Luc apologetically. It was a gesture she'd made countless times on dates. Not that this was a date. *Oh God, just shut up.* "Yes." She managed a smile. "Do you watch the show?"

"Oh my God," said the other girl. "*Yes.* We're, like, your biggest fans. Could we have your autograph?"

"And would you mind if we took a photo?" asked her friend.

Lily was always happy to take the photos and sign anything that wasn't a body part, and would have done it even if it wasn't a sensible PR move. The studio came down hard on anyone who was caught out being rude to fans. It was just preferable if it didn't happen while she was out with someone—anyone—else, who also ended up having their evening disrupted.

"Of course." She signed the backs of the receipts they immediately thrust at her, and posed between them while their boyfriends dutifully took their phones and snapped the photos.

"Thank you *so* much," gushed one of the girls, while the other chipped in with "You're so much nicer than I thought you'd be! You're such a bitch on TV. It's awesome."

Lily thought she heard a muffled sound from Luc, but held on to the smile until the group departed, the girls chattering about how amazing it had been to meet her.

They were still within earshot when one of the guys said dismissively, "What's the big deal? She's probably dumb as fuck."

"With that face and those tits, who cares?" the other guy said jokingly. "Like *you* wouldn't fuck her."

Maybe *not* boyfriends, then.

Lily heard that sort of thing so often and was so distracted tonight that it hardly registered. She would have gone back to eating her fruit salad if Luc hadn't stiffened so visibly. He actually started to rise from the table, and Lily shot out an alarmed hand.

The tabloids were already full of false allegations; it would hardly help the cause if he beat the crap out of two stupid kids in a posh restaurant.

"Don't even think about it."

"They shouldn't—"

"What? Look at my body and mentally halve my brain size? Talk sexist shit in public?" She picked up her fork again, carefully examining the tines. "Wouldn't have put you down as a hypocrite. A number of other things, but not a hypocrite. For God's sake, would you please sit down?"

He did, reluctantly and sensibly, but turned his scowl on her. "What the fuck is that supposed to mean?"

Lily suddenly remembered why she'd never been going to call him on this.

"Well?" he pushed, obviously in a foul mood now, despite the soothing, festive atmosphere.

He was *famed* for his ice-cold temperament. It was like nobody had ever spent more than five minutes with him. The man started steaming like a kettle on a regular basis.

She sighed and made a mental apology to Jamie. Not that she was going to let Luc extend his influence anywhere near the usefully loose-tongued teen. "For someone who once referred to me as a Marilyn Monroe impersonator who probably needs direction to tie her shoelaces, you're awfully quick to judge."

There was an extremely long pause. Amazingly, a faint, ruddy tinge spread across his cheeks.

"Well, I'm glad you're not going to deny it. I was fairly sure you weren't a liar as well as tactless."

"How the hell," Luc asked at last, his voice a warning purr, "did you know that?"

She could almost *see* him filtering through the people who'd been present that day, weighing company loyalty and likelihood to gossip, and jumping to the right conclusion.

"You don't by any chance have a relative or a very youthful admirer who wields an extremely slow tea trolley?"

She couldn't help grinning, but made a "lips sealed" zipping motion. "Sorry, Watson, my sources are top secret. And have diplomatic immunity. So don't go guns-blazing after any more adolescents, please."

She wasn't sure what reaction she expected—probably more anger—but he suddenly returned her smile. The fine lines around his eyes crinkled. Sexily. "The cheeky little bastard. One of your network of spies, is he?"

Her phone whistled in her clutch with a text message, and Luc nodded at it as he began to eat his dessert, which was enviably boozy and full of chocolate. "Go ahead. Wouldn't want you to miss any important intel, MI5."

It was a text from Trix, with a link to a website. "You're getting some good press for once," Lily said, reading. "Bet you're glad you didn't right-hook an Oxford undergrad now." She passed him her phone. "Margo Roy made a statement through her PR rep. You're great, she's great, nobody cheated. Trix must have thought I'd be interested," she added lamely, when he turned a sharp glance on her.

His face was blank again as he thumbed through the article. His own phone began to ring in his pocket before he'd finished reading, and they copped a sour look from a couple who were obviously trying to have a romantic meal in peace.

Luc frowned. "I'm sorry, I'm going to have to take this. Are you okay here if I step out for a few minutes?"

"I imagine I can bear up under the loss of your company for five minutes. I'll practice being silent. But you'd better take your chocolate with you. I'm not sure my willpower is strong enough to withstand the temptation yet."

He was gone so long that Lily had time to finish her

depressing dessert, thank the waiter who removed her plate, and check all her emails.

She was playing Sudoku when the game paused for an incoming call. The next-table lovebirds bristled.

"Sorry," she murmured to the neighbours, and "Hi, Peter," into the receiver.

"Lily?" her agent queried cautiously.

"Yes."

"Why are you whispering?"

"Vocal hygiene."

"I see. Right, well, terrific news. Kathleen Leibow-itz's casting director has requested your reel for *Blithe Spirit* next August."

"You're kidding."

"You're up for consideration for Edith," Peter whis-pered back. It was obviously contagious, like yawning.

"Doesn't Kathleen Leibowitz have a blanket mora-torium on all TV actors?"

"Apparently she's prepared to make an exception for a principal in a Savage play." There was satisfac-tion in Peter's hushed voice. "This is the beginning of good things."

Lily's stomach jumped, but the rush of nerves didn't dampen her growing smile. She was still trying to keep it under wraps a few minutes later, when she ended the call and went in search of Luc.

He was in the foyer, off the phone now and striding back in the direction of the restaurant. "Hell," he said when they met halfway. "Sorry. I didn't mean to just abandon you in there."

"It's fine. Is everything okay?"

Stupid question. He was clearly hanging on to the last threads of his temper.

"We're short a leading lady."

"What?"

"That was Bridget's agent. She's quit."

Two rounds of good news in ten minutes. The universe *did* like her. Although it wasn't so flash for him. Or the production as a whole.

Lily abandoned the whispering. "But—this role…it could be the biggest performance of her career. Why would she bail?"

"In her opinion, the biggest role of her career will involve running around in circles screaming while Los Angeles disappears under a tidal wave."

"She can't take a film role. That would be in total violation of her contract."

"Yes, it would. However, by the time that fact is thrashed out in court, we'll be casting for the next production run. And Bridget's flight to the States left half an hour ago, which makes it a little difficult to either force her back to rehearsal or have her killed."

"I don't think homicide, however justified, would do much for your PR problems."

"Good point." Luc released a long breath, rested his hands on his waist and looked down at the floor. Eventually, he exhaled again and nodded towards Lily's phone. "It's a good thing Margo is feeling charitable. Because I'm about to require a monumental favour."

He said nothing more while he walked her back to her room, but stopped her when she opened the door and turned to say good-night.

"By the way, MI5." Humour flickered briefly across his face. "Before I get caught up in what's likely to be a complete shitstorm of hassle—I'm sorry."

She cocked her head.

"I'm sorry for what was repeated to you after that casting meeting. I'm sorry that I said it in the first place. I'm very sorry that it's such an everyday occurrence to you that you barely blink an eye when a couple of little fuckers make totally inappropriate comments almost to your face. I wholeheartedly apologise for being a prejudiced, sexist dick."

She was too taken aback to respond for a moment; then, slowly, she smiled.

"It's all right," she whispered. "You wouldn't believe the things I said about you behind *your* back."

Chapter Six

The tug of the spotlight was strong. Apparently not even the beauties of Italy and the sole company of a gorgeous husband could win out against the temptation of returning to the stage. Margo Roy and Alberto Ferreti were coming back to London, and she was taking over as leading lady in *1553*.

Lily was feeling a hundred different emotions at once about that, and she had no idea what Luc was thinking. She kept glancing at him as they drove. They'd left Oxford before ten o'clock, after eating breakfast separately in their rooms. Well, she'd eaten toast and more fruit salad, silently mourning the death of coffee, but she suspected he'd spent most of the time saying icy things into a phone receiver. Or possibly coaxing things, as difficult as that was to imagine. It was no secret that Margo had been offered the role of Mary weeks ago and had turned it down. A few people in the cast who particularly disliked Bridget had mentioned the fact multiple times over the weekend at Aston Park. Bridget's complexion had become increasingly purple.

Margo had obviously changed her mind. Whether it was to benefit her own career or a sacrifice for Luc, she had already signed an emailed contract.

"They're flying into London tonight," Luc had said briefly, before turning his attention to the tricky road conditions.

Snow was falling lightly again. It was soft and pretty, and totally at odds with her turbulent thoughts.

From the perspective of her career, this was one of the best things that could have happened. She was going to be working with one of the best actors in the business. And public interest in the play was about to go sky-high, partly because Margo had considerably stronger pull power than Bridget, and mostly because it was going to get Luc and Margo back in the same room.

And that was the part that was making her just a little bit twitchy, with absolutely no justification.

She relieved her tension with a period of active vocal exercise, which involved belting out the current playlist on her phone. It was ninety-five percent Michael Bublé Christmas, with a bit of Bon Jovi and Adele thrown in as a palette cleanser.

Luc looked pained.

"Hey." Lily paused in her carolling. "I can sing."

"Amazingly," he agreed, "you can. I just wish you'd sing something else."

Obligingly, she switched to Boney M, and got an audible groan.

"Try not to sound totally gobsmacked, by the way," she said, returning to the Canadian vocal gloriousness. "I told you that everything on my skills sheet is true. I've wanted to go into theatre since I was sixteen. I obviously took singing and dance."

"I shouldn't be that surprised," Luc conceded. "A lot of people have radically different singing and speaking voices."

She was determinedly in the festive Bublé zone; there was no space for annoyance.

"Your father's estate is nearby, isn't it?" he asked out of the blue, probably to put a stop to her decking the halls with boughs of holly.

She frowned through the fogged-up side window, trying to see where they were. "Mmm. Yeah, it's only about twenty minutes away, near Chesham."

"Is he there or in London at the moment?"

"Or in Monte Carlo or Zanzibar? You never know with Jack. But I think he is at Kirkby. He texted me a while ago that he was heading there for some kind of pre-Christmas schmoozing."

"Your dad texts?" Luc was suddenly amused. "I think mine still uses a rotary dial."

"Jack usually wrangles the latest iPhone a month before it goes on sale." Which was one bit of canny networking she wouldn't mind him sharing with his loving daughter.

"Are you going to Kirkby for Christmas?"

There was a full cast rehearsal until the late afternoon of Christmas Eve, but their Saint Nick of a director had grudgingly agreed to a day off on Christmas Day.

"No." She'd never spent Christmas at Kirkby. She couldn't even imagine it. Eating Brussels sprouts while Charlotte averted her eyes. It sounded like the recipe for a stomach ache in more than one respect. "Jack's going to Venice to finalise a business deal."

He had offered to fly Lily out as well, but she would literally be in and out, and she knew what he was like in dedicated work mode. She'd see him for five minutes and then end up eating Christmas dinner in a hotel dining room. Same deal with her mother, who was on tour in Austria. She'd rather curl up on the couch with Trix and *The Wizard of Oz*.

"Do you want to stop by now, then, and say hello?"

She looked up. "Seriously? I thought you'd be itching to get back to London to start knocking lawyers' heads together."

He bit back a smile. "Such a way with words you have. That's exactly why I'm prepared to procrastinate for a couple of hours. Right now, I'm liable to say things I'll regret. I need some breathing space." He nodded towards the upcoming exit. "Yes? No?"

"Well." She *would* like to see her father before Christmas. She'd figured it would be the New Year before they managed to match their schedules. Or that she'd see him for ten minutes on his way to the airport. "I'll have to check if Lady Charlotte is home." She reached for her phone to send the text.

Luc navigated the turn off the motorway. "Why?"

Because she wasn't allowed in the house if her father's wife was there. It wasn't something they usually vocalised. To misquote Captain Barbossa, it was more what you'd call guidelines than an actual rule.

"Um…"

He shot her a disbelieving glance. "Are you seriously telling me that you're banned from the grounds when her Ladyship is gracing the place with her presence?"

"She's not the Wicked Stepmother from panto. If I showed up unannounced, I'm pretty sure she wouldn't lower the drawbridge and release the hounds. It's just always been kind of an understanding, that Jack keeps me a separate part of his life and doesn't rub her face in it. Which I do get."

Although it hadn't been quite so easy to understand as a child, why she couldn't go to her dad's other houses.

"That Lamprey keeps you his dirty little secret, you mean." Luc was pissed off again. On her behalf. It was very warming. Slightly alarming.

"Well, it's hardly a secret, is it?" she pointed out. "It all gets dredged up as muddy backstory every time someone takes a photo of me with a new man."

Speaking of which, she'd be surprised if…

With her thumb, she switched from messages to the net.

Yes. Good old *London Celebrity.* Never failed to spy an opportunity for clickbait.

Luc Savage and Lily Lamprey spotted leaving Oxford hotel, fuelling speculation as to why Margo Roy sought a bit of Continental consolation. Sources say the director and his leading lady were "all over each other."

Just your basic blatant lie, then. "All over each other" was apparently code for "walked eight feet apart and spoke to other people on their phones." The site was slipping—someone had missed an ideal opportunity to use the words "illicit weekend." The *LC* reporters usually loved their flowery clichés.

And to be strictly accurate, she was not the leading lady. She would be located safely under both Margo and Freddy in the programme.

Unenthusiastically, she flicked through the article. She never understood why they listed in excruciating detail what she was wearing. If people had eyes to read the words, they could see for themselves in the thirty-five near-identical photos that she was wearing a black wool coat, tights, pointed ankle boots and "just a hint of makeup."

She was wearing quite a lot of makeup. Her brain had refused to turn off last night and it showed in her under-eye bags today. Luc braked to let a van turn into a side road, and she held up the phone for him to see.

He dismissed it with a passing glance. "Inevitable. They've been running around like ants hoarding crumbs ever since Margo's elopement. I think this would make you my sixth rebound fling." He caught her knee-jerk reaction and rolled his eyes. "In the *press*. Not literally. Christ."

No. She couldn't really imagine him casually *flinging*. Constantly meeting and making plans with new people took a certain amount of time and effort. Making a half-arsed commitment to someone so that you didn't go home to an empty bed at night was probably much more convenient. It was a bleak picture that was continuing to emerge, his so-called epic romance.

He was right, though. These kinds of blog posts had been inevitable since the first rumours had leaked of her casting. The highly unlikely casting that was still provoking "What the fuck?" reactions from anyone who'd seen even ten minutes of *Knightsbridge*. In the past week, she'd seen headlines linking her with almost every man involved with the production. She'd have to have a personal assistant and a time machine to manage that many dates.

Her agent and Amelia kept repeating, ad nauseam, that she had to expect that level of scepticism and derision until opening night. At which point, Amelia confidently believed, she would silence the nasty speculation in the only way possible: by taking the stage and killing it.

No pressure.

"'When you consider her predecessor,'" she read aloud, "'the talents that Lily displays so amply on *Knightsbridge* are obviously equally potent in real life. It's nice to see a girl who knows how to use her biggest assets to advantage.'" She scrolled back up to the byline. "Cheers, Claire Barham. Really flying the flag for your fellow woman there."

Luc accelerated again. "The press is going to make false allegations left and right, but you can't let it affect your performance."

You'd better not let it affect your performance was the emphatic subtext.

"You already know how good you're going to have to be." He didn't soften the warning. "A lot of critics will be taking their seats on opening night salivating at the prospect of seeing a car crash firsthand."

It was amazing, really, that people didn't hire him out for motivational speaking.

"People don't like to be proven wrong. You have to be so good that even a hint of a critical review will just look like sour grapes." Without looking away from the windscreen, Luc reached out and touched her hand briefly. She hadn't realised she was restlessly plucking a hole in the loose threads of her tights. "You can do it."

He sounded so sure now. And she didn't want to disappoint him.

"The rumours will die down eventually," he said, a little too evenly. "They'll move on, pick on someone else."

Their eyes met.

"Right," she said. "It's just one of those things."

"Occupational hazard."

"Happens all the time."

She turned Michael Bublé back on, but didn't feel like singing along this time. She looked back at her phone. "We're all good. Charlotte is out for the day."

"Good."

She had the distinct impression they would have been going on to Kirkby even if her father's wife had been standing at the front windows with a pair of binoculars and a flamethrower.

It was a longer drive than usual on the icy roads and past noon when they crossed the boundary of her father's ancestral estate.

Luc's face went totally blank when they crunched to a stop outside the house. He'd obviously never seen a photo of Kirkby. If he'd been expecting something along the lines of Aston Park, he was rapidly re-evaluating.

When they were out of the car, he remembered how to speak. "How much do the neighbours hate your father?"

They stood looking at the enormous, futuristic steel-and-glass box that had been built over a torn-down Georgian mansion. Her father had unique taste in architecture.

Whoever hadn't listed the original Kirkby House was probably still face-palming.

"How did he even find an architect to do this?" Luc seemed torn between fascination and revulsion. Pretty much the universal reaction to Kirkby. It was a monumental feat of ugliness. The house looked like an interplanetary prison. "Or was it multiple architects? Or did he just grab a sledgehammer and a screwdriver and do it himself?"

Lily couldn't answer. Her stomach was doing its usual Kirkby acrobatics. She associated her very few visits to this house with feeling like Jane Eyre going into the Red Room. She wasn't supposed to be here. It was a piece of childhood knowledge that still cowed her steps as a grown woman.

"God." With no warning, Luc put a freezing-cold palm on the back of her head and pressed warm lips to her forehead. "Don't look like that." He butted his nose gently against hers. "Come on, MI5," he said, releasing her with a stroke of her hair. "Where's the nobody-fucks-with-me woman who walked into my office and stood her ground relentlessly?"

There were excellent, rational reasons why she ought to keep her distance from him.

Yet right now, she really wanted to shove her face into the space between his ear and shoulder, and just hibernate there. She'd never experienced an attraction quite like this before. Usually if a man was off-limits for any reason, she mentally shrugged and moved him out of that box in her mind. She didn't have prickling, driving instincts constantly nudging and needling, and saying inappropriate things.

It didn't feel fleeting and solely physical. It didn't feel like infatuation.

It felt like…recognition.

That was the most unsettling part.

The concern in Luc's expression turned wry. "That look isn't helpful, either. Especially when we're standing right outside your father's house."

At least he'd provided a distraction. Nervous tension replaced by sexual tension.

She shook her head. "What are you doing to me?"

"Back at you."

Just for a moment, Lily reached out and placed her palm against his chest, resting it there, imagining she could feel his heartbeat through the thickness of his coat. He stood still, then caught her fingers in his when her hand slipped away. He tugged gently, pulling her forward one step at a time until she was standing beneath his chin. Lowering his head, he rested his cheek against hers.

"It's going to be all right," he said into her ear. She didn't know if he meant the next few minutes, or the next few months, or the rest of her life.

She closed her eyes, smelling him, breathing in sync, feeling her body relax.

He kissed her ear, her forehead again and, so briefly, her mouth. Then, sliding a hand through her hair and cupping her cheek, he murmured, "Enough."

She stepped away.

Her skin glowed with warmth where he'd touched her. She breathed easier.

Enough.

Jack Lamprey was a slight man, with hair that had once been a familiar silvery blond and was now pure white, a high forehead and a wrinkled baby face. It was as if someone had left the Gerber Baby out in the sun too long. His eyes were the same deep, dark brown as Lily's, but they gleamed with mischief. He was fifty years older than his daughter and his eyes were somehow younger. There was rock-solid, quiet strength in Lily, even when she was doing her best to drive Luc insane.

Jack eyed Luc speculatively over Lily's head as he hugged her. He ruffled her hair. "It's a sad day when you bring a Savage to lunch, pet. As Christmas presents go, I think I'd return this one forthwith."

"Nice to see you again too, Lamprey," Luc drawled. He strongly suspected that Jack had been standing at a front window a few minutes ago. Their last meeting had been brief, but the elderly man's attitude had radiated amusement then. There was a definite edge this time that spoke of a protective father rather than a half-hearted family feud.

"Yes," Lily said repressively. "I heard you're fairly well acquainted with Luc's family."

They were startlingly alike to look at, but what translated into almost ridiculous beauty in Lily didn't sit so well in a male septuagenarian.

"'Luc,' is it? Very informal, aren't we?" Jack lifted bushy eyebrows, then deliberately let his smile turn reminiscent. "Ah, yes. Darling Célie. How is your charming mother, *Luc*?"

It would take more than that to provoke Luc at this point. There was already the constant barrage of innuendo and abuse from Byrne. More important, first and foremost, there was Lily, who had tipped his world upside down, without permission, in about five minutes flat. The bar had been raised.

He smiled back. "Much the same as ever. It's interesting. *Charming* is the exact word she uses about you. She often sits down with a glass of wine and tells the story of how well you took your rejection."

Jack's laugh was genuine. When he bowed in a visual

touché and the barbed smile turned into a real grin, the infamous Lamprey charm burst out like a power surge. The explanation of his success with women, Célie Verne excepted, didn't lie solely in a Swiss bank account. He could have written the book on winning friends and influencing people. His many friends would just be well advised to keep their eyes open and their wallets closed.

"As you and your brother owe your existence to my rejection, you ought to be praising the skies that your distressingly monogamous mother has such poor taste in men. My old friend Cameron is well, I assume? Still behaving like a pair of cooing young doves, are they?"

"Jack," Lily said before Luc could reply, and the lingering mischief in her father's eyes faded into fondness.

He took pity on her. "Well, baby, how's work? Have you shot your final scenes yet? Do I need to steel myself for blood and gore?"

"Final days on set Thursday night and Friday." Lily seemed relieved to draw the focus away from Luc and his family. "No gore. A lot of flailing and choking, and cosmetic bloating. The execs at CTV weren't exactly thrilled when I resigned. Poor Gloria is going to meet an ugly end. Don't tell anyone; I'll get sued for breaking the confidentiality clause." She suddenly made a face. "Have you started watching the show again? Awkward, Jack. Really awkward."

"I record it and get Mrs. Hastings to tell me when it's safe to look." Jack coughed. "PG-rated, father-friendly scenes have been rather far and few between, recently. I think it's a good thing you're moving on. That role was always fluff and filler." He fixed Luc with another of those assessing stares. "I'm very pleased that you'll finally be working with a *professional*—" there was definite emphasis on the word "—who knows what he's doing."

"Why, Jack," Luc said. "I'm touched."

"Be as touched as you like," Jack retorted. "Just don't touch anything you shouldn't. Savvy?"

"Oh my God." Lily squeezed her eyes shut, then looked at Luc. "If you're starting to feel homicidal again, I feel I ought to remind you whose idea this was."

"That was a momentary outburst in unusual circumstances. I believe my usual subtitle is 'cold, heartless bastard.'" He ignored Jack's scowl as they excluded him from the conversation. "My self-control is legendary."

"Oh, I've noticed."

Jack was watching them narrowly. "Oh Christ," he said, in resigned tones. "A *Savage*."

It was a welcome interruption when the front door opened and a group of chattering people came in, until Luc realised they were led by Lady Charlotte Lamprey. She was a familiar figure from the press and public events, a physically lovely woman in her fifties with a butter-soft way of speaking and expensive taste in clothing. Her sculpted face froze when she caught sight of Lily, and Luc immediately tensed in response. Like he was a fucking mother hen.

Or a man who didn't want to see his woman hurt.

He fully echoed Jack's sentiments: *Oh Christ*.

Jack smiled at his wife and his own body remained relaxed, but his hand curled about his daughter's elbow in a silent show of support.

It improved Luc's opinion of him significantly. After what Lily had said in the car, he'd been under the impression that Lamprey was a crap father as well as a substandard husband. However, despite his obvious faults, he clearly cared about her.

"Hello, darling," Jack said mildly. "I didn't expect you back so soon."

"Obviously," Lady Charlotte murmured. Her lovely, silken voice managed to be far more grating than Lily's technically flawed tones. Her smile didn't reach her blue eyes as she looked first at Luc and then somewhere to the left of Lily's ear. "Hello, Lily."

"Hello, Charlotte. It's nice to see you again." If he'd ever doubted Lily's abilities as an actor, she would have swept over his scepticism now. She was warm, she was believable, she had just enough polite distance so as not to seem an imposition. "This is Luc Savage. Luc, this is Lady Charlotte Lamprey."

The whole discreet scene hit a wrong note. There was tangible tension in the air, and he could understand why Lily avoided this house.

He could also understand, as Lily did, why her presence would be a painful and embarrassing reminder of a liaison Lady Charlotte would prefer to forget, but his loyalty in this instance had a single focus. And she was struggling beneath the carefully perfected mask.

Lady Charlotte's handshake was unenthusiastic. She obviously wanted them both the hell out of her house, but she was a politician to the core. "It's a pleasure to meet you, Mr. Savage. I've worked with representatives from your company in the past, and your charitable contributions have been very much appreciated, I assure you."

He wasn't aware that he'd made any charitable contributions to her campaigns. However, Maria was in charge of their annual tax write-offs and she was fairly vocal around the offices about women's rights, usually when she was about to ask for a pay raise, so it sounded probable enough. He'd always approved of Lady Charlotte's political activities in theory, without thinking much about her as a person.

He'd spent his career observing body language and directing the construction and display of a character, and he saw the moment when her own mask cracked. A flash of indecision and torment was quickly swallowed up by the experienced civil servant.

It seemed cruel to both women to prolong this visit. Nobody was winning anything in this situation.

When the small talk faltered, he said casually, "I'm sorry this has to be such a flying visit, but we really ought to get back on the road. We're due in London this afternoon and I don't want to risk an accident in this weather."

"Oh, you aren't staying for lunch? You're very welcome." Lady Charlotte was all smooth politeness again. She voiced the barefaced lie without batting a lash. He could have used her on the stage.

"Of course they're staying for lunch." Jack was visibly reluctant to sacrifice his daughter's company, even for his wife's peace of mind, but Lily stepped in then, equally firm.

"We really do have to get back to London." Her eyes briefly held Luc's before she smiled at her father. "Next time."

A silent, poignant look was exchanged between husband and wife before Jack gave in.

He walked them outside to the car, under the scrutiny of the interested house guests. The snow was falling again, swirling down in light, erratic patterns, glinting in the grey light. It dusted Jack's head and shoulders as he stood there in his shirtsleeves, suddenly looking every one of his years. The ageless rogue was gone; a tired old man had taken his place.

"I'm sorry." Regret threaded through the abrupt words.

Lily blinked rapidly as snowflakes settled on her lashes. She glanced back at the house before she stepped forward to wrap her arms around her father's neck. "It's okay, Jack."

Luc just barely heard the murmured words; the acoustics of the still, icy landscape carried them to his ears.

"Love you, pet," Jack said gruffly, returning her hug. "Reckon I was unjustly rewarded for my sins when I got you, wasn't I?" He flicked her cheek with the back of one finger. "We'll have lunch in London before I go to Venice, shall we? Put on our glad rags and drop a few quid at Claridge's?"

"Yeah." Lily smiled back at him. "Call me and we'll do that."

There was an odd note in her voice, a dash of resignation underscoring her response.

Luc didn't think she was expecting lunch at Claridge's anytime soon.

Of course you forgot about the reservation. Margo's voice was an ironic echo in his memory. *So did I. I ate a sandwich in the green room between scenes. I don't know why we bother. If there was a twelve-step programme for workaholics, we'd be too busy to go.*

He moved his head in a jerking movement. It was one of those uncomfortable moments in life when the mirror cleared for a moment and the reflection wasn't pretty.

When they neared London, the snow turned to rain, drumming heavily against the car windows. Lily didn't seem to be in the mood for Christmas music any longer. He would have preferred endless hours of nonstop Bublé to the sight of her glum face in his peripheral vision. It had been his suggestion that they stop at Kirkby and he felt directly responsible for dragging her day down into the depths as well.

He dealt with a lot of temperament, but patient coaxing and support wasn't his forte. He usually found that a matter-of-fact "get over it and do your job" worked equally well in rehearsals. Actors tended to take a drop of sympathy and run with it all the way to hysteria. He actually *cared* that Lily was hurting, though, and she wasn't the type to indulge in self-pity.

Before he could think of something bracing to say— "Sorry that your family life is like something out of a Jackie Collins novel"?—she spoke, as if to herself, staring out the window at the rain. "Jack danced with me in the rain once. When I was about seven."

That sounded like exactly the sort of irresponsible thing Jack Lamprey would do with a small child. Probably hadn't even put a coat on her.

"Hmm," Luc said non-committally.

"I stayed at his London flat for two weeks. I had a nanny, but I remember he came home early from work on my birthday. It was pouring with rain outside, but he said you have to dance in the rain at least once."

Luc was fairly sure you *didn't*, particularly if you weren't a fan of head colds, but again, it sounded suitably sentimental and unnecessary of Jack.

He didn't think she would appreciate a rational reply, so he said, truthfully, "He obviously loves you. Whatever his faults. And we all have those, in one form or another."

"I have noticed that most men do, yes." He was relieved by Lily's return to lightness, after he'd checked that it matched the expression in her eyes. "I, however, like most women, am perfection in human form."

Close enough to it.

Painful. Physically painful that his mind was even capable of producing a *thought* that fucking lame. He wouldn't have said it out loud for a million quid and a write-off of his mortgage. It wasn't even true. She was a disruptive nuisance. He expected to go completely grey before the run was over.

"No arguments?" she teased him, and he grinned briefly.

"Whatever my many masculine faults, I do have a sense of survival."

It was still raining when they got back to her mews flat and he carried in her year's supply of luggage, but her living room was quiet and warm, and smelled like someone had been doing Christmas baking.

"Is Trix here?" He put the suitcases down by the couch.

Lily looked up from her phone, but kept texting with one hand. "No, she's got training all afternoon, then a show tonight. I'm just letting her know I'm back safely, despite the snow and dodgy company."

"I'd be offended, but you did spend the weekend with Bridget and Dylan, so there's plenty of room for my ego to shift the blame." He heard a faint beeping in the flat as Lily smiled at him and smoothed back her sodden hair. When wet, it darkened to matte gold.

"I'm guessing that after the read-through tomorrow,

I'm going to find you a slave-driving nightmare, so I'll say thanks for everything now, while I still feel nice."

"And I'll acknowledge that, overall, you were slightly less irritating than Bridget."

He wasn't aware of walking, nor of her moving, but somehow they ended up within touching distance.

"Jocasta will be in touch with you directly to arrange a schedule around rehearsals." He could smell her perfume over the scents of cinnamon and cloves. "It's going to be intensive."

"I can handle it." She kept looking at his mouth.

"Keep the cockiness. You'll need it." He hesitated. "I'll see you in the morning, then."

"Yes. Enjoy knocking heads together. I hope you get everything sorted."

Their fingers brushed, came apart and then tangled together. Her breath was quick and shallow, warm against his face.

When the door suddenly banged open and hit the wall, Lily made a noise like a strangled duck and almost shoved him into the coffee table in her haste to propel herself out of his hold.

"Wow," Trix said from the doorway. She was wearing reindeer leggings and a lurid Christmas jumper, and looked half-asleep. "Imagine how awkward that could have been, if I'd opened the door *normally* just now, cleared my throat twice, still not been heard over the screaming sexual tension, and then had to go back into the hallway and come in again super loudly."

His blood having made a swift migration south, it took several moments for Luc's brain to connect the dots and realise that when someone sent a text message and a beep immediately sounded, it usually meant that the other phone was not currently in a dressing room at the Old Wellington.

Lily blinked at her friend, managed to look both incredibly sexy and a little like a stunned haddock, and flushed to the tips of her ears. "What? Um," she said, and ran out of ideas.

"Yeah." Trix tugged on a loose stand of bubblegum-coloured hair. "I was going to ask if you wanted me to put the kettle on. But I strongly feel like maybe my training *wasn't* cancelled this afternoon and I'm needed at the theatre urgently."

Lily seemed totally lost for words, which would have seemed like the answer to a prayer when he was watching her TV reel, and underlined the cliché that you ought to be careful what you wished for.

"Go ahead and make the tea," he said to Trix, when the silence became screamingly loud. "I'm already late back to the office."

She was scrutinising him closely. "Would you like a cup before you go?" Her tone was wary and overly polite.

He felt the small movement that Lily made at his side, an immediate rejection of that idea. He touched her arm in a fleeting gesture of reassurance. "I appreciate the offer, but I've got a meeting with my solicitor and a backlog of paperwork waiting for me."

He already had a dull headache building in his temples, which seemed natural enough, since he'd clearly lost his mind.

"I'll see you tomorrow." Lily seemed to read the mangled remains of his thoughts, which were bitterly self-condemning. "My fault as much as yours." It was a low, unequivocal statement.

Professionally, he was in a more powerful position, and given his current PR problems, his behaviour was rash at best. Some might say morally reprehensible and totally fucking hypocritical.

"Hardly."

When the door closed behind Luc, Lily released a quick breath. "God. It's finally happened." She sat down on the couch. "Gloria's pulled me over the edge. Best start locking up the vicars now."

"Interesting weekend, I take it?" Trix went into the kitchen and switched on the kettle, watching her over the bench as she opened a new packet of biscuits. She cleared her throat. "I'm trying to think of a way to phrase this tactfully. Did you tumble arse-over-tits into a snowdrift and suffer some sort of catastrophic head injury?"

The words themselves were teasing, but her tone was not, and Lily didn't smile. "I get all morally superior about the media reports and then do this. Because I can't help myself. It's pathetic."

"It's not *pathetic*. It's radically out of character, but—" Trix looked down and seemed to realise what she was wearing. "I wore my reindeer PJs in front of Luc Savage. That could have been really embarrassing if I hadn't caught him making sex eyes at the staff."

"Fuck." Lily rested her forehead on the heels of her palms. "He's my boss."

"That fact only just occurred to you?"

"I'm hoping that if I repeat it enough, my brain might untangle all the crossed wires."

Trix said nothing while she brewed their tea. Lily rubbed her thumbs in slow circles over her temples, as if she could hypnotise her racing thoughts into stillness, and listened to the cosy clinking of pottery, which she usually found calming.

When Trix came around the bench and passed over a steaming cup of tea, there was a cracker sticking out of it at an angle, already dunked. Like the chocolate flake in a 99, only dry and depressing.

"I found them in the cupboard," she said. "Conveniently vegan. Although you probably intended to smother them in cheese, which would have defeated the purpose. And herbal tea. No dairy or caffeine for the voice, right?"

"Or alcohol, chocolate or curry."

"Just like being back at boarding school." Trix sat down on the couch and curled her legs beneath her. Her movements were flexible and graceful, as if she were one of those dolls with elastic limbs and could just casually loop her knee about her neck if she wanted.

"You slept with vodka and Milky bars stuffed under your mattress at school." Lily bit the corner off a cracker. She couldn't remember buying these, which could mean they'd been in the cupboard since she'd moved in. It wasn't too bad. Although it was slightly concerning that a vegan cracker tasted like fake chicken.

"Most of which you nicked." Trix stirred a spoonful of sugar into her tea, still watching Lily closely. "Do you want to talk about it?"

"My history of petty theft? I think it's mostly behind me. I haven't even opened any doors on your advent calendar."

"Lily."

Lily snapped the corner off her cracker and toyed with it, tapping it against the side of her mug. "It's just—

attraction." The statement—the lie—seemed to loiter in the air, returning a sceptical, silent *Oh yeah?* Deliberately, she shrugged it away. "He's a good-looking man, my sex life has been on the backburner recently, and things—bubbled over. It's nothing. As soon as I get stuck into rehearsals, I'll forget all about it."

Her conscience heaved a loud sigh and stalked off in exasperation.

It would have been a decent performance, if she'd been playing to a different audience.

In her best Gloria voice, Trix said silkily, "Who cares about my professional reputation? I'm so starved for a man and he's ever so dreamy." She snorted. "As if."

"You couldn't even *pretend* that you don't know me that well."

"Despite that brazen lie about your dried-up husk of a sex life, you've never come close to compromising your job for an *attraction*." Trix took aim and fired. "And thanks to your mother, you usually sprint away from workplace relationships like you're outrunning a swarm of wasps."

Lily looked at the remains of her cracker and imagined choking it down like a mouthful of dust. She set it back on the saucer before she met Trix's steady gaze.

Hot-button topic. Nobody enjoyed having their neuroses pointed out to them.

Her mother was a driven, intelligent woman. A talented, successful singer. A witty conversationalist, well informed and charismatic. And Lily loved her.

She *didn't* love that Vanessa had unapologetically used influential men to advance her career for almost thirty years.

Dating a club promoter had brought her into Jack

Lamprey's sphere. An affair with Jack had propelled her from backup singer to headline act.

Lily had been an unexpected extra.

It was do-or-die survival of the fittest, from Vanessa's perspective. If you wanted to reach the top of your profession and stay there, you kept a cool head and made shrewd choices.

"It's snakes and ladders in this business, darling." Laughter in her mother's voice. *"You go to school, you work hard and you take advantage of the shortcuts when they come along. Just be careful you don't get bitten."*

Networking, as one paper had called it sarcastically, to her mother's intense amusement, had opened doors for Vanessa, but it was her talent that kept her on the stage. She would have got where she wanted to be regardless. Her voice had always been able to silence every conversation in a noisy room, whether it was a backstreet pub or an arena. In a good way, unlike when Lily spoke.

Vanessa was currently living with the chief executive of her record label, whose existence she had ignored until his promotion. Perfectly nice man. Highly unlikely to last.

Lily could still remember, word for word, what her mother had said when Lily had started going out with her first boyfriend. *"Flesh and blood, that's everything. That love is forever. Men—men are lovely. For a while. It never lasts, kiddo. And it's nice if you're left with something more than memories and a bruised ego."*

As a person: total delight to be around. As a role model for romantic and sexual relationships: not ideal.

Lily couldn't control Vanessa's choices, but she was

in charge of her own. Just because the media was convinced she was going to follow in her mother's slightly
erratic footsteps, and just because she'd inadvertently
put a face and voice to the most notorious gold-digger
on primetime TV, it didn't mean that she had to play
to type in real life.

She was already crossing a line with Luc. The whole
dynamic was uncomfortably familiar.

Yet even thinking that also felt weirdly like a betrayal.

She was going to destroy herself with stress before
this show even opened.

"I don't understand it," she said slowly. "And I can't
explain it. But it won't go any further."

Ideally, she would have sounded cool and certain
when she said that, not depressed.

"I hope not." Concern licked at the edge of Trix's
blunt words. "Because you've had one dream since we
were at school and it didn't involve taking your clothes
off. Either to play a complete numpty like Gloria or
to hop into bed with your director. You're finally on
the precipice of turning your career around. And if
you want to start shaking off the shadow of Gloria the
Homewrecker, at least until the special-edition DVD
box set comes out, you probably shouldn't be making
return sex eyes at a man everyone thought was all but
married to the most beloved actress in Britain until a
couple of months ago."

"Jesus, Trix. Tell me how you really feel."

"I made the worst decision of my life this year, and
God knows how far I would have sunk if you hadn't
tried to talk sense into me, over and over again. You
didn't half-arse around the point."

Lily didn't reply immediately. She hadn't held back at the time, but she trod more cautiously around this subject now. "I'm not arguing, but—the circumstances aren't exactly the same."

"No. In this case, there'd be professional implications as well as personal ones."

Which pretty much covered the spectrum of her own reservations, but wasn't what she'd meant. "I should have said, the men aren't exactly the same."

Trix's fine-boned features set into unreadable lines. "They're both forty-something workaholics. Used to being in charge."

And the similarities ended there.

Lily gave up on hedging. She was incapable of going soft on Dan St. James. "Dan could have been younger than you and he'd still have had the control issues."

"You don't know what Luc is like outside of work. You hardly know him."

Lily's otherwise uncooperative brain acknowledged that fact. A less rational part of her instinctively disagreed. The Romantic poets would call it her heart; realistically, it was probably her hormones.

"Maybe not, but—Luc isn't Dan. God, I'd be even more worried about myself if I really thought he was anything like Dickhead Dan—" Flushing, she cut herself off. "Sorry."

It was a tiny flicker, but the first time she had seen Trix smile when they'd been anywhere near this subject. "It used to slip into text messages when you were getting really heated." That scrap of a smile faded. "It was one reason why I was glad I kept a second phone."

It was in the past now, thank God, but that whole situation could still infuriate Lily. It had been a horrendous time, with Dan slinking about like a manipulative octopus, wrapping his tentacles about every aspect of Trix's life, trying to cut off anybody who could see what was going on.

They'd come within inches of losing their friendship altogether, when Trix had still been so wrapped up in him that she'd listened to every poisonous word that dripped off his forked tongue.

Lily had disliked him the first time they'd met; six months in, she'd never detested anybody so much in her life.

"I'm just thrown," she said eventually, veering away from the subject of Dan before her brain imploded with residual rage. "I thought I'd be fighting Luc professionally throughout the whole process, however short it turned out to be. I thought that if I managed to do this, it'd be *despite* him. I didn't expect—"

She hadn't expected Luc Savage, the insufferable, insulting twat, to be *Luc*, the man who had suffered through an awkward cuddle to comfort her when she'd almost vomited from Kirkby nerves.

"It's just—temporary." She did manage firmness this time, although the words were very quiet.

Trix still looked worried. "Is it? I've never seen you like this. You *blushed*. You're usually so unflappable around men. I'm not surprised most of them find you intimidating."

"They don't."

"Uh, they *do*. You only see the crap that's written by strangers. The people we actually know, guys we meet—most of them spend two minutes with you and want to run home to Mummy."

Lily choked on the mouthful of tea she'd taken to

ease the dryness in her throat. "Thanks a *lot*. You make me sound like the White Witch from Narnia."

"You're not *cold*. You're just very self-contained. Erring slightly on the side of cynical."

"Cynical?"

"You're never surprised when your mother ends a relationship. You expect it to happen, and it does. Every time. You love your dad, but you don't have much faith in him. You expect to be let down. You aren't exactly Little Miss Trusting. Which I don't think is a bad thing," Trix added hastily, seeing Lily's expression. "I mean, you were never taken in by Dan. Right from the beginning, you told me to be careful, and you were right. It was a fucking mess, and I still can't believe that I just let it…spiral."

Absently, Lily shook her head. "I think that's why people like Dan are so dangerous, though. Anyone could fall for the charm offensive. He worked by stages, one step at a time, so your warning signals never went off. He never bothered to manipulate me. He saw me as some sort of twisted competition for your attention from day one. I bet he used to say all sorts about me, in a really light way, like he was joking." She saw from the tinge of colour in Trix's cheekbones that she was right. "You can't blame yourself. He's a career manipulator. I bet he was a vicious little shit at school, always playing people off one another and tugging the strings. It's emotional abuse. Bullying should be illegal."

The unfamiliar traces of hardness fell away from the downward curve of Trix's mouth. "I do blame myself."

Lily reached out and took her hand. "I know. It makes me want to strap him to that table with the industrial laser in *Goldfinger*."

"And you wonder why men run away crying."

Lily bit her lip. "Cynical?"

Trix squeezed her fingers. "In the most lovable way." She added softly, "Just—don't lose yourself looking for something that's not really there."

The door closed behind his legal team and Luc jerked open a desk drawer, sifting through the contents for painkillers. He could deal with a headache; he didn't need it turning into a migraine. The tablet on his desk buzzed with an incoming call.

Margo.

He answered while he swallowed a couple of tablets dry. "Hi."

"Hi." She sounded exactly as usual, voice perfectly trained, emotion carefully restrained. He'd never been able to tell her mood from a phone call. She'd been good at covering it in person as well, but he'd directed her enough times to recognise her tells. "I'm downstairs—okay to come up for a minute?"

"Shouldn't you be killing time in an Italian airport about now?"

"The concierge at the hotel was a fan of Alberto's." He thought he heard a hint of a smile that time. "He got us a free upgrade and an earlier departure time."

Luc suspected that was a metaphor for Ferreti's life in general. Most people regularly experienced delayed flights and bad customer service, and most people didn't bounce when they walked.

"I have a meeting in twenty minutes," he said, checking his schedule. "First free window I've had today. Nice timing. Come on up."

She came into his office a few minutes later, after

one obligatory knock. For some reason, that single knock seemed to punctuate their new relationship. He hadn't seen her for a while. If she came to his house now, she'd knock on the door, when she'd once had a key. After the breakup, she'd removed her things so efficiently that she hadn't left behind so much as a stray hair tie—and he'd spent so little time at home the past couple of years that he hadn't built up enough memories of her there to make it seem empty now.

The behemoth of a man walking behind her gave Luc one hard stare, barked, "I'll wait outside," and spun on his heel.

Luc looked at Margo quizzically as she shut the door. "Assistant, bodyguard or overzealous fan?"

"He combines the roles of driver, coffee purchaser and fan buffer."

"You didn't come across him in Rome, by any chance? Slaying lions in the Colosseum?"

"I found him in Shoreditch, bench-pressing twice his own body weight."

"He really felt it necessary to follow you up here?"

"Are you kidding? I told him I was going to discuss business with my ex. It was difficult to talk him out of packing nunchucks."

He sat on the edge of his desk as he surveyed her. She looked tanned and relaxed, her hair falling in a shiny black bob. It was surreal. He felt like she was an old colleague or a friend he hadn't seen in years. It was hard to believe that a few months ago he'd been living with her. Sleeping with her.

She was studying him with equal fascination. "You look—different."

"I know, it's bizarre. Eight years, and I feel like our entire relationship was some sort of surreal dream."

She blinked. "No, I mean, you're actually *different*. You're even acting differently. You would never have said something like that when we were together. It wouldn't have occurred to you. To analyse our relationship in any way."

That was uncomfortably true, and he realised it belatedly. He shrugged, deliberately casual. "There was never a need. We always got along well."

"Yes, we did. Which I've since realised was another symptom. We never argued when we were a couple. People who love each other argue. People who *hate* each other argue. People who aren't invested enough to bother just get along."

"Don't tell me there's conflict in paradise already," he said ironically. "It must be difficult to argue with the personification of a Tickle Me Elmo."

She pressed her lips down on an instinctive smile. "God, you're such a git. Why did I ever overlook that?" She set her bag down on his desk and took a seat in a spare chair, crossing her legs. "Catch me up, then. What did you say to Bridget to send her scurrying for the hills? She didn't even make it to the read-through. That must be a new record."

His jaw clenched with a surge of renewed irritation. "She's defected for an action flick. And is trying to avoid contractual obligations by arguing that my recent bout of bad press is damaging her career by association."

Margo tilted her head. "I have noticed that most of the mud is flying your way. I'm surprised. My press agent was on standby. I thought I was going to come off as the guilty party."

"You did, for about three days. Happily, you're now being congratulated on escaping my reign of tyranny."

"I just wrapped a shoot with Michael Trevayne. His directorial style makes you seem like a veritable teddy bear."

"Thank you for that unlikely comparison, but I think they're referring to our relationship outside of work."

"We hardly saw each other outside of work."

"As a rebuttal, I'm not sure that would do either of us any favours."

Margo frowned. "Most of the vitriol seems to be coming from *London Celebrity*. Have you been ruffling feathers over there?"

Luc made a noncommittal sound. He and Margo had never discussed the Byrnes. His grandfather's less than sterling character wasn't exactly pillow talk. "Personal differences with the editor." He changed the subject. "I was surprised you were prepared to take the role after all. It was a fairly adamant 'no' during the initial casting."

"Well." Her tone was generous. "I did feel that I owed you some loyalty after all these years."

"Or you had a serious case of stage itch."

"Might have been a bit of that too." She widened her eyes at him. "Is there a member of your company who *isn't* courting media attention at the moment? With the possible exception of Freddy, who's such a crowd-pleaser that even that sourpuss critic on *Wake Me Up London* just verbally pats her on the head. Dylan Waitely generates enough scandal for two. There are probably so many skeletons in his cupboard that bones fall out when his maid puts the washing away, although he disgraces himself in public so often that nothing short of murder would damage his career at this point. And Lily Lamprey from *Knightsbridge*. I also saw that." She looked at him meaningfully. "I'm not surprised the press has run wild with rumours on that one. A bit unexpected?"

Also not a topic he wanted to discuss with anyone right now, and very definitely not with his ex-girlfriend.

"She's good," he said briefly. "Once Jocasta whips the vocals into shape, she'll be very good."

Margo looked intrigued. "I watch *Knightsbridge*, and I can't say I've been overly struck by Lily's work in it, but I trust your judgement. And it's certainly one way to build interest. I don't think you've ever had such rampant speculation about a show before."

"You know that the media attention is going to go into overdrive after the press release goes out tonight and everyone knows you're on board."

Her mouth tipped up at the corners and a faint gleam lit her blue eyes. "I know."

"And you look so bothered about it."

"Well, I have got feelers out for another big film role next year. After we close, naturally. Having cut my honeymoon short, I have no plans to pull a Bridget and jump ship. However, I can't say that all the attention recently hasn't—helped things along, professionally."

"So glad I could assist."

"As if you haven't been rubbing your hands with glee watching the pre-sale numbers rise."

"I can sell out a production without needing half of England to read that I've been brutally dumped for an opera singer because I'm the West End's answer to Sauron, thanks."

She laughed. "It's nice, you know, just being back to this. I like you a lot more when I don't have to worry about why I'm not in love with you."

As compliments went, it was fairly backhanded, but he'd take it.

Chapter Seven

After all the nerves and build-up, the read-through was almost boringly normal. The surroundings and core cast were different, but otherwise it was very much like the CTV table reads, down to the snack selection and dirty jokes from the younger male actors.

Lily stood by the refreshment table during the break, looking around.

They would be rehearsing here in the studios at Savage Productions for the next few weeks, before they moved to the Queen Anne for the madness of technical week. Hell Week, as the crew called it.

Then—because Luc was one of the few West End directors who refused to hold previews—they were opening cold, with no test run. There would be no opportunity to gauge a response from the public before the critics were given free rein; any problems would have to be ironed out during tech week.

Reality was sinking in for everyone concerned. Lily was still fielding a bit of hostility from certain members of the company, but most people were focused on their own lines and cues today. The party atmosphere was over. This was work.

If there *were* side glances and murmured speculation, most of it was aimed at Luc and Margo.

She had been trying not to watch them, but her eyes kept travelling back when they were talking and making notes on their copies of the script. She hadn't expected them to do anything to feed the gossip, but she could usually spot a poker face—it was in the genes—and she'd expected to sense some underlying tension.

There was nothing. It was exactly as Freddy had said. They might have been friendly but distant acquaintances, not people who knew intimately if the other snored and what they looked like asleep.

"Nice work." The comment was warm, and Lily looked up from the juice bar and returned Margo's smile.

"Thanks." She filled a glass with pineapple juice and stood back to let the other woman grab a cup of coffee. Obviously Margo didn't worry, or didn't have to worry, about caffeine. Another member of the vocally blessed. "I have a lot more work to do with Jocasta, though."

"She's a miracle worker," Margo agreed. "I worked with her when I first started in theatre, right out of drama school. I had no vocal stamina back then. I lost my voice halfway through an am-dram production of *Chitty Chitty Bang Bang*. One of the worst nights of my life."

Oh.

Well, if Lily should have learned anything by now, it was the dangers of making assumptions.

"I can't remember you ever being anything but word-perfect," she said ruefully. "I was reminding myself that I should feel inspired, not psyched out."

Margo pulled a face. "It's just experience. I've been

doing this a bit longer than you have." She caught sight of the folded newspaper Lily had been reading and tilted her head to read the headline. "Well, God, don't read rubbish like that. Of course you're going to psych yourself out."

"I know. I'm not sure why I do it to myself." Lily turned the paper over, smothering the paragraphs about how she was bringing down the tone of the whole production against the tablecloth. "And I don't know why it's worse when it's printed in a paper than online. The online stuff *stays* there, even if the news moves on. This will end up in the bin, or the fire, or stained with fish-and-chip grease. But when someone actually takes the trouble to print it out…"

"You're entirely correct, though. It's going to end up in the bin. Right now." Margo tossed it into the nearby rubbish bag. "Just stop reading it. It's never going to be productive. Even if they're saying good things, you'll find something negative. Or you'll turn it into a negative, think that you're on a good streak, it can't last, it's only going to disappoint people more if you fail. You can't worry about all of that or you will break."

She made it sound so easy. She was totally right, but it didn't seem that easy. It was partly the new medium. Lily was used to cameras and highly edited scenes; there was amped-up pressure with the live immediacy of theatre, and it was going to take a while to get used to that. It also *meant* so much. She had been so sure for so long that this was what she wanted to do that the self-doubt was creeping in again, and it didn't help when it seemed like the rest of the theatre world agreed with her.

Before she could stop herself, Lily glanced over at where Luc stood in conversation with his stage manager. He turned his head for a moment, on cue. It was only the slightest altering of expression, probably not discernible to anyone else in the room, but it doubled the number of butterflies in her stomach.

"Some people must find *you* fairly intimidating to be around," Margo said, to her embarrassment. "Or to stand next to."

That was the second time Lily had heard the word *intimidating* in as many days. It was bizarre, the way different people saw the same situation. When Lily had arrived this morning, a member of the legal team had brought paperwork for her and Dylan to sign. He'd greeted her in a tone that just crossed the line from kind to patronising, and then addressed all his questions to Dylan, as if she would be incapable of even understanding what he was asking, let alone answering for herself. When he'd left, he'd all but patted her on the head and offered to change her tyres for her. She hadn't felt intimidating then. She'd felt like a mannequin.

"I've never seen men literally trail off mid-conversation when someone walks into a room."

Lily tucked a loose strand of hair behind her ear. Her cheek felt hot against her hand. "I'm sure they didn't."

"I'm sorry, I'm embarrassing you. I imagine it's difficult to know what to say to stuff like that, if you don't have an ego the size of Europe. And you must get comments on your looks fairly often."

"Well, it is the only thing worth noticing about a woman." She grimaced. "Sorry. Sore point."

"Valid point."

Lily shrugged. "I've been working in the TV industry for several years. There's obviously a lot of focus on looks. The management and the makeup and wardrobe teams have no problem giving a detailed analysis of your appearance to your face, and that's never going to be a stream of compliments."

"Oh, I know. And I think there's even less room for unconventional beauty and quirky character faces in the TV studios than in the British film industry. But you do have quite an extraordinary face." Margo added frankly, "I expect that's why the tabloids take such pleasure in criticising your acting ability and your body. It makes people feel like you're still a real person if you're a half-wit with hips."

Lily had to laugh then. Margo had been completely single-minded from the moment they'd opened their scripts; five minutes in, it had been impossible to imagine that anyone else could ever have played Mary. She was stubborn and prejudiced, loyal and manipulative, and occasionally, unexpectedly, very funny. The flawed, lethal queen. But out of character, she was so direct that it was impossible not to like her.

"I assume you're leaving *Knightsbridge*?" Margo was checking out the biscuit selection. "Do you see Party Rings?" Lily pointed at one of the platters. "Excellent." She offered the plate and Lily took one as well. "Don't answer that. You probably can't say anything contractually until your exit episode screens."

"Fair assumption." Lily licked a smear of pink icing from her thumb. "I'm shooting certain scenes tonight and tomorrow."

"Really. I don't suppose Steve Warren is directing?"

"I'm pretty sure he is."

"I filmed my first guest role with him, in my early twenties." Margo chewed thoughtfully. "Is it a closed set? I don't suppose I could tag along?"

It *was* a closed set, due to the "secrecy" of her departure, which had been pretty widely guessed since fans of the show knew she would be performing a heavy West End schedule for the next six months, but Margo had probably had open access anywhere she wanted to go for at least ten years.

"Do you want me to ask?"

"Would you?"

Unsurprisingly, Lily got the go-ahead to bring the famous film star to work with her. When they arrived at the CTV studio late that afternoon, accompanied by Margo's walking mountain of a bodyguard, the assistant who brought the confidentiality form for Margo to sign was humbly apologetic. Margo gave her triangular sphinx smile and signed both the form and an autograph.

Shooting Lily a mischievous look, she murmured, "I'm going to quite enjoy the regal persona for the next few months. I just finished playing a Roman slave. My husband is going to find things a little different on the home front with this character."

It kind of figured that Margo would be an extreme method actor.

When he spotted her, irascible Steve Warren fawned all over his most successful protégée. After that disturbing sight, it was a relief when Ash was his usual, unfazed self.

"Is this the new status symbol? The next step up from a Chanel bag?" he teased as they stood off-set, waiting for the production team to give the all-clear. "Just tote a BAFTA winner around with you?"

"Apparently she used to work with Steve and wanted to say hello."

"Strange woman."

"I really don't think he *purposely* gave you a triple chin."

Ash scowled. "People keep screenshotting it on Twitter. I'm a fucking meme."

"Hang in there. You get to show off your muscles today. Although why Edward is walking around shirtless on a Sunday afternoon when the house is full of elderly parishioners…"

Ash flexed his shoulders and pecs. "A little post-sermon treat for them."

"I think I'd rather have the jam and scones, myself."

They were filming the scenes out of order, so her emotional final sex scene and argument with Chris Blakely, who played the duke, was tomorrow. Today was the discovery of her body by Ash. The script had changed, which she should have suspected, to avoid any spoilers leaking to the public. The garter-belt strangling had been scrapped; she was now going to drown in an enormous vat of champagne. It seemed massively unlikely that the Victorian-minded duchess would order a literal *tank* of champagne for a church fête, but whatever. Lily wasn't paid to critique the writing.

The crew had erected a glass diving tank, filled it with water, and tinted it with pink dye that would show up as a muted gold on screen. They were doing alarming things with ropes and pulleys. She couldn't help feeling that one of the people she'd pissed off in Head Office had really enjoyed coming up with this. Legally, they had to provide a body double for anything that could end in an insurance claim, but she was going to have to be underwater for at least a few seconds. She'd once had to shoot a pond scene where they'd used green dye and it had clung to the fine hairs on her arms. For three full days, her skin had looked like mouldy bread. Hopefully the pink residue would just look like a heat rash.

Nobody had bothered to heat the water, she discovered when she was lowered into the tank on the end of a pulley, like a giant hooked salmon. It had probably been tepid half an hour ago. In the December air, it had turned freezing.

They also hadn't anticipated that the pump in the bottom of the tank would cause her dress to fly up over her head the moment she was submerged. The silky fabric clung to her face and blinded her in sequinned green. It happened so quickly; suddenly, she couldn't see, hear or breathe, and her body instinctively jerked. Her leg dislodged the clear tube that was providing gentle streams of bubbles and it wrapped around her ankle.

Outside the tank, people were shouting; she heard the muted echo under the water. It was probably less than thirty seconds before somebody was in the water with her, knocking against her, hands touching her ankle, and her head broke the surface, but by that time she'd inhaled several gulps of water.

Every time she coughed and sucked in a breath, she got a mouthful of wet silk. And she still couldn't see.

Her brain stuck on a revolving chorus of *getitoffgetitoffgetitoff.*

Strong arms pulled her clear of the tank, and someone finally unwound the sodden dress and dragged it off. She was lowered to the ground, where she sat shivering in the period-appropriate and now totally seethrough cami-knickers.

"Jesus Christ." Steve's moustache filled her stinging vision, and she scrubbed at her eyes. Her hands came away tinged with pink. "Are you all right?" He didn't wait for her to answer, but turned to roar at someone, "What's happened to the fucking medic? And why the fuck didn't you do a test shot with the dress?"

An arm came around her. She looked up at Ash. As her mind started to clear from the rush of adrenaline, she wasn't sure which of them was shaking.

"Fuck," he said. It seemed to be the shared reaction. "You okay?"

She looked down at her unnaturally pink palms again. "Yeah. I think so."

He took the thermal blanket someone brought out and wrapped it around her, then refused to move while the set medic took her vital signs and listened to her lungs as she coughed.

Lily eventually became aware of Margo hovering nearby, eyes anxious, voice exasperated as she spoke into her phone. "I don't *know* what happened, Luc. I was outside in the hallway. Writing down your vitally important schedule." She lowered the phone to speak to Lily. "Are you all right, Lily?"

She could hear Luc's muffled voice. She couldn't make out the words, but the sharp urgency came through the speaker.

"Yes." She was starting to feel more embarrassed than shaky, which was probably a good sign.

Not only had she writhed around in a giant fish tank and granny panties in front of the entire crew, they'd recorded the whole thing.

"She said she's okay, Luc." Margo sounded even more harassed. "Yes, she's talking. And breathing. She seems fine now." Sarcastically, she added, "I don't think you need to worry about recasting Elizabeth as well."

Whatever he said in response made her look at Lily and then cast her gaze upward in a bid for patience.

However, half an hour later, when Luc strode into the studio, tense and furious, her eyes stopped rolling and opened wide. Lily saw the astonishment first and then the speculation, before her attention was taken up by Luc. He dropped to a crouch in front of the chair that someone had brought out for her. His hands settled on her knees. His grey eyes were intent on her face.

Which was probably still the colour of Calpol. She was waiting for the medical clearance so that the makeup team could turn her skin a pasty, bloated white-blue instead.

If she'd wanted less glamour—score.

Luc studied her, his own face pale, and then released a long breath. "You're okay." It was a statement, but there was a note that sought reassurance, which she responded to.

"I'm fine."

His index finger hooked hers, and Lily caught sight of Margo's arching eyebrow.

Awkwardly, she moved her hands away, but he had already turned his focus on Steve, who had got over his initial shock and was now reviewing the footage of the incident.

"We might be able to use this," Steve mused, and was lucky that Luc couldn't actually laser people's heads off with a single look.

Without asking permission, he rose and joined Steve at the monitor. To really cap off the crappiness of her day, he watched over the other man's shoulder. His jaw tightened so much that the skin went completely white.

"Use that footage," he said emphatically, "and you'll be hearing from my lawyers."

Steve jumped and automatically scrabbled to turn off the monitor. "…Savage? What the fuck?"

"My question exactly." Luc's tone was glacial. His eyes returned to Lily, scanning her again from head to foot. "What the fuck? What kind of bullshit safety measures did you take?" He took in the tank and pump system. "For Christ's sake. One simple stunt and you almost fucking drown her."

"We had her out of there in seconds—" Steve was reduced to defensive rambling. He was still retorting things about test shots and stunt doubles when Luc walked away mid-argument.

"Are you up to finishing this tonight?" he asked Lily, and ignored Steve's immediate "Do you know how much it costs to shoot one scene? The medic has cleared her. We're getting the shots tonight."

"Are you up to it?" Luc repeated evenly, looking only at Lily, and she nodded.

Setting aside the blanket, she stood up, testing for any lingering shakiness. She felt okay. The heavily sugared tea had helped. The medic had waved aside her half-hearted protest about the caffeine. She hadn't taken much persuading, even though she suspected Jocasta wouldn't accept anything short of awakening from a coma as an excuse for breaking the vocal hygiene diet.

Basically, this wasn't the first time she'd attempted something semi-athletic and ended up looking like a complete prat.

"I'm good," she said, to both Steve and Luc, who was still being tall and intimidating. If he ever got bored with directing, he'd make a steamroller of a theatrical agent. Nobody would try to sneak cleverly worded clauses past his clients. If Peter were more like him, she could probably have left *Knightsbridge* a year ago and there wouldn't be footage of her flailing about in large pants.

Luc continued to stand there scowling, watching every move that the technicians made as they redressed the set.

It was uncomfortable, to say the least, putting the nightmare wet dress back on and returning to the freezing water, but her own self-respect wouldn't let her plead out of the scene. Bad enough that the entire room had witnessed her earlier freak-out, either catching the live show or crowding around the monitor for the action replay; she wasn't letting an obviously faked, stunt-double death scene air as her last body of work on the show. It had been her first acting job. She hoped it was the worst performance she ever gave, but she'd still invested four years into this role.

A grip had taken out the pump, so this time she was able to keep her dress at thigh level and her eyesight as clear as it could be underwater. She kept having to come back up for air and to hear Steve's barked instructions, so after the initial "I don't want to do this" flight-or-fight instinct, it quickly became so repetitive and annoying that she forgot the residual fear.

She was treading water at one point, her arms hooked over the edge of the tank, when she saw Luc and Margo. She swiped a tangled clump of hair from her eyes. Luc was watching her; Margo was watching Luc with great interest.

This whole situation was getting more complicated by the day.

Taking another deep breath, she pushed back into the water and found the clear grip on the side that would keep her suspended a few feet below the surface. Her wrist slipped through the loop, keeping her hand and arm floating in dead eeriness. She messed up a couple of takes by holding her breath with her cheeks puffed out. Ash was obviously rattled by what had happened, since he screwed up even more times than she did and he was usually a one-take wonder.

Finally, she was able to get out of the tank to shoot the last scenes, where the audience would be left with the flattering memory of her artificially swollen cheeks and blue lips.

Ash, kneeling at her side on the wet floorboards, heartbroken, muttered, "For some reason, I'm having flashbacks to the night we realised you're allergic to shellfish."

With her tongue, she moved the foam pads to a more comfortable position around her teeth, and covertly lifted her middle finger. He snickered.

It was almost ten o'clock when they finally wrapped. Luc and Margo had both disappeared at some point, but Luc knocked on her dressing room door while she was creaming off the makeup.

Wordlessly, she stood back to let him in. The room was a generous size compared to the cupboards they put the bit parts in, but he shrank it to mouse-hole proportions.

When he slipped his hands into his pockets, the thin wool of his jumper pulled tight over his shoulders and outlined the breadth of his upper arms. His sleeves were pushed up to just below the elbow, and his face was lined with fatigue. His jaw was beginning to shadow with beard. She'd only ever seen him clean-shaven before.

"Well," he said. "You know how to go out with a bang, at least."

She sat back down at her vanity table before she lost all touch on reality and hugged him. "Or a damp fizz." With a muslin cloth, she scrubbed off the last of the greasepaint. Her face was red from the cleansing. "They aren't using the first footage, are they?" She never wanted to see that while flipping through channels.

"Not anymore."

Looking at his expression, she wasn't surprised that Steve had changed his mind.

"How are you now?" His eyes were unreadable, but the skin around his mouth was still taut. Abruptly, he said, "You scared the hell out of me."

She was intensely aware of the rhythm of her fractured, rapid breath. "I know. I'm sorry."

"I was on the phone to Margo when she said all hell broke loose in the hallway and some kind of alarm went off."

God, they'd sounded an *alarm*? Like what, the big red fail button?

"'Oh my God, Lily's drowning,'" Luc quoted acidly, and managed to replicate Margo's usual pitch exactly. He made an exasperated sound. "I didn't even know where she was at that point."

"What did you think, that I'd fallen in your courtyard fountain or something?" Lily took refuge in sarcasm. She clasped her hands together tightly, watching her knuckles flex.

"I didn't know what to think," Luc snapped. He

shoved one hand through his hair, a gesture he'd made a number of times by the look of it. "I heard *Lily's drowning* and my heart just about fucking stopped. And Margo chose that moment to become incoherent for the first time in her life."

She didn't think this time. She just got up and went with the hug. When her arms slid around his waist, he held her tightly and his hand came up to cup her head. She'd blow-dried her hair and it was sticking out like a dandelion puff, so his fingers caught in the fine strands and tugged painfully.

And then, because obviously some kind of public service text went out as soon as they got within two feet of each other, Margo appeared in the open doorway.

"Oh." She stood still, staring at them. "Sorry. Didn't mean to interrupt." Her voice sounded odd.

She started to back up, but Lily stepped out of Luc's arms. His hands tensed for a second as if he were going to hold on to her; then he let them drop away.

"You're not interrupting."

It was a ridiculous thing for her to say. That couldn't be passed off as anything but an emotional cuddle.

Margo didn't respond. The look on her face was one that most people saved for a bad opening speech at the Golden Globes.

Also as usual, Luc's phone rang, which somehow increased the tension instead of breaking it. He pulled it from his pocket and looked at it. "Sorry. I've been waiting for this."

He had the grace to hesitate. Their gazes locked. He seemed to debate further speech.

And then the lucky bastard left the room.

How very male.

"Well." Margo was a bit red in the face, as well. "That explains why Luc went all shifty when I mentioned the recent media attention." Her lips compressed. "Okay. Feeling a little stupid. It didn't even occur to me before tonight that those particular stories were true. I was starting to wonder earlier, when he showed up like that, but—*Luc*, having an affair with one of his actresses." She frowned. "A fairly young actress."

"We're not having an affair," Lily said at once. Touchy. Skating the edge of truth at this point. She closed her eyes for a second. "Technically."

"It's none of my business if you are." Margo sounded troubled. "Oh God," she said after a moment, and scrubbed the back of one hand over her forehead. "I'm sorry. I never cast myself as the witchy, dog-in-the-manger ex. I'm not jealous." She seemed to turn the words over in her mind, testing them. "I'm not jealous," she repeated, more decisively. "It's just—I like you, and you don't seem like the type to— *Ugh*." She cut herself off with a frustrated noise in her throat. "Just…don't get hurt, all right?"

"Luc wouldn't hurt anyone." Lily spoke quietly, but without hesitation.

"Not on purpose," Margo agreed. "But he's not— The theatre is everything." Her gaze was unflinching. "It will always be the theatre first, everything and everyone else second."

That was something that had crossed Lily's mind more than once in the past few days. For that reason, as if shying away from a direct hit, she asked the question. "For you or for Luc?"

Margo made a small movement, a slight inclination of her head. "For both of us." She read Lily's mind. "Yes, I'm married now, and I adore my husband, and I'm happier than I've ever been. But." She lifted one shoulder. "When Luc rang and offered me this role again, I didn't hesitate. We always were a little too alike. Alberto is a very generous man. He accepts that my work is a part of who I am."

There was something about having a conversation with Margo that occasionally made Lily expect to hear a director snap "Cut!" and order that they read the scene again, approaching it from a different emotional angle.

"Ambition isn't your sole prerogative," she couldn't help pointing out, a bit drily, and Margo looked at her thoughtfully.

"No, it isn't. And the theatre is obviously where you want to be."

Was there a slight off-note in those words?

Everything in Lily revolted against the implication she read into that. "I would never use a man, or anyone, to advance my career."

"I didn't think you would," Margo said, and it was very definitely an exit line. "Which is exactly where you differ from Luc and me."

Chapter Eight

Lily was still troubled by Margo's parting shot when she got home the following night. The rest of the *Knightsbridge* cast had given her a send-off with a chocolate cake and several rounds of cocktails that she couldn't eat or drink, so her defences were especially low.

Trix was in the living room, doing leg stretches in front of the TV. She was still wearing her coat. She was always wired after a performance; it took her a good two hours to wind down each night. That was obviously only a side-effect of performing live. Lily was usually so knackered after a day of filming at CTV that she fell asleep on the couch by nine.

Trix grabbed the remote and paused the screen. "Hey. You look…not like someone who just finished a job they hated."

"I didn't *hate* it," Lily said automatically. She stooped to switch on the Christmas tree lights.

"You got hammered at your twenty-second birthday party making a drinking game out of how many ways Gloria could have died through sheer stupidity. You knocked back about sixteen shots of tequila. That was, like, a week after the pilot episode aired. You hated it."

Lily dropped her bag on the coffee table and herself

down on the couch. "Ah, tequila," she said reminis-
cently, and Trix grinned.

"The journey from Lorelei Lee to contralto painfully dry, is it?" she asked, and Lily threw a cushion
at her. "Seriously, what's up? Please tell me it's not
Senõr Surly and his sexy scowl. You weren't even at
rehearsal today."

"It's nothing."

"So you keep saying. Increasingly unconvincingly."

Lily stared at the frozen TV screen. "Do you want
to go out?"

Trix's fingers paused partway through unbuttoning
her coat. "'Go out'?" she repeated, stressing every syllable, as if Lily had suggested that they go to Regent
Street and do their Christmas shopping nude.

"Yes. Go out. Relax. Unwind. There's a new club
in Mayfair. Dylan Waitely said he's put my name on
the list."

Trix's eyebrows almost disappeared into her hair.
"*Dylan Waitely?* Dylan I've-had-sex-with-over-a-thousand-
women-because-I-owe-it-to-my-enormous-cock Waitely?
Who are you and what have you done with Lily? You never
go to Central London nightclubs. And you're not even allowed to drink."

"Mocktails."

"But—it's half past eleven." Poor Trix was actually
stuttering.

"It's Friday night."

"Yes. Exactly. I have my biggest show of the week
tomorrow. And you have rehearsal all afternoon. What
the hell?"

"I just—" Lily jiggled her crossed leg, bouncing her
foot. The fairy lights on the tree were blurring into one

pulsating circle. She blinked away the halo. "I don't know. I feel really restless tonight."

"Yeah, well, you know what doesn't usually help with anxiety? Drunken crowds and conceited dickheads."

Lily looked at her. "One hour."

Just for tonight, just for an hour, she wanted music and festiveness and a distraction. She didn't want stress and confusion and other people's words superglued to the front of her mind.

"The theatre is everything. It will always be the theatre first, everything and everyone else second."

"Flesh and blood, that's everything. That love is forever. Men—men are lovely. For a while. It never lasts, kiddo."

Trix stared back and then groaned. "Oh *God.*"

Lily was going to smell like Dylan's aftershave for the next month. He'd latched on to them as soon as he spotted her through the crowd and had insisted on introducing them to half the people in the club. Apparently it had been necessary to keep his arms around them the whole time. Giorgio Armani had seeped into her pores.

They finally managed to escape to a booth in the back of the room, and Dylan traipsed off somewhere to break a few more marital vows.

Across the table, Trix finished her drink and reached for Lily's glass. "I'll admit it. It's not nearly as bad as I thought it would be. A Dylan Waitely haunt, I was expecting strobe lighting and suspiciously sticky floors."

The floors were polished marble. There was a lot of crystal and copper, a live band, a Christmas tree that would have looked at home in the foyer of the Savoy, and at least a dozen familiar faces, which explained the amount of photographers outside.

"I'm a bit drunk," Trix said wonderingly.

"That would explain why you were doing salsa to Band Aid."

Trix swallowed a mouthful of water. "And you look like you're having about as much fun as I expected. I.e., none."

"No, it's good. I wanted a distraction." Lily watched the political anchor for CTV's morning show attempt some serious moves. "Mission accomplished."

With the odd exception—like when she received her first review in the *Guardian* on her twenty-second birthday, or when she totally lost her head over a man who was probably thinking about floor plans and lighting angles right now—she avoided camera-bait clubs like the plague. A few hours of dancing with strange men never seemed much recompense for inner-city taxi fares and the inevitable tabloid commentary. She preferred going out for a drink at their local pub, where no one tried to get a photo up her skirt or prayed to the paparazzi gods that she tripped over her heels and fell into a gutter.

Jacko Clubs's TV starlet daughter looking a little worse for wear, leaving X club with X.

She also preferred just relaxing at home. With Netflix. And Jammie Dodgers.

Sanity was returning.

"Would you like to tell me again why we're here?" Trix asked. "When there's clearly a ninety-five-year-old woman trapped in that gorgeous body, just waiting to get out and nap?"

It *was* actually worth the discomfort and boredom

to see Trix acting like herself. She'd been dancing and flirting and laughing in her old way, not with the brittle, defiant edge she'd adopted since the breakup with Dan.

"Lily." The change in Trix's tone made Lily look up. "It's about minus five degrees outside, there's black ice everywhere, and we're here. In five-inch heels. How deeply are you in?"

She didn't have to explain what she meant. Even when Lily was making an effort to set everything aside for a couple of hours, he was lurking in the back of her mind. The sudden turn in the conversation just seemed to follow on from her silent conflict.

Fortunately, there was very little chance that Trix was going to remember anything that had happened after her fourth mojito. Lily still wasn't entirely comfortable discussing this. They both thought she was walking a dangerous line, but for different reasons. Dan St. James was well out of the picture, yet he was still managing to put a shadow of constraint between them.

When she spoke, it was more to herself than Trix. "Even if we didn't act on it until the show closed, the press would take the story, slant it in the worst way possible and drag it out every time I did *anything* newsworthy. I've seen it happen to Mum for years. She doesn't care." Lily gripped the edge of the wooden table. "I pretend I don't care, and then I don't show my thighs in public for four years."

Trix looked at her unblinkingly before her gaze dropped to the water glass. "You didn't add anything to this while I was dancing, did you?"

"Like what?"

"Like ninety proof vodka. What do your thighs have to do with anything? Not that they aren't lovely."

"Thank you. And never mind."

It wasn't just the tabloids and anonymous hate comments. It was what they fed into. In the theatre, in the studio, on a film set, everything had an impact. It wasn't a good look if you were sleeping with your director, who cast you in your first West End show, in a role that seemed light years beyond your ability. Especially when there was a...parental precedent. Although she wasn't shoving all the blame onto her mother. Her own over-eagerness had locked her into the contract with CTV, thus leading to the world's worst case of typecasting.

You could get away with dating a co-star—if they were single and born in the same decade. That was good promo for the show. The bosses loved it. Until the inevitable breakup, when fans went into meltdown on social media and the backlash hit. Lily had seen it happen enough at CTV that she'd never wanted to go anywhere near another actor romantically.

Nobody was high-fived for having a fling with management.

She couldn't help feeling that it *would* be the equivalent of a fling, however long it lasted. Luc had already spent eight years in a relationship that, in the end, had obviously been a poor second to his career. Did anyone think he was going to do an about-face for her sake? Just because they had enough chemistry to charge a power station and an unexpected connection. A strong connection.

It was all her lifelong deal-breakers in one man. It was like she'd made a list and the universe had laughed in her face. Nemesis had come along, called her a talentless bimbo, and made her like him.

"By the look on your face," Trix said, shaping each

word with painstaking care, "I'm guessing you don't need your own lecture on toxic relationships."

"You were singing Luc's praises not long ago." She was dancing through a minefield where he was concerned and she still felt compelled to defend him against the smallest slight.

"As a *director*. Not a roll in the hay that could derail years of hard work."

A wave of exhaustion rolled over her. She rubbed at her eyes, probably smudging her mascara everywhere. It had been a bit naive to expect a change of scene to provide a magical epiphany. She'd paid ten quid for mineral water, had her arse squeezed by Dylan, and watched a load of strangers kissing under the mistletoe. Every time, her mind had helpfully produced the memory of Luc's lips against her pulse.

"Okay." Trix pushed out of the booth and stood on unsteady feet. "I'm seeing six angels on the top of that Christmas tree and they're all waving at me. I have to pirouette on a high wire tomorrow night. Tonight. Whatever the time is, if I don't sober up in the next few hours, you're going to be spending Christmas at my bedside in Intensive Care."

Hastily, Lily got up and grabbed her arm when she teetered. They almost made it outside without incident, but their luck ran out at the door. Dylan reappeared, even more drunk than before, and insisted on escorting them to their Uber with a lot of showy gestures for the cameras.

Lily put up an arm against the flashes, finally managed to wrest herself from Dylan's helping hand and slid into the backseat after Trix. With her hand on the door, she looked up at him. "Thanks, Dylan. See you tomorrow."

He smiled at her. His long hair was loose and his pupils were so dilated that his eyes looked black. "Sure, Freddy."

"It's Lily."

"Whatever."

It was dark and blessedly quiet in the taxi. When the car pulled away from the curb, Lily dropped back against the headrest.

They crawled through the traffic at an approximate speed of half a metre per hour, coming to a complete halt in the chaos near Oxford Street.

"Hey."

Lily looked sideways at Trix.

Her friend was pale in the gloom and the lights outside were casting multi-coloured prisms on her face. She didn't slur a single syllable when she said, "You could be overthinking this. You said it yourself. You'll get over it. He's just a man. You have lines to learn. Corsets to stuff your breasts into. The Spanish Armada to thwart."

"The Spanish Armada was 1588."

Too much detail for the number of mojitos consumed. It threw Trix off her stride.

"Sorry." Lily leaned back and closed her eyes again. "Not important."

"Where was I?"

"Something about stuffing my breasts into corsets."

"You're under a lot of stress at the moment. It could be affecting your judgement."

That was distinctly possible.

"Maybe it's just a crush."

"Yeah," Lily said softly. "Maybe."

* * *

"On the bright side," Amelia said cheerfully, removing a partially chewed pen from her mouth. "Truly horrific rehearsals usually mean a stellar opening run."

Luc looked up from the latest script revision, where he was scrawling notes in appropriately slashing strokes of red ink. "The superstition is specific to the final dress rehearsal. It's also a total fallacy. Truly horrific rehearsals mean actors who can't keep their lines straight even though their scripts are two inches from their faces—and who apparently can't tell left from right. *Freddy!*"

In the performance circle, Freddy stopped mangling her monologue and glanced over warily.

Silently, with his pen, Luc pointed at the opposite side of the studio. She glanced over and then down at her feet, formed an "Oh" with her mouth and went to re-enter from the currently improvised stage left.

David whistled in frustration, swung his feet off the chair in front of him and sat up. "There are currently two dozen six-year-olds around the corner doing a better job at rehearsing the Tiny Tots' Nativity Play. The last time I saw Freddy flub an entire scene, she was eleven and had a bad case of the mumps. She's our workhorse. Solid. Dependable."

"While I'm sure any teenage girl would *delight* in being compared to a Clydesdale—" Amelia examined the remains of her pen "—it's the first time they have to speak *and* move simultaneously. It's always like watching newborn kittens work out where their legs are." She looked at Luc. "Although considering that at least one of our highly paid professionals is sweating enough morning-after whisky fumes to anaesthetize an elephant, you're being relatively Zen there, Captain."

"I'm trying to keep my blood pressure somewhere south of Neptune until at least the dress rehearsals." Flipping to the next page in the script, Luc raised his voice again. "That was your cue, Freddy."

Freddy pushed a handful of hair behind her ear and checked her script, frowning. "But—Oh. Sorry!"

"Just pick up from the beginning of Scene Three."

Laughter on the sidelines became smothered giggles and whispers.

"Quiet," snapped one of the assistant producers, and the noise level dropped.

David grunted. "Lamprey's doing a halfway decent job."

Luc made another note on the script and glanced over at Lily, who was running lines in the other practise sphere with Margo and David's assistant. Unlike Freddy, Dylan and the rest of Group B, who were clutching their lines like kids with teddy bears, Lily and Margo were almost off-book already.

Lily was moving well, confidently conferring with Margo. She was smiling between scenes and had so far only had one momentary nose-rubbing lapse into insecurity. There were tired shadows under her eyes, however, as if she hadn't slept well. She was wearing a black jumper and leather jacket that hugged the soft curves of her upper body and added to her pallor.

"She still sounds like she's got a collapsed lung," David added, before anyone could accuse him of optimism.

"Jocasta Moore will be here this afternoon." Amelia settled her laptop on her knee to bring up the schedule. "Lily's booked for two hours of voice training after the lunch break. One until three. Also at that time, you're taking Freddy and Dylan through Act Two, scenes three and four, Margo's working on the opening monologue with Luc, and Padma is overseeing the understudy read-through. All three principals in Studio A at three o'clock, so you can start blocking the confrontation scene. Luc, you've got a lunch meeting with the financial advisor from Weston & Crimm at noon. And wardrobe wants measurements before five."

"Shit, what time is it now? Magalie's got the new costume sketches for me upstairs." David shoved back his chair and took off at a trot, dodging around Margo and Lily.

"Hey." On the floor, Dylan broke off his scripted argument with Freddy to ad lib a few complaints of his own. He whistled at one of the interns. "You with the glasses. Shut those blinds, would you? The sun's right in my eyes."

The panicked-looking intern looked from the floor-to-ceiling windows and electric shutter system to the management conclave, and wavered. "Um…"

Luc tossed his script down on the table. "James, carry on with your work. Dylan, take two steps to the right. Crisis averted."

Dylan scowled, but moved into the shadow cast by the projector screen.

"We're breaking for lunch soon," Amelia called. "Try to hold it together. There's light, soup and some truly excellent scones at the end of the tunnel."

When the noise resumed, she quirked a brow at Luc. "Reckon we could traipse around to St. Barnabas and offer them a swap for the Nativity? Give them Dylan, and we'll take whichever kid permanently haunts the naughty step off their hands. I think we'd still come out on top." She frowned, following the straying path of Luc's gaze before he could look away. "Is there a problem with Margo and Lily now? I mean, other than the sense of your universe imploding as your past and future mattress buddies rub shoulders and chuckle together."

Coffee sloshed from the cup Luc had just picked up. Swearing, he thumped it down on a piece of scrap paper and shook spilled drops from his hand. "Could you give some sort of warning before you say things like that? It would help to avoid the third-degree burns."

"FYI, the starchy expression and tight lips are not attractive *and* they don't cancel out the emoji heart eyes every time you look at her."

He ripped open a sugar packet and poured it into the coffee.

"That was your cue to say 'I have no idea what you're talking about,' with stalactites hanging off every syllable."

He finished the coffee before he replied. "Sorry. You don't usually require a response when someone flips the lunacy switch."

"Ah. So we're just going to ignore the elephant in the room?"

"I believe it was already knocked flat by Waitely the walking distillery."

Amelia looked over at Dylan. "He drained a bar dry last night and is managing to speak in iambic pentameter. I have two glasses of wine with dinner and I can barely decipher the *TV Guide* the next day. I'm so freaking old."

"Join the club."

She hummed in her throat. "Speaking of Dylan, I see

Lily's doing her part to dispel any totally false rumours by generating new ones."

He exhaled loudly and set his cup down. "What?"

She turned the laptop screen in his direction. It was filled with a photo of Lily, dressed up for a night out, surrounded by a horde of photographers and Dylan Waitely's arms.

"Apparently Lizzie and Guildford had quite an evening at the Primavera last night." Amelia studied him, fascinated. "Got a little tic in your jaw there, maestro?"

He looked down at the screen for several more seconds. Then he turned the laptop around and picked up his script again. "Co-star hook-ups are inevitable."

"Uh-huh." Amelia circled her finger near his temple. "I think a vein just popped."

Luc flipped to the current scene. "So, we're going ahead with those lighting changes in the first act."

Amelia's eyes continued to burn a hole into his profile before she sighed. "I don't know why I bother."

"It's a mystery to us all." Luc started to flag the new directions, but after his third error, he set his jaw and let the end of the pen rest against the paper. His gaze travelled from Dylan to Lily, still at opposite ends of the room.

Amelia bent to speak close to his ear. "I like her. She seems to bring out the best in you."

Turning the page with his left hand, Luc shook his empty cup in her direction. "Black, one sugar, thanks."

"Not right at this moment, admittedly." Amelia lifted the cup by the rim. "But in general—you seem… I think you've smiled more this week than you have in the past five years. Watching you together, it's like a couple of leopards circling one another with their hackles on end. Then, when you expect the fur to fly, they start purring. Heads rubbing instead of butting. Making each other laugh."

"Leopards laugh?"

"Well, I thought about using hyenas, but I don't want to insult Lily. Her problem is more soft and breathy; she doesn't manically cackle."

They were now about one animal metaphor away from a full zoo.

Luc closed the script and looked at her, not feeling much like smiling. "Are you having some sort of breakdown?"

"No, but thanks for your concern." Amelia crossed her arms, letting the handle of the coffee cup dangle from one hooked finger. "You've been so…shut off for a long time now."

"Amelia—"

"It's not that easy to find, you know. A person who makes the hard work worthwhile."

Luc did know. It wasn't something that had been on his mind until very recently. He hadn't been aware that he was missing—

He couldn't deal with this right now. And his leopard obviously had no intention of dealing with it either, since she preferred to spend her limited spare time in London nightclubs with the inhabitants of the monkey cage.

Deliberately, he said, "I have no idea what you're talking about."

"Maria, however, flipped her shit after we walked into whatever was going on in the study at Aston Park, and is about ready to have her shipped off to Siberia, so discretion, Obi Wan, discretion."

* * *

"We're breaking for lunch." Padma, the assistant stage manager, stuck her head into the side studio where Lily and Margo had been discussing their confrontation scene. "Lily, there's paperwork for you to sign in David's office."

Lily sat on what looked like an old church pew to put her boots back on. "Where—"

"Eighth floor."

"Three doors down from Luc's office." Margo tied the belt on her coat and smiled at her. "If you did a private read there while he did his impression of a cyborg, I'm sure the location is emblazoned into your nightmares. Nice work this morning, by the way."

Lily hesitated. "Thanks."

"Look." Margo played with the ends of her belt. "I want to apologise for the other night. I was a bit—thrown. The whole thing took me by surprise."

"It's really not—"

"It was bitchy." Margo's smile twisted. "Luc's personal life is none of my business now. Blame it on ego. Even when you've moved on, you'd prefer to think that your ex is mostly happy but still shedding the occasional tear into his pillow. Not breaking multiple traffic laws to get to the side of a semi-drowned, twentysomething blonde."

"Margo—"

"I'm out. I promise. Whatever is going on between the two of you is between the two of you. And probably every gossip columnist in the city with a dubious grasp of ethics." She slung her handbag over her shoulder. "Anyway, I have a lunch date with my husband." Her smile turned more affectionate. "It's his birthday. He's got a big concert at the Majestic on Christmas Eve, so we're sneaking in a double celebration at Claridge's."

"Sounds great." God, it was almost Christmas Eve already. Claridge's reminded Lily of the visit to Kirkby and her father's suggestion of the meal that would never eventuate. Which in turn reminded her of Luc, holding her, his body solid and warm, his arms comforting around her, his breath and his lips against her neck. The dual feeling of safety and...tingles.

Margo stopped at the door. "I just want to say—I *am* sorry for the things I said. At least, for the way I said them. But I stand by the warning. Just—don't expect something from Luc that he's not capable of."

She had really nailed the leading lady routine of exiting with a flourish and the last word.

Trying to leave all the angst behind in the studio, Lily took the lift up to the eighth floor. The elevator was the quirkiest part of the building. The text of Shakespeare's tragedies wrapped the wood panelling in tiny lines of gold lettering. Presumably, if it broke down somewhere between the conference rooms and the management suites, there was the immortal *Hamlet* bloodbath to remind you that however bad the situation might seem, it could be worse.

The doors slid open at the executive reception desk, where an administrative assistant was talking to a tall man in a suit. He thanked her, tapped his hand against the countertop and turned around.

And the melodrama just came crashing right back in.

Lily froze.

There was an extended, startled pause.

"Lily." A definite sneer appeared in Dan St. James's

eyes. He was as square-jawed and expensively barbered as ever. "Fancy meeting you here."

She wondered if her own hair was starting to rise on end like a hostile Chihuahua, or if it was just prickles of intense, unadulterated loathing. "Dan. Horrifyingly small world, isn't it?"

This was London. There were millions of people living here whom she would never encounter during her lifetime. She'd hoped Dan would become one of them.

The assistant was watching them curiously. Lily automatically backed up to a position where the other woman would at least have to put some effort into eavesdropping.

"Well," she said in Dan's general direction. "See you around."

There were several other things she'd like to add, but not anywhere near her workplace. She headed for the hallway that led to Luc's and apparently David Benton's offices.

Behind her, Dan asked, "How's Trix?" and her steps faltered.

Her response was equally cold. "She's great. Thanks for asking."

"Give her my love."

She started counting to ten, and gave up at three. She turned around. "Your *love*. Right."

He came up to her, looking down on her. He'd had plenty of practise doing it metaphorically, so doing it literally was probably a cinch. "I see you haven't lost the attitude. Something to work on." He lowered his head so he was looking into her eyes and slowed his speech to enunciate every letter. "Do you need me to write that down so you can remember? In tiny little words? Spelled phonetically?"

The assistant at the desk was all but craning her neck and cupping a hand behind her ear. Lily glanced at her, bit down hard on the retort that was clawing up her throat, and stepped back.

Professional. She was a professional.

Dan followed her, still right in her face. "Trix has a lot of baggage. Naturally enough, given her unfortunate childhood. Being handed off from one foster home to another, dumped at boarding school on scholarship, it's got to mess with your head."

She assumed that he had a reason to be in Luc's building, besides pushing her closer to the edge of grievous bodily harm.

"Correction," she said. "Trix *had* excess baggage, for almost a year. Fortunately, she wised up and left it on the curb."

He dropped any pretence of a smile. "With a little help from you. What exactly are you doing here?" he asked, pre-empting her exact same question. "Learning how to act like even more of a bitch?"

"Wow. It must be a relief that you don't even have to *try* to hide the inner demon anymore. Good for you. Embrace the truth. Live in the real world. Pour yourself a nice glass of holy water."

"You—"

"Just to see what happens."

"Listen, you interfering little bi—"

Luc's voice came from behind Lily. "I think everybody in a five-hundred-metre radius is listening. And I'd strongly suggest that you don't finish that sentence."

She felt the burn in her cheeks as she spun around.

Luc's eyes clashed with hers before his gaze sliced back to Dan, who was visibly trying to get his temper under control.

"Mr. Savage." Dan cleared his throat and tested out his most plastic smile. "I'm Dan St. James, from—"

"You're a financial advisor from Weston & Crimm."

"That's right." Dan started forward with his hand extended, ignoring Lily now. "I have to say, we don't usually meet with clients on a Saturday, but obviously for you, we were—"

"I assume you have colleagues."

Dan blinked, his hand hovering in the air. "I'm sorry?"

Luc spoke in the same slow, drawn-out syllables that Dan had used on her. "I suggest that you go back to your office, drop your boss an email and tell him or her to send someone else. By the end of business hours on Monday. You can add a postscript that if their second attempt at competency also speaks to a member of my company like that, we'll be contracting a different firm." He paused. "A postscript is a sort of written afterthought to include information not previously mentioned. It's usually abbreviated as 'P.S.' Do you need me to write out those letters for you phonetically?"

Lily bit down on the inside of her lip and tried to pretend that the noise that erupted from her chest was a cough.

Dan was opening and closing his mouth like a grouper. His face was a violent shade of crimson. "I—"

"Monday. Before five." Luc turned away. His voice was tight as he addressed Lily. "I'd like to see you in my office." He walked back down the hall without waiting to see if she followed. She could suddenly sympathise a little more with Mitchell the Wolf-Whistler.

Leaving Dan to his futile spluttering, she caught up with Luc at the entrance to his suite. His secretary must be at lunch and would be disappointed to learn that she'd missed the opportunity for another judgemental stare-and-sniff. "Now?"

"Sorry," he said sarcastically, and held the door open, "are you late for another public slanging match?"

She slipped past him into his office. "I'm sorry. That was completely unprofessional."

"Yes. It was." Luc sat on the edge of his desk. He was doing his best two-dimensional Gertrude Stein again. Crabby as hell. "I'd appreciate it if you'd keep your personal life out of—"

"I know. Inappropriate. Unprofessional. Profuse apologies. Won't happen again."

He looked at her levelly.

"Although," she added, "if by 'personal life' and that charming tone, you're implying something other than mutual, overwhelming hatred—very wrong track."

"As long as I don't come across a similar situation between you and Dylan Waitely at any time during this run, it's not my con—"

"Sorry?" She stared at his tense face before enlightenment dawned. "Seen photos of us at the Primavera last night, have you?"

A muscle moved in his jaw, but he said nothing.

"Well. I did kind of bring that one on myself. Having said that—what was it you said about expecting and *ignoring* all sorts of insinuating crap in the press?"

"I think that was more of a factual play-by-play than an insinuation. If you're going to leave a Central London club hanging from Waitely's neck, it's not much of a stretch for even the single-celled organisms who take up desk space at the gutter press to smell a story."

They glared at one another.

"You're jealous." Lily's accusation tailed into slight uncertainty, but he didn't even hesitate.

"Yes, I am." He sounded even more pissed off than before.

"And mad."

"Apparently it tags along with the jealousy."

She felt a bit unsteady. "Dylan helped Trix and me to a taxi. And by 'helped,' I mean played up to the cameras like he was doing a Charlie Chaplin skit and then accidentally kicked me in the back of the leg when I opened the car door."

"Sounds about right."

"I neither arrived nor left with him."

"Sensible."

"*Technically*, however," she continued, taking a slow breath, "it would be none of your business if we were boinking like bunnies, as long as it didn't affect the show."

"It always affects the show." Luc was still scowling. "Co-stars jumping into bed inevitably ends in tears and tantrums and a PR disaster."

"Cynical society, party of two," Lily murmured.

"What?" he snapped. He stood and shoved a hand through his hair.

"Nothing. I agree with you. Didn't mean to interrupt the rant."

"*I'm not*—" Luc looked at her. He shook his head, once, a quick jerk to the side as if he were dislodging an insect or other minor irritant. She heard the rush of air as he forcibly exhaled. "I don't know what I'm doing with you. I don't even recognise myself when I'm around you."

He might have been reading from the transcript of her own jumbled thoughts, so it shouldn't have hurt.

Again, as he had in the snow outside Kirkby, he reacted instinctively to whatever expression she was totally failing to hide. He reached out and cupped her cheek, his hand warm and strong, and she closed her eyes.

She curled her fingers about his wrist, stroking her thumb over the hairs she felt there, tracing the strong lines of the bones.

"People say things," she said quietly. "And write things. All the time. And even if every other person in London believed them, *I* need to know that they're not true. I need to know I'm not that person. My reputation does matter to me. And it's not only the implications for *my* career, going forward." She tugged his hand away from her face, although their wrists stayed linked between their bodies. His fingers tickled as they traced patterns on the tips of hers. "This wouldn't do your reputation any favours either."

He didn't pretend otherwise. He was similarly frank as he released her hand. "No, it wouldn't."

"Especially given what's already being said. About you. And your overly active casting couch."

"I've been accused of running a production like a despotic, lecherous automaton, not of senility. I haven't forgotten."

"I don't…trust this." She hadn't intended to say that, and he didn't look impressed.

"I'm surprised you're standing within tumbling

distance of my couch, then. Although I suppose since you've already secured the part—"

"I've already had one encounter today with someone who gets his kicks from twisting people's words and using them as weapons. Do me a favour. Rein in the inner prat. He's been so delightfully *quiet* since he made that comment about the blow-up doll and retired on a low note."

She rubbed her forehead. "I'm not talking about your ethics. From that perspective, you don't just *look* like Atticus Finch. I'm sure you abide by union rules regarding sick days and work hours, support equal pay and civil rights, and only throw members of your company down on your desk in exceptional circumstances. I unreservedly believe you. As, I'm sure, would Atticus, if we ignore the existence of *Go Set a Watchman*."

"The moment of desktop insanity was a first." Luc looked her up and down, and did a very flattering groan-and-curse combo. "Specific to one particular bane of my existence. Thanks for the vote of confidence. What don't you trust?"

That this could end in anything but a professional headache and a personal heartache.

That he would ever let anything jeopardise his plans for the theatre.

That if covert desk-tumbling and unsubstantiated rumour became confirmed fact, it wouldn't matter if Lily *owned* that stage on opening night. Even if she were magically so brilliant that she made Margo look like a rank amateur, she'd still end up cementing the public and industry image she'd been carrying for the past four years and would prefer not to heft around for the rest of her career.

Landed first serious stage role. Slept with director. Nobody would be picky as to the order in which those statements went.

She had fenced herself into a very small box when she'd taken the role as Gloria, and enforced it by showing up for contractual interviews with the only face she had and a voice she was still trying to de-porn. Hooking up with her director would undermine any belief that she might be able to earn a role on her own merit. It would limit her chances of receiving genuine respect and a fair trial from future casting agents and directors.

All for an intense attraction that might end up being a...*failing proposition*.

She stood in total silence.

Luc's follow-up question, when it came, was unexpected. "What's the connection with corporate Ramsay Bolton out there?"

It took her a second to catch up: story of tabloid-Lily's life. When his question registered, she snorted. Dan even looked a bit like the *Game of Thrones* character. "I'm sure it's a daily disappointment to Dan that he doesn't possess an army of serfs to torture, maim and carry out his every self-centred whim."

Luc's mouth lifted at the corner. "Are you sure I was on the wrong track earlier? I'm sensing just an edge of hostility."

"He's Trix's ex. He's an emotionally abusive, manipulative wanker. With a fixation on the tax expectations of overseas hedge funds that I find highly questionable."

"Hedge funds."

"Have dinner with him sometime. He'll either be talking about his offshore investments or he'll be making passive-aggressive comments about his girlfriend to slowly whittle down her self-esteem, one acidic little criticism at a time."

"As tempting as that sounds, if I want the conversational equivalent of having sections of my brain removed without anaesthetic, I'll schedule a shareholders' dinner with your godfather." Luc was still watching her. "Trix's ex?"

"Unfortunately."

"How old is Trix?"

"Twenty-six."

"I see," Luc said. "And you're also twenty-six?"

Lily narrowed her eyes slightly. "Yes."

"Mmm. And Dan is—"

"Not twenty-six."

"No. I'd say he's somewhere around my age."

"Quite possibly. Are we going to arrive at your point anytime soon?"

"No point." Luc's voice was bland. His expression was not. "Just an observation."

"That some of us are twenty-six and some of us like to make leading comments?" Lily took his vacated seat on the edge of the desk. "Dan treated Trix like absolute dirt, tried to take over every aspect of her life, and systematically suppressed her personality. It was not because he was older. It was because he's a complete bastard. I in no way mentally house you in the same pigpen just because you were born in the same decade."

Her prejudiced view of the situation was focused elsewhere.

Luc leaned back against the office wall, one ankle crossed over the other, putting some space between them. It was probably wise, given their habit of stroking, groping, and every other verb that involved bodily contact when they were alone in rooms that contained desks.

"I think it's pretty obvious that my opinion of you is in a different stratosphere." She tried to ease the mood. "I don't throw out comparisons to Atticus Finch lightly. He was my first boyfriend."

"He's fictional."

"When I was ten, that was a minor drawback, easily outweighed by the staunch devotion to human rights and penchant for natty waistcoats." She pushed off the desk and stood up. "If I've apologised sincerely enough for the ruckus in reception, there are papers I have to sign in David Benton's office."

Luc didn't move from his position against the wall. "I assume that's a subtle hint you don't want to discuss this anymore?"

She looked back at him from the doorway, her hand resting on the wooden frame. A stream of weak winter sunlight was creeping along the carpet, highlighting a path towards his booted feet. He was tense beneath the casual stance.

She sought for the right words. "I—"

He smiled, just a twist of his mouth. "Have papers to sign. Got it."

She bit her lip. "I'll see you back in there."

Chapter Nine

The Majestic had always been one of Lily's favourite theatres, partly for the domed ceiling, which wasn't quite as impressive as the Sistine Chapel but still merited a cricked neck. It was very close to the Dramatic Arts Institute, so she'd been to a lot of productions as a student. She'd never been to the Christmas Eve concert, though, and hadn't planned to attend this year. Unfortunately, Margo was still trying to build bridges and had asked what she was doing tonight. Since her parents were both out of the country and Trix had to work, Lily's plans involved vegan mince pies and *Love Actually*, and she'd been too distracted by David and Dylan's eggnog-fuelled shouting match to invent something more pressing.

Fatal mistake.

The foyer was packed, people standing shoulder to shoulder in their winter coats, their combined voices buzzed and happy.

"We're in the family box," Margo said into her ear. She pointed to the marble staircase that led to the upper levels. "I'm just going to duck backstage quickly. Meet you up there?"

She slipped between two women in fur coats and pearls, and was swallowed up by the crowd.

There were still thirty minutes before the concert was due to start. Lily turned to the closest person, one of the men in the party, and indicated in the direction where she was fairly sure the bar was hiding. "I'm going to grab a glass of water before it starts."

She would prefer something with at least a one-percent alcohol volume, but Jocasta's ban on all fun food and drink was helping her vocally. With only a few weeks to go, she wasn't going to risk backsliding just because everybody in sight had either mulled or sparkling wine in hand.

"Oh, let me," said the helpful gentleman who'd already offered to take her coat, buy her programme and, after two glasses of wine in as many minutes, father her children.

"Thanks." Lily extracted her wrist from his hand. "But I need to use the bathroom too." Before he could make any suggestion about escorting her there and probably following her into the stall, she escaped.

Murmuring apologies, she edged through the crowd. There were at least forty people queuing for drinks, but one of the bartenders recognised her and served her first, which earned her a glass of wine she couldn't drink and the violent antipathy of four dozen opera fans.

She was elbowed to the edge of the crowd and looked around for a place to leave the wineglass. Despite the chaos, she was enjoying the atmosphere. She loved the theatre. Any theatre. It was a stark reminder that in less than a month, she was going to be backstage, hearing a similar audience buzz from the other side of the curtain.

A group of businessmen pushed past and she stepped

out of the way. Turning around, she came face-to-face with Luc.

"Oh!" She quickly whipped the glass back before the wine sloshed on the strip of white shirt showing between the edges of his coat.

"Lily." He looked down at the wine.

"I'm not drinking this. I'm just—holding it."

"Right." He looked very chiselled and freshly showered. His hair was still damp. "I didn't know you were coming tonight." He glanced around. "Are you here by yourself?"

"No." An usher walked past with an empty tray of glasses; hastily, she handed off the wine. "I'm here with Margo."

He did have an exceptional poker face. "You're here with Margo."

"We were talking at the studio earlier and she invited me along tonight. Are you here to hear Alberto, too?" It seemed to take the concept of friendly exes to an extreme, but it *was* Christmas Eve, and the season of peace and goodwill, and so forth—

"While I'm sure that listening to Alberto's rendition of 'The Little Drummer Boy' will be the highlight of my Christmas, my mother is also performing." The hint of a smile crept into his eyes. "And when she has a concert in London, it's full family attendance on pain of death."

He pulled back his sleeve to look at his watch. "I'd better get in there. My father will have been here for at least an hour, and my brother can't get away from work until nine, so he's already bagged the late card tonight. If you're with Margo's party, I assume we're going the same way? Family box?"

She nodded, and he stepped back to let her go first. When she got trapped after three steps, with her nose almost buried in the wet wool covering a stranger's broad back, he switched strategies and led the way, reaching back a hand to snag hers. She was totally unsurprised when he managed to get them to the staircase in about fifteen seconds, parting the crowds like a dashing, twenty-first-century Moses.

He kept hold of her hand while they climbed the staircase to the third-floor boxes, which she appreciated, given the height of her heels and the slippery surface, and released her when they reached the red-carpeted entryway. It was much quieter up here, with just a few voices coming from behind the heavy curtains that partitioned off the private seating.

She looked down the hallway. "Which—"

"In here." He parted the first curtain and held it open for her.

The family box was larger than the standard, with seats for about twenty, most of which were filled already. The balustrade looked right over the stage. Lily peered down at the stands, watching as people continued to mill inside and find their rows. Large Christmas trees lined the outer perimeter and ushers walked around giving out hand-held lanterns and candles in small silver dishes.

One appeared in front of her face, already lit, and she turned to take it from Luc. Her smile faltered when their eyes met.

"Thanks." She looked down. "You don't have one."

"They drip wax."

"So you thought you'd just offload it on me?"

His lips curved.

"Luc!"

She jumped. A familiar man raised his hand in greeting and got up from his seat in the front row. He had a sweep of silver hair and, she realised when he was close enough, Luc's grey eyes.

"You're here. On time. It's a Christmas miracle." Cameron Savage's booming, cavernous voice had always reached the farthest seats in a theatre without needing electronic aid. The moment he spoke, it was like hearing his Lear and Julius Caesar come back to life.

He turned to Lily with a smile and a barely noticeable glint of surprise. "And you brought someone." He looked at her more closely in the dim light. "Oh, you're our Elizabeth! Lily, isn't it?" He shook her hand firmly. "Cameron Savage. Fifty-percent responsible for inflicting your boss on the unsuspecting actors of London. We almost got another player in the family, but he was always better at giving orders than following a cue."

Luc rolled his eyes, and she got back enough of her composure to laugh. "It's nice to meet you, Mr. Savage. Merry Christmas."

"And a very cordial same to you, young lady. Call me Cameron."

"'Our' Elizabeth?" Luc enquired.

The resemblance between them was even more marked when Cameron grinned. "Did I say 'our'? I meant 'your.'" He turned back to Lily. "So, you're Jack Lamprey's daughter."

"For my sins."

"For *his*, I'd imagine." The words were sardonic, but his smile was warm. "I hope you're sitting with us?"

"Lily came with Margo's party." Luc's arm brushed hers as he pulled off his coat.

"Really? You're here with Margo." Cameron was obviously intrigued. "Well, I suppose the two of you must have plenty to talk about." His face was pure innocence, but his eyes gleamed with gentle teasing. "Rehearsals, and so forth."

Lily could see why he and her father had been friends at one time.

Margo still hadn't returned by the time the theatre lights started to dim and the noise level dropped to hushed whispers. Mr. Helpful and Handsy arrived with another glass of wine, however, and edged towards the empty seat next to Lily.

She wavered before getting up, slipping along to the other end of the row and sliding into the seat next to the Savages. "Sorry. Are you saving this for your brother?"

Luc glanced down the row. "Unwanted admirer?"

"Apparently our children will have my looks, his brains, and excel in science at Harrow."

"Stay put. Alex has gone on to a Christmas party in Notting Hill. If you turn up more than an hour late, you can't complain if you're seated next to the clinically insane."

"Thank you. The save is much appreciated. It almost makes up for the fact that I have hot wax dripping down my wrist."

The houselights went out, leaving only the fairy lights, lanterns and candles—hundreds of glowing pinpoints through the stands and up the tiers. It was beautiful, and when the curtain went up and the orchestra began to play, Lily was pulled into a rare experience of pure warmth and contentment, where nothing existed beyond the music and the atmosphere.

Alberto was listed in the second part of the programme, but Célie Verne opened the concert and returned repeatedly throughout the first half. She was charismatic and popular with the audience, coaxing and demanding that the crowd join in, until five thousand or so voices swelled the harmony of "O Holy Night."

In the candlelight, Lily looked up at Luc. Her gaze moved over his jawline and profile, travelling over the inky black hair with the threads of silver. He turned his head and looked down at her.

He was sitting only inches away, but neither of them made any attempt to cross the divide. She could see the slow, steady rise and fall of his broad chest as he breathed. His face was a mystery of shadows and flickering light.

As everyone around them sang, with mixed ability but plenty of enthusiasm, they watched each other's eyes and sat in silence and stillness.

When the houselights came back on for intermission, it was like being shaken out of a deep sleep. She blinked several times, disoriented, and focused on Cameron, who was getting to his feet on Luc's other side and smiling down at her.

"What did you think of Célie?" he asked proudly. "Isn't she wonderful?"

"Yes." Lily found a return smile. Sincerely, she added, "Incredible."

"She's an extraordinary woman, my wife. Looks of a Raphael Madonna and a mind like a steel trap. And the left-hook of Joe Frazier. But she could have had a face like a dropped pie and the voice would still have sealed the deal. It was love at first word. If I remember correctly, it was a four-letter word, but nobody else can make an obscenity sound like the first note of 'Casta

Diva.' My girlfriend before Célie had vocal cords like deflating bagpipes. Her Christmas Eve rendition of 'Silent Night' caused livestock all over Derbyshire to flee for the hills. I'm going backstage for a few minutes."

Lily stared after him as he finally drew breath and left. "There's just the faintest strain of Simon Cowell running right through your family, isn't there?"

Luc stood up to stretch. "I don't think I've ever suggested that your voice would cause a farmyard stampede."

"Don't think I've forgotten the Helium Barbie comment, Backtrack Ken."

"I issued a blanket apology for all sexist comments, inadvertent or intentional. And I told you after rehearsal this morning, there's definite improvement. Twice, in your response to constructive criticism, you almost hit an F below middle C. And the accompanying gesture the second time was an inspired piece of method acting."

The box continued to empty out, with everyone presumably heading towards the bar or the loo. A note of awkwardness drifted back in.

"No sign of Margo," Lily said. "Or your brother."

"Margo is probably still propped on Ferreti's knee backstage. And Alex is probably propped up on a bar in Soho by now."

"Will your mother not mind that he missed her performance?"

"Outwardly, no. Wait a few years and then check her autobiography. The chapter on achieving stardom despite family neglect."

Lily laughed. They wandered out into the hallway to stretch their legs, and she remembered her favourite part of the Majestic. "Is the Canali necklace still on display on the second floor?"

Luc leaned against the wall with his eyes closed, looking exhausted. There was a definite pause before he answered. "No. It's been moved."

"To?" she asked suspiciously.

"The Tower. Lots of tourists and Beefeaters, hours of queuing, totally inaccessible."

"If you're going to lie, you could at least put in some effort and make it semi-believable."

"Maybe it's been moved to where it belongs."

"The dramatic arts museum?"

"A pound store."

"Bossy *and* droll. Form an orderly queue, ladies." She grinned. "I'll see you back in there."

When she was halfway down the marble stairs, her heel slipped. She grabbed hold of the railing, and a hand caught her around her waist.

Luc hauled her back to an upright position and kept a steadying arm around her until they reached flat ground.

She cleared her throat. "You did not *know* that was going to happen."

"The odds weren't in your favour."

The walls of the second-floor gallery were lined with locked glass displays. Lily found the one she was look-ing for in a central position on the far wall. A framed portrait of Elisabetta Canali—once known as Edmund Cane—was mounted above a collection of letters. And, nestled in a velvet box, the Canali necklace.

Lily touched a fingertip to the glass.

Luc continued to look underwhelmed. "I wouldn't have pegged you as the type to go misty-eyed and sentimental over the dusty contents of someone's dresser drawer."

"It's a beautiful necklace."

"It's a hideous necklace."

She bent down for a closer look. "Only aesthetically."

"Call it masculine stupidity, but I would have thought aesthetics were sort of the point, if you're going to walk around with something slung around your neck."

"Ironic, coming from someone wearing that tie."

"Funny, funny woman."

Lily studied Elisabetta's painted features. They were sharp and blade-like. Her eyes seemed to stare out of the canvas like lasers.

"Considering that the Elizabethan portrait tradition favoured round faces and arms, and artists softened their subjects to the point where most of them looked to be from the same family of pillows," Luc said, "Elisabetta Canali must have been a walking hatchet."

"Feel free to go away now and leave me to soak up the inspiration in peace."

"Canali is your inspiration? The woman pretended to be a man for fifteen years, enjoyed middling success, and then died falling through a stage trapdoor. With your hit-and-miss ability to remain vertical, I'd suggest picking a different role model. Sarah Bernhardt, as far as I'm aware, never failed to spot a giant hole in the floor."

"Elisabetta Canali would have been arrested and imprisoned if her gender had been discovered. *That's* how dedicated she was. She defied all of society's rules and conventions to break out of the box and be the person she wanted to be."

"Hiding behind a costume," Luc said. "Onstage and

off. Her entire adult life. Until she *fell through a trap-door.*"

"Would you get over that?"

"I'm not sure you realise how uncommon it is for that to actually happen. Even centuries before the Health and Safety Executive insisted that we put up signs and hand out a leaflet. Unless the woman was legally blind or just blind-drunk, she doesn't get a pass."

"Well, some people did drink about a gallon of alcohol a day back then. They didn't trust the water was clean. Probably wisely. I've seen diagrams of the London sewage system." Lily touched the glass cabinet again. "Anyway, Elisabetta had the…somewhat ugly four-leaf clover necklace made as a symbol of perseverance. To show that if you search long enough and work hard enough, you'll eventually find what you're looking for."

"No, she didn't."

"What?"

"It was in the arts column of the *Quarterly* last year. Elisabetta Canali was found out by George Berry, who was essentially the Elizabethan equivalent of a stage manager. Instead of having her thrown in the stocks, he took a fancy to her *Terminator* stare and legendary mean streak, and started writing her love letters, which were found in somebody's attic. He commissioned the clover necklace for her. The symbols of faith, hope and love, the poor bastard. And the fourth leaf: luck. Although some might say he would have brought her more luck by—oh, I don't know—closing the trapdoor."

"Is that true?"

"Apparently."

"Oh." Lily stared at the necklace anew. "So it was a symbol of—love."

"It's a symbol of bad taste. Given, I suppose, in love. Or at least unlikely and possibly one-sided infatuation."

"She wore it," Lily said slowly. "It was found on her body, under her costume. It's not something a man would wear. Even in a time when every self-respecting alpha male wore tights and frills. You wouldn't risk blowing your whole cover, when that much is at stake, for unrequited infatuation."

Luc shrugged. "I guess she believed in taking risks in every aspect of her life."

She looked again at the necklace. "I guess she did."

"Right." Luc took her by the shoulders, turned her to the left and gave her a gentle push.

"Where are we going?"

"Intermission ends in four minutes. Just enough time to divert past the Sarah Bernhardt portrait so you can soak up some inspiration from a woman who could actually act."

"One of Sarah Bernhardt's most iconic roles was in a play that folded after one night and was banned in three cities."

"Yeah, well, fortunately it's not 1910 and I haven't cast you as a highly sexualised Judas Iscariot. Provided everybody sticks to Starkey's script and keeps their clothes on, I don't think you'll have to cross a picket line."

The final carol was a full-audience rendition of "Silent Night" performed in near-darkness as most of the candles had gone out. A single spotlight illuminated the mirrored star above the stage. It would have been very affecting if Lily had been able to lose the mental image of animals, shepherds and Wise Men fleeing the holy stable in panic while Cameron Savage's one-time girlfriend warbled out the lyrics.

In the foyer afterwards, she met Célie Verne and Alberto Ferreti, and was soundly hugged by both. Alberto was a big bear of a man with a beaming smile, a lot of sex appeal and an endless stream of positivity.

"Bit of an adjustment for Margo," Célie murmured in Lily's ear as she embraced her. Her speaking voice still had the gorgeous French lilt. "It must have been like consciously uncoupling from Eeyore and eloping with Baloo."

Lily almost died of laughter in the middle of the Majestic. The others all looked over. None of them had heard, but Alberto laughed with her anyway, deep and booming. The expression on Luc's face only sent her into another spiral of giggles.

Célie was smiling at her. "Oh my goodness, you're like your father. You light up exactly the same way when you laugh. Although you've managed to take his looks and put them together in a much more pleasing way." She angled her head in a darting, bird-like gesture. "How is your father?"

"He's—Jack," Lily said, smiling back. "I don't think you'd find him much changed."

"He was the most terrible rogue," Célie said fondly. "And he made my Cameron *furieux*, which is always fun. Are you spending your Christmas with him tomorrow or with your very talented *maman*?"

"Neither," Lily said, before she could think better of it. "I'm going to my friend's charity performance. She's a dancer in *The Festival of Masks*."

"And then you will have your lunch?"

"Yes," Lily lied firmly. There was a speculative gleam in Célie's eye. It was exactly the expression Margo had assumed when confronted with the holiday orphan, and she could guess where this was leading.

Célie studied her for a second longer. "You have no plans," she announced. "You will come and have Christmas lunch with us."

Hastily, she shook her head. "Thank you so much, but—"

"Nonsense." Célie turned and beckoned her family over with an imperious finger. "Luc, this young woman is one of your star players. It's disgraceful that you're abandoning her to spend Christmas by herself."

"I'm not—" She flushed hotly when Luc frowned. "Really, I have plans."

"Darling child," Célie said. "I was once the mother of two teenage boys who regularly tried to pretend that they spent their Saturday nights studying. I know when I'm being lied to. You're coming to us. Isn't she, Cameron?"

"Of course she is," Cameron Savage agreed promptly, tucking his hand through the crook of his wife's elbow. His eyes, glinting with mischief again, were fixed on his son.

"Before my parents forcibly abduct you," Luc said, ignoring them, "*do* you have plans?"

"I'm going to watch Trix's charity performances for the children's hospital."

"So, you're going to spend Christmas Day, your one day away from the theatre, in the back row of a different theatre, watching the same series of acrobatics and improvised panto multiple times in a row?"

"It's for charity," Lily said loftily.

"So you've said. Very commendable. And probably a good reason why you shouldn't be taking a sick child's seat."

Yes, well. There was that point.

"Come to us," Célie urged. "It'll be great fun. We always have friends and colleagues join us."

Luc's car keys jingled like bells as he pulled them from his pocket.

"Luc will pick you up at eleven." It was more of a royal command than an offer.

To be polite, Lily kept her resigned sigh inward. It resonated silently through her entire body. "That's okay. I have my car. Thank you."

"*Merveilleux*. Champagne at eleven, turkey at two."

"I don't know what I've done to get to the top of Santa's 'nice' list," Alex said, champagne glass in hand as he looked out the kitchen window, "but the embodiment of my favourite fantasy just appeared on the street."

"Somebody dropped off a beer fountain and the world's largest round of camembert?" Cameron didn't look up from the oven.

Luc grinned and pulled the cork from a bottle of Australian Shiraz.

"That's my second-favourite fantasy." Alex knocked back the rest of his champagne and continued to peer through the lace netting. "Please be here for me."

Mark Campbell joined him at the window. His features, which he'd always been able to mould like playdough into whatever character part the Royal Shakespeare Company required, lifted and creased into a smile. "Are we referring to the Audi R8 or Miss Great Britain?"

Luc's movements hitched before he held a glass of red in his father's direction.

Cameron finished prodding the unfortunate turkey in the backside with what looked like an extendable backscratcher. "Cheers." He took the wineglass. "Get away from that window," he said to Alex and Mark, "and stop staring at the poor woman like she's a zoo exhibit. You'd think neither of you had been let out in public before." He carried a bowl of crisps to the table. "And if Miss Great Britain is a platinum blonde and dressed like she just stepped out of *The Matrix*, forget about it. She's Luc's."

"I'm sorry." Alex dropped the curtain and swung around. "She's *Luc's*?"

Luc poured his own glass of Shiraz. "She's a member of my company whose family is out of town."

Cameron's smile was bland. "That's what I meant."

"I'm this close to taking back that case of Scotch."

Alex frowned. "Catwoman is here for you?"

"Catwoman is here for lunch."

"She has a name, chaps," Cameron said reprovingly.

The doorbell rang. Luc heard his mother's voice and then Lily's greeting in the hall.

She followed Célie into the kitchen, her eyes going straight to him. A wash of pink appeared along her cheekbones. She was wearing slim black trousers, a tight black jumper and her lethal-weapon boots again, and did look capable of scaling the outside of a sky-scraper. "Um, Merry Christmas." She held up a bottle of Drambuie and a huge box of chocolates. "Provisions. A small thank-you for having me."

"Totally unnecessary, but much appreciated." Cameron took them from her. "And a very happy Christmas Day to you. Have you met Mark Campbell? Mark, Lily Lamprey." They exchanged greetings and he added, "Help yourself to crisps."

"Thank you. Salt and vinegar?"

"Is there any other flavour?"

"I believe there's an urban legend that some people prefer them plain."

"Philistines." Cameron offered her the bowl. "Glad you're here. We're seriously short on people with taste and brains. This is Alex, by the way, my elder son."

"Thanks for *that* segue." Alex held out his hand. With a spark of private amusement, his gaze skated towards Luc. "Alex Savage."

Lily switched the crisps to her left hand and returned the handshake. "Lily."

"I believe you've signed your life away to my despot brother."

"Well." She also flicked a glance at Luc. "The next few months, anyway."

"Champagne or shiraz?" Luc asked her. He looked at the bottle she'd brought. "Or Drambuie?"

"No alcohol, remember?"

"One glass and I won't tell Jocasta."

"How very un-despotic."

"It's the constant, mind-numbing refrain of Mariah Carey. It's weakened my defences."

When lunch was served, he sat down next to Lily and realised why his mother had, at the last minute, decided she had to have named place-settings for the first time in years.

"Don't forget to pull your crackers." Célie was already wearing a pink paper hat and examining her prize and joke.

Luc shook his head. "Have you started mentally tracing your steps back to yesterday yet, when you agreed to let yourself in for all of this?"

"Hey, I enjoy a good cracker joke." Expectantly, Lily held her cracker out to him.

"I think that's an oxymoron." Unenthusiastically, he pulled on the other end, and it came apart without a sound.

"That was a bit anticlimactic." Lily tipped the contents onto the tablecloth.

"Probably preparing you for the experience of what's inside."

She unwrapped the coiled joke and found her prize. "Cool. Nail clippers." Smoothing out the joke, she read it. "Huh."

"If it's anything about chickens, turkeys or reindeer crossing the road, I don't want to know."

"It's not a joke, Ebenezer. It's a proverb. Of sorts. Maybe there was a mix-up at the cracker-joke-and-fortune-cookie factory." She read it aloud. "'Life is like a treadmill. Exercise is good for you.' I'm slightly offended, but not so much that I'm not going to eat these roast potatoes." She picked up her knife and fork.

"Lily, you're not wearing your hat," Célie said.

"Oh, they never fit." Lily's eyes were reflecting the dancing light of the candle flame. "My head's too big."

"I'm sure it isn't—" Célie stopped when Lily obligingly tried to put on the red paper hat and it immediately tore in half. "Oh dear."

"Never mind." Cameron speared a Brussels sprout

and glared at it. "You know what they say. Big head, big…" He trailed off, puzzled.

"The saying is big *feet*, Dad." Alex reached for the bowl of cranberry sauce. "It's not really appropriate when you're referring to a woman, and it's definitely not appropriate at the dinner table."

Lily lifted her napkin, very rapidly, to cover her mouth.

When they'd reduced the contents of the table to crumbs, Luc avoided the post-turkey party games by offering to stoke the fire in the lounge. He was looking into the flames when Lily came through from the living room and perched on the arm of the couch. She was holding a gift bag.

He shot her a sideways glance. "I see you managed to escape from Charades hell."

"My ten-minute attempt at *The Luminaries* flopped. Mark did *Fablehaven* in about ten seconds. My ego is dead." She coughed. "I excused myself to get a glass of water. But your parents are snogging in the kitchen. I didn't really want to squeeze past them to the tap."

"Sorry. Any first-time guests should probably be issued a warning at the door." Straightening, he pushed his hands into his pockets and studied her. She looked… at home here.

She obviously hadn't wanted to come. Anyone without ironclad proof of a prior commitment was likely to fall victim to his mother's relentless hospitality, and he hadn't seen any way to fend off the press gang without drawing even more attention to their…situation.

But even when she wasn't in the same room, house or city borough, she seemed to have become a constant presence in his life.

Possibly a necessary one.

"It's nice." She reddened. "I mean, not the walking in on them part, and I'm glad I didn't take a second longer to fail at Charades because…hands were going places…" He winced. "But your parents love each other. A lot, obviously. It's nice."

"Mmm. The occasional couple does make it in this business."

"Apparently so. Your parents. Paul Newman and Joanne Woodward. Kermit the Frog and Miss Piggy."

"And a few others." The mention of the Muppets reminded him of the library at Aston Park and the oversized pink jumper. Evidently, when she broke away from her favourite sleek black, she did it in a big, fuzzy way. "Although I think Kermit's back on the market."

"Figures."

"So young. So cynical."

"Statistics back me up, Methuselah." She played with the handles of the gift bag. "It obviously takes something very…special to survive the media attention and work schedules. Public opinion. Travel. Career flops. Clashing egos."

"Apparently so."

The bag started to crumple in her grip and she looked down. "Oh. Here." She held it towards him. "Season's greetings. I'm sorry in advance."

He took it from her quizzically. "Sorry?"

"You're a very difficult person to buy for. And I didn't know if I should, or if it was inapprop— Anyway, it's Generic Man Present 101. I'm sorry."

He opened it and took out a bottle of cologne. "This is what I use," he said slowly.

"Yes. I—know."

He turned the box over in his hand. "You wear something vanilla."

"Diptyque Eau Duelle," she supplied automatically, then eyed him. Her cheeks flushed again.

"Thank you." He slipped the box back into the bag. "I was almost out."

She made an effort to be casual. "At least I saved you a trip to Selfridges, then. Not a total gift fail."

He picked up the wrapped parcel he'd left on the wooden dresser and passed it to her without a word.

She looked at it, and at him, before she slipped her fingers beneath the wrapping paper to loosen the tape. "You didn't have to—A book?" Pulling out the faded hardcover, she turned it to see the spine. Her smile returned and she shook her head. "*Surfeit of Lampreys.* Funny, funny man." She opened the cover. "Luc. It's a first-edition." She turned a page. "Oh my God. It's signed." Her finger hovered over the signature as if she was afraid to touch it. "It's *signed.* Is this real?"

"Well, I didn't personally witness Ngaio Marsh pulling out her ink pot and refilling her pen, but the extremely possessive owner of Ocelot Books in Covent Garden tells me it is legit, yes. And since he just about requested photos of the bookcase it was going to before he'd hand it over, I chose to believe him."

She touched her thumb to the signature, staring down at it. "Thank you."

"You're welcome."

There was a faint tap at the door to the back hallway, and Luc turned to see Alex standing there, his expression inscrutable.

"Sorry," his brother said. "But Mark's looking for Lily. Apparently he offered to show her the collection of RSC memorabilia he carries around in his car. He's in the conservatory, Lily, if you want to make a quick exit out the back door and avoid an hour of anecdotes about Brian Blessed."

Lily seemed to hesitate, looking again at Luc before she stood, holding the book to her chest. She smiled weakly at Alex. "No, that's okay. I did want to see them."

"He's on his fourth Drambuie," Alex warned her. "You might want to pour yourself a glass to deaden the pain."

He waited until she was gone before he snorted.

"What?" Luc said flatly.

His brother pressed the tips of his fingers together and raised them to his mouth. "Oh, haven't the mighty just come *crashing* down?"

"She works for me."

"Clearly."

"I mean, *she's on my payroll*."

"I know," Alex agreed gleefully. "That just makes the whole thing so much better. In fact, my vindication could only be exceeded if she was your secretary. All that shit you gave me about Jillian."

"Your *nineteen-year-old* ex-wife? Whose middle name you still don't know? I stand my ground."

Ignoring the interruption, Alex finished with triumph, "And you're nailing some little blonde-haired chorus girl."

He probably couldn't punch his brother in the face on Christmas Day. "I'm not *nailing* anyone. And I don't hire chorus girls, blonde or otherwise. It's not fucking *42nd Street*."

"You just exchange expensive presents with everyone in the cast, then?"

"Just peered through the crack in the door, did you?"

"She couldn't look more like a midlife crisis if you'd found her draped across the bonnet of your Porsche."

Hell, Christmas came around every year, and what was a bruise or two. "She's a woman, not a cliché. A fully grown woman whom I'd happily let kick your arse if she were still in the room. And I don't have a Porsche."

"By the look of your new girlfriend, it's only a matter of time. Red *is* a little too cliché. I suggest black."

"For your eye?" Luc offered, and Alex's grin widened.

"I have to say, Dad's Christmas dinner is always pretty good, but this year—" He kissed his fingers like a self-satisfied chef. "Even with the hangover, *so* worth the drive."

Cameron shouted from the living room, "Queen's speech!"

Alex nudged Luc's foot with the tip of his loafer. "Wouldn't want to miss that. I love a good chat about morality. Although—do we think it might seem a bit dull after the raging hypocrisy of your effort?"

His brother was the only Savage in several generations who hadn't gone into the entertainment business, but he didn't lack the family bent towards melodrama.

Swinging around, Luc headed for the kitchen instead, where his father had opened one of his new bottles of scotch earlier. Alex followed, still laughing into his hand, like he was fucking Muttley from the old *Wacky Races* cartoon.

Exit, pursued by snickering hound.

Chapter Ten

"Again. From the diaphragm." Jocasta patted her own middle as an unnecessary visual aid. Lily might be struggling to pull all the minute details of the performance into one cohesive character, but she was fairly clued up on body parts. She didn't think her diaphragm was located in her foot.

She repeated the line, deepening the vowel sounds and feeling as if she were doing a meditation exercise. Minus any feeling of relaxation.

"Hmm." Jocasta folded her arms and nodded. The plastic bird perched on top of her cloche hat echoed the movement. "It'll do."

Lily breathed out through her mouth, spontaneously this time, not measuring every inhale and exhale. *It'll do* from Jocasta was high praise.

"Although," Jocasta scolded, checking the clock, "you're ten minutes late for your costume fitting."

Lily had mentioned that she was due in the wardrobe department at two o'clock. She had mentioned it, in fact, every fifteen minutes for the past hour. Jocasta's exact words after her last reminder had been: "Nobody is going to care what you're wearing if you have the diction of Boomhauer on a bender."

Lily's smile was tight-lipped as she thanked Jocasta for the voice session and yanked her wool cardigan back on, wrapping the ends behind her back ballet-style. She was just going to have to take it off again on the second floor, but even though the Savage Productions central heating was a lot more generous than they'd had at CTV, London had entered the January phase of winter. Bleak skies and freezing-cold rain, without the festiveness of Christmas to cheer things up. Even inside the building, it wasn't warm enough to run between floors in her vest top.

"Stop! Turn," Jocasta ordered, and Lily swung around in the doorway. "Take a deep, slow breath."

Lily glanced at her watch. "I don't—"

"Deep. Slow. Breath. In. Out."

She let out a short, impatient breath first, and then followed the direction. And again. And again.

Some of the tension left her body, and Jocasta nodded. "You're starting to lose your temper."

"I know." The general level of stress all around the building was escalating. Shit, as Freddy had put it succinctly this morning, was getting real. "I'm sorry."

"It's perfectly normal. It's the downward roll towards tech week. And then it's going to be speed bumps and delays and potholes, and every other uncomfortable part of a rocky road, while David Benton and the production team nitpick and harangue and drive everyone into a nervous breakdown. Luc will turn into a human iceberg and rarely raise his voice, but prepare to defrost your ego with a hairdryer if you screw up in front of him. Which you will. Everyone will. And then you'll pull it together." She spoke briskly, the decree laid down and absolute, and dismissed Lily from both the room and her mind.

Pull it together. Lily's breathing quickened again as she hurried down the stairs as quickly as safety and her boot heels permitted, and it wasn't the physical exertion.

She'd been trying to pull it together for weeks now, and particularly since Christmas.

She was failing on all counts.

There was another press article today about her impending failure and equally colossal hips. There was Margo, who made knowing faces every time Luc worked through lunch or appeared to have slept in his office. And there was a signed Ngaio Marsh novel on Lily's bedside table, personally tracked down in an obscure rare bookstore, that threw her into an emotional mess every time she thought about it.

Lily expected the costume fittings to have begun by the time she slipped into the wardrobe department, but most of the cast were still sitting stretching, running vocal warm-ups or sipping water. Or, in Dylan Waitely's case, looking into the wall-length mirror and smiling.

A worried-looking Amelia ended a call on her phone. "Lily, hi. Sorry, we're running a bit behind. Magalie needs Luc to approve the final costume changes, but he never showed for their meeting, and now he'll be out for the whole day, so we're postponing last fittings until tomorrow."

Lily set her bag down on the floor. "Luc's not here? Is everything okay?"

By which she meant "Has he been hit by a car or bitten by a black mamba?" because she didn't think even the phone-it-in directors took a day off this close to showtime unless they were in the Emergency Room.

She felt terrible for even silently semi-joking about the hospital when Amelia said, "Célie Verne has had a heart attack. Luc was on his way in today when he got a call from the ER."

"Oh my God." Lily's breath caught. "Oh God, is she—"

"She's alive, but that's as much as I know. Luc didn't really have time to talk. His father is in Edinburgh and trying to get a flight back, and his brother's in Nottingham, so he's dealing with it all himself. And, well, it's Luc," Amelia added ruefully. "He isn't much for spilling his guts at the best of times." She frowned. "I was going to head down there, offer some moral support, do a coffee run, but my nanny is leaving at three on the dot today. The rest of the staff are flat-out, and Margo has a photo shoot. I don't think she would be prepared to risk the media circus if she went to the hospital, particularly without her husband. I doubt Luc would appreciate her turning up any—"

"I'll go." Lily didn't even think about it. Her mind had been running in chaotic circles since the first day she'd walked into this building, but now her heart took over. "Which hospital?"

Amelia looked at her long and hard, and told her.

She took a black cab. Even outside of rush hour, the traffic was horrendous. It was after three o'clock by the time she reached the hospital in west London. She got out of the car and found herself in the middle of a throng of photographers.

Fuck. She hadn't even thought. She should have used a side entrance. She wasn't even wearing a bloody coat. No hood to pull up. In her driving need to get to Luc, there hadn't been space to worry about—

It took an eighth of a second for someone to spot her. Cameras started snapping.

"Lily, are you here to see Luc?"

"Is Margo inside? Is it true that you got into a fi—"

"Any news on Célie's condition? Is she expected to recover?"

"How's Luc coping?"

"Is she dead?"

Ducking her head, Lily pushed past and went inside. She was followed to the lifts before a security guard advanced to ward them off. When the doors slid closed and the lift began to rise, she released a breath into the welcome silence.

It took her a few minutes to find the right nurse's station on the fifth floor, the cardiothoracic unit.

"Célie Verne?" she asked the woman behind the desk, and was fixed with a basilisk stare.

"Press are restricted to ground-floor reception."

"I'm family," she said, without missing a beat. "She's my aunt."

The steady glare was becoming almost hypnotic. "Do you have ID?"

She started to think of an excuse, but changed her mind. "Yes." She fumbled through her bag, found her wallet and showed the nurse her driver's licence.

"This says Lamprey."

"That's right." Lily didn't blink. "My mother was a Verne."

This was where she held her breath, crossed her fingers and prayed she wasn't dealing with a music buff.

The nurse's eyes narrowed to glittering slits. At last, she barked out, "She's currently in surgery. When she comes out of theatre, she'll be taken to the ICU."

"And where is—"

"Round the corner, take a left, waiting room on the right." The woman turned back to the computer, dismissing her as effectively as Jocasta had done, but without the bobbing plastic bird on her head to rob the moment of actual coldness.

"Thank you." Lily stepped out of the way of an orderly pushing an elderly woman in a wheelchair. Walking rapidly down the corridor, she rounded the corner, took a left turn and came to a halt in the open door of the family waiting room. It was empty except for Luc, who sat in a chair by the window, leaning forward with his hands dangling loosely between his parted knees, his eyes unfocused. His face was grey and taut.

For the first time, Lily stopped and let her brain catch up with her instincts. She was almost knocked back by a rush of uncertainty. This was a family crisis, and a moment when Luc probably *wanted* to be alone, and what right did she think she had to—

His gaze switched to her face. He was so far away mentally that it took an agonising moment for him to register her presence. And then his eyes closed, and he was on his feet and striding towards her, and she was yanked into his arms.

She held him to her, wrapping one arm around his head as he buried his face in her neck. His breath was ragged and rapid against her skin. She felt the shudder that went through his solid chest and tightened her hug.

They stood like that for a long time.

Eventually, he tugged her back so he could look down into her face.

"I came as soon as I heard," she said quietly. "It's only just occurred to me that I might be in the way."

His hand came up and cupped her cheek. "No." It was all he needed to say.

"I'm so sorry, Luc." His back was warm and hard against her arm. "Has your mum had problems with her heart before?"

"A bit of angina. But she eats pretty well, she still exercises. Takes care of herself."

"Your father's coming?"

"He was giving a drama lecture in Scotland last night, but he's getting the next available flight back. He calls every twenty minutes or so. Not that there's much to tell him."

Acting on instinct again, Lily reached up and pressed her lips to the spot beneath his ear. "And Alex is in Nottingham?"

"Amelia?" Luc's mouth quirked when she nodded. "He was, but he should be here anytime now."

"Good. I'm glad you'll have support."

He traced circles on the inside of her wrist with his fingertips. "So you're just here for the bad coffee?"

"No, I just have a thing for the smells of soup and antiseptic." She gave him a tiny smile. "Should I stay? You can say if you'd rather be by yourself, or alone with your brother." She nudged him gently with their linked hands. "He probably gives better hugs than I do."

"Oh, I'm sure," Luc said, deadpan. "However, one member of the family in surgery is already too many and I can't speak for my actions if he kisses my neck." He touched his forehead to hers. "Stay."

She saw the flash of movement at the open door from the corner of her eye and caught a glimpse of the woman standing there with a huge camera in her hand. Then her old friend the admissions nurse herded the paparazzo out of the way with a sweep of her arm and a bark of "I said *this area is for family and registered visitors only. Get outside before I call security. Get.*"

Lily took back everything she had previously thought about the gem of a woman.

"Hell." Luc looked as if he were coming out of a daze and falling into an even bigger nightmare. "Have the press got hold of this already?"

"As if you don't have enough to worry about. It was probably inevitable that someone would recognise your mother, but it's unforgiveable that they're actually coming into the ICU."

"And you. She saw you." Luc released her. "I'll get onto the solicitors, put a block on any photos—"

"Too late. I came in through ground-floor reception and caused quite a stir. There's probably a frame-by-frame record of my bolt through the lobby by now."

He turned sharply. "You came in through the front?"

"I was in a hurry." There would be repercussions in the distant fog that was tomorrow. Right now, she couldn't think beyond this room.

"You were in a hurry." He was still looking at her, his expression inscrutable. "To get to me."

Lily twisted her hands together. "Yes."

"I think we just issued a press release confirming that our relationship is not strictly professional."

She took a deep breath. "Probably."

He shook his head slightly. His eyes were intent. "Are you okay?"

"It's not my mother in the hospital. I think I should be asking you that."

"You were fairly vocal about avoiding this exact situation."

She ignored the twist of unease in her stomach. "Your mother had a heart attack. Kind of seemed more important."

He started to say something else, but Alex arrived then, looking harried and wild-eyed.

"What happened? How is she?" he asked before he was even through the doorway.

Luc dragged his eyes away from Lily's face, tension in every line of his body. "She's still in surgery. No word yet."

"It was a heart attack?" Alex pulled open the buttons of his overcoat with one hand. He was restless and edgy, pacing back and forth. "Where was she?"

"It was a heart attack. She was at home. Their cleaner called the ambulance and did some sort of emergency first aid, and we owe her a phone call and a massive increase in salary."

"Well, who's looking after her? Where's the doctor?"

"Hopefully in the operating theatre." Luc kept his voice level, until Alex's agitated gaze stopped darting about the room and focused on him. Categorically, he said, "Mum's tough. She's a fighter. She'll be fine."

"She's seventy." Alex shoved one unsteady fist into his trouser pocket. "She's not a young woman."

"Do you want to tell her that or should I?" Luc asked, and Alex gave a lightning flash of a grin.

"As Célie would say, she didn't raise a couple of imbeciles. I'd end up in the bed next to her, in traction." He seemed to notice Lily for the first time. "Lily. Hello."

"Hi. I'm sorry that you had such a bad end to your trip."

"You're not kidding," Alex said fervently. "I'm just glad it wasn't last month, when I was in the States. Even

two and a half hours in the car seemed like a lifetime."
He looked a bit surprised. "It was good of you to come.
No rehearsal today?"

"I'm done for the day." She hesitated. "I would have
come anyway."

"On a personal level," Luc said, "I appreciate that. As
your director, I feel I ought to condemn your priorities."

She turned quickly, but the expression in his eyes
was the opposite of censure. She swallowed, recall-
ing that his brother was three feet away and watching them critically, and that they probably wanted to
speak privately. "I'm going to find some hot drinks.
Any requests?"

"Anything with enough caffeine to wire the control
board at NASA." Alex pulled off his coat. "Thank you."

"Got it." She tilted her head enquiringly at Luc.

"Coffee would be good," he said softly. "Thanks."

She went to the café on the second floor and waited
for ten minutes before ordering, to give them some
space. When she came back with a tray of triple-shot
espressos and a bag of muffins, they were sitting at
opposite ends of the small waiting room. They both
looked stressed, but there was no obvious hostility, or
any black eyes or bloody noses, so she assumed it was
just habit to claim their own territory.

She passed out the coffees and offered the muffins.

"Maybe later." Alex raised a smile. He held up the
coffee cup. "Cheers."

Lily wondered if she ought to take the third row of
seats, under the window, to keep everything discreet
and…geometrical, but set the cardboard tray and the
paper bag down on the magazine table and sat down
next to Luc.

He came out of his reverie and touched her knee. "Thanks for the coffee."

"Any news?" she asked tentatively.

He shook his head.

"I'm sure she *will* be fine," she said quietly, addressing them both, and Alex gripped his coffee so tightly that the cup bent.

"Of course she will." His tone was brisk and unconvincing. "She's a wily old bird."

It was quiet in this part of the hospital, away from the general wards. There were none of the usual hospital sounds of machines beeping, room alerts buzzing, dinner trays rattling in trolleys. Nothing but the clock ticking and the occasional distant ring of the phone at the nurses' station. Lily leaned her head back. She usually tried not to make too much skin-to-germ contact with furniture and reading material in hospital and doctors' waiting rooms, but this was the ICU, so probably most of the thousands of people who had sat here over the years had been perfectly healthy.

Just cold and afraid.

Cameron rang a few minutes later and Luc took the call, standing in the corner of the room with his head bowed as he spoke steadily and reassuringly to his father.

Alex put down his cup and clasped his hands between his jiggling knees. "God, I hate waiting." His breath was a hiss of sound. "Especially this kind of waiting."

He was probably talking to himself, but she answered. "I know. I wish I could do something to help."

There was a long pause before he asked, "How are you at poker?"

"Excuse me?"

"You're Jack Lamprey's daughter, right?" He reached forward and picked up the box of playing cards on the table. "I'm guessing you probably know how to play poker."

She acknowledged that with a resigned gesture. "I don't often play, but yes. I do know my way around a pack of cards. I think I could recite the rules of crib-bage at five."

Alex raised his hand, balancing the box between two fingers. "Care to take pity and help me preserve my sanity?"

"What would we bet with?"

He reached into his pocket and produced a large bag of Skittles. "Conference swag."

It was the most genuinely friendly look he'd given her yet. "Go on, then." She got up and moved to a closer chair while he started dealing the cards.

Luc, still on the phone, looked over and raised an eyebrow. She shrugged in response.

When he ended the call, Alex asked without looking up from his hand, "Do you want me to deal you in?"

Luc sat down again and stretched out his legs, closing his eyes with a tired sigh. "No, I'm good. You two carry on."

Lily was watching him when his eyes flickered open and met hers. He shook his head but smiled at her.

Later, when the windows had turned black and reflective, the artificial light in the room seemed stark and clinical, and she and Alex were on their fourth hand of poker, he got up and went for a walk. Before he left the room, he bent and pressed a kiss to her temple.

It was almost ten o'clock before a weary-looking surgeon came into the waiting room, still wearing scrubs under his white coat. The three of them were crashed out on the same row of chairs. Lily sat curled under Alex's coat, her legs tucked beneath her and her head resting on Luc's shoulder. He had his iPad on his lap and was flicking through work emails. His free hand played with her hair, twisting a lock around his finger. Alex's arms were folded, his legs splayed, and his head tipped back at a ninety-degree angle.

"Célie Verne's family?" the surgeon said from the door, and they all jerked upright. Luc and Alex got to their feet at once.

"Yes," Luc said. He was totally expressionless, but Lily saw his fingers twitch, curling into a loose fist. "Is she—"

"How is she?" Alex asked quickly.

"It was a complicated procedure, but your mother came through it well. We removed the blockages and repaired the affected arteries using blood vessels from her thigh. There were a few—difficult moments," the surgeon said obliquely, "but she's stable now and resting comfortably."

"And she's going to be all right?" Alex pressed.

"We expect her to make a full recovery."

Lily got up and stood behind Luc. She touched his arm lightly, and he put it behind his back to grip her fingers. He offered his free hand to the doctor.

"Thank you." His words were stilted with the intensity of his relief. "Can we see her?"

"Just for a few minutes, please. We'll keep her under sedation until the morning, give her body a kick-start on healing, but she'll be closely monitored throughout the night and you can speak to her in the morning."

"We should stay, though?" Alex looked at Luc, but it was the surgeon who replied.

"It's up to you, but I would suggest that you head home after you've seen her, get some rest and come back in the morning. It's highly unlikely that there'll be any change before then, and we'll be keeping her in for at least a week, so it's going to be a long haul. Obviously, we'll be in touch immediately if any complications arise, but—everything is looking good and working well."

"I'll stay," Luc said when they were alone. "You go home." He looked at Lily and squeezed her fingers. "And you definitely go home. You must be exhausted. Alex will give you a lift." It wasn't a suggestion.

"Alex doesn't have his car," his brother said, and suddenly looked equally forceful. "Because he had a company car and a driver and only had to sit in the backseat, twiddling his thumbs. Meanwhile, you've been here for hours and were probably up working at some ungodly time. *I'll* fulfil the role of family watchdog for once. You're taking your leading lady home and getting some sleep. I'll kip in the waiting room and see you back here in the morning."

"Fuck off," Luc said calmly. "I'm staying."

"Oy. I have seniority. Arrived on the planet first, pulling rank now. Get lost. You look like shit. And what about Lily? Just going to shove her in a taxi at ten o'clock at night?"

"Lily," she inserted, "is perfectly capable of calling her own taxi and getting herself home."

Luc looked at her silently. He turned to his brother. "You'll call me if there's a problem."

"I believe I do have your number, yes." Alex smiled

at Lily, who pulled free of Luc's hold to put her hands on her hips in exasperation. "Thanks for humouring me with poker."

"You're welcome. Thanks for the use of your coat."

"You're an appalling card shark, and if we'd been playing for money I'd have to sell my house tomorrow, but I appreciate the distraction." He paused. "And I wanted to apologise."

Lily frowned. "What for?"

Alex seemed to be talking to Luc as much as to her. "Just—sorry."

Luc inclined his head, obviously responding to some sort of obscure Man Speak.

She glanced between them. "Should I ask?"

"Please don't," Alex said. "Anyone who bids that aggressively is bound to have a violent streak."

While they went to find their mother in the recovery ward, Lily dug her phone out of her bag.

An attempt to contact her mother sent her straight to voicemail, but her father finally answered on her second try. "Hi, baby." He sounded distracted. "Just a moment." After a couple of minutes he came back on the line. "Sorry. There's a conference call to Seoul taking place on my desktop. I've left them to yell amongst themselves."

"You shouldn't still be working after ten o'clock at night. It's not healthy."

"Aren't you preparing to spend months overthrowing Jane Grey until at least half past ten?"

"Yes, but I'm not—"

"Old?" Jack sounded amused. "I won't be taking up skateboarding anytime soon, pet, but there's a bit of life in the old bones yet." There was a rustling noise, as if he were turning over papers. "Not that I'm not thrilled to hear from my pride and joy at any hour, but is there a reason you're calling your crypt-keeper of a father at prime party hour on a Friday night?"

Lily sat down on one of the hard seats. "I just wanted to—check in."

Jack's voice turned sharp. "What's the matter?"

"I'm at the hospital. With the Savages. Célie Verne had a heart attack today." Unless the news had appeared on the stocks report, she doubted if her father had heard.

"Célie? Is she all right?"

"Sounds like she's going to be."

"Good. That's good." The pause was heavy and meaningful. "*You're* at the hospital, eh?"

"Don't start, Jack."

He sighed. "Do I infer that a little reunion with the beauteous Célie and her humourless husband is in my future?"

She stared fixedly at a poster diagram about the sugar content of vending-machine food; she doubted if people waiting in this particular room would be that concerned with the calorie count of Dairy Milk. "Possibly."

"Well, if *possibly* becomes something a little less hedging, let me know. I'll wait until Cameron's had time to get over the shock. Seeing me wouldn't help. The man was always overly dramatic. Holding a grudge for decades. All those years pretending to be Lear went to his head."

"I can see that reunion is going to go really well."

"How did you manage to get past the family-only barricade?"

"Told them I was her niece."

"Christ. What does that make me? Cam's brother? Do you *want* me to end up in the cubicle next to his wife?" Jack hummed. "Still. Proud. Savages play by the rules; Lampreys get things done. Don't comfort your cousin too enthusiastically. People will look at you funny."

"That ship has sailed."

"Lily—are *you* all right?"

"Yes. I just wanted to…"

"Check in," Jack finished quietly.

"I'll let you get back to your squabbling business-men." She frowned. "Go to bed before midnight."

"Go to bed alone."

"I'm hanging up now."

She was grateful for the semi-tinted windows of Luc's car when they got on the road without being bothered by the media. She saw a few photographers still waiting outside the main doors, probably hoping that Margo was going to make an eleventh-hour appearance.

When they reached the street by her mews, Luc turned off the car engine and they sat in total darkness.

She rolled her head tiredly to the side. He had one wrist resting on the wheel and was leaning back against the headrest with his eyes closed.

"You okay?"

"Mmm-hmm."

"Feeling like a cross between a coiled spring and a deflated balloon?"

"Sounds accurate."

"I'm so glad your mother is going to be okay."

"So am I."

Lily bit her lip. "If you've got enough momentum left to walk a few feet, do you want to come in?"

He opened his eyes.

"It's late," she said. "It's Friday night and the traffic between here and Kensington will be nuts, and you look half-dead."

"If that's your idea of a pickup line, it's probably lucky you were born with that face."

"I don't make passes at barely conscious men who've just left their mother's hospital bedside. Trix moved out after New Year's and I have a spare room. I also have disposable razors and Pop-Tarts."

"Well, in that case…" Luc unsnapped his seat belt. "You're sure?"

"*Mi casa*, etc."

"Then *gracias*, offer gratefully accepted."

Inside the flat, she switched on the heat pump and the kettle before she dropped to sit beside him on the couch.

Tucking one leg beneath her, she took a deep breath. "Look—"

His mouth cut off whatever she'd been going to pull from her lagging brain. The jolt of sensation was a physical shock. The kiss was searching, more slow and affectionate than the explicitly sexual desk-roll in Shropshire, but still broke her breath into pieces and kicked her heart somewhere into her throat. She wrapped her arms around his neck, and he pulled her into his body, tugging her lower lip between his teeth, nudging it open. His tongue slid against hers and her belly clenched down hard.

She had to pull back when the pinpoints of light behind her closed eyelids became less about hard, warm hands and lips, and more about a lack of oxygen. They stayed close together, mouths almost touching, his nose brushing hers.

"You've had a traumatic day."

"Very. It's ending on a much better note than it began."

"It really wasn't a pickup line."

"I know."

Their mouths clashed back together. He picked her up with one arm, swinging her under his body and lowering her to the cushions. His weight was heavy on her, the thick muscle of his thigh flexing as his knee parted her legs.

"Wait." She tore her mouth away. Her heart was thumping against his palm.

His breath was equally ragged. His chin rubbed against hers as he turned his head. "No?" His voice was a husky blur.

"Yes." She pulled the back of his shirt free of his belt and traced her fingers up his spine; he instinctively pushed back into her before he caught himself with a groan. She tried to remember why she'd interrupted his fairly inspiring moves. "But not here. I suggest we either move this down the hall or do a synchronised barrel roll onto the floor, because this is a very anti-sex couch. It gets extremely hostile and tries to perform an inner-spring lumber puncture on whoever's on the bottom."

He trailed kisses up her neck. "And you know that because…" he murmured into her ear, and nipped the lobe sharply.

She paused, feeling the light trail of hair that furred upward from his belly. "The sales guy at IKEA mentioned it. He was very conscientious."

"Smart." Luc kissed her again. "Saving all of your acting ability for the show."

She had to take her hands off his buttons to let him untie her cardigan and pull her vest top over her head. He tossed them aside, and she pulled the edges of his shirt apart and pressed a kiss to his shoulder. His skin was warm and smooth, moving tautly over the joint as he shrugged the shirt off.

Her hair caught and tugged on the cushions when she arched to create a space for his hand between the couch and her bra strap. The lace went slack and gravity took over, and his mouth followed the falling curve of her breast. His tongue curled around her nipple, and she made an embarrassing sound in her throat.

He sat up on his haunches between her thighs, his chest heaving, to remove the rest of their clothing. His coordination was impressive; the choreographers at *Knightsbridge* would have loved him. When he swept her legs over his shoulders and bent his head, her vocal cords started producing noise that bordered on feline. Somewhere, Jocasta's misbehaving-client alarm was going off with a vengeance.

Running his hands up the backs of her thighs, a part of her body she'd never appreciated until this moment, Luc said indistinctly, "Anti-sex couch, huh?"

She managed to speak despite having swallowed her tongue. "What?"

Luc slid his hands around her waist, lifting her to kiss her belly button. "How far away is your bedroom?"

He smelled like Christmas cologne and all good things. "Too far."

"Option B, then."

Before she could take a breath, he rolled them off

the side of the couch, twisting so that he took the fall, landing on his back on her sheepskin rug and startling helpless laughter out of her.

Sprawled against his chest, she said against his mouth, "I was joking about the barrel roll."

"Well, you have vocal issues. Who could tell?"

She dug her elbow into his ribs and he grunted. He was smiling when he kissed her again, which was such a relief after the horrendous evening that she could over-look any rude comments. He deepened the kiss, his hand twisting in her hair, supporting her neck. Lily rocked into him, shivering as he ran the pad of his thumb down the line of her spine.

"Fuck," he said suddenly against her cheek.

"Yes, please."

"I don't have anything." His chest and belly rose rap-idly beneath her questing fingers, and he swore again when she ventured lower.

"I beg to differ," she said, grinning, and he caught her wrist with a strangled laugh.

"Protection, smart-arse."

She pushed her hands against the floor, straighten-ing her arms on either side of his ears. "You don't keep one in your wallet?"

"I keep credit cards in my wallet. I'm not sixteen years old and I'm not that optimistic."

"Well, thanks to your middle-aged pessimism, I'm going to have to get up. And I'm naked."

He pulled her back down and kissed her neck. "Oh, I noticed."

"And so will the Bradleys across the street. I forgot to close the curtains." She spotted her handbag on the coffee table. "Balloon animals."

Luc paused with his lips on the underside of her chin. "Another of your infamous circus skills? I think the acrobatics might be more useful right now."

She managed to grab the bag without leaving the circle of his arm. Plunking it down on his chest, she sat back on his hips and searched through the accumulated mess until she found the condoms. "The sixteen-year-old males at CTV—some of whom are chronologically thirty-five—had a habit of making condom poodles. It wasn't safe to leave them alone with anything inflatable. I confiscated these the same day I auditioned for you."

He swung the bag aside and sat up, which did delightful things to his abdominal muscles. "You brought condoms to the audition?" He took the box from her. With his free hand, he caught hold of her ankle and tugged her leg to hook around his waist. The slide of their skin prickled the sensitive nerves of her inner thigh.

"The only reason they would have left the bottom of my bag that day was if I'd filled them with water and aimed at your head." She rested her cheek against his shoulder. She was starting to feel shivery and clenched her teeth so they didn't chatter. The adrenaline fog that had taken over in the wardrobe department this afternoon was clearing, the room sharpening. Awareness was setting in of exactly whose chest hair was tickling her. There was a sprinkling of freckles under her cheek. There was rustling of foil.

She hadn't been nervous about sex in a long time.

This was Luc, and this suddenly felt very—*different*.

"Okay?" he murmured in her ear. Gently, he smoothed her hair, his fingers lingering on her skin, and nuzzled a kiss on her temple. "Lily, we don't have to—"

"No." She ran her hand over his chest, stroking over his heartbeat. "I want to."

"You're shaking."

"I know." She pulled his mouth back to hers and he kissed her for a long time, slowly at first and then increasingly deeply.

His lips travelled back down over her collarbone and breast before he looked into her eyes. The muscles in his supporting arm were taut as he started to push forward, stopping when she winced.

"Lily?" It was barely a rasp.

"Yes," she said thinly, on a sharp breath. Her legs quivered around him. "Move."

He did, hooking her knee higher so he could thrust deeper. His first movements were slow and careful, a rhythm her body found and followed easily, but the friction quickly became so intense it was almost uncomfortable.

Her senses narrowed to the feel of him, hard inside her, agonisingly tense around her, the clamminess of her palms and the wetness between her thighs, the low sound of her name. Her breath hitched and she scrunched her eyes shut, grinding her hips into his and making uncontrollable little sounds in her throat.

He held her tightly, one arm still circling her waist, the other slanted up her back. They caught at each other for snatches of kisses when their mouths crossed paths, but their lips were constantly moving and murmuring over ears and jawlines and beads of sweat. She leaned into him, twisting her forehead against his as the pressure built.

"*Lily.*" He shuddered, his fingers digging into her curves.

It wasn't a distant battle for satisfaction; it was… together. Her and him, and them together.

Until the finale. She'd never had a quick trigger, even when she was going it solo with mechanical assistance. It took some mutual handiwork, once he'd regained the use of his brain and motor skills, to keep things fair and equal.

Her hips arched violently, pressing up into his curled fingers, and she covered her mouth to muffle a stream of four-letter words.

While she was trying to catch her breath and stop orbiting somewhere around the ceiling, Luc let his forearm fall across his eyes. "I might have known you'd be hard work in every respect."

Without turning her head, she patted consolingly in his general direction. "B for effort, but A+ for execution."

"What do you mean, *B for effort*? I think I've got carpal tunnel."

Lily jerked and clutched at her ribs. "Don't make me laugh. My abs feel like I've been doing the 30 Day Shred for about three years." The sheepskin rug felt like heaven on her bare back as she stretched. She rolled onto his chest and smiled down at him. "And I'm not sure you should be capable of saying anything at this point, except maybe 'Thank you, universe,' or 'My God, is this woman even human?'"

His arm slipped around her and his sleepy grey eyes crinkled. "I thought that went without saying."

Reaching behind her, she felt around in her abandoned bag for tissues. He took care of the unsexy but necessary, then pulled her back into his arms and kissed her, his mouth warm and lingering.

She sighed against his lips. "I suppose we'd better move. Do us all a favour and stay between me and the window. Marta Bradley does her neighbourhood watch routine on Friday nights, looking for so-far-nonexistent thugs and hooligans, and if she's going to cop an eyeful, it should be of you. You've got a nicer butt."

Luc raised his eyebrows and bent forward to look over her shoulder. "Demonstrably untrue." He yawned. "Why are we moving, again?"

"Shower, toothpaste, memory-foam mattress for your decrepit back." She squeaked when he lazily snagged one of the fallen couch cushions and whacked her on her inferior behind. "Joke, Old Man Time, joke. But I'm not sleeping on the floor. I'm fairly sure that walking tomorrow is going to be difficult enough. Interpret that correctly and reinflate your ego."

"Hey." Luc sat up and caught her hand in his. His hair was tousled and there was a definite element of male smugness in the air. But his expression was suddenly serious. "We do need to talk about that."

"About your ancient yet surprisingly agile back?" she asked lightly, tugging her hand free. She knew they needed to talk, and tomorrow she would need to *think* about quite a lot of things, but right now she just wanted to sleep in cosy, cuddly denial.

"Among other things."

"I know. But not tonight. I'm not sure how you're still conscious, but I don't think either of us is in the right headspace to—"

"Turn the afterglow into an autopsy?"

Despite the note of tension, she smiled. "You're so my kind of person."

"Mmm." Luc nipped at her ear. "Who'd have thought?"

He stood in one swift movement, totally naked, tossed her equally nude body over his shoulder and carried her out of the room. She wheezed and grabbed hold of his ribs to steady herself.

"Point taken," she said to the base of his spine. "Mocking the elderly is insensitive and not funny. You clearly have the body of a twenty-year-old and the maturity of a six-year-old."

"I'm not sure that fantastic sex has the best effect on you."

"Yeah? Well, when Tarzan did this to Jane, she at least had leaf and loincloth support and wasn't in danger of being smothered by her own breasts."

"Bedroom?"

"Last door on the right. The blood is rushing to my head."

In her bedroom, he flipped her back upright and lowered her to the bed, and she rolled over to turn on the lamp. "For the record," she said, flopping back with a sigh and letting her limbs loll, spaghetti-like, "if you're going to recreate an iconic scene, I'd prefer you think Richard Gere and Debra Winger, not Van Gogh's *Miners' Wives Carrying Sacks of Coal.*"

The mattress depressed as he followed her down, resting his weight on his hands. He ran the tip of his tongue between her lips, taking things from casual peck to full snog in two seconds flat.

She reached up for him, quite willing to continue postponing the consequences of her actions, but he broke away, kissed her cheek, her throat and her knuckles, and stood up.

"I'm going to ring Alex. I'll pull your curtains and spoil Marta's fun. After I've stood in your freezing-cold hallway for a few minutes. I'm not comfortable speaking to anyone in my family in this particular state."

"Okay. I'm going to take a quick shower."

He paused in the doorway. "Don't make it too quick."

"I hate to crush your newfound optimism, but my shower is the size of a matchbox. If I drop the soap, I have to stand on the bathmat to have space to bend forward."

"If you're trying to put me off coming in, you might want to rethink your approach."

When she could hear him down the hall in the lounge, she glanced at the bedside table, where she'd left her iPad on charge. Her hand reached for it without waiting for permission from her common sense.

The third thumbnail on the *London Celebrity* site was a headline about Célie Verne's heart attack. The fourth thumbnail was a slightly blurred shot of her and Luc in the waiting room.

Headline and hook: Sex Sent Me to the ER: Lily Lamprey rushes to comfort her *1553* director at his mother's bedside, fuelling rumours that the *Knightsbridge* starlet was the catalyst for Savage's shock split from Margo Roy. Do we diagnose a case of life imitating art for TV's most notorious man-pincher?

Lily woke up the next morning in her own bed, in her own room, and for several seconds had absolutely no idea where she was.

Next to her cheek, her hand flexed on hard muscle and warm skin. Her eyes shot open. She moved her feet a little, testing the territory beneath her toes.

"I'm on top of you," she said blankly. Her voice was low and hoarse for about ten seconds a day; it was her short-lived time to channel Kathleen Turner, but mostly she was the only one around to appreciate it.

"Yes, you are." Luc sounded wide-awake and amused.

He was lying on his stomach, with his head resting on his folded arms. She was stretched full-length on top of him, her legs tucked along his, her stomach in the curve of his back.

"Did you put me up here?" she demanded, still trying to stumble back into awake and functional, and felt his snort echo through his spine.

"Did I pick you up in the middle of the night and somehow attach you to my back like a squirrel monkey? No."

"I climbed on your back in my sleep?" She scrubbed at her eyes. "And you didn't wake up?"

"Apparently I was exhausted and you need to attend some sort of clinic." He stretched and she rose and fell with him. "I was actually relieved when you started drooling on my neck. I called Alex, my father and my mother's surgeon half an hour ago, and you still didn't move. I was starting to think I'd have to visit the narcolepsy unit as well as the ICU."

He managed to turn over beneath her without throwing her off the side of the bed. She looked down into his tired face. "How's your mum this morning?"

He tucked her hair behind her ear. "According to Alex: awake, demanding breakfast and recreating the longing stares and melodrama of the *Casablanca* reunion scene with my father."

"He's back?"

"His plane got in at 4:00 a.m. He went straight to Mum's room."

"And they let him in?"

"Do you remember my father?"

"I take your point." Lily kissed his chin and slid off him to turn on the lamp. It was still quite dark outside, yet not acceptable to be asleep: the worst part of winter. "Sorry. You should have woken me up so you didn't have to make your calls in the dark. Half-buried."

Luc pushed up and tucked the pillow behind him. She wasn't exactly a *waif*, but she didn't think the wince was necessary when he straightened his back. "I tried to wake you up. You kicked me."

"I did not."

"Nailed me right in the Achilles tendon." He started flipping through his emails. "Forewarned is forearmed. Protective padding and possibly some sort of helmet wouldn't hurt when sharing a mattress with you."

She tried to keep her voice level. "That would seem to imply a repeat performance or two."

His expression didn't change, but she didn't miss the sudden stillness of his body. He turned his head and regarded her steadily. "I think that would be up to you."

"No, I think the whole concept of a relationship would imply mutual participation. Particularly the parts that require a mattress and a helmet."

Luc rubbed his hand over his chest. She liked the dusting of hair there; she now knew from experience that it felt really good against her skin. "You were great yesterday."

"Well—" she began modestly, buffing her nails against her collarbone, and made him grin.

"There *was* that. I may also have meant at the hospital. You were a rock. And a much-needed buffer. Alex and I would probably have ended up killing each other if you hadn't systematically stripped him of his self-esteem one royal flush after another." Any trace of levity left his voice. "But the situation did act as a bit of a—catalyst."

The choice of word reminded her of the tabloid headline from the night before.

He touched her cheek. "I don't want you to feel—forced to stay in a situation that's going to be…messy."

Lily looked down at their sheet-wrapped nakedness. "I think it's a little late to backtrack now."

Something flickered in his eyes. "Do you *want* to backtrack?"

Crossroad: bare-chested, concerned Luc on one side, iPad full of stranger hate on the other. After this, however opening night turned out, her current reputation of stage-climbing homewrecker probably wasn't going anywhere. And there was still a little voice in her head whispering things like: *Playing second-fiddle: better get used to it.* The voice sounded quite a lot like Margo.

She mentally shut her eyes and stepped off the edge of the cliff.

"No. I don't want to backtrack." Years of habit refused to be kicked aside that easily and made her add in a rush, "But—discretion wouldn't hurt."

"I wasn't planning to seduce you in the orchestra pit."

She didn't smile. "And you? You weren't thrilled about the age difference and the work conflict either."

"No, I wasn't," he freely agreed. "The timing is still bloody awful, and I'd feel a lot more comfortable if you were forty years old and pursuing just about any other career, with the possible exceptions of politics or stand-up comedy, but—"

Her fingers curled around his.

"But," he said, his thumb rubbing hers, "I made the mistake once of defining you by a label, or in this case a number, and narrowly avoided getting smacked in the face by a condom water balloon." His tone had lightened, but he wasn't smiling either. "As a strategy, blind denial and ignoring the situation is not working."

"That's a very directorial way of putting it, but no. It's not." She gestured with the sheet. "Clearly."

He smoothed over the line of her eyebrow. "I was expecting a mediocre actress and ten minutes of my life I'd never get back, not a woman with the impact of a Lancaster Bomber. When the press referred to you as a bombshell, I assumed they meant the outside package."

"I'm sure there's a compliment in there somewhere." She hunched her shoulder in a ticklish flinch when Luc sneaked a kiss on her neck.

"It was buried—" he switched direction towards her lips "—but it's there."

Before he could kiss her mouth, she said, "Why did your brother apologise to me last night?"

He went still again, before he rolled out of bed and reached for the trousers he'd slung over her chair last night. As he zipped them up, his stomach muscles working above the leather strip of his belt, he glanced up at her through a ruffled fall of hair. "Given everything else that happened in the past twenty-four hours, I thought that might have glanced by."

"It would really simplify things if you just assume from this point on that *nothing* will glance by."

Luc shook out his shirt. "Alex recently went through an expensive and entirely predictable divorce. I was fairly outspoken on the subject of his ex-wife. When you came over at Christmas, he saw it as divine retribution."

"I'm going to need a footnote."

"His ex-wife is nineteen."

"Oh."

"But I believe we established at Aston Park that you're not a teenager. You're a veritable pensioner, knocking on the door of thirty." Luc finished buttoning his shirt and tucked it into his trousers, then fastened his belt.

"The family precedent rears its ugly head again."

"What was that dark-sounding mumble?" He sat down on the edge of the bed to put his shoes and socks on.

"Nothing." She picked at the sheet. "You're heading into the hospital?"

"I'll stop by on the way to the studio, then go back during the lunch break and after the afternoon rehearsal."

"So you'll be at rehearsal this morning?"

"If Mum's on the mend, missing another day isn't really an option. We're two days out from tech week."

"Don't remind me." Lily slammed an imaginary door on the image of Margo's silent, eloquent nod. This wasn't putting work above family; he'd be back and forth nonstop between the hospital, the Queen Anne and every floor of his office building all day. He was honouring his commitments. "Would your parents mind if I visited in a few days, once your mum is up to it?"

Luc's expression eased a little as he looked over his shoulder. "I'm sure she'd appreciate that. Although I wouldn't expect to have much free time for anything but eating and sleeping next week, and even that's not a given."

She took that to mean she'd better get up now before she was late for her early voice session with Jocasta. Throwing off the sheet, she swung her legs to the floor and stood up, stretching while he watched with obvious appreciation.

"The industry press party tomorrow night." She pulled open her wardrobe door and sifted through the racks, looking for something warm. "Are you going?"

"Shit." He stood up and slipped his phone into his back pocket. "I forgot. Hell Night."

Her head popped through the neckline of her jumper and she pulled her hair free. "I thought it was Hell *Week* in your snazzy theatrical lingo, which doesn't start until Monday."

"Tech week isn't hell, it's just insomnia and organised chaos. *Hell* is sharing small talk and tiny plates of food with the media and all the people who've ever annoyed me in every theatre in the West End."

"So—that's a misanthropic 'no' on the party attendance, then? You do have a pretty good excuse to skip it."

"Unfortunately, it's part of the package. Especially when we're opening cold. Inviting the actors we didn't cast in the actual production ensures that at least some of them will show up on opening night, and getting most of the theatre critics in London drunk helps drain some of the poison from their pens before they see the play. It doesn't build so much goodwill if we lure people to the Savoy with the promise of canapés and champagne and then don't bother to show ourselves." His eyes narrowed. "I'm guessing from the way you're clutching at your nose that you'd rather I don't speak to you or walk within six feet of you in public."

She immediately dropped her arm to her side and smoothed out her frown. "No. We're doing this, so— feel free to come within at least three feet."

"I know it's not an ideal situation, Lily, but—we'll figure it out."

"I squash you into the mattress for one night and you cross completely into glass-half-full territory." Her smile felt a little tight. "That *London Celebrity* journalist was right. My womanly wiles *are* potent."

"Ignore the press."

"Says the man who's shelling out a fortune to seduce them with Bollinger and smoked salmon."

"I have no intention of seducing any of them." He bent and kissed the tip of her nose. "And *London Celebrity* aren't on the guest list. I have to go. I'll see you in Southbank shortly."

In the doorway, without looking at her, he dropped a verbal bomb. His voice was so low that it almost went over her head instead of hitting the target on the left side of her chest. "It's second nature to pull apart a performance, isolate and slice out the dead weight, piece it back together. I also know what it feels like when there's that very rare click and it's just—right. It works. From the first line of the first scene." A nerve ticked in his jaw. "It doesn't often happen onstage, and I didn't expect to ever experience it offstage."

She didn't move. Or breathe.

He still didn't turn when he said, "Drive safe. And don't be late. I'm fairly sure that plastic bird on Jocasta's head is concealing some sort of weapon."

She heard his footsteps in the lounge and the front door opening before he called, "Take a breath before you pass out."

She sat down on the edge of the bed and exhaled.

Chapter Eleven

"And then I said to him, 'Simon, if it was good enough for Vanessa Redgrave—'" The woman in plaid, who was either from the Palladium or *Town and Country*, took a gulp of champagne and kept talking, and Lily nodded at intervals and hoped that her eyes weren't actually glazing over.

"Laurel!" Amelia joined the one-sided conversation, Maria Finch following a second later. They were both wearing cocktail dresses and carrying Cosmos. Amelia widened her eyes meaningfully at Lily before she completed the save. "There you are. I was just talking to Angela Fox and she wanted to go over the—" She hooked a firm hand under Laurel Somebody's elbow and steered her away into the crowd.

"Dreadful woman," Maria said, watching them go. "I hear she's being considered for Marie Antoinette. Putting her anywhere near a guillotine is just tempting fate." Her gaze sharpened on Lily. "Where's Luc?"

Lily swirled her cranberry juice and reminded herself that she was supposed to be an actor. It shouldn't be difficult not to tense up every time someone mentioned him. Which so far had been approximately every three minutes. "I think he had to stop by the Queen Anne."

"But he's coming?" Maria pressed, obviously assuming that Lily was now fully informed of his schedule. Which she was. He had texted her half an hour ago when he'd left the hospital. "He has things to do here."

"He's coming."

"I almost didn't make it myself, after all the calls I've been fielding today about Célie Verne and your headlong dash to the ER. We need to have a meeting on Monday."

"'We,' meaning—"

"You. Me. Luc. Possibly Margo too, although I suppose that could be slightly awkward."

Just a tad.

"We can thank whichever studio lured Bridget away to LA, because this whole situation would have been a *disaster* if Margo wasn't attached to the project." Maria finished her drink. "She has a very strong fan base, all of whom would be boycotting the show otherwise. From what I can gauge, public sentiment is in her corner. Luc trades her in for a younger model, and she marries the romantic Italian on the rebound."

"I didn't even *know* Luc when—"

Maria dismissed that with a finger flutter. "Doesn't matter. Nobody will believe you. Fortunately, with you and Margo both in the cast, we're getting a massive boost in sales. We'll discuss opportunities for the two of you to appear at a few events together. If it looks like you're pretending to like each other, it'll keep people interested in what's going on backstage."

"We *do* like each—"

"Actually," Maria said thoughtfully, "the whole thing was marketing genius. Luc certainly knows how to sell out a show. He's driving me into an early grave, but the numbers are looking *great*." She frowned. "Dylan has his hands all over a waitress. In front of fifty members of the press. Super."

She made a beeline through the crowd. Dylan's wife was filming another reality show in the depths of the jungle somewhere, a fact he'd referred to as a "get-out-of-jail-free card."

Lily swung around, sighing, and almost spilled her drink.

Despite Maria's implication, with all its sledgehammer subtlety, she didn't believe Luc would manipulate this situation for publicity; she doubted if he was enjoying his rapid descent from the highest pillars of the British theatre industry to the dregs of typical bloke having early midlife crisis. Any more than she was enjoying being the *catalyst* for dragging him down.

Unless bad press negatively affected his work and company, however, he didn't seem to care that much what people were saying—and it was probably true that their increasingly battered reputations were sending pre-sales through the roof.

She needed to channel that attitude. It was a party, the last big gathering before opening night. She was supposed to be networking and repairing some of the damage, and ideally enjoying herself. Trix had provided a distraction for the first half hour, but Lily had lost track of her after David Benton had pounced and introduced her to a famous blogger.

The candlelight and string quartet could have created a peaceful atmosphere, but were no match for a room heavily populated by actors who had been trained to project and were all trying to dominate their circle.

The waiters in white tie were having trouble navigating the crowd with their trays of glasses and finger food.

She finally spotted a flash of pink, and grinned when she saw Trix at the bar, gesturing with a glass of wine and talking intently to Leo Magasiva, the show's hot makeup artist. Lily had spent three hours with him this week while he transformed her into the narrower-featured, red-haired Elizabeth. He was one of the top special-effects artists in the city. The brief for *1553* wasn't much of a stretch for a man who could probably turn a Victoria's Secret model into a creature from *Pan's Labyrinth* using the contents of her handbag, but Luc evidently wanted and was prepared to pay for the best.

Leo wasn't exactly chatty, but he'd been professional and polite, his big hands had been gentle as he worked, and he'd been unexpectedly kind when someone had brought in the latest gossip column.

Blunt, but kind. *"Load of bullshit. You're going to nail this. Fuck them."*

From what she could see now, he was perfectly happy to stand there, head cocked, eyes intent on Trix's face, listening to whatever her friend was saying in her old animated way.

"Hey."

Lily turned, still smiling. "Hey, Freddy." She looked from her co-star's topknot of escaping ringlets to her dress. "You look gorgeous."

"Thanks." Freddy toasted her with her cocktail glass. "I would return the compliment, but I think it's redundant. How's your night going?"

"Good."

"Mmm-hmm. And the truth?"

"I feel about as popular in this room as a tax investigator."

"Yeah," Freddy said sympathetically. "Little tip from a West End veteran: banging your director is kind of a rookie mistake."

"Thank you."

Freddy looked into the crowd. "I see our competitor for the crown is playing the role of the heartbroken but resilient ex tonight. Probably why she left the fit husband at home. No reminder that she's not exactly crying into her celibate pillow. I like the little downcast glances and lip-bites. Really grab that sympathy vote."

"I thought you liked Margo."

"I do like Margo. But—and I mean this in the most flattering way possible—if I'm a veteran, she's the freaking Yoda of the theatre. She can blow most of the people in this room out of the water performance-wise, and she knows how to work the publicity machine like a pro. She's smart, she's nice, but don't get in the way of her career. She's also human, so I'd take anything she says to you on the subject of our esteemed director with a pinch of salt."

Lily hooked her thumb over the rim of her glass. "The breakup was mutual and I really don't think she regrets it. She seems pretty satisfied with her husband." She paused. "Away from the cameras, anyway."

"I was in the studio next door when Alberto paid her a little visit at work on Wednesday night. *Believe me*, I know she's satisfied, and I'd rather not have had the full audio experience through the wall." Freddy rolled her eyes. "But come on. Even if a breakup is amicable, who really wants to think their ex is getting something from a new partner that they obviously didn't inspire themselves?"

Margo had said something similar, in an open and self-deprecating way, right before she'd followed up with the kicker about Luc's single-minded devotion to cues, lighting and profit margins.

"Mmm." Lily took a sip of her drink.

"Well, anyway, I'm sure you've been around the block a few times," Freddy said cheerfully, and Lily's cranberry juice went down the wrong way and almost came back up her nose when she choked on a spontaneous laugh. "I doubt you need my words of wisdom."

"You wouldn't think so." Wryly, Lily wiped juice from her chin and checked her dress for stains. "I haven't exactly been myself lately."

"Sex that good, huh?" Freddy asked, interested. "He does have kind of a Gregory Peck thing going on."

"No comment."

"You're even starting to sound like him." Freddy's gaze drifted over to the bar. "At least you *have* a sex life, even if it's turned you into a professional pariah. I see my most promising prospect prefers pink-haired women the size of his thumb. I'm depressed." Her roving eyes lit on someone behind Lily. "Hey, it's the Troys, plural."

"And the Carlton, singular." The male voice was deep and intensely dry. "Which is usually more than enough."

Lily knew Richard Troy by sight and reputation, like most of London. The amount of awards he'd won was roughly equal to the number of people he'd alienated. At any other time, she might have been intimidated; right now, it was quite nice to have some company in the bad-press pen. She already knew and liked his wife.

Lainie Graham had guest-starred on *Knightsbridge* several months ago, and Lily had got the intel from Ash this week that she'd been contracted for a multi-episode arc next season.

"Hi, Lainie," she said. "How are you?"

From the loose circle of her husband's arm, Lainie returned her smile. Her green eyes were warm. "A little disappointed. I was hoping we'd be working together again, but we seem to be doing a career switch."

"Yes." Lazily, Richard stroked circles on his wife's hip. "But I believe the correct order is soap opera to stage, sweetheart, not the other way around." He nodded at Lily. "Congratulations on the escape from improbable storylines and truly dire writing. Although choosing a Savage play for your debut was a dive straight off the deep end."

"Into the deep end," Freddy corrected.

"If you say so."

"Do I sense a little hostility?"

"Shall we say that Richard and Luc Savage didn't exactly hold hands and skip through the wings when they worked together?" Lainie grinned. "I'm still *so* sorry that I wasn't in *The Importance of Being Earnest* to witness those interactions in person. It must have been like watching a Monty Python skit. Or Bert and Ernie, if they'd lost all their joy in life."

"If that babble is meant to imply some sort of temperamental similarity," Richard said, "I think it qualifies as grounds for divorce."

"Oh, it wasn't," Lainie assured him. "I don't think you're at all alike. Luc Savage knows how to control his temper." She widened her eyes at him. He shook his head, but a smile played at the corners of his mouth. His arm slid around her fully, tugging her into his chest.

"Okay." Freddy glowered. "Ernie's not even here and I still feel like a fifth wheel. I'm going to continue preparing the critics for my upcoming brilliance, before the overwhelming coupledom makes me vomit." She peered at the dregs of her drink. "Although it's possible the vodka might contribute."

Richard watched her go. "She needs to hire an interpreter to walk two steps behind her and translate into English."

"Lainie!" A guy in a tweed suit swooped in to kiss Lainie's cheek. The scent of his cologne was so strong that it caught in Lily's throat; she took another swallow of juice and tried to breathe shallowly. "You look gorgeous."

"She looks a lot better from a distance," Richard said frostily. "Preferably from the other side of the room."

Lainie turned and stared at him. "I beg your pardon?"

"That didn't come out right." He scowled at Tweedy's hand, which was still fastened around his wife's elbow.

The other man wisely removed it. His eyes fastened on Lily and brightened. "Hello, there."

Lainie was trying not to laugh. "Sorry, Rafe, it sounds like Lily's elbow is spoken for as well. Do you know each other? Lily, Rafe Talbot, assistant director at the Fallon. Rafe, this is Lily Lamprey, 1553's Elizabeth I."

Lily looked up quickly. The Fallon was Kathleen Leibowitz's theatre.

"Lily Lamprey. Right, right. Shame about that not working out."

Her professional smile faltered. "I'm sorry?"

"The shortlist for *Blithe Spirit*? You were up for Edith."

Were up for it. She almost saw the little bubble of anticipation with Leibowitz's name on it drift past and pop.

"Yes," she said, slowly. In every sense of the word, she'd been up for it.

Lainie glanced at her with concern. Richard's expression hadn't changed; he still looked as if he'd rather be at home in bed.

Right now, going home, crawling onto Luc's bare back and yanking the quilt over her head sounded like a good idea to Lily.

"Pity, but Kathleen's kind of a purist, you know? Old-school. Classical training, you live for the theatre, you keep your nose clean. She's all about the 'artistic integrity,'" Rafe said with air quotes. "No publicity that isn't generated by the quality of the performance. She once fired a lead on the first night because of a minor shoplifting incident, can you believe that?" He flicked something from his cuff. "You see how it is."

It took all of Lily's classical training to allow her to hold on to the dregs of her smile. Inside, she wasn't sure whether she was more disappointed, embarrassed or pissed off, and hoped that an intense combination of all three couldn't shrivel vital organs. "Yes. I see how it is."

There was a slightly awkward silence after the bearer of bad news left to hunt down another martini.

Lainie cleared her throat. "You know, Alexander Bennett is casting soon for the autumn season at the Metronome. I'm happy to put in a good word."

Lily tried not to visibly cringe. Now she was being

thrown a pity bone by the kind-hearted and far more professionally popular. Brilliant.

"Well, don't kick her when she's down, darling," Richard drawled. "I think her evening has taken enough of a curve without having Bennett inflicted on her, as well."

That did draw a small smile from her. "Thanks," she said to Lainie. "Couldn't hurt. Although I'm having a bit of a…PR issue at the moment."

Lainie seemed to be trying to find a way to phrase it delicately. "I did notice you've been providing a bit of light relief from all the important but depressing news that people should actually be reading."

Lily sighed. "As long as it's benefitting someone."

"If it helps, I think it's benefitting your current show at least. The room is buzzing."

"I've noticed."

"Not much fun when the arrows are all pointing in your direction? I think you've temporarily dethroned Richard. Although he has an interview next Friday, and I don't think he's ever got through an hour at the BBC without using the words *fucking* and *moron*, so that's bound to result in at least one unfortunate headline."

"I'm standing right here." Richard's voice was mild.

"I know. Your hand is on my butt." Lainie looked at her astutely. "I know it can be difficult trying to tune out the criticism—"

Richard's hand came up to tweak Lainie's ear. "I'm not sure you're really in a position to give advice on dealing with bad press. You could stand under the Shaftesbury Memorial Fountain and burn the national flag, and Rupert Murdoch's minions would still print 'Isn't she sweet.'" He brushed his lips against her temple. "If

I remember correctly, Tig, your impressive ability to con the British media into overlooking your faults is the reason we've somehow ended up sharing a wardrobe."

"Careful." Lainie put her hand over his. "If you keep showering me with these excessive compliments, we're going to nauseate everyone in the hotel."

"Tig?" Lily asked.

Lainie's cheeks turned the same shade as her hair. "Tigger."

Lily's gaze moved to the sleek red ponytail. "Because of your hair?" Which was not orange, but—well. Men.

"Um. No. It's because I—"

"Bounce." Richard grinned properly for the first time, which completely transformed his angular, brooding face. "She likes to bounce on…things."

"Richard."

"Tig."

Lainie buried her nose in her cocktail glass, hiding her glowing cheeks behind it, and Lily produced a hasty cough.

"How convenient." The new voice was strident and mocking, managing to cut through the drone of conversation around them like a buzz saw. "Two of my most profitable headliners posing in one picture frame."

The man who joined their circle was on the latter side of middle age, lean and silver-haired with piercing eyes and a contemptuous mouth.

Richard reluctantly removed his gaze from his wife to look at him, equally coolly. "If you're going to interrupt a private conversation, you might as well introduce yourself."

"Zach Byrne." He didn't offer a handshake. Wisely, he also didn't venture near Richard with the air kisses that half the guests in the room seemed to prefer. "Editor-in-chief of *London Celebrity*."

Lily stiffened, all lingering amusement doused. Lainie's eyes narrowed, and Richard murmured sardonically, "Well, they do say that admitting your problem is the first step back to a decent life."

The Burned by *London Celebrity* club obviously had a wide membership.

"We're just missing your patron," Byrne said to Lily. His lips twisted. "Did I say 'patron'? I'm sorry. As I age, I tend to mix up my words."

Richard lifted a brow. "That would at least *partly* explain the garbage you print."

Byrne's attention didn't waver from Lily. "I meant 'director.' No sign of Savage, I see. I'm surprised he's not here. Keeping up appearances. Keep trying to scrub the shit off the family name."

"I'm sure you can think of plenty more lies and innuendo without requiring his actual presence."

"From where I'm standing, I'm not seeing anything that needs a retraction."

"Do you see your name on an invitation from where you're standing? Because I'm fairly sure you didn't get one."

"Interesting tone. Apparently pre-production at the Queen Anne doesn't include media training."

"Why exactly are you here?"

"Our theatre critic was mysteriously left off the guest list. I rectified the omission for the public good. Even stopped by personally, just to show there's no hard feelings on that score."

"'The public good?'" Lily repeated. She looked at his champagne flute. "Drinking alcohol paid for by a man you seem to have some kind of petty personal vendetta against is somehow benefitting the public?"

"It's always been the responsibility of journalists—"

"Taking wild liberties with the definition of *journalism* there."

"—to keep bloated egos in check. If there weren't social commentary, people like the Savages would get away with murder."

Lainie coughed. "Is it just me or is this conversation heading into the realms of *The Perils of Pauline*?"

"If Byrne was connected to Savage & Byrne, the most spectacularly unsuccessful production company in West End history," Richard said, as if Byrne weren't standing right in front of him, "one of the revenge plays might be a better reference. The moral is usually that an obsessive persecution complex leads to multiple people being skewered. However, I assume he's not a complete sociopath as well as a bad writer, so hopefully he'll cling to the cliché that the pen is mightier than the sword."

"Really?" Byrne jerked his thumb at Richard. "Someone voluntarily invited *him* to a party?"

Lainie patted her husband's hand. "Never mind. I still like you."

Byrne smiled humourlessly. "My father invested everything into that company. Johnny Savage extorted everything *out* of that company. We ended up penniless, and the Savages continue to act like the cocks of the walk. Luc Savage built his business with dirty money, profiting off others' hard work and naive trust." His eyes returned to Lily's face and he put a certain emphasis on the word *naive*. "I don't think he ought to get a completely free ride. Do you?"

Lainie frowned. "Johnny Savage?"

"Cameron Savage's father." Richard's very blue eyes were shaded with cynicism. "The black mark on the family name. We all have one. Most of us have several."

"No," Byrne said. "We do not *all* have one. There are actually entire families of decent, moral people."

"Possibly." Richard didn't sound impressed. "But I think you've scotched any chance your family had to that claim."

"My conscience is clear. I doubt if Luc Savage can say the same."

This was the first Lily had heard of any of this. By the sounds of it, Luc's snotty reaction to her father's business practices was even more uncalled for, but she didn't have to consider before replying. "Whatever Johnny Savage did or didn't do, it's not a reflection on Luc. He's honest—" uncomfortably so "—and hard-working." Troublingly so. Unequivocally, she returned Byrne's cold gaze. "People aren't genetically programmed to repeat their grandparents' mistakes."

Or their parents' mistakes.

His patrician features were derisive. "I almost feel sorry for you."

"If you hadn't grossly abused your position, I might say the same."

Byrne shook his head. "If the Savages and their… associates—" he might as well have just said *playmates* "—choose to behave in ways that increase our website traffic on a daily basis, I'm hardly going to look a gift horse in the mouth. A little recompense is due." He drained his glass and saluted her with it. "Best of luck for opening night. I'm reserving plenty of space for the review."

As she watched him stride away, Lainie's opinion

was succinct. "What a dick." She tugged on Richard's tie. "Is he the slimebag who headed the exposé about your father?"

Richard was playing with the end of her ponytail. He tugged back. "I think that was his less bitter but totally moronic predecessor who shagged the Minister of Agriculture."

"Education," Lainie and Lily corrected at the same time.

Richard's expression was priceless. "You know, it's amazing how much you can get done if you don't read the intimate details of other people's sex lives in constant, minute detail." To Lily, he said blandly, "This profession is also a lot easier if you don't get bogged down in the social media shit."

"Oh, I believe you."

Lainie checked her watch. "We should probably get going. But in a totally sincere, non-dick way, best of luck for Hell Week and break a leg on opening night."

"Are you coming?"

"I am. Richard's doing another run at the Globe."

"Of course."

"I always found that was the worst part about having friends in the theatre. You can never go to each other's opening nights because you're working the same hours a few streets over."

That was true; Trix was gutted that she was going to miss Lily's debut, but you didn't hand over to an understudy unless you were physically unable to move, speak or get out of bed. She'd promised to come to the after-party.

Richard touched Lainie's lower back to nudge her in the direction of the doors, seemingly itching to get out of there, but before they were swallowed by a sea of silk and diamonds, he turned back. "I wouldn't expect a rave review from Byrne's paper unless you justifiably snap after tech week and beat Savage senseless with your curtain call roses, but you wouldn't have scored principal billing if you weren't capable." A faint smile appeared in his eyes. "Personally, I'd rather decapitate myself with a blunt teaspoon than work with Savage again, but he knows what he's doing. And he's more businessman than artist. He thinks and acts with the success of the production in mind."

So people kept telling her.

Richard tucked his wife's hand through the crook of his elbow. "Prove them wrong. It's always more entertaining to win over the sceptics than to come in as crowd favourite. And one tip: play to the public, not the critics. They've paid a lot of money, they're out for a good time, and once that curtain is up and they're caught in the plot, most of them will be backing you."

Lily watched them leave, a little wistfully. Their minds were clearly moving to the night ahead; they were so engrossed in one another that they didn't notice cameras turning in their direction, recording intimate glances and lingering touches.

Finding somewhere to stash her glass, she went to join the queue for the bathroom. When she'd washed her hands, she came back out into the plush hallway and paused beside a statue of Apollo to adjust a loose strap on her shoe. Snatches of laughter and joking conversation drifted around the corner from the men's room.

"...bit out of character for Savage."

"Hell, what's the point in having your own theatre if you can't install a few little treats for yourself?"

"She can audition for me anytime she likes. Lucky bastard."

She remained hunched over her foot for a second, then straightened and shook out her skirt. Leaning beside the wall sconce, she exchanged stares with stone Apollo. "You're the god of the plague. Think you can manage a ninety-degree angle with one of those arrows?"

Luc stood in front of the fireplace, watching Lily wander restlessly around his lounge. She stroked the spine of a novel in one of the inbuilt bookshelves that lined the walls before moving on to touch the wooden frame of a landscape. She'd already done a rapid circuit of the entire ground floor, drunk the cup of peppermint tea he'd given her, and turned on the TV.

She offered him a poor attempt at a smile. "If this was my house, I don't think I'd ever go out."

"Shame about those annoying things like food and mortgages and vitamin D," he agreed, and stepped out of the way to let her pace past him.

He could imagine this being her house. He could imagine waking up every morning in her mews flat. The fact that he could clearly imagine both of those things was either a sign that the mammoth task of getting the QA up and running had tipped him over the edge, or—

She rounded the coffee table on her next circuit and didn't see the footstool. He jerked forward and caught her before she smacked her head on the corner of the table, twisting so that they both landed on the couch. The fall knocked the wind out of her; she wheezed and accidentally caught him in the ribs with her elbow.

Or he was in love with her.

She was too young for him, she was contracted to his company, she was probably going to knock him unconscious at some point, and he was completely in love with her. He'd known in the hospital, when he'd been sitting in the empty waiting room, listening to the muted footsteps in the corridor, trying to keep an iron fist around his mind, and he'd looked up to see her standing there. Looking edgy and uncomfortable, and like his only source of comfort. The realisation hadn't knocked him sideways in the best dramatic tradition. It had just slotted neatly into place, a sense of recognition, acknowledging it at last.

If he followed the playbook, and in most of his friends' footsteps, he was now supposed to see his recently regained single life bowing out for good and run like hell in the opposite direction.

He'd actually *missed* her when he'd been caught up at the theatre this evening, for only a couple of hours. She made him happier than he'd been in a long time. Ever, maybe. He liked his life—and his own company—a hell of a lot more when she was in it. He was done running away from this.

Lily, however, looked as if one false move—or one more run-in with the ugly side of the press—would see her bolting towards Heathrow.

It had always been in his nature to push for what he wanted—and he'd never wanted anything as badly as he wanted her. This was the first time he was so wary about pushing too far, too fast, that he was holding back. He was fighting his own instincts.

He also had a company of people whose immediate livelihood depended on a solid opening, so on a purely practical level, he really couldn't afford to send one of his principals into an emotional tailspin this close to curtain.

She was a very good actor on the stage, but when she wasn't reading from a script, every movement and every word that came out of her mouth seemed to stem from instinct. Occasionally with unfortunate results. He saw the way she looked at him, and the way she reacted when she thought he was hurting. And her aversion to the outside circumstances bordered on the obsessive, so he doubted if she would have set foot in his house if she weren't invested.

But life wasn't a film. Problems didn't disappear and "The End" wasn't emblazoned across a lingering embrace the moment people succumbed to the inevitable and found the right moment to verbalise it.

He wasn't thrilled about the increased media attention on anything except the play, but he found it a lot easier to ignore than Lily did. He did understand, to an extent, why she was struggling. If their relationship affected anyone's career, it was likely to be hers. He was more established than she was, and there was a double standard to contend with.

He doubted if his own attitude towards her before they'd met had helped.

Despite that, she was blowing it out of proportion. She was stealing scenes from Freddy at every rehearsal and steadily climbing her way to secondary lead status. If she held out through tech week and put in the opening night performance he expected, she was extremely likely to secure another role in the West End after the run ended.

She kept reading all the bullshit she should be ignoring by now, and he didn't think that was the only thing bothering her.

She still lay sprawled half under him. When she'd re-inflated her lungs, he propped his arm against the back of the couch so he could see her face. "Did something happen tonight that I should know about? Because you're never the most restful person, but you were a little… overly cheerful at the Savoy for someone who was drinking fruit juice, and ever since we got back you've been acting like you're in a dentist's waiting room."

She pinched the end of her nose. "Not exactly. You missed seeing Richard Troy and Lainie Graham."

"Reason to be grateful to my contractor after all."

"I like Lainie."

"I was referring to the only actor who made directing Bridget Barclay seem like a holiday in Bora Bora, not the unfortunate woman who has to live with him."

"Richard seemed nice enough, in a brusque way. And at least he never broke his contract."

"If Troy had quit, I wouldn't have sued. I would have broken out the party poppers."

There was a short silence.

"You also missed the encounter with the editor of *London Celebrity*, which was probably fortunate for all concerned."

He'd been tracing his fingers up and down the length of her thigh, but at that, his hand flattened and his grip tightened. "Zach Byrne was there?"

"He was there, he'd had a bit too much to drink and he was very—Hamlet."

He realised he was squeezing her leg and relaxed his hold with a murmured apology. "I'm guessing the conversation centred around the main reason I wasn't on his Christmas card list."

"Yes, it did." Lily pushed up on her elbows. "It maybe should have come up in an earlier, private conversation? I've never exactly been popular with sites like *London Celebrity*, but things have been getting a little intense in that corner."

"*Gutter* would be a more appropriate word. There's a lot of useful, occasionally even responsible reporting in this country. Then there's *London Celebrity*, which was absolute trash even before Byrne started using it as a personal hit list." Luc sat up. "I ought to have talked to you about my grandfather." He watched her closely. "To be honest, I'm surprised you didn't know. You're usually impressively well informed. Jack certainly knows. He's been needling my father about Johnny for years. And you spend so much time reading that garbage I assumed you would be aware who's slinging most of the mud."

Lily dragged her tangled hair back and held it in a ponytail. "Was that you making a very subtle point?"

He couldn't completely repress his frustration. "The point is, stop reading the bloody tabloids."

"It's probably a little easier to ignore when, with one exception, you're starting to get just the faintest hint of a pat on the back, while I look like an opportunistic homewrecker who's sleeping her way up the ladder."

"I'm aware of the double standard. And before you say anything, in no way condoning it."

She opened her mouth to retort, but suddenly sighed and covered her face with her hands. Bringing up her knees, she rested her head against them, her loosened hair falling forward. She was quiet for almost a minute before she raised her head. "Sorry."

Luc moved his arm, sliding it beneath her legs, and scooped her into his lap. He wove his fingers through her hair, feeling the silky texture. "So am I. I didn't mean to snap."

"I don't want to argue with you." Lily tugged his tie loose and his top button open. "I especially don't want to argue with you over Zach Byrne." To the hairs on his chest, she said, "It's just—a blur at the moment. Everything's changed so much in such a short time that I'm still trying to work out where I am now."

He found a tight knot in her neck and moved his thumb in massaging circles. "If you figure it out, clue me in. I could use a few directions myself."

"Ironic."

"Incorrigible."

"Are you planning to do anything about Byrne?"

"Dad and I have both offered the family financial compensation at different times. Byrne is far too bitter to accept it. I understand *why*; Johnny's behaviour towards Alan Byrne was atrocious. It's a case of too little, too late where money is concerned—and hell, *I* wouldn't have touched Johnny's bank accounts, even if he'd left anything in them, so I don't blame Byrne for rejecting what he wants to believe are Johnny's dirty profits. It's the way he's choosing to vent his anger that's the problem."

"Are you going to take legal action?"

"If it gets any worse where you're concerned, yes. Although even if we won a case against him, there are countless ways to insinuate without crossing the line into actual slander, so…"

"So, basically, as long as he's editor, his paper is

going to continue painting you in the worst possible light."

"And dragging you down with me? Pretty much."

"Great." She shifted on his lap and their combined weight bumped the remote control she'd left on the cushions. The muted volume came back on, loudly. Broadcasting a familiar voice. "Shit."

She grabbed for the remote and aimed it at *Knightsbridge*, and he swiped it from her hand and held it out of reach.

"Luc," real-life Lily said at the same time her screen character made a sort of purring noise and slunk up the aisle of a church. "Change the channel."

"I'm making amends. I made snap judgements about your work on this show without a fair trial."

"Seriously, change the channel."

He curved his hand around her forehead, holding her back as she tried to make another grab for the remote. "I've told you repeatedly that you need to have more confidence. Even if you think something was shit, *you* can't say that. Own your work." He watched the screen over her squirming. Screen-Lily was talking to the co-star he recognised from that fucking awful day at CTV.

"And I heard you. Self-confidence. More power to me. Swell." Lily looked at the scene again and groaned. "But I remember this episode *very* clearly and in about fifteen seconds that suspender belt is coming off. What happens next barely made it past the censor board. I do not want to watch my fake orgasms with the man who's providing me with real ones, and I really don't think you want to see that either."

"I've directed a sex scene or two throughout the past

couple of decades. I do get the difference between fiction and reality."

"Is that right?"

"That I understand the concept of acting? Yeah, I think I've just about got it down."

Lily raised her hands in surrender. "Okay."

They watched in silence, until Luc said scathingly, "A *baptismal font*? Sacrilegious *and* uncomfortable. Neil Forrester's writing?"

"I think so."

On screen, her co-star shoved his hands beneath her sequinned dress and tore it open. The bastard lowered his mouth to her breast.

Luc lowered the remote and switched to the weather channel.

Lily twisted in his lap to look at him.

"I need to make sure it's not going to snow tomorrow. The schedule is packed."

"I told you it would be weird."

In bed, in the early hours of the morning when they should have been asleep and were emphatically not, he settled his body more comfortably on hers, enjoying the softness and warmth of her and the slick glide of their skin. Her thighs gripped his sides; he could feel the glancing touch of her feet against his legs.

Her heels pulled up and dug in when he slowed his thrusts and angled deeper, and her broken breath fanned the side of his neck. Against the chaos they'd made of the sheets, their entwined fingers gripped tighter.

He freed one hand to trace down over her breast and ribs, relearning the silky curves of her hip and stomach, brushing against himself as he found her with his thumb. She jerked the hand that was still linked with his, sliding their arms up towards the scattered pillows, and arched beneath him. He was rapidly becoming addicted to the sounds she made.

When she finally shuddered and clamped down on him, he groaned and ground his hips into hers, searching out her mouth with his. She kissed him back, sliding both arms around him, her short nails digging into his shoulder blades as the tension in his body locked ferociously and his brain went into blinding white stasis, registering nothing but extreme pleasure.

They lay in a tangled, breathless, sweaty heap, his lips nuzzling at her ear, his body a dead weight on hers. He was half-aware that he was crushing her into the bed, but couldn't gather the energy to move until her legs loosened their grip and went slack around his hips. When his heart stopped trying to shove forcibly through his chest, he shifted to her side.

Gently, he rubbed his knuckles over her arm, playing with her fingers, lifting them to his mouth. "You can talk to me, you know," he murmured, and felt a hint of tension return to her body.

"I think the dirty talk usually comes a bit earlier in the proceedings. But if you're that set on it, give me a second. I think I forgot how to make a sentence even before you rolled me into the headboard." She stretched, sweeping her sweat-dampened hair away from her neck. "Sexy. You. Fuck. Huge. Harder. Me."

He couldn't help smiling. "Lily."

The forced lightness in her expression faded. She slid her hand from his shoulder to his chest, sending sensation shooting through him. "It's just—so easy when I'm with you. And then I remember that other people and other things exist, and it all gets a little more complicated."

Luc studied her conflicted features. "Lily, *did* something else happen tonight?"

Her dark eyes met his.

After a brief hesitation, she shook her head, and when she tugged him down to kiss him again, he tried to ignore the trickle of unease that edged through his belly.

If the past few weeks had seemed like a blur, tech week was like being caught in *The Wizard of Oz* tornado, with people and props and sets flying about her in a whirlwind. Lily stood in the wings, watching Luc and David slowly drive Freddy and Dylan demented, making one scene adjustment after another. Every day, the play evolved into something a little bit different, a little bit better. Sometimes significantly worse, then they backtracked and tried a different approach. It was exactly as Jocasta had predicted: fireworks from David, icicles from Luc. Backstage was chaotic, the dressing rooms were already a mess, and the construction crew was putting final touches on the foyer.

They were almost there.

Luc came offstage, clipboard in hand. He surveyed her from headpiece to buckled shoes, and she swept out her voluminous skirts and curtseyed.

"Practising for your standing ovation?"

"You think I'm going to get one?"

"If you turn in another performance like this morning, I'd say you've got a shot." A small smile lit up his tired eyes. "You're buzzing."

"I love this." She swished from side to side. "I feel

like I just drank about sixteen shots of espresso. Who needs actual caffeine?"

"The stage bug is a lifelong disease." His expression was torn between amusement and affection. "I'm glad to see you're the type where the pressure translates into adrenaline, not a nervous breakdown. Long may it last."

"And the vocals?"

"Marilyn has left the building." He stepped back out of swatting reach of her fan, and sobered. "Seriously, I couldn't have hoped for better. Jocasta was actually smiling this morning. You should be very proud."

She felt a flush of warmth in her cheeks, the glow adding to the fizz of excitement in the pit of her stomach. "I am." She gestured around them. "And look at this place."

"I've been looking at this place for months. I can see fifty-pound notes layered over every square foot."

"Luc."

He relented and looked out of the wings as well, where the state-of-the-art lighting system illuminated the huge stage and the glimpse of rising balconies, beautifully restored carvings and the gold dome ceiling. "It's not bad, is it?"

"Not bad? It's fucking amazing." She touched her palm to the wall. "*You* did this."

"Me and about two hundred builders, restorers and architects."

She smiled at him. "I'm so proud of you."

He almost reached for her; she saw the muscles flex in his shoulder and his arm partly rose before he swore under his breath. "I'm not kissing you at work."

"I should hope not." She adjusted her headpiece. "I'm the future Virgin Queen. I have a reputation to uphold."

Not *much* of one, but still…

She was *not* going to worry about the reviews right now. Performance first, then panic about the critical reception. Enjoy having this job before stressing about ever finding another one.

Luc checked his watch. "I have a meeting with Maria. You're back on in ten minutes. Don't miss your cue."

"Have I ever?"

"You have been known to make an unexpected entrance. I'm still reeling from the impact of the first one."

By the time they were halfway through the afternoon dress rehearsal, Luc's responses were getting sharper and more monosyllabic. He was unusually impatient when Margo made a rare error and Lily caught him raising a hand to his temple.

When David finally held up his script and called time for the day, Lily gathered her skirts in one hand and joined Luc where he stood in the orchestra pit, making last notes into a spreadsheet.

"Here." She held out a bottle of water and a box of painkillers.

"Hmm?" Luc automatically took the water she thrust under his nose, but barely looked away from the iPad he held in the crook of his arm. "Thanks, sweetheart."

Lily blinked. If there was ever a sign he was paying no attention to her whatsoever… She shot a glance over her shoulder to make sure no one else had heard that. Their relationship was the worst-kept secret in the West End—there was so much media attention now that a distant cousin in Ireland had called a couple of days ago to get the scoop firsthand—but they were at least *trying* to keep things professional in the theatre.

She cleared her throat. "Could you look at me for a second, please?"

He made another note, lifting the chilled water bottle to press it against his forehead. "What?"

"Eye contact. Could you make some?"

He finally looked up, frowning, and she saw the lines of pain around his mouth and the strain in his eyes.

"You have a migraine."

"I have a headache." He checked the time again. "And back-to-back meetings."

"I went through a stage where I got hormonal migraines every month. I recognise the face. If you're not in full-blown pain yet, you're heading that way. You should have been lying down in a dark room an hour ago."

"I don't have time for a migraine. I can't reschedule these meetings."

"I don't think you can reschedule a migraine, either."

"It's not a migraine. It's a headache. You don't look like you're underwater, and I don't feel like tearing my head off with my bare hands." Luc noticed the box of painkillers she was still holding. "I'll take a couple of tablets, drink some water and get a taxi. It'll be fine."

"Luc." His chief financial officer, a striking grey-haired woman whose name Lily couldn't remember, appeared in the stalls, looking impatient. "The meeting with Hannigan and Fischer is in twenty minutes."

"Right." Luc winced when his phone rang. Lily was beginning to hear his ringtone in her dreams. He answered it, his eyes still shadowed with pain. "Savage. Hold on a second." He covered the speaker with his thumb. "Two more days and press night is over, and we'll all be on a more regular schedule." Even with a headache, his voice was different when he spoke to her. Warmer.

"You seriously think you can make what I assume are important financial decisions with a migraine?"

"It's not a migraine," he said again, and she shook her head. "I have to go." He ignored his CFO's foot-tapping. "Are you—"

"I'll go back to my flat tonight." She looked at him for a few seconds longer. "If you can still see well enough after the meetings—"

"I'll be there."

Three words she'd heard countless times in the past. The magical promise, confidently spoken. Easily broken.

Lily was lying on her bed, propped up against every pillow she owned and trying to concentrate on the TV, when a FaceTime call came through from her mother. She was always happy to see Vanessa's face, even on a digital screen with a bad connection.

"Hi, hon." Vanessa's hair had changed colour since Lily had last seen her and was now jet black. Her movements were slow and fragmented, and there was a strange line bisecting her left cheek. "You look tired."

"Long day. You look blurry. Where are you?"

"Sydney."

The camera went out completely then, which was probably fortunate since Lily was fairly sure the feeling in her stomach was reflected in her changing expression. "Australia? I thought you said Austria."

"I was in Austria, but I got an offer to do a last-minute performance here in Sydney. Some stock magnate's birthday party. You wouldn't believe how much she's prepared to pay." The visual came back; Vanessa rolled her eyes expressively. "Some people have money to burn."

"That's great." Lily wound a loose thread in the quilt around her index finger. "When is it?"

"Saturday."

"You're not coming to opening night, then."

"No. I'm sorry, darling. The guest list at this event— my agent thinks it could open up a whole new market for me." Her mother rubbed at her nose. "But I'll be back in London in a few weeks and I'll definitely come to see you then. Every night that I'm there."

It was a little harder to smile this time. "Sure. That'll be great."

"I mean it. A few weeks, a month tops, and I'm there. I'm so excited for you. I know how long you've wanted this." Vanessa pursed her lips. "And from what I've been reading, we have a lot to catch up on. Luc Savage?"

The thread around Lily's finger broke before it could cut off her circulation. She tried to will away the heat creeping up her neck before it could appear in her cheeks. "Yeah. Well. That's been a bit—unexpected."

"Dating your director? I'll say." Vanessa arched a brow. "Try a complete turn-around on your usual attitude. When you were five years old, you used to stand in my bedroom doorway, watching me get ready for dates and *tsking*. Until you started coming home from your dad's house with bags of sweets you'd won playing poker, I thought I'd given birth to Queen Victoria. What happened to the golden rules?"

They'd fractured on an antique desk and shattered into pieces in a hospital waiting room.

Lily could only shake her head, unsmiling, and the trace of sarcasm disappeared from her mother's voice.

"I met him once. For about five excruciating minutes at an opening. Small talk and questions on my side, zero personality and monosyllabic answers on his. It was like having a conversation with Siri."

"Maybe he had a migraine," Lily muttered.

"I hope you're not getting in over your—" Vanessa turned her head, and Lily heard the muffled sound of another voice. "Shoot. I have to go. Call me on Sunday night, okay? I want to hear all about the first show. Jack's going, I hope?"

Lily kept her face carefully neutral. "He says he is."

"Good. That's good." The other voice spoke again and her mother blew a hasty kiss at the camera. "Got to run. Love you."

The screen returned to the desktop before Lily could respond.

Slowly, she flipped the leather cover closed and returned the iPad to the dressing table. She was reaching for the TV remote when the front door buzzed. It was just after nine, too early to be Luc. Frowning, she got up and pulled on her dressing gown, wrapping it across her chest as she padded down the hallway to check the peephole.

She took one look and immediately fumbled for the lock.

Luc was leaning against the wall with his eyes closed. He'd been pale earlier; he was now a nice shade of green.

Without opening his eyes, he said tightly, as if he didn't want to open his mouth, "I'm—"

"I can see." She slipped her arm around his waist,

taking his weight as she tugged him away from the wall. "Come on."

His hand came up to the side of her head. "You can say 'I told you so' at any time." He was still speaking as if his teeth were stuck together.

"I never say 'I told you so.'" Lily kicked the front door shut and steered him towards the bedroom. "I don't know if you've noticed, but people tend to find that annoying." His face was alarmingly close in colour to a courgette. "Bedroom or bathroom?"

He swallowed before he answered. "Bedroom. I just need to lie down."

She helped him to the bed, then hastily turned off the TV and the lights, leaving only a lamp on in the hallway so that neither of them walked into a wall if he needed the bathroom. He sprawled across the mattress, his arm shielding his eyes, and she stood looking down at him. Her heart twisted; it was a reaction that was almost physical.

Carefully, she unlaced his shoes and tugged them off, then undid his belt and pulled it free, and went to work on his shirt buttons. His stomach was taut above the waistband of his trousers; all his muscles were locked tight in defence against the pain. She stroked his warm skin with the backs of her fingers. "Can you lift up for a second?"

The protesting grunt came from deep in his chest, but he eased up enough that she could take his shirt off completely. He caught her hand as she went to put it on the chair. "Lily." She could hardly see him in the dim light, but his grip was tight. "Thanks. I'm sorry about this."

She squeezed his hand. "I'll be right back."

In the bathroom, she wet a clean flannel. She brought it back to the bed and climbed onto the pillow mountain behind him, and Luc rolled over to lie between her legs, resting his cheek against her thigh. He hooked an arm under her bent knee and mumbled something unintelligible when she pressed the cold flannel against his forehead.

"How bad?" she asked quietly, stroking his hair.

"Ready to rip my head off anytime now."

He fell asleep after about twenty minutes, heavy against her legs. Lily sat in the near-dark, watching where the strip of light from the hallway touched his cheek. Even in sleep, he wasn't relaxed, and she rubbed his back gently, trying not to wake him.

She leaned her head against the pillows and closed her eyes, listening to him breathe.

At some point, she must have fallen asleep, because she woke to the whisper of her name in her ear and lips brushing hers. She opened one eye. The room was still dimly lit; she could see a glimmer of very grey light through the crack in the curtains. The lamp in the hallway had been turned off.

There was a crick in her neck. Kneading at the muscles there, she turned in the circle of Luc's arm and blinked up at him. He was sitting on the edge of the bed, dressed, smiling down at her as he played with her hair.

"You're up," she said, and yawned. "How do you feel?"

"Lucky, grateful and intensely sorry that I have an early start and can't express the first two emotions properly." He bent and kissed her again, his mouth lingering on hers. His fingers stole underneath her pyjama top to caress her hip. "Thank you."

"You didn't have to thank me the first time." She found it easier to fix her gaze on the base of his neck, where his pulse beat, than to meet his eyes. "I think it comes with the job description."

"I've read your contract," he said drily. "I'm fairly sure there was no clause that mentioned sitting up half the night with the semi-comatose."

"Yeah. Well." She put her hand over his where it rested on her waist. "Are you sure you're feeling okay now?"

"Completely back to normal."

His phone rang.

Lily sighed and pushed up on her elbows, dislodging his hold. She couldn't keep the edge of irony from her words. "So I see."

Chapter Twelve

Lily barely recognised herself.

She stood in front of the full-length mirror, smoothing her hands over her hips, following the line of the thick brocade gown. The heavy gold velvet moulded over her corset and led into the stiff white ruff that doubled as a chin rest. The red wig was pinned so tightly that it was pulling up her forehead. She had to dig her fingers underneath and create a bit of give to avoid looking permanently shocked. She also had the cheekbones she'd always wanted, thanks to Leo, who had remained characteristically silent but overdrawn her eyeliner when she'd snuck Trix into the conversation.

She turned at a tap on the door. "Come in."

The vibration of voices and flurried movement in the hallway and adjoining dressing rooms rose to a loud rumble. Padma came in with a clipboard tucked into her armpit and her arms loaded with flowers.

"Thirty-minute warning, Your Highness." She smiled at Lily as she handed over three bouquets and a wrapped parcel. "You're now in social media lockdown. Phone on silent, no internet, no psyching yourself out. House rules."

Lily set the flowers and gift box down on her vanity table. She stroked the velvety petal of a red rose. "Did someone think I needed a reminder of that rule?"

Luc had addressed the whole company an hour ago, thanking them for fulfilling his every expectation—with a note of sarcasm directed at Dylan—but it was management policy to leave the cast alone to focus in the final stretch before curtain. He had to do the pre-show networking before he took his place in the lighting box to watch the first public performance. Before she'd come downstairs, he'd touched the back of his finger to one of her visibly trembling hands and said, "You've worked incredibly hard, you had one hiccup in the final rehearsal and recovered from it well, and you thrive under pressure. You've made this role your own. You can do this. Unless I see you checking Twitter before or during the show, in which case this is your understudy's big night."

"Luc may have mentioned something." Padma ticked off something on her clipboard, then looked up and winked. "I believe his exact words were 'If there's something electronic in her hand, ask her how she feels about a new role picking popcorn out of seat cushions.'"

"Sounds about right." Lily checked the card on the red roses and ran her fingers over Luc's name. "I left the iPad at home and I'm about to turn off my phone."

Padma gave her a thumbs-up and kept jotting things down on her sheaf of papers. "Final wardrobe check in fifteen minutes. First cue in twenty-five."

"Got it." She was still holding on to Luc's card, and Padma tucked the clipboard back under her arm and looked at her understandingly.

"Nervous?"

"Eighty percent excited, twenty percent absolutely fucking terrified."

"Enjoy the excitement, use the fear." Padma nodded at the open bottle of water on the table. "And don't drink too much water, because in that costume you're going to need four extra hands and a pair of pliers before you can use the loo."

"You're not kidding," Margo said from the open doorway. She gripped the wide skirts of her gown to manoeuvre inside the room. "It took me a quarter of an hour just to get out of the stall. If you haven't gone yet, I think you'll have to wait until intermission."

"Right. I'll leave you to it." Padma paused to straighten Margo's bodice, then saluted them with her pen. "Break a leg, ladies."

The noise level outside was still rising. People would be taking their seats now. The paparazzi had been circling the red carpet since late afternoon. The front-of-house staff had already reported the arrival of several of London's toughest critics.

Lily pressed her palm against her tightly-bound ribs and took as deep a breath as the corset would allow. Level of terror: creeping up towards an even fifty percent.

Margo touched her arm. "You're a few hours away from critical acclaim. This is the first night of a long, successful career in the theatre. And it's the oasis between the rehearsal slog and the realisation of exactly how many more times we're going to have to say these lines. This is the fun part."

Lily exhaled. "Thanks."

Margo grinned. "We've got this."

"Amen, murderous cousins." Freddy stuck her dark

head into the dressing room and peered around. "Is this the royal gathering? Or is it half-sisters only?"

Lily laughed. It was difficult to catastrophize when Freddy was around. "Come on in."

"All one big dysfunctional family here." Margo shifted to make room for her. Luc's architects had been reasonably generous with the dressing room space, but their clothing filled most of it.

"Cheers." Freddy lowered herself to a stool, holding on to her waist. "Dylan's in my room and if he makes one more suggestion about consummating our fake marriage, I'm going to have to cut straight to my second costume change. This dress is so tight that I'm just not sure what would *happen* to the vomit." Her gaze fell on the collection of flowers. "Hey, nice haul." She touched the bow on the yellow roses, then noticed the gift box. "*Yes.* Luc's sent down his first-night presents. He gives the best 'thanks for doing everything I said' goodies. Last time, it was top-shelf bubbly and a *very* generous shopping trip to Harrods. My shoe collection wept with gratitude."

"Another pair of Louboutins is in your future." Margo adjusted her bodice again. "Champagne and gift cards are Luc's trademark."

A heavy bass beat shook the wall to their left, and Freddy's head shot up. "That little fucker. He's got my iPod again." Leaning over, she thumped her fist against the panelling. *"Waitely. For the last time—paws off!"*

"'What is she but a foul contending rebel, and graceless traitor to her loving lord? I am ashamed that women are so simple.'" The quote from *The Taming of the Shrew* was muffled but audible.

"Try Dogberry's speech instead, dickwad," Freddy

snapped back through the wall. "'Masters, remember that I am an ass; though it be not written down, yet forget not that I am an ass.' It's like Shakespeare knew you personally." She rolled her eyes and tapped the wrapped parcel. "Too early to break out the alcohol?"

"I'd say so." Lily leaned towards the mirror to remove a ball of dried mascara from the end of her lashes. "But you can add my bottle to your stash later if you like. I'm still on a booze ban for the duration."

"Cruel and unusual punishment, but it's working. Your vocals are solid." Freddy studied her. "Although, I have to say—hair-wise, red is really not your colour. It's like Wilma Flintstone just discovered static electricity. Is this the least attractive you've ever looked?"

Lily grinned and turned away from the mirror. "I have a long track record of falling off curbs, down stairs and out of bed. When your cheekbone swells right over your eyelid and your bottom lip is hanging past your chin—that's tough competition."

Margo made a startled sound. "Damn. That reminds me, I have to double-check the first scene amendment with David. What time is it?" She twisted to see the clock. "Shit. Shit, shit. See you both up there."

She hoisted up her skirts and went sideways through the door, almost colliding with a group of laughing soldiers on their way to the wings.

Freddy blinked. "Which part of the droopy-lipped Cyclops image reminded her she had to speak to David?" She stood up and accidentally knocked the yellow roses with her elbow. "Oops. Sorry." She caught them before they fell. "Gorgeous. Luc has a great florist."

Lily tore her eyes from the battered copy of the script

that had been lying abandoned on her table for several days now. All of a sudden, her brain was convinced that she'd forgotten every word that was printed in it. "Mmm? Oh. No, the red ones are from Luc."

"Really?" Freddy turned, looking wickedly delighted. "How about that?"

"What?" A slight blush was warming her cheeks already. Whenever Freddy produced that expression, an embarrassing remark was likely to follow.

"Luc has a routine when it comes to gifts. He always gives the principal cast yellow roses. Even when he directed Margo during their relationship: yellow roses." Thoughtfully, Freddy cupped a red bloom between two fingers. "And he gave you red ones. Beautiful, glossy, crimson red." She brought the flower to her nose. Her lips were twitching. "How very interesting."

Clearing her throat, Lily got up and reached for the card on the yellow roses, looking for a distraction. She ripped open the small envelope. "These are from my dad. He's—" The rest of the words fell away as she read the short note.

Looking down at the short, apologetic sentences written by a stranger's hand, she felt almost distant as she separated out her emotions in that moment, examining each one. Disappointment. Resignation. Very little surprise.

Freddy poked the rose back into the bouquet and looked at her with concern. "Problem?"

Carefully, Lily slipped the card back into the envelope and smoothed the torn edges. She tucked it back under the gold ribbon that encircled the wrapped stems. "Not exactly. My father's had to fly to the States on business."

"He's missing your debut?"

"Well, my friend Ash is planning to illegally film the whole thing on his phone, so I guess he can catch the low-res replay."

Freddy ignored the blithe words. Her voice remained serious and her eyes sympathetic. "Sorry."

Lily shook off the simmering disappointment. "So is he. Very. But a lot of people are relying on him. Business comes first."

"Still sucks."

"Yeah." She found her hand playing with the corner of Luc's card again. "It does a bit."

Her phone started vibrating on the table, which reminded her that she needed to turn it off.

"I need to start my vocal warm-up." Freddy squeezed Lily's arm and winked. "See you in the sixteenth century."

Lily reached for her phone. She was about to switch it off when she saw the number of the incoming call. She recognised that number. It contained several repetitions of the numeral six that she'd always found ironically appropriate.

Her stomach twisted.

"Safety checks complete, sets in place, props accounted for, all teams on standby, front of house running like clockwork, every influential critic in the city has been spotted circling the foyer, and no reports of nervous breakdowns in the dressing rooms." David paused for breath, standing by Luc as they both surveyed the final activity on the stage. There was a ruddy flush of exhilaration under his skin. Thousands of people were finding their seats in the stalls beyond, their combined voices and rustling coats and possessions rising into a droning hum. "I think we may yet do this thing." He turned and extended his hand. "Congratulations, mate."

Luc clasped David's hand. "Very much a combined effort. And in a couple of hours, I won't have the slightest hesitation in passing this one into your care—lock, stock, barrel and Waitely."

"When do you start pre-production for the autumn season?"

"Monday."

"The conveyor belt begins."

"For the sake of my mortgage, long may it continue." David stroked his chin. "So Waitely's all mine, huh?"

"Every job has its ugly side."

"David." Margo squeezed past a couple of grips, holding her heavy skirts above her knees to keep the hems from dragging on the floor.

"If you've contracted some sort of illness," David said uncompromisingly, "it had better not be contagious. Because as long as you're conscious, you're going on that stage."

Margo held up a torn-about, sketched-over piece of paper. "I need you to clarify the final amendments to the Tower monologue."

A stagehand walked past, hissing, "Twenty minutes."

"Luc." It was Amelia this time, and at the unusual grimness in her tone, David and Margo broke off their hurried conference.

Luc looked into Amelia's eyes and a jolt of apprehension went right down his spine. There was a certain highly specific expression that nobody ever wanted to see in the face of someone speaking their name. His response came out in a clipped staccato. "Is it my mother?" She'd been in her usual form this afternoon, sitting on his father's lap and issuing a stream of complaints that she was going to miss the opening, but—

"No. It's Lily's father."

For a split second, the tension in his body began to drain; it immediately racketed back. "Jack? What's happened to him?"

"He's had a stroke."

His mind levelled out and went completely blank. Then, flatly, he said, "You've got to be kidding me."

"Hudson Warner just rang. He can't get through to Lily's phone."

"No. I told her to keep it off until after the performance." He felt as if he'd gone on autopilot.

"He's still on the line," Amelia said. "And he wants to speak to you. I've transferred the call to the props office."

Adrenaline started to kick-start Luc's brain again. "*Fuck.*" He bit the word out. It was the only venting of emotion he could allow himself. "Which hospital is he in?"

"He's—"

He didn't even let her finish; he was functioning on instinct and there was only one possible course of action. "Alert Kirsten," he said sharply to David. "Quickly. Tell her she's going on tonight."

"Luc—"

"We're opening with an understudy?" David looked horrified. "On press night?"

"We don't have a bloody choice. And you're in charge as of now."

"What? Where are you—"

"I'm taking Lily to the hospital." He ran through

a rapid-fire mental checklist. "You'll have to change Elizabeth's first cue in the second act. Kirsten's repeatedly had trouble with it in rehearsal; we'll play it safe. Let Magalie and the wardrobe team know. Padma—" He spoke to the hovering, wide-eyed assistant. "Has Kirsten been through hair and makeup?" The answer had better fucking well be yes. He'd run a policy of full understudy preparation for years, ever since one of his Lady Macbeths had come down with violent food poisoning during intermission. He'd rather keep the understudies on a higher pay grade than issue mass refunds of tickets.

"Uh, yes. Yes, she has," Padma stammered.

Margo was looking between them with worried eyes. "Luc. You can't leave. There's an audience out there full of investors and critics and press who are expecting you to be here. You have to be here."

"My active role in this production ends after tonight."

"Yes. *After* tonight." Margo was obviously juggling concern and utter disbelief. "You're expected to be here. We need you here."

The words came from the very heart of him. "Lily will need me more."

"Luc—" Amelia tried again.

Margo's eyes held his, and finally, he saw the glitter of recognition and resignation. "I see." There was a wealth of meaning in the words. She added softly, "And you need to be with her."

It was as if a final door was closing between them, a sort of mutual silent apology for everything they had never been to each other.

"Yes," he said. "I need to be with her."

"Luc." Amelia finally broke through with sheer exasperation. "Luc. He's dead."

He was very aware of his own heartbeat in that instant. "What?"

She visibly swallowed. "It happened about an hour ago. He was on a flight to Chicago. There was a doctor on board who did everything she could, but apparently he died within minutes. They couldn't resuscitate him." She hesitated. "He was a fairly elderly man…"

"Where is he now?"

"Luc, he's gone."

"His body." His voice was terse and impatient, and he took a deep breath. "Where have they taken Jack's body?"

"They landed in Chicago about twenty minutes ago. Warner's making arrangements to have his body returned to London on the next available flight."

"Luc." David gestured at the clock. "I'm very sorry to hear about this, but there are two thousand people out there expecting to see a play that's been hyped into the stratosphere, and the curtain is due to go up in fifteen minutes. If we're making changes, we need to make them now. Am I alerting Kirsten?"

Luc stood in silence, breathing slowly in and out, trying to clamp down on his racing mind. She would be shattered. However fragmented her relationship with Jack was, it would devastate her. The cracks in their history could make the loss even more difficult to bear.

And if he did this… If he did this, she would be furious. Absolutely, justifiably furious. He bowed his head, debating, second-guessing his decision. At last—"No."

"No?" Amelia repeated. "But—"

He spoke through the knot of tension in his stomach. "There's nothing Lily can do, and nobody she needs to

support. Her mother's out of the country as well." She
had slipped that piece of news in over breakfast, and
tried to pretend that it hadn't bothered her. "And she's
not close to her father's wife. It'll be hours before the
return flight touches down. She can't even go to—sit
with him yet. This is her shot. If she doesn't appear for
the press tonight, she's out of the reviews, she's probably out of contention for casting negotiation with other
theatres. All the hard work, almost none of the payoff."
Harshly, he made the call. "Don't tell her."

"Luc…" Amelia was shaking her head, but Margo
nodded.

"If there's nothing she can do right now, all you're
doing is sabotaging her future. And we can't open this
level of production with an understudy. It'll undermine
everyone's performance."

Luc shot her a look, then addressed David, Amelia
and Padma. "She's not told until later. I want that order
down the line. Jack Lamprey is a public figure." He
clenched his jaw. "Was a public figure. If this isn't out
in the media already, it's only a matter of time. I want
Lily kept in a bubble tonight. This news does not reach
her. Is that clear?"

David and Padma nodded, but Amelia frowned. "Are
you sure about this, Luc? It's her dad. She has a right
to know."

"Whatever happens onstage, her night is going to
end in pain and grief. She should at least have this."

Amelia took a deep breath. "Okay. I'll put the word
out quietly. You'll tell her? After?"

"Yes. I'll tell her." Luc balled his right hand into a
loose fist. Keeping this from Lily, acting behind her
back on such an intensely personal matter, was a physi-

cal crawling sensation on his skin. It was a betrayal at a fundamental level, but the only thing he could protect now was her career. Her performance tonight would go a long way towards silencing the worst of the industry prejudice. Her career was important to her; it might seem like nothing for a while when she heard about her father, but eventually it would matter to her.

Maria rounded the corner from the back offices in a clatter of heels. "I just heard. Tell me we're not opening with Kirsten."

"Lily doesn't know," Amelia said. "And she won't know until after the show."

Maria's eyes narrowed. "It's out in the press. People will assume she knows." It was as if she had a PR machine tattooed on her forehead; Luc could almost see her inputting the facts and clanking out possible outcomes. "Still works. We can spin the public sympathy vote. Strong work ethic. The show must go on. Kept a stiff upper lip and rocked it anyway. I can use this. No show tomorrow, thank God. We'll have to think about next week. Might be best to pull her for five or six performances. There's a line between brave and callous that you don't want to straddle."

Rolling his eyes, Luc turned away. "I need to speak to Warner, get the facts, ask him not to break the news to Lily. Props office?"

Amelia nodded. As he walked past her, she caught his arm. "Luc," she murmured, "I don't think Lily's going to thank you for this."

He was damn sure she wouldn't.

Lily could only think of one reason why Dan St. James would be calling her, tonight of all nights, and her heart was a heavy thump against her ribs when she answered. "What? What's wrong with Trix?"

Trix ought to be backstage at the Old Wellington right now, and Lily couldn't imagine why she would be with Dan under any circumstances, but—

Dan's voice was smooth and deep. "Ah. A question with many possible answers."

She curled her fingers tighter into her throat for support. "Has something happened to Trix?"

"Trix?" he repeated blandly. "No. Why? Has she been talking about me?"

The dissipating rush of anxiety left her with unsteady legs and emerging anger. "Why are you calling me?"

"Call it a peace offering of sorts. I heard the news and wanted to express my condolences personally. I'm sure you had all sorts of hopes about tonight—"

"I have no idea what you're talking about."

There was a small pause. When he spoke again, she could hear the fizz of surprise behind the malice. "Your father, of course."

For long seconds, she physically felt as if the costume was strangling her. Her nails dug into soft skin under the ruff.

"It sounds as if it was very quick, at least—"

With shaking hands, she ended the call. Fumbling, she brought up a web browser and ran a news search, hoping, hoping… God…

The top results almost cut her off at the knees.

She was trembling so badly that she clicked on the wrong link at first, had to backtrack to the ones that said her dad was dead.

She read a paragraph, two, three—and had to drop the phone and press her forehead against the edge of the table. She took a deep breath, and another, swallowing down on the ball of nausea.

She wasn't sure how long it was before she straightened and picked up the phone, selected her contacts list and scrolled until she found Hudson Warner's number. He was supposed to be in Chicago with Jack.

She closed her eyes when he answered. "Hud?"

"Lily." Hudson's voice was thick with suppressed emotion. "Did you get my flowers? I'm sorry again that I can't be there toni—"

"Hudson."

He broke off the stream of unconvincing pleasantries. "Oh hell. You know."

She couldn't speak. When she got words out, they cracked, all of her training shot. "It's true, then."

"It's true, pet. I'm sorry." Hudson cleared his throat several times. "It was very quick, Lily. Seconds. He didn't suffer. I swear to God."

"Is he—" She pressed her palm over her face. Oh God, she wanted Luc. She'd never wanted anyone's arms so badly in her life. "Where is—"

"He's here with me in Chicago. I've arranged for his… I've arranged a return flight. He'll be home by tomorrow night."

No. He wouldn't. He'd never be home again.

A heavy knock on her door was followed by the shout of: "Ten minutes, Lily!"

"Was that your stage call?" Hudson asked, startled. "I thought Savage must have decided to break the news and take you out of tonight's show after all. Are you sure you're up to this? I don't think anyone would expect you to—"

She was existing in a strange, cold bubble where

reality couldn't quite penetrate. The meaning of those statements didn't immediately register. When it sank in, it was as if frozen fingers slipped around her heart and closed tight.

"Savage?" she repeated. "Luc... I don't— What do you mean?"

Hudson came back slowly and cautiously with his own question. "Lily, who told you what happened?"

She mangled a laugh and a sob. "About the last person I would ever want to hear *any* news from. Google filled in the details. What did you mean about Luc?"

"I couldn't get through to your phone," he said warily, "so I called and spoke to a member of Savage's team and then to Savage himself. He asked me not to speak to you personally until later tonight. I understand he's issued a blanket order that you're not to be told anything before or during the performance, so that you can focus."

"Luc said that." She stood up and turned around, gripping the edge of the table. "Luc knows that my father died tonight, and he's forbidden anyone to share that minor fact with me until his prize show is over, so I don't miss a cue or lose my train of thought during the monologue."

"I'm not exactly Savage's biggest fan, but I really don't think that's the slant to put on his intention—"

It was either cut him off rudely or cry into the receiver. He would be more bothered by the tears. "I have to go."

"Lily—"

She ended the call and this time did turn the phone off. No access to social media or well-meaning friends. Luc would be relieved.

For two, possibly three precious minutes, she just stood there. Her dad. Jack—sarcastic, mischievous, affectionate, selfish Jack Lamprey was…gone. She couldn't— Oh God. She couldn't even imagine it.

He'd been in his seventies. He could have—She'd always seen him in her mind, still making trouble into his nineties.

Oh God. Dad.

Something smacked against her door, partly shaking her out of her daze, although when she opened it she felt as if she were trying to push through a wall of water. A lady-in-waiting was limping towards the stairs, rubbing her thigh.

Lily walked over to the full-length mirror and stared again at her unfamiliar reflection. Bowing her head, she pressed her hands over her face, feeling as if a thick layer of ice was forming over her skin.

Lampreys get things done. She could hear Jack saying it, with that wicked lilt.

Against her forehead, she balled her hands into fists.

She could do this. For the next few hours, she was Elizabeth. She lived in a different time; she had never known Jack Lamprey… She faltered, and steeled herself. She had never known Jack Lamprey.

And if the men in her life acted like self-absorbed pricks, she could just throw them in the Tower or order a swift beheading.

More deep breaths, in and out, moving her hands down to press her fists against her stomach, before she turned and strode swiftly through the doorway.

Upstairs, she walked into an almost tangible wall of nerves and excitement, and the atmosphere of organised chaos made it easier to lock herself into character. Margo's quick glance at her, hastily averted, was a small stab through her armour, but she kept her own gaze fixed firmly on the wings.

When the curtain went up, routine and muscle memory were her saviour. She had made these movements, reacted to these cues so many times in rehearsal that her mind and body responded automatically.

The call boy signalled, and she stepped out in front of her first full house, and into the political instability of 1553.

It was close to perfect. Miles better than the final rehearsal. The cast were in full control; the audience was engaged. From the principals to the one-liners and the bit parts, every actor was cue-ready and holding up their end.

Lily was stealing the show. She was working the audience like a seasoned pro, and they responded beautifully to every tense moment and unexpected quip.

About twenty seconds after she first took the stage, Luc closed his eyes briefly.

When the lights went up for intermission and the room appeared to undulate as people got to their feet or stretched in their seats, David released an audible sigh. "So far, so fantastic."

At his side in the lighting box, Amelia whistled. "Lily. Holy shit. Talk about exceeding expectations." She shook her head. "God, it's such a shame this night is going to be ruined for her."

Luc scrubbed his hand roughly through his hair. "She knows."

"What?"

David looked at him sharply. "This is the strongest performance she's turned out—"

"She knows." He spoke without a shred of uncertainty. He knew Lily. He knew the body language of all his actors, but above all, he knew Lily. She was hiding it well. Superbly. But he'd heard it in her voice, seen it in her face, from her opening line.

A small crease appeared between Amelia's brows. "Are you sure?"

"I'm sure."

"Should we—"

Luc turned in his seat. "Padma, go backstage and make sure Lily's left alone. If she doesn't speak to anyone, nobody speaks to her. Let her focus." Grimly, he looked back at the closed curtains and the milling stands. "If she's doing this, let her do it her way."

It was a dream. She'd actually had this dream more than once in the past. Standing in front of a West End audience, many of whom were on their feet, taking her bow with the rest of the cast. The direction of the house lights had changed, so that she could clearly make out individual figures and faces, all of them strange. Margo's hand was dry, holding hers tightly; on her left, Privy Councillor Brian Halsey's palm was slick with sweat.

The applause went on for a long time. The lights started to blur her vision.

She should be enjoying this moment. She couldn't wait to get off the stage.

Finally, the curtain went down and stayed down. Lily dropped Margo's hand and wove through the mass of people between the main stage and the wings. A few of the cast and crew smiled and congratulated her, but in general there was an odd, awkward vibe that she would have found disconcerting if it weren't for Dan St. James's last act of spite.

Nobody stopped her on the path to her dressing room. Inside, she carefully detached her headpiece and started removing hairpins. It was a relief to pull the wig free and lay it back on its stand. Her movements were a little more flustered and jerky as she yanked at the laces of her bodice, suddenly desperate for air.

Luc came in quietly, without knocking, and closed the door behind him. They stood, staring at one another, as she kept loosening her dress, one row of cords at a time.

At last, he said, "Lily." Just her name. Heavy with regret and worry, and a dozen emotions she couldn't name.

"How could you?" Her voice broke and she stopped to steady it. She didn't want to cry right now.

At that first sign of tears, Luc came to her, reaching for her, but she made an instinctive, defensive gesture, and he stilled.

"I'm sorry." His hand lifted again, futilely, and he clenched it so tightly that his knuckles blanched. "I'm so sorry."

"What for?" She heard the harshness of her words almost from a distance. "My father's death, or that you tried to keep it from me for the sake of your fucking profit margins?"

His head went back at that, a physical reaction, as if she'd hit him. "Lily—God. No. Christ, no. That's not—"

Again he reached for her, and again she moved her hands, backing away. "After everything— God, Margo *said* it would always be the theatre first with you, she *warned* me, but I didn't think you'd…" She swallowed down the rising tears. "I didn't think you'd…"

His jaw was iron-tight. "Lily—"

"It was *that* important to you to open with the core cast? You actually issued some kind of gag order? Everyone in the theatre can know what happened to *my* dad, but keep Lily in the dark until she's done her part? Like a fucking trained seal?"

Luc was breathing just as quickly, but obviously trying to stay calm. "You have no idea how much I hated—There was nothing you could have done. The plane won't arrive back for hours. There's nobody here who needs you to be with them. I wanted you to have tonight." He thrust his fingers through his hair. "I wanted you to at least have this."

"Right." She didn't even try to hide the scepticism. "That decision was entirely for my benefit." Pressing her fist to her forehead again, she made a strangled noise. "God. I'm over here, getting pulled down into shit and rumours every day because of this, losing opportunities—"

"What opportunities?" he asked tightly.

"I was up for a role with Kathleen Leibowitz. Turns out she's not that tempted by tabloid trash."

"Don't fucking call yourself—"

The door opened again; if someone had knocked, she hadn't heard it through his harsh response and the white noise clouding her brain. In a daze, Lily turned. When she saw Ash's face, usually filled with humour and now creased with concern, something pinged in her chest.

"Lily." Ash made an abrupt, cut-off movement, as if he were going to open his arms to her, and she realised he was probably holding back as a mark of respect to her relationship with Luc. "I'm so sorry, kid."

"You heard?"

"I think everyone's heard. The prime minister's re-leased a statement expressing his condolences to—" Ash flushed.

"To Lady Charlotte?" For the first time, with a rush of guilt, Lily wondered how the other woman was cop-ing. She didn't know if she ought to call her, or if that would make things worse. She assumed she would be allowed to attend the funeral. Another lump formed in her throat and she had to fix her gaze on the wall to the left of Ash's ear. There was a small crack in the plaster that Luc's construction team had missed. "That's very politic of him. The whole House of Lords is probably having a quiet party. A lot of pacemakers had to work overtime when Jack attended a session."

"There's a lot of press outside. And about fifteen people in the hallway clamouring to speak to you," Ash said to Luc, who swore viciously. "I've got a car wait-ing out back. If you want to make a quick exit now—"

"Yes." She didn't hesitate. She wanted to be at home. The adrenaline that had carried her through the perfor-mance was wearing off, and she just wanted to crawl into bed. "I want to go now."

Ash looked at Luc again. "I can take her home and wait with her until you—"

"I'm coming now." Luc's reply was uncompromising.

She forced herself to meet his gaze; he was watch-ing her intently. "You have a duty here. The show's a hit. You might as well follow through." He was very pale. She could hear herself saying these things, and she couldn't seem to stop. She was aware that she was hurting him, which made her stomach and her heart seize with pain, but she was *just* holding it together.

If she opened up completely, let herself feel it all, she would fall apart.

Ash looked extremely uncomfortable. "I'll take her home."

Luc's grey eyes were dark and conflicted. His jaw shifted. "I'll follow you." He came towards her, and she felt the warmth when he slipped her coat around her shoulders. "I'll be there. Soon."

She tore her gaze from his, and let Ash slip his hand through the crook of her arm and steer her out the door. The walk through the theatre, pushing through the laughing party atmosphere backstage, putting her hand up against the camera flashes before Ash's driver opened the car door for her—it was all a haze.

She felt as if her brain didn't start functioning until they were halted somewhere in traffic and she became aware of how cold she was, even with the wool coat and the car heating on full blast.

Ash put his hand over hers. "I know this probably doesn't mean what it should right now, but…you were bloody amazing out there. Every person backstage was singing your praises." He nudged her, very gently. "Spine of steel, my friend." He was so very, very serious. Ash, the jokester, without even a hint of a smile. Just one more surreal element in a night of unreality. "I'm so fucking proud of you, Lily."

"Thanks," she said quietly, and felt absolutely nothing.

Chapter Thirteen

It was shaping up to be the most commercially successful opening of Luc's career, and one of the worst nights of his life. He gave perfunctory thanks to the investors and VIPs for their support, and a statement to the press that was both guarded and sincere. He expressed the condolences of the company on the death of Jack Lamprey and emphasized how very proud they were of Lily. He ran the media gamut in less than fifteen minutes and delegated the rest of the PR hassle to Maria and her team.

Ignoring the prying questions of the waiting paparazzi, he left the theatre and headed straight for Lily's flat. Traffic congestion was fucking awful and he had even less patience for it than usual.

He sat behind another build-up at a red light, knocking his fingers against the steering wheel. He wanted to be with her. Every instinct was telling him that it was his *right* to be with her. And it was a toss-up at this point whether she would even open the front door to him, let alone want him to touch her or offer any kind of physical comfort. He doubted if he would ever forget the image of her stricken face, or the knife thrust of realising exactly *how* badly she had interpreted his actions.

Margo had told her that the theatre would always come first with him. That had never been true where his family were concerned. It was almost laughably untrue now.

When he finally pulled up outside her mews, Trix was getting out of a taxi. She glanced over her shoulder as she paid the driver. They met at the intercom.

"How is she?" Trix asked a bit stiffly, pressing the button. Her coat was unbuttoned and she was still wearing her costume underneath. There were smears of greasepaint on her cheeks.

"Not good," he said, as someone buzzed them in and the outer door clicked open.

When Ash let them into the living room, Luc could hear the shower running.

"Lily's in the shower," Ash confirmed unnecessarily. He looked as tired as they all probably felt.

"How is she?" Trix asked again, pulling off her coat. She headed straight for the kettle and switched it on.

"She's in shock." Ash turned to Luc. "She must have always known that she'd lose Jack while she was relatively young, but—you're never really prepared, are you? She's not thinking straight, and she doesn't know what she's saying."

Luc nodded once. "I know." Abruptly, uncomfortable with discussing Lily behind her back in any more intimacy, he asked the question that had been lurking behind more immediate concerns. "Did she say how she found out?"

He hoped to God she hadn't had to read about it online. This situation was bad enough.

A slight flush rose in Ash's cheeks. "Uh…yeah. She said…someone called her."

At the kitchen counter, Trix's eyes narrowed. "Why did you look at me when you said that? *I* didn't tell her."

"Dan told her."

Trix had been lifting down a mug from a high cupboard; her hand froze in mid-air. "Excuse me?"

"Your ex-boyfriend called her on the pretence of offering his condolences, really to rub it in that her chance of a big opening night was shot, and scored the unexpected bonus of catching her completely off guard." Ash looked as if he'd swallowed a glass of acid. "He's a dick. Your taste in men leaves a lot to be desired."

"Dan St. James called Lily? At the theatre?" Trix's face was flooding with a far more violent shade of red.

"Yes."

There was a tense moment before Trix set down the mug she was holding, walked around the counter and picked up her coat. Slipping it on, she started buttoning it. Her movements were precise and calm.

"What are you doing?" Ash asked warily.

"I'm going to speak to Dan." Trix considered. "Possibly murder, maim and/or castrate him. We'll see how the verbal evisceration goes first. Tell Lily I'll be back in an hour. If she needs me before then, call me."

"I don't think you should—" She was already stalking towards the door, and Ash swore. "Lily will unman *me* if I let you go around there alone."

Trix fixed him with a scornful look. "Dan's not *dangerous*. He's a cowardly, spiteful shitbag who gets his kicks spreading poison, and enough is enough. I have several things to say to him and they're all long overdue. And let's be real—in the extremely unlikely event that things did get physical, you would be absolutely no help."

Ash groaned. "You realise I'm still going to have to come with you." He raised his hands when Trix scowled. "Look, my money's on you, Rambette, every time, but seriously—Lily will lose her shit and she's got enough to deal with tonight. I'll wait in the car if you like, but I'm coming." He grabbed his keys. "I'll drive." He looked at Luc. "Look after her."

"Goes without saying." Luc lifted an eyebrow at Trix. "If there's anything left of Ramsay Bolton when you've finished with him, feel free to send the remains my way."

Her expression was still banked with fury, but her lips suddenly eased into a minuscule smile. "Ramsay Bolton? Was that Lily?"

It belatedly occurred to him that, dick or not, he was referring to her ex-lover. "Uh—no. It wasn't. Sorry."

"God," he heard her mutter as she left with Ash. "It's like peas in a pod." Before the door closed behind them, she issued a direct warning. "Don't make things worse for her."

Luc glanced grimly down the corridor before he went into the kitchen to finish making the cup of tea. When he took it into Lily's bedroom and set it on the bedside table, she was still in the bathroom.

He was sitting quietly on the edge of the bed, his linked hands resting between his knees, when she padded across the hall with a comb in her hand and a towel under her arm. Her hair clung wetly to her neck and shoulders, dampening the soft knit top of her pyjamas.

Averting her eyes, she crawled past him onto the bed, thumped the pillows into a tower and tugged roughly enough at a knot that even he winced.

Without a word, he twisted, bringing one knee up

on the mattress, and took the comb from her hand; she sat perfectly still while he gently worked it through the satiny tangle. She wouldn't relax against him and he could see the tension in the graceful lines of her back.

"Thanks," she said in a low voice when he handed her back the comb.

"I know you're angry with me." He touched his cheek to hers. She almost reached for him. Her hand half rose before she stiffened again. "And I'm sorry. I really am so fucking sorry. About all of it."

Her skin rubbed his when she turned, making them both shiver. She swallowed and at last raised her lashes. Her eyes were swamped with grief and guilt, disappointment and misery, and the sound that rose in his throat was involuntary.

Her words were harsh, radically unlike her usual soft vowels and teasing humour. "It's not like I shouldn't have expected this, right? He was in his seventies. He was an old man."

Luc ran his thumb over her knuckles. There was a painful knot in his throat. "He was your dad."

"Yeah, but—" Her voice cracked a little. "He was never a very hands-on father. His follow-through was shit. He was hardly ever there. It's not like I'm going to be—to be missing—much—"

She covered her face with her forearm, and Luc curved his hand around her head, cradling her. "I know," he said into her damp hair. "I know."

She kept her arms folded in tight to her chest, but she didn't pull away. Luc stroked her hair and her back, listening to the sound of her ragged breathing. It was one of the most frustrating, powerless feelings in the scope of human experience, to watch the person you loved suffering and be unable to take the hurt away.

This should have been a watershed night in her life for a very different reason.

Lily was the only member of the cast who'd had no family support in the audience tonight. Her parents had shown where their priorities lay, clearly not for the first time.

Given her history—and his—he could hardly be surprised that she was sitting stiffly in his arms right now, not exactly radiating trust.

When she put her hands up to cover his, holding on to him for a few seconds before she put him away from her, he knew what she was going to say before she opened her mouth.

His instinctive "no" clashed with her soft "I need you to leave."

"I'm not leaving you alone." He didn't reach for her again. He respected her need for space to that extent. Not enough to put several city boroughs between them when she was hurting and still in shock.

"I won't be alone. Trix and Ash are—"

"Taking Dan St. James apart, one home truth at a time."

"What?" Lily's shadowed eyes focused. She made a move as if to get off the bed, and he shook his head.

"They'll be back soon. And if anyone needs to be worried about that visit, it's St. James."

Her lips lifted in the tiniest scrap of a smile. "Is Trix on the warpath?"

"If he knows what's good for him, he won't open the door."

He recognised the look that was creeping over her

beautiful, blotchy face. It was classic Jack Lamprey, as televised during confrontations at the House of Lords: totally immovable.

"Luc."

"No." He spoke through gritted teeth. "You can be as pissed off at me as you like, but—"

"Please." Her voice broke again on the word, and she might as well have tightened her cold, white-knuckled hand directly around his heart. "Just—not tonight."

He bit down hard on what he'd been going to say next; it obviously would have been absorbed into the impenetrable wall she'd built around herself.

He stared at her, his jaw working.

She pressed her palms over her eyes. She was trembling. He wanted to touch her. He wanted her to turn to him for whatever comfort he could offer.

Right now, it seemed he was causing her even more pain. She'd completely shut herself off, every taut muscle locked in self-defence.

"I need to think," she said huskily, lowering her hands to her lap. She interlocked her fingers, holding *herself* in a firm grip as if she couldn't trust anyone else's touch. A sheen of tears was trapped in her spiky lashes. "I'm tired, and I have some stuff to think about. I really need to be alone for a while."

"Lily." His voice was raw and painful.

"Please, Luc. Just…go."

Wrong was firing through every nerve ending. Leaving *anyone* when they were this upset: wrong. Leaving his lover—Leaving the person he loved more than anyone, when she was shaking and on the verge of tears: totally fucked up.

"We'll talk tomorrow." Lily progressed to wrapping

her arms about herself in a full hug. He couldn't isolate a single emotion in her eyes that made him feel okay about this. "Tomorrow. I promise."

His abdomen was clenched so tightly that it was starting to cramp. "All right." He forced himself to stand up. He pushed his hands into pockets, holding himself almost as stiffly as she was. "Tomorrow?"

She nodded, a tear slipping down her cheek. He watched it track a path to her jaw and disappear.

"I'll wait in the living room until Trix gets back." He wasn't compromising on that. "And I'll have my phone. If you need me, call me. I don't give a shit what time it is."

Her head nodded; every other part of her body told him not to get his hopes up.

When he turned at the door, she was holding the cup of tea he'd made, looking into it as if she'd lost all memory of what it was. On the English crisis scale, step one was drinking a cup of tea. Forgetting the entire concept of tea was off-the-charts stress.

He sat in the semi-darkness of the living room for a long time. He went back several times to check on her, and was relieved when she finally dozed off. Her head was bent at a neck-cricking angle against her immensity of pillows. Quietly, he walked over to the side of the bed and lifted her, as gently as he could, settling her down more comfortably. He took the furry comforter from the end of the bed and draped it over her.

He didn't tuck back the loose strands of hair or kiss her exposed ear, or do any of the things he would have last night. Only hours ago, when they'd still been on speaking terms and her bare legs had been tangled with his. He looked back at her once, then returned to wait for Trix.

It was almost two o'clock in the morning. He was starting to wonder if he'd been too flippant about her ability to handle Dan. From the little he'd seen of the other man, he'd written him off as a classic bully, too self-serving to risk violence, but—

The intercom buzzed. He released a breath and went to open the door for her.

"Is she asleep?" Trix's movements were steady and assured as she unbuttoned her coat; even he could see there was something different in her. Closure, perhaps. For her sake, he hoped that didn't mean St. James's head was now mounted on the end of Lady Justice's sword at the Old Bailey.

"Yeah." Exhaustion settled into the depths of his body. He sat back down on the edge of the couch. "I've been checking on her. She dropped off a while ago, thank God."

"I'm glad. I made Ash head home. He means well, but he's a real pain in the arse when he's trying to be sincere." Trix hung up her coat and turned to study him.

"No bloodshed, I see."

"It was a narrow escape. For him." She lifted her chin. "He won't be a factor in my life or in Lily's ever again."

"Good for you." He meant it sincerely.

"Is there a reason you're sitting out here by yourself? That's quite a big bed Lily has in there."

Luc didn't respond, but his expression must have said a good deal.

"Did she kick you out?" Trix didn't sound all that surprised.

A little tightly, he said, "She wants some space until tomorrow, to think things through."

People usually meant one thing only when they asked for space. He glanced back down the hallway, fighting the overwhelming urge to go in there, press close to her, hold her, and demand—something.

That was what *he* needed. This was about what she needed.

Which apparently wasn't him.

Lily's cheek felt sticky and sweaty where it rested on her hand. It was that godawful experience when reality took a moment to settle. For a few seconds, she felt light and well-rested; then she remembered and her stomach swooped.

It was on pure instinct that she reached out for Luc. Instead of warm, spice-scented skin and taut muscle, her arm encountered delicate bones and feminine softness. Her eyes shot open. Trix looked solemnly back, her tousled pink head resting against her folded arm.

"Hey." Lily's voice was like sandpaper.

"Hey. You slept."

She swallowed. "It really happened. All of it."

"Yeah." Trix gripped her hand. "It did."

She drew in a shaky breath and looked at the clock. Almost eight. She pushed the fluffy mess of her hair behind her ears. Last night felt like the shreds of a nightmare, but every word and sickening moment was sinking back into her consciousness. "Did Luc leave?"

"He waited until I got back." Trix hesitated. "He waited a long time. And he didn't want to go."

Lily stared at the cold, abandoned cup of tea on the bedside table. "I know."

There was an odd pause, as if Trix was unsure whether to say more, before she squeezed Lily's shoulder. "Are you hungry? Toast? Tea?"

"Tea. Tea would be good. Thanks." She tried to shake free of the remnants of ice that had paralysed her. "I can get it."

"Lily." Trix stood up with a pursed-lipped frown that would have put the sternest of their boarding school teachers to shame. "I'm fully aware that you've spent most of your life trying to look after everyone around you, and the only reason you let people hold you up last night was because you were in shock. But I'm telling you right now. You're grieving. You're allowed to be sad and you're allowed to lean. Now run a hot bath, get in it and let me make you some fucking toast."

After an instant of sheer surprise, Lily—unbelievably—felt her lips twitch. "Am I also allowed to be intimidated?"

"Just call me Rambette." Trix pointed at the door. "Bath."

"Yes, ma'am."

She ran the bath hot enough to scald and emerged from it a nice shade of blush pink. While she dressed, she tried to concentrate on breathing and stillness, but constantly battled away thoughts of her father, thoughts of Luc, tossing and tumbling and jumbling, all of them making her feel sick. Sad. Guilty.

Angry.

She stopped, startled, in the doorway to the living room, and Margo looked up from where she sat on the couch.

"Lily." She stood and ran her hands over her hips, smoothing down her expensive wool dress. "I'm sorry to intrude this early. How are you?" She winced. "That's always a ridiculous question, isn't it?"

"I'm—" Lily started to come out with the conventional social lie, but broke off. "I honestly don't know."

Trix came out of the kitchen holding two cups of tea and balancing a plate of toast on her forearm. She'd paid her way through drama school and dance training by waiting table and tending bar, and her skills were holding. She set everything down on the coffee table and looked between them. "I'm going to take a shower. Nice to meet you, Margo."

"Yes, you too." Margo seemed distracted, but she produced her infamous smile. It faded when Trix discreetly made herself scarce. "Luc's not here?"

Lily sat on the edge of her favourite armchair and reached for one of the cups, wrapping her hands around the warmth for comfort. "No," she said baldly.

"I see." Absently, Margo sat down again and picked up a piece of toast, glanced at it, put it back on the plate. "Lily, I'm very sorry about your father."

Another stab of pain. "Thank you."

"It's amazing that you performed as well as you did. You stole the stage last night. It would have been an incredible show under any circumstances, let alone… this one." Her gaze was steady and sincere. "We're all unbelievably proud."

Lily tightened her grasp on the cup. "Everyone came through last night."

"Yes. It was one of those rare instances of magic. It's such a shame that—" She pressed her lips together. "I *am* sorry to come here so early and so soon after—It's just that—"

This was the most flustered Lily had ever seen her.

She was usually utterly in control of her voice and body, and apparently emotions.

When she did get out a complete sentence, it seemed to be totally irrelevant. "Luc did a beautiful job renovating the Queen Anne."

"Yes…"

"But I think he skimped on the insulation in the dressing room walls." Margo coughed. "They're not soundproof. At all."

And the light dawned.

"You heard us. Me. After the show."

"It was a little difficult not to." Margo sat forward on the couch, her hands clasped tightly. "I realise I'm probably the last person you want commenting on your relationship with Luc—again—but… I think you need to know, and he wouldn't have wasted time trying to justify himself when you were that upset. When Luc got the news from Amelia last night, he thought your father had been taken to the hospital for treatment. He thought you'd need to be with him, and he didn't hesitate. Not for a second. He told David to put Kirsten on in your place and take over immediately, so that he could go with you."

Lily set down the tea before she spilled it. She had to steady her voice as well. "He was going to sub in Kirsten? And leave the theatre before the show even started?"

"He was prepared to miss the entire thing, delegate full control to his team. Lose all the satisfaction of seeing everything come to fruition. The opening night of his theatre, not just of the play. His dream for years." Her eyes flickered. "He said you needed him more."

Lily had been on the verge of tears before; she almost broke completely then.

"I'm…glad." Margo took a deep breath. "That he has that. I'm glad for him. For both of you."

Lily's hands were shaking. She curled them tightly into fists.

Margo cleared her throat. "Maybe I shouldn't have come, but—"

"No." Lily looked up. "No, I'm glad you told me. I… don't like being left in the dark."

"He didn't want to hurt you. Fifteen minutes to curtain and it was like his mind went straight down to your dressing room and never left your side. It's a rarefied little club, the people who mean that much to Luc. To *that* extent, it might be a club of one." She collected her bag and her coat. "I'm going to go."

Lily stood, as well. "Margo…"

Margo spoke abruptly. "I brought your flowers and presents over, by the way. I saw them when I passed your dressing room and I thought—I don't expect you'll have a shortage of flowers this week, but I thought you might want some…happier ones around."

Lily looked over at the dresser, where the clusters of roses were stacked carefully next to the wrapped box of champagne from Luc.

Margo touched his crimson roses on her way out. "They're beautiful." She paused and slanted a small smile back at Lily. "Gorgeous colour."

Lily closed the door behind her and stood with her hand resting against the wood, before she turned and picked up the bouquet of roses.

Beneath it, looking slightly bedraggled, a few blooms

askew and shedding buttery petals, were the yellow roses her father had sent her.

A tear tickled along the side of her nose.

Luc stood outside the closed door for several moments before he knocked.

When Lily opened it to him, she was very pale. Her skin had a strange papery fragility and her eyes were bloodshot.

She reached for him.

She came into his arms, her hands sliding beneath his coat, fisting in his jumper against his back. She shook once, a compulsive shudder; he tightened his grip, pulling her into the curve of his body.

His heart was beating in a disjointed series of jerky thuds.

He knew, as he had known last night, what she was going to say. It was like being on an express train, heading for the worst destination he could imagine; he wanted to alter the course, to turn back, and he couldn't.

There was a cliché about unstoppable forces and immovable objects that was about to derail his best hope for happiness.

Her scent and her body were familiar, but it was as if *Lily*—everything that really made Lily who she was— had retreated deep within, trapped in a frozen little box. She was cuddling against him, her breath warm into his neck, her fingers clutching at him almost desperately— and it felt like goodbye.

She took a deep, tear-clogged breath and stepped back. Just a single step.

"Don't do this." His words came out in a rasp, as if

they'd been torn from him with a serrated blade, and she swallowed.

"Luc. Margo told me what happened last night. When Hudson called." She shook her head. "I'm so sorry. For what I said. How I acted."

He rubbed her wet cheek with his thumb. His hand was unsteady. "You had every right to be angry. My reasons for trying to keep you in the dark weren't what you thought, but I still went behind your back. I knew that was inexcusable."

"You did it for me." She touched his chest. "I do believe that."

He heard the silent *but*…loud and clear. Harsh words of protest were a corrosive burn deep in his gut, but he looked into the immensity of pain in her eyes and they never made it to the surface.

"Until last night, you've never been anything but honest with me." She made a quick, negative gesture when he started to speak. "I don't mean that as an accusation. I know you were thinking of me; you were doing it for me." She took another long breath, releasing it in a shaky rush. "But I still thought—I never doubted, even for a second, that you'd done it for the show."

It hurt, as it had hurt last night, and his expression obviously revealed that.

Her voice hitched. "I should have trusted you, and I didn't."

"I don't think you've ever had much reason to trust the people who—care about you, have you?" *Care about*. It was a pathetically watered-down substitute for how he really felt, but he'd never spoken the words aloud before, and to use them now… She wasn't ready to hear them. They would disappear into emotional blackmail. "Your parents…" He couldn't continue that, inflict even more pain. It didn't need to be reiterated, anyway. "Even Trix."

If Trix was still in the flat, she was giving them space. He hoped she wasn't listening to this.

"Trix?" Even in her grief, Lily was loyal. "Trix has been amazing."

"But when she thought she was in love with St. James, she turned her back on you. For a while, at least." He touched her white knuckles. "And it hurt."

Lily didn't look back towards the bedrooms, so he assumed Trix had gone out. Blotchy pink appeared in her cheeks and down her neck. "Dan makes a game of manipulation. I never blamed Trix for—"

"Didn't you?"

She closed her eyes for a moment, her lashes tangled black fans against her skin.

"It's completely understandable, Lily," he said evenly. "She was probably the only constant in your life for a long time."

She spoke in a rush. "She said I was cynical. She was right." Her expression was tormented—and achingly sad. "I think the very fact I jumped to that conclusion last night—after *everything*—is proof that I need to… sort myself out."

He didn't move his gaze from hers. He forced the word out. "Alone?"

She probably couldn't see him clearly through her tears, but she left her hands balled at her stomach, pressing into her ribs as if she needed the support. "Yes."

"No."

Her mouth curved, just a fleeting, blurry distortion of a smile. "I knew you would say that."

"Good. Progress."

"Luc. I'm a mess right now."

"You're beautiful." His statement had nothing to do with her physical appearance, and her face softened a little.

She laid her hand over his, and he turned his wrist to entwine their fingers. "I don't even know how I feel. I'm sad." Her voice fractured again. "And I'm so *angry*, and I feel guilty that I feel angry, and I just... I need to come to terms with—everything."

"Lily—" *I love you. I need to be with you. When you love someone, you work through things together. You support each other. When it's hard to stand alone, you take someone's hand.* There were a hundred things he could say to her in that moment, but—

She was crying harder, but in utter silence. "I don't want to hurt you," she said at last, and it was a broken vow. "And I feel like I'm just going to hurt you again and again."

Their hands were their only point of contact; she was holding his fingers so tightly that her nails dug into him.

She was grieving, she was confused—and she was stubborn as hell. She needed to find some peace in her-self, and he couldn't force the issue.

Or it really would break them.

With his free palm, he cupped her neck, dragging her up on her tiptoes so that her forehead pressed against his. "I can't walk away from you." Her lips moved; he pressed his over them. It wasn't a kiss so much as a seal on his words. "But I'll always try to give you what you need. And if that's—" It was hard. It was so fuck-ing hard. "If that's to not be with me—then I'll leave.

But I'm here." He shook her, gently, just once. "I'm here, Lily."

Her tears were wet against his wrist.

"And I need to know you're...okay," he said roughly. "So—text me."

She touched her wet lashes. "Text you?"

"Every night. Just one word. A fucking emoji if you like. Just—text me."

He could hear her breathing.

Softly, she said, "For how long?"

For however long it takes.

His gaze went from their linked hands to the conflicted expression in her eyes. "That's up to you."

Chapter Fourteen

Lily's paternal grandmother had given birth in the middle of someone else's wedding. Jack Lamprey had entered the world with a roar, lived like a rocket burning a trail through the sky, and at the end, disappeared silently into the night. There was no funeral. *I'm not giving all the bastards a public forum to gloat and paying for the privilege*, he'd written in a letter to his lawyer. By his own request, he was cremated and his ashes released into the wind from the rooftop of Lamprey Enterprises.

Lily stood off to the side of the small gathering, her hands tucked into the pockets of her black coat, her hair whipped back by the breeze, watching the grey dust catch on the crossing currents and scatter, the last remnants of her father dancing out towards the black strip of the Thames and the lights of Tower Bridge.

Her eyes were dry. She hadn't cried since the morning she'd pushed Luc away and put that look in his eyes.

Her dad was a black shadow on her heart. She felt as if the moments of love and humour and affection were slipping through her fingers, falling into the depths of everything that was permanently lost now.

Being apart from Luc as well—it *hurt*. It physically hurt.

She texted him every night, just the one word: Okay. It was an acknowledgment that she was safe, that she was coping, that she was…okay, in the most literal, un-emotional sense of the word. Otherwise, it was almost farcically untrue.

She wasn't okay. She was a fucking disaster.

Not onstage. She'd missed two performances, then gone back to work two weeks ago. It was getting her through. She didn't like herself much right now, so it was a relief to escape into the persona of a stranger for a few hours a night.

With the exception of *London Celebrity*, she was apparently getting a lot of accolades and sympathy in the press. Freddy was cutting out the good reviews and leaving copies in her dressing room for her, usually accompanied by a packet of biscuits and a series of old books with increasingly bizarre titles, her very sweet attempt at keeping Lily's spirits up.

Lily hadn't looked at a single newspaper clipping. It was amazing how much priorities could change in such a short space of time.

She had seen Luc only once, across the busy green room. His jaw had clenched when she'd turned away. He was working mostly from his office building, putting things in motion for the next production.

Life went on.

He texted her back every night, just the single letter: X. A signature. A kiss. A mark on a map, pointing the way to where the good things were.

"Terrible shame about Jack," an elderly man said to her. His faded gaze was curious and contained no recognition, but he was too polite to ask who she was. Most people who read the tabloids were well aware of her existence, but her birth had never been openly advertised among the Lamprey family's intimate circle. "Quite a character, he was."

"Yes, he was."

"Hard to believe he's gone."

Yes. It was.

Lady Charlotte was also dry-eyed, standing stiffly next to a woman Lily thought was her sister. Her clothes and makeup were faultless.

Over the heads of Jack's closest business connections and a few family members, her eyes locked with Lily's.

Lily didn't move. She barely felt as if she were breathing.

Charlotte said something to her sister, who looked across at Lily with an inscrutable expression, then edged smoothly through the crowd.

She stopped about six feet away. Her gaze went from the tips of Lily's black heels up to her face, where it lingered; a quiver of emotion passed over her own. "Lily." Her body was tense, but her voice was brisk. "I need to speak you with you, please. Not now. Could you come to my office on Monday?"

A fog of Lily's own breath was blown back by the bitter wind, curling around her. "Yes. I have to be at the theatre by five at the latest, but—"

"Early afternoon? Two o'clock?"

"That's fine." Lily searched the other woman's face, looking for some hint as to what she was feeling, what *Lily* ought to be feeling, but it was utterly blank and businesslike.

Charlotte inclined her head. "I'll see you on Monday, then." She raised a slim hand, gesturing to the rest of her family, who began to move towards her.

It took almost ten minutes for the work associates to follow them inside; they were talking shop.

When she was alone under the spotlights and stars, forty floors above the ground, Lily took a deep gulp of the cold air and looked back towards the twinkling bridge.

In the beams of light, she could see tiny specks, still spinning.

Even when he wasn't in the theatre, Luc's presence dominated the Queen Anne. Lily could hear his voice in her mind while she waited in the wings; she could see his aesthetic and his hard work in every detail of the architecture. She avoided the foyer. The Italian tiles gave her a bittersweet tug in her stomach.

When she rose from the full-cast bow after the Thursday night performance, she shouldn't have noticed the woman in the third row. Her brain was usually so wired from adrenaline that it skittered over details.

Her gaze arrowed straight to her mother's face.

Margo shot her a questioning look when she accidentally clenched her hand. The applause and audience noise blurred into the background. She was very aware of the constriction around her ribs and the dampness of sweat under the weight of the wig.

Downstairs, she changed back into her street clothes. She was pacing her dressing room when the knock came.

Her mum slipped inside, closing the door behind her. She looked the same as ever. Dark, sultry, graceful, all the things Lily wasn't. When she lifted her arms, the loose sleeves of her bright silk dress fell away from her elbows like butterfly wings.

Lily returned the hug, still feeling oddly distant.

Vanessa pulled back to scan her face. "You were wonderful. Not that I expected any less. How are you, darling?"

"I'm…okay."

Her mother frowned. "I'm sorry it's taken so long to get back. I wanted to be here when they scattered his ashes." Wryly, she corrected herself. "Not actually at the service. I'm not quite that tactless. But I should have been here for you afterward. Was it—"

"It was what Jack wanted." Standing in her mum's presence, smelling the perfume she'd been using for at least twenty years, Lily's hard-won composure cracked a bit. The words spilled out before she could swallow them. "To be blown all over London. He isn't even having a headstone. Even in death, he's inaccessible."

There was a slight pause before Vanessa spoke again. "Are you finished here? Should I follow you home?"

There were lines around her eyes that Lily had never noticed before. Although she'd never actually thought of her mother as young. Vanessa had probably been born with that cool pragmatism. Jack was the one who had seemed ageless.

"I'm done." She reached for her coat and bag. "Are you staying with me?"

"For a few days, if you'll have me." Vanessa's discreet cough was jarring. "Unless it'll be a bit crowded?"

"No." Lily's response was short, and she tried to temper it. "It's just me at the moment. Is—" Oh Christ. Her mind temporarily blanked out. "Is…your partner with you?"

She hoped not. She wasn't in the best state of mind to play hostess.

Vanessa lifted one of her straight eyebrows. "I'm a solo

act, darling. Always have been, always will be. If the name you're desperately striving for is Milo, however—no, he isn't. We've parted ways."

Lily registered that without even a glimmer of surprise.

It was almost midnight when they got home, and Lily was so exhausted that she missed the keyhole three times before she managed to unlock the door. She stumbled through the process of getting fresh towels for the guest room, kissed her mother on the cheek, and collapsed face-first into her pillows. She was usually grateful for the extreme energy drain after the performance. It was better than lying awake thinking about her father and wanting Luc so badly that she ached.

It wouldn't work. Unless she could just...*let go*, open her mind, open her heart, stop expecting disappointment, it would be a shell of a commitment. Easily shattered.

She reached for her phone to tap her usual token Okay into the message field, but her thumb hovered over the screen. She rested the cool plastic against her forehead. Then, before she could second-guess herself, she typed My mother's here, and sent the text.

The response came back in about twenty seconds. Good. About fucking time. Talk to her.

She looked at the words until they blurred into the same muddle as her thoughts. Okay.

X.

Lily had inherited her hair colour from her father, but the fine texture was all Cray. When she set a cup of milky coffee in front of her mother the next morning, Vanessa's black hair was sticking out in a fluffy mass.

"Lifesaver. Thanks." She was sitting sideways in the chair, her legs crossed, effortlessly elegant. She swallowed a mouthful of coffee before resting the cup on her knee. "No Luc, then?"

Lily's hand slipped and her butter knife scraped against her plate.

"You're a photogenic pair. Looking *very* cosy lately. I was expecting to find him a permanent fixture." Vanessa's eyes were searching. When Lily was unable to suppress a tiny flinch, her expression changed. "Christ. Don't tell me he's chosen a time like this to end it. He can't be that much of a bastard."

Lily's throat felt dry and rough, as if her unwanted toast were lodged back there instead of going cold on the plate. She spoke from the most protective part of her heart. "He's not a bastard. He's..." Stubborn. Bossy. Loyal. *One of the best friends I'll ever have.*

"He didn't end it." She pushed the plate aside. "I told him I needed space."

Time alone to clear her head, she'd said. The memory of his eyes that day had kept her company ever since. He'd curled his hands into fists to keep from reaching for her. God.

Vanessa raised an eyebrow. "That one's as old as the hills, and usually reserved for the men with easily bruised egos. From what I've seen, it would take an air force squadron to decimate Luc Savage's ego." She picked up a piece of toast. "Still, his reputation isn't exactly glowing, and your star is well and truly on the rise. I realise your career isn't top priority right now, but thinking ahead—If you want maximum leverage from the reviews, it's probably a good idea to cut ties where he's concerned."

Lily's mind was across the river in Southbank; it took a second to hear that as anything but words. She emerged from the fog, at first absently and then in a wrathful rush. "I didn't cut ties because of my career." She hadn't cut ties at all. The microscopic, repetitive text messages were a tiny but vital link she couldn't seem to sever. "My relationship with Luc has never had anything to do with *networking*."

Vanessa was totally unfazed by Lily's tone. She kept eating toast while she reduced the most meaningful, complicated experience of Lily's life to a professional fuck-up. "Regardless of why you got into the relationship, it hasn't done you any favours. This isn't a kind industry, or a fair one. You came into it by choice, with your eyes open. You need to make smart decisions."

She wiped her buttery fingers on a napkin, then reached for her handbag and pulled out her planner. She was using a magazine clipping as a bookmark, a cut-out photo, which she removed and placed on the table. With her fingertip, she flipped it around to face Lily.

Lily looked down. It was like stepping into Alice's rabbit hole and falling right back into the hospital waiting room that night. Everything she'd felt then, she felt now. Worry. Stress. Need.

Her hand brushed her mother's when she pulled the cutting closer. It wasn't the shot that *London Celebrity* had run. This one was crisper and zoomed in on their faces. The silent connection, crystal clear for all to see. In that moment of stress and urgency and honesty, she'd been stripped bare. There had been no acting then. No self-deception.

Just…love.

Unmistakable. Beautiful. Miraculous.

And, on its own, not enough.

Vanessa spoke very evenly. "Don't let infatuation cloud your judgment."

Feeling as if she were moving in slow-motion, Lily raised her head. She looked at her mother. "Is that what you see in this photo? Infatuation?"

Vanessa's mouth, oddly pale without lipstick, was a rigid curve. "I see a woman with a very bright future about to make a mistake."

A few heartbeats of silence went by; they watched one another.

Lily pressed her palm hard against her thigh. "Like you did? With Jack?"

She had always wondered. Vanessa's affair with Jack had followed an established pattern, in all but one respect. As far as Lily was aware, there had never been another married man. Her mother was always upfront about her motives, and she didn't usually trample on other people's happiness.

Vanessa said nothing for a long time. Then she released a sighing breath. "*You* were never a mistake. I could never truly regret what happened with Jack."

"It didn't hurt your career, either." Hateful words that Lily wished wouldn't jump to the forefront of her mind, but it wasn't something her mother ever denied.

"No, it didn't. But it—cost me."

"Did you have feelings for Jack?" She kept all emotion out of the question, but her nails bit into her leg.

Vanessa's small movement was quickly shackled into stillness. "For a very short time, I lost my head over Jack. And a good deal of self-respect." Fleetingly, her mouth twisted. "I know you don't approve of the choices I've made, Lily-bit, but I don't usually have difficulty looking at myself in the mirror."

Lily-bit. Jack's old pet name for her. Lily hadn't heard it since she was a child. The lump in her throat was painful.

"There are people who have a unique ability to inspire feeling without letting it touch them." Vanessa rested her fingers over the tabloid image of Lily's face. "Don't sacrifice everything that really matters for a short-term fling."

Fling. The word roused an echo of memory. *It would only be a fling. It wouldn't last. I'll never let my guard down. He'll always have other priorities.*

Her desperate attempt at denial, because she was afraid to take a chance and risk the most devastating failure of her life.

She and Luc could hurt each other in a way that Zach Byrne could only aspire to. She *had* hurt him. First when she hadn't trusted him. A thousand times worse when she'd turned away from him.

He wasn't the one who had taken without giving back.

"It wasn't a fling," she said quietly. "And it did matter."

"Then what was it?" The question was woven with cynicism. Flyaway hair aside, they looked nothing alike; yet just then, Lily could see her own reflection in her mother's face, and it was a physical shock down her spine. "Love? With a man who's probably made his priorities very clear."

Lily looked at the hardness in her mother's expression for a beat longer before her eyes returned to the photo. "He did make it clear. All the time. With everything he did. I just didn't want to see it."

Vanessa's voice was drenched with exasperation. "Empty promises and grand gestures? Lily—"

"No." She felt a familiar burning behind her lashes and swallowed the tears back. "There was nothing dramatic about it. He knew what the potential consequences were, and he just—acted. In a way that seemed totally natural to him. Even at the worst moment, he put me first." It was still hard to believe. "And after everything that's happened between us, I still didn't trust him. I was...so *tired* of being an afterthought that I lashed out."

That knife-edge sharpness wavered. "You were never an afterthought, Lily."

Lily didn't look away from Luc's profile. "Was I a first thought?"

When Vanessa at last replied, the words were very quiet. "Is that what you think you are to Luc?"

Lily moved her hand, stroking her thumb over the photo before she curled it around her mother's. "I think—" She took a deep breath. "Yes. I do."

Vanessa rubbed her fingers, but her features were taut. "Bit of a role reversal for us, isn't it? I think you're being very foolish." A shadow passed over her face. "And Jack would have agreed with me."

The news of Lily's first serious boyfriend had resulted in a letter from Jack outlining a prenup in layman's terms, followed by a short scribbled note: *Live alone. Bring them in for fun. It's less complicated, less expensive, and you'll have much more drawer space.*

With a faint smile, Lily released her grip on her

mother's hand. "Probably. But I think I need to start listening to the right voice."

"Savage's?"

"Mine."

Her mother got up and stood looking down at her. She shook her head. Then, without a word, she kissed the bridge of Lily's nose and went to take a shower.

Lily was grateful for that timing when someone pressed the intercom button and she picked up the phone to hear the last voice she would have expected. The clipped tones brought her out of her reverie with a bang. It was like having a glass of ice water thrown in her face.

"Lily? It's Lady Charlotte. May I come in, please?"

After checking that the shower was still running, Lily buzzed her in. The three of them had never been in the same room at one time. It was a circumstance she was happy to avoid indefinitely.

As she opened the front door, she glanced down at her crumpled pyjamas. She was trying to smooth her hair when Charlotte walked into the flat, her back straight and chin held high.

"I'm sorry to intrude so...early." Charlotte looked at the pyjamas, then at the gold watch on her slim wrist. Her tone suggested several things about people who weren't dressed by nine o'clock in the morning. "I realise your performances run quite late into the evening."

Lily offered Charlotte a cup of tea, which was refused, and a seat, which she took gingerly. She showed no interest in her surroundings, sitting rigidly, obviously intending to complete her business and leave as soon as possible. All signs pointed towards her news being unpleasant.

Lily sat opposite Charlotte and couldn't help another hasty look over her shoulder. Had the water stopped? The last thing she needed was her mother sweeping out in her silk robe.

"I'm sure you're wondering why I'm here."

"Well…"

"I know we had scheduled a meeting for Monday, but I decided it would be better to—"

Lily wondered if she'd been about to chuck the etiquette books out the window and say "get it over with."

Charlotte opened her leather briefcase and removed a few papers. "Jack's solicitors will handle the details of his will, of course, and the probate process will take some months." Without any obvious emotion, she said, "Naturally he's made provision for you."

"I really don't nee—"

"You're his only child." Again—nothing. Not even a quiver. Lily supposed she'd had a long time to perfect this persona. "You're entitled to a share of his estate." There was a slight pause. "I've started clearing out his study, however—"

Lily had to suppress a wince at that.

"—and I came across a couple of things that I thought you ought to have now."

With a tinge of wariness, Lily accepted the papers. "What are they?"

"This is a contract Jack put into effect a couple of weeks ago, validating his purchase of Hudson Warner's shares in the Queen Anne Theatre, to be transferred into your name on your next birthday." Charlotte's expression was still inscrutable. "I believe you'll be twenty-seven." With the slightest edge, she added, "Doesn't time fly?"

Lily stared down at Jack's and Hudson's signatures. "Excuse me?"

"After you visited Kirkby in the company of Luc Savage, Jack decided to buy out Hudson's shares in the theatre. He said you ought to have a stake in the family business."

Lily couldn't breathe properly; her lungs were working overtime to keep up with her heart. "Jack said..." After seeing her with Luc for quarter of an hour, at a time when they hadn't even been properly together, Jack—*Jack*—had...

"He discussed it with me first. He was always very open about his business affairs."

Lily looked up quickly. For that single second in time, Charlotte shot her a very human, very dry look.

"Jack said that if you—" Charlotte cleared her throat. "And I quote, 'must handcuff yourself to a Savage and throw away the key and your sanity, you ought to at least have leverage in the boardroom.' I had a few qualms, but he said you knew what you were doing." For the first time—possibly ever—she made direct eye contact. "He said that whatever has happened in the past—" her voice faltered "—and whatever happens in the future, you would be okay."

At the age of four, Lily had made a rule that she didn't cry in front of Lady Charlotte.

A tear slipped out and crept down her cheek.

Charlotte's words turned brisk. "I'm sorry there aren't any scrapbooks or many mementos to pass on, but Jack wasn't a sentimental man."

"This is enough."

He'd bought into a Savage family business. For Jack, it didn't come much more sentimental.

Charlotte pulled a photo out of the briefcase. "He did keep this in his wallet. I thought you might want it."

Lily took it and turned it over. It was creased and almost twenty years old. She remembered Jack taking it. He'd broken away from their improvised waltz and gone to get the camera, capturing Lily midspin in the rain, her face tilted up to the sky, her arms flung wide, a huge grin on her face.

The wetness on her cheeks now wasn't rain and her smile wasn't joyful and carefree, but the unfurling of warmth in her chest was the same.

Charlotte locked her case and stood up. "The lawyers will be in touch about the rest of the settlement."

Lily got up, holding the contract and the photo. "Thank you." It was husky and heartfelt.

"I don't expect we'll meet often in future." It was a very polite warning. "But I—" To Lily's astonishment, Charlotte lifted a hesitant hand to touch Lily's hair, rubbing the silvery colour between her fingers. The grief that slashed across her face was so quick and so intense that Lily's breath caught. For the second time, their eyes met. "I wish you every success, Lily."

Lily exhaled, and it was as if she were blowing out a bitter little flame that had burned for a long time. "Thank you. Same to you." She looked down at the papers again, and this time, it felt like it might be the truth: "I'll be okay."

When she closed the door behind Charlotte and turned to lean against it, her mother was standing in the entrance to the hallway.

Lily's hand tightened on the contract, rustling the paper, and Vanessa came forward to take the photograph. She studied it in silence. A small smile creased the corners of her eyes. "Apparently Jack was unpredictable until the end."

"Apparently so."

"He could have at least put a fucking coat on you. It *was* raining."

With a choked laugh, Lily slipped her arm through her mother's and rested her head against her shoulder.

Vanessa reached out and set the photograph on the dresser, propping it against a vase. "I still feel that Charlotte was absurdly naive if she thought Jack Lamprey would magically embrace monogamy, but I didn't want to be even half responsible for putting that look on someone's face ever again." Her voice cooled. "Not that it excuses the way she's treated you. I own responsibility, but she lost most of my sympathy a long time ago."

"It's difficult for her."

"I know it is. But you were a child. My baby. Not an easy target for her anger at Jack. She did her best to come between the two of you for years. Although Jack played his own part there." Vanessa's hand came up to cover hers. "You're like your dad in a lot of ways. Some good, some—slightly concerning." She grinned when Lily straightened and rolled her eyes. "You might even be a little like me." Her smile faded. "But I should never have pushed my prejudices on to you. It was unfair. You have a very different temperament." The green in her eyes suddenly seemed much brighter than the brown. "A much more generous heart, that doesn't deserve to be kept locked away."

Lily shook her head. "There are things I've blamed you for, and it was on me. I let myself think that way. I let things affect me that—in the long run, they're just not important."

"I do love you, Lily. More than I think you know."

Tears blurred Lily's vision. "I love you too."

"What I said before…" Vanessa cupped her cheek. "I just don't want you to get hurt."

"I might get hurt." She felt utterly calm and certain when she spoke. "But it'll be worth it."

"It's a huge gamble. For yourself and for your career."

"Well." Lily dabbed under her eyes with her sleeve. She could feel a tiny spark of humour creeping back. "I *am* half Lamprey."

Vanessa cast her gaze heavenward. "Yes." She nodded towards the gift-wrapped box on the dresser, still sitting where Margo had left it. "And when you decorate your flat with unopened presents, the Cray genes clearly didn't dominate." She made the transition to a lighter subject smoothly. The Cray genes also shied away from excessive emotion. "Who's it from?"

"It's my opening-night present from Luc." With everything that had happened, Lily had never opened it. She still wasn't allowed to drink, and she'd forgotten to give it to Freddy.

"And you never opened it?"

"It's champagne and a gift voucher for Harrods, apparently. I haven't been in the mood for shopping." She lifted it and removed the paper, pulling the tape carefully, trying not to rip something Luc had given her, although she doubted he'd wrapped it himself.

"Well, I'm happy to take both off your hands if they're going spare." Her mother looked questioningly at the items that appeared. There was a wooden casket of extremely expensive wine and a black leather case… that did not look like it contained a gift voucher.

Lily opened the lid and looked down at the necklace nestled on padded velvet.

Vanessa leaned forward. "Oh my. That's—"

The smile started somewhere in Lily's heart. "Hideous," she said through another bubble of astonishing, misery-shattering laughter. She slipped her fingers under the glittering diamonds. "It's hideous."

It was a clover, almost identical to the Canali necklace in its spectacularly tacky setting, but…only three leaves. A small card was attached. She opened it and read the short message in Luc's familiar scrawl, and the jolt of emotion actually made her hands tremble.

For an actor far more talented and slightly less clumsy than her idol. Three leaves only. The faith, hope and love are yours, MI5. You don't need the luck.

"Is that a shamrock?" Her mother looked understandably confused. "From Luc? Does that mean something?"

"Yes." Lily closed her hand around the necklace, holding it tightly. "It means a hell of a lot."

More than she would ever have thought possible.

"What now?" Luc didn't look up from the contracts he'd been trying to read for the past hour. Forget deciphering legal terms: he was so distracted that he was barely comprehending vowels.

He'd known, right from the beginning, that she would be a completely disruptive pain in the arse.

He worried about her. All the fucking time. And he missed her like hell.

All the fucking time.

Grimacing, he tossed the papers aside. Amelia read that as an invitation and lowered herself gracefully into one of the chairs opposite. She was holding a newspaper.

"Unless Waitely's actually killed someone, I don't want to know about it."

"How much sleep did you get last night?"

"Enough." Fuck-all.

"Did you even go home?"

He had, for a few hours, although it would have been more convenient to have slept in his office suite.

Margo's absence might not have left a shadow in his house, but every corner of it now smelled like Lily's perfume.

"You've been working eighteen-hour days." Amelia's eyes were anxious. "I'm worried about you. You can't maintain a pace like that. You'll have a str—"

His lips twisted. "Stroke?"

He *was* working longer hours than he needed to at this stage of pre-production. In theory, it kept his mind occupied. Some days, like today, even the new show couldn't distract him.

"Have you talked to her?"

One-word and one-letter texts. Except for last night, when she'd stretched to four words, and he was so bloody in love with her that he'd actually taken heart from that pitiful progress.

"No. She needs time."

Which he'd respected, but his decision to step back and give her the space she wanted was grating more every day.

Lily struggled with trust—because every person she

might have leaned on tended to step back and go their own way at the last moment.

So effectively walking out on her, even at her insistent, tear-sodden request, seemed like a massive fucking mistake now.

He was tapping his pen against the desk with increasing pressure; it suddenly broke.

Amelia sighed. "I see we need to buy pens in bulk."

Luc shoved back his chair and stood up. "Tell Carly I'm out for the rest of the day."

"Before you go—" Amelia chewed on her lip and extended the paper, which he only now saw was *London Celebrity*. "I think you ought to—"

"What? I had someone assassinated? I'm planning to rob the National Trust? Just throw it in the recycler. Who keeps *buying* that? If we have a subscription, I'm going to—"

Amelia flipped open the paper, thumbed through the pages and held a headline under his nose.

He looked down at it, and his lips compressed. He read the first three paragraphs before he rolled the paper into a tube and tucked it under his arm. "If anyone needs to reach me, I'll have my phone."

"Keep in mind that you'll be giving *London Celebrity* excellent copy if you murder their editor."

"That's a trade-off I may be willing to make."

The *London Celebrity* offices were only a few blocks from his own building. If there weren't a banking highrise blocking his view, he and Byrne could have looked directly at each other's mirrored windows like a couple of melodramatic comic book foes.

When he reached the glossy foyer, he walked straight

to the lift and jabbed the button for the top floor. He'd be extremely surprised if Byrne didn't have the penthouse.

The glass-and-marble box shot upwards smoothly, giving him a clear view of every floor he passed. Gutter journalism was obviously a lucrative business.

In the most convenient moment of the past fortnight, Byrne was standing talking to his secretary when the doors pinged open. He broke off his conversation when he saw Luc. His face, which was evidently capable of producing a decent facsimile of a smile in more congenial company, iced over.

"Savage." Byrne didn't move from where he stood. "How did you get past security?"

"Am I on the undesirable list?" Luc asked sardonically. "I walked through the front doors and got in the lift. If you *have* security, you might want to look at how much you're paying them."

Byrne's gaze flickered to his avidly listening secretary, before he opened a heavy oak door and gestured with exaggerated pseudo-courtesy. "Since you're here, I suppose you might as well come in."

Luc walked past him, took one brief look around the plush office, and concentrated his attention on the so-called human element.

"To what do I owe the pleasure?"

Luc pulled the rolled-up paper from beneath his arm and tossed it on the desk.

Byrne walked around to stand behind his nameplate and flicked the paper over with his pen. "Today's issue. So kind, but we do have a few spares."

"I have something far more important to do today, so I'm going to make this brief." Luc met the cold blue stare with equal calm. "Even by your standards, trashing the character of the recently deceased is low. Advising that the city celebrate his death is atrocious. Jack Lamprey may not have had *your* flawless moral character," he said ironically, "but he wasn't a criminal, and he has a grieving family who don't need to see this."

Byrne's smile made Luc's hand itch. "Ah, yes. His family. Would we specifically be referring to the lovely Lily? She's rather like a one-woman production of *The Wizard of Oz*, isn't she? Dorothy's pretty face and the Scarecrow's unfortunate plight. 'If I only had a brain.'"

Luc kept his expression bland, although the hand he'd tucked into his pocket also curled into a fist. "I want the online version of that article taken down within an hour."

"*Do* you? How disappointing for you—"

"If I see anything remotely similar appear on your site or in print again, I'll have my legal team comb through every defamatory word you've approved over the past few months, I will compile a watertight case for slander, and I will *destroy* you in court." Luc continued to speak over Byrne's retort. "I'm aware that you've been trying to push me into that corner, presumably to generate even worse publicity for my family and increased sales for you. I would happily have avoided this situation. It's a fucking waste of time, it's a drain of resources, and yeah—I *do* still feel that you had a valid grievance against my grandfather."

Byrne's nostrils and lips were white and pinched. "How magnanimous of you to admit it."

"Against my *grandfather*," Luc repeated. "Who died a long time ago. I don't appreciate constantly paying for someone else's sins. You've had that experience yourself."

"Meaning what, exactly?"

"Meaning that, yes, your father was the victim of a conman. However, *he* made the decision—with utter recklessness—to put his family's entire livelihood at risk by investing in one of Johnny Savage's businesses. Johnny's track record was no secret. Your father let himself be blinded by false promises, but his own choices bordered on criminal stupidity."

Byrne's face flushed a dangerous shade of magenta and he took a step forward. Luc profoundly hoped that he wasn't going to end up in a one-sided fistfight with a sixty-five-year-old man—or have another heart attack patient on his hands.

He tempered his tone, but didn't soften the message. "It took years of saving and investments, with my *own* money, to restore the Queen Anne, but no matter how much that project meant to me, it would never be worth risking my family's financial security." Pointedly, he added, "I assume you have insurance against litigation here. You wouldn't be paying out of your children's pockets if I took you to court."

Byrne didn't deny that, but his fury was still palpable. "That doesn't change the fact that your grandfather got away scot-free."

"Nobody gets away scot-free." Luc had seen photos of his grandfather, taken late in his life. He'd been an alcohol-ravaged, debt-ridden wreck. His eyes had been pools of…nothing. No humour, no love, no life. "Every action has a consequence. One way or another." He held the other man's gaze. "And for the record: I'm sorry that happened to your family. I also understand why you refused compensation. But where you're concerned—my conscience is clear."

Byrne's hands were still balled into fists.

"If writing one lie about me after another changes something for you—go ahead." Luc's voice lowered. "But if you continue to go after my family—and you can include the Lampreys and the Crays in that category—I *will* retaliate."

The tension in the room was like the clashing of metal.

Luc turned and left the room, almost knocking over the secretary who had rolled her chair dangerously close to the door.

He jabbed at the lift button.

"Savage."

He turned. Behind him, the doors opened, and he reached back to hold them.

Byrne's mouth stretched into something that wasn't quite a smile. "She was similarly vocal in her defence of you."

Luc didn't let so much as a flicker of what he felt cross his face. "She's a formidable opponent."

He stepped into the lift.

"I'll see you in court."

"That's up to you."

The doors slid closed.

The lift doors opened and Lily stepped out into reception. The same receptionist who had witnessed her meeting with Dan St. James a hundred years ago looked up without curiosity.

Amelia, standing in conversation with her assistant, also looked up. "Lily!"

"Hi, Amelia." Lily glanced down the corridor. The car ride here had seemed interminable. She wanted to—

She had to see him. "Is Luc in?" She started towards his office without waiting for a reply.

"No." Amelia almost ran to intercept her, stumbling when her high heels caught in the thick carpet. "He's not."

"Oh." He wasn't answering his phone, either. Her heart was racing. She pressed the heel of her hand to her chest. "Is he in a meeting?"

"He's—" Amelia studied her narrowly. "Why?"

"Because I—" She couldn't say this to Amelia. After everything she'd put Luc through recently, she owed these words to him alone. "Do you know when he'll back?"

The other woman suddenly looked profoundly uncomfortable. "No. I don't."

Lily focused on her properly. "Why, where is he?"

"He's gone to the *London Celebrity* offices."

For fuck's sake. "What have they printed about him now?"

Amelia's lips parted, but nothing came out.

"Amelia?"

"It's not about Luc. It's about…your father."

The receptionist, abandoning any pretence that she wasn't listening, leaned forward and offered her a print copy of the tabloid, open at the correct page. Lily read the headline.

"It's—" Amelia began bracingly.

"It's more tabloid rubbish." Lily let herself feel the rush of pain; then, deliberately, she closed the paper. "It's spiteful, it's biased and it's not true."

Amelia continued to study her with concern, but finally a hint of a smile appeared in her eyes. "Good for you."

The full meaning behind Amelia's earlier statement clarified. "What do you mean, he's gone to the offices?"

"Luc didn't take that piece of 'journalism' quite so philosophically. He's on the warpath."

"Well," Lily said. "Shit."

"Indeed."

"And where are…"

"About ten minutes' walk away."

On her way past the increasingly large group of staff at the reception desk, Lily tossed the paper in the bin. "By the way—who keeps *buying* this?"

The *London Celebrity* office building was a lot classier than its product. Sewer journalism obviously brought in the pennies. Lily walked straight past the reception desk towards the lift.

She reached for the button, but the doors opened before she could touch it.

She almost heard an audible click as things slid into their right place.

"I probably ought to be surprised," Luc said, "but your dramatic instincts always were solid."

He tucked a hand beneath her arm and steered her firmly away from the lift. "If you're planning to go up and disembowel Byrne, would you consider letting the legal team handle him instead? It'll be less messy and I'd rather you weren't carted off to jail. It's been bad enough having a couple of boroughs between us."

Lily checked him out from sleek head to shiny shoes. "I'm here to stop *you* being arrested for assault. I don't see any bruises."

"In the unlikely event that I got into a physical fight with a senior citizen, I would bloody well hope you wouldn't see any bruises. I'm not *that* fucking old." Luc's grey eyes had been like ice when the lift doors had opened; now they were warming with the light she loved. "I was on my way to your flat after this."

A smile began to flutter to life.

In hindsight, he'd been amazingly restrained waiting this long.

"I was on my way to your office."

She saw Luc's chest rise in a breath that looked slightly uneven, and she hated that tiny betrayal of apprehension.

"Luc—" God, how did she even begin? What kind of words could just bridge the gap *she'd* forced?

His gaze suddenly moved to her chest and fixed there, which—okay, didn't really seem the moment to be focusing on her breasts, but... She suddenly remembered what she was wearing. It was amazing it had slipped her mind even temporarily. It wasn't exactly a wallflower.

Luc reached out and touched the clover necklace, his palm resting against her heart. He cleared his throat. "For the record, if I'd intended it to be *worn*, I'd have given it to someone I can't stand, not the woman I—" Their eyes locked again. If hers were reflecting how she felt, they ought to be steady and clear. "The woman I love."

Her heart was beating so rapidly and heavily it might have been trying to press into his hand.

Luc gestured with his head. "You realise we're standing in gutter press HQ right now. If we're going to give them copy, we don't necessarily need to bring it directly to them."

"I don't care."

He shook his head, but she put her hand over his and gripped his fingers.

"I really don't." She gathered the last vestiges of her courage. "I'm so sorry, Luc. For everything. My head's been all over the place. Jack's—Dad's death just seemed to be the final straw. And I was so *angry*. I felt like I'd been waiting for him, for—something, my whole life, and suddenly it was just gone. He's just gone."

Luc stroked her fingers. "I know."

"He loved me in the only way he knew how, and it's—enough."

"You deserved a hell of a lot more." He spoke roughly, but his touch was gentle.

"I've had a hell of a lot. I still do. I shouldn't ever lose sight of that." She hooked her thumb around his. "And I hope I haven't completely fucked up the best part."

His hold tightened in a compulsive movement. "I know it's been difficult to…trust in this. In us. My relationship history leaves a lot to be desired, and probably reinforced any doubts you already had." Luc stopped, grasped for the right words. "If I say that this is different—that what's between you and me is different in every way imaginable— it sounds like a line." He lifted their entwined thumbs, as if they were doing an eccentric version of a pinkie promise. "It's not. You've changed absolutely fucking everything. And I'll be there for you as long as you'll let me."

She was not going to cry again. She was turning into a bloody sieve.

"I know." Her voice was crackly. With her free hand, she grasped a handful of his shirt to pull herself up. She placed a tiny kiss on his lower lip. "Did a bit of shopping at the pound store, did you?"

He grinned. "Well, I looked, but their selection was a little too tasteful. I finally found a jeweller who agreed to make it on commission, as long as his name is never associated with it."

"I love you." It was something she'd said to very few people; she'd never meant it so profoundly. "God, I really love you—"

He swallowed the last words with his mouth, kissing her deeply, dragging her into the sheltering warmth of his body. His tongue thrust against hers, and she wriggled her trapped arms free, wrapping them around his neck.

Again and again, he kissed her, stroking her, nipping at her, loving her.

Right in the midst of tabloid central.

When the need for oxygen became dire, she pulled back, sucking in a deep breath, and stayed on her tiptoes. His tousled hair tickled her skin.

"In case it wasn't clear," he said, "I love you like hell."

She believed that. No doubts. No second thoughts. Complete trust.

It was freeing and hopeful.

And it was more than enough.

Epilogue

Autumn, in the Lake District, in a forest of all places.

Lily rubbed her nose against the curve of Luc's neck. His hand slid down her back, shaping her hip. His lips nuzzled her ear.

"How's the birthday been?" he murmured, and she smiled without opening her eyes.

"Contender for best ever. You got it into the top three by two o'clock in the morning. And we didn't even spill any bath water on the floor. We've got skills."

"And bruised elbows."

"And my knee is making a weird clicking sound when I walk. Still worth it."

Luc nudged her head with his until she looked up. He kissed her. "*Contender* for best ever? Bathtub sex in a tree house hotel in the Lake District. Come on, I climbed a tree for you. Credit where credit's due."

"I did go to Disneyland Paris for my seventh. There were fireworks, a cupcake with my name on it, and I got a hug from Goofy. The bar is set pretty high."

"How about I light a candle, write your name on a Curly Wurly from the minibar, and throw in another couple of orgasms?"

"Might push you over the edge." She kissed him again, and felt his body shift against her, his arms pulling her even closer.

"One question."

"The answer is yes. I do think staying in a tree house means you should have worn a loincloth to dinner."

"Different question." Luc cupped her face, stroking his thumb over her cheekbone. "You know I love you."

She didn't think that would ever not do things to her heart. She raised her fingers to his chin. "I know."

"You'll always be my priority. Nothing and no one will ever be more important to me."

"I know," she said again, quietly. She touched his mouth. "Back at you."

"You drive me up the wall, and I can't remember what life was like before you strode into it, opened your mouth and fucking horrified me, and turned everything upside down."

"It probably involved more sleep." She grinned when he closed his teeth lightly on her thumb. "Sorry. Go on. You were generously overlooking my faults—"

"You're the love of my life."

She took a quick breath through her mouth.

His wrists locked at the base of her spine and he rocked her, gently, from side to side. "There's very little I wouldn't do for you."

"I'm realising that. You actually booked the tree house."

"Exactly. We're talking compromise. Commitment. If we were hanging off the side of a cliff and the rope was only strong enough to hold one of us, I probably wouldn't let you plummet to your death."

"Thank you. Crossing abseiling in the Grand Canyon off the list for our next holiday."

"And even though you've crossed over enemy lines and contracted yourself to the Metronome," he went on, "I *will* actually sit through at least one performance of an Alexander Bennett play, even though I would usually rank that experience alongside a root canal."

"He had really warm and cuddly things to say about you as well."

"But." Luc looked down at her through the steady stream of rain. Their hair was soaked and her dress was plastered to her breasts—the one part of his very unexpected and poignant gesture that had changed his expression from Martyred to Interested. "The reality of the rain dancing is even worse than it sounded in theory. How many ranks do I drop if I suggest we go inside now? We're probably a lot less likely to drown thirty feet above the ground."

Lily smoothed her hair out of her eyes and pushed her face back in his neck. "Soon."

"Hell," he said, and rested his cheek against her head.

"This is so nice," she mumbled. "There's something about the air in the Lake District. Goes to my head."

"The champagne might also have something to do with it."

"There *are* benefits to being between shows." She tucked her chilled fingers inside his collar. "And you haven't made a single work-related phone call yet."

"Arguing with Amelia and wrangling contract negotiations for hours, or bathtub sex with the most beautiful woman I've ever seen. Tough decision."

"I give it one more day. And you can lay it on as thick as you like. We're still not going inside."

They stayed in each other's arms while the rain dwindled to a light drizzle and the cloudy sky turned dark. The lamps in the tree house above cast a warm glow that touched them with light.

"I miss him," she said softly, and the cradle of his arms tightened.

"I know you do."

"I got a birthday present from him."

He pulled back to look at her. "What?"

"He arranged it as a surprise. I got the official confirmation from his solicitor today." She straightened. "Luc. I can *feel* you bracing yourself."

"A surprise arranged through Jack's lawyer? I assume it's at least legal, then."

"Oh, it's legal."

His eyes narrowed. "Why do I suddenly have the *Jaws* theme music in my head?"

"As of five o'clock this evening, Hudson Warner's shares in the Queen Anne have been transferred to my name. When you turn your phone on, I expect you'll have several calls."

"Excuse me?"

"Jack offered to buy him out the day we went to Kirkby. Right after we left. He told Hud that I needed a stake in the family business."

"Your father said that? Last December?" Luc's expression was unreadable.

She tugged on one of his shirt buttons. "Yes."

"Wise man, Jack Lamprey."

"Yes, he was."

Suddenly, he grinned. "No more calls, meetings, dinners or helpful little suggestions from Warner? I thought this was supposed to be *your* birthday."

She looped her arm back around his neck. "I wouldn't get too excited until you see my list of suggestions for the next shareholder meeting."

"Your list?"

"I jotted some things down while you were in the shower."

"Is that right?"

"One word." Lily made a sweeping gesture with her free hand. "Vaudeville."

"Three words. Cause for separation." He trapped her hand against his heart. She could feel it beating beneath her palm.

"Don't worry. I'll be a good counterbalance." Her lips turned up in a tiny smile that found an echo in her chest. "Savages play by the rules. Lampreys get things done."

"Jack?"

"Like you said. My father was a wise man."

Luc's fingers slipped between hers. Their rings glinted in the dim light. "And Lamprey-Savages?"

Her smile grew. "Despite reports that I've left you for Dylan Waitely and you're consoling yourself with the woman who does the baking segment on *Wake Me Up London*, the Lamprey-Savages are pretty damn spectacular. Up to their ears in scandal, rumour and sin, but nauseatingly happy."

"I noticed on the hotel register that we're still giving you top billing."

"Savage-Lampreys? If you *want* to sound like a vicious marine parasite..."

"When you put it that way." Luc turned his attention to her neck, pushing back her wet hair to feather a kiss in the hollow beneath her ear. He paused. "You're really going to come to shareholder meetings?"

"Is that a problem?"

"No. Great. Can't wait."

She slipped her hand under the clammy fabric of his shirt to feel the muscles shifting beneath his warm skin. "You never know. It could be a side career for me. Corporate Barbie."

He winced. "You're never going to let me forget that, are you?"

"I probably will eventually." She waited a beat. "By the time I'm ninety and you're a hundred and fifty, I'll—"

He tilted her into a dramatic dip, her hair touching the muddy ground, his grin against her mouth, and her laughter broke through the stillness of the night.

* * * * *

Keep reading for an excerpt from
ACT LIKE IT by Lucy Parker, now available at all
participating e-retailers.

Chapter One

Almost every night, between nine and ten past, Lainie Graham passionately kissed her ex-boyfriend. She was then gruesomely dead by ten o'clock, stabbed through the neck by a jealous rival. If she was scheduled to perform in the weekend matinee, that was a minimum of six uncomfortable kisses a week. More, if the director called an extra rehearsal or the alternate actor was ill. Or if Will was being a prat backstage and she was slow to duck.

It was an odd situation, being paid to publicly snog the man who, offstage, had discarded her like a stray sock. From the perspective of a broken relationship, the theatre came up trumps in the awkward stakes. A television or film actor might have to make stage love to someone they despised, but they didn't have to play the same scene on repeat for an eight-month run.

From her position in the wings, Lainie watched Will and Chloe Wayne run through the penultimate scene. Chloe was practically vibrating with sexual tension, which wasn't so much in character as it was her default setting. Will was breathing in the wrong places during his monologue; it was throwing off his pacing. She waited, and—

"Farmer!" boomed the director from his seat in the front row. Alexander Bennett's balding head was gleaming with sweat under the houselights. He'd been lounging in his chair but now dropped any pretence of indifference, jerking forward to glare at the stage. "You're blocking a scene, not swimming the bloody breaststroke. Stop bobbing your head about and breathe through your damn nose."

A familiar sulky expression transformed Will's even features. He looked like a spoilt, genetically blessed schoolboy. He was professional enough to smooth out the instinctive scowl and resume his speech, but with an air of resentment that didn't improve his performance. This was the moment of triumph for his character and right now the conquering knight sounded as if he would rather put down his sword and go for a pint.

Will had been off his game since the previous night, when he'd flubbed a line in the opening act. He was a gifted actor. An unfaithful toerag, but a talented actor. He rarely made mistakes—and could cover them better than most—but from the moment he'd stumbled over his cue, the additional rehearsal had been inevitable. Bennett sought perfection in every arena of his life, which was why he was on to his fifth marriage and all the principals had been dragged out of bed on their morning off.

Most of the principals, Lainie amended silently. Their brooding Byron had, as usual, done as he pleased. Bennett had looked almost apoplectic when Richard Troy had sauntered in twenty minutes late, so that explosion was still coming. If possible, he preferred to roar in his private office, where his Tony Award was prominently displayed on the desk. It was a sort of visual aid on the journey from stripped ego to abject apology.

Although a repentant Richard Troy was about as likely as a winged pig, and he could match Bennett's prized trophy and raise him two more.

Onstage, Chloe collapsed into a graceful swoon, which was Richard's cue for the final act. He pushed off the wall on the opposite side of the wings and flicked an invisible speck from his spotless shirt. Then he entered from stage left and whisked the spotlight from Will and Chloe with insulting ease, taking control of the scene with barely a twitch of his eyelid.

Four months into the run of *The Cavalier's Tribute*, it was still an undeniable privilege to watch him act.

Unfortunately, Richard's stage charisma was comparable to the interior of the historic Metronome Theatre. At night, under the houselights, the Metronome was pure magic, a charged atmosphere of class and old-world glamour. In the unforgiving light of day, it looked tired and a bit sordid, like an aging diva caught without her war paint and glitter.

And when the curtain came down and the skin of the character was shed, Richard Troy was an intolerable prick.

Will was halfway through the most long-winded of his speeches. It was Lainie's least favourite moment in an otherwise excellent play. Will's character, theoretically the protagonist, became momentarily far less sympathetic than Richard's undeniable villain. She still couldn't tell if it was an intentional ambiguity on the part of the playwright, perhaps a reflection that humanity is never cast in shades of black and white, or if it was just poor writing. The critic in the *Guardian* had thought the latter.

Richard was taunting Will now, baiting him with both words and snide glances, and looking as if he was enjoying himself a little too much. Will drew himself up, and his face took on an expression of intense self-righteousness.

Lainie winced. It was, down to the half sneer, the exact same face he made in bed.

She really wished she didn't know that.

"Ever worry it's going to create some sort of cosmic imbalance?" asked a voice at her elbow, and she turned to smile at Meghan Hanley, her dresser. "Having both of them in one building? If you toss in most of the management, I think we may be exceeding the recommended bastard quota." Meghan raised a silvery eyebrow as she watched the denouement of the play. "They both have swords, and neither of them takes the opportunity for a quick jab. What a waste."

"Please. A pair of blind, arthritic nuns would do better in a swordfight. Richard has probably never charged anything heavier than a credit card, and Will has the hand-eye coordination of an earthworm."

She was admittedly still a little bitter. Although not in the least heartbroken. Only a very silly schoolgirl would consider Will Farmer to be the love of her life, and that delusion would only last until she'd actually met him. But Lainie had not relished being dumped by the trashiest section of *London Celebrity*. The tabloid had taken great pleasure in informing her, and the rest of the rag-reading world, that Will was now seeing the estranged wife of a footballer—who in turn had been cheated on by her husband with a former *Big Brother* contestant. It was an endless sordid cycle.

The article had helpfully included a paparazzi shot of her from about three months ago, when she'd left the theatre and been caught midsneeze. *Farmer's costar and ousted lover Elaine Graham dissolves into angry tears outside the Metronome.*

Brilliant.

The journo, to use the term loosely, had also complimented her on retaining her appetite in the face of such humiliation—insert shot of her eating chips at Glastonbury—with a cunning little system of arrows to indicate a possible baby bump.

Her dad had phoned her, offering to deliver Will's balls on a platter.

Margaret Ward, the assistant stage manager, paused to join the unofficial critics' circle. She pushed back her ponytail with a paint-splattered hand and watched Richard. His voice was pure, plummy Eton and Oxford—not so much as a stumbled syllable in his case. Will looked sour.

Richard drew his sword, striding forward to stand under the false proscenium. Margaret glanced up at the wooden arch. "Do you ever wish it would just accidentally drop on his head?"

Yes.

"He hasn't *quite* driven me to homicidal impulses yet." Lainie recalled the Tuesday night performance, when she'd bumped into Richard outside his dressing room. She had apologised. He had made a misogynistic remark at a volume totally out of proportion to a minor elbow jostle.

The media constantly speculated as to why he was still single. Mind-boggling.

"Yet," she repeated grimly.

"By the way," Margaret said, as she glanced at her clipboard and flagged a lighting change, "Bob wants to see you in his office in about ten minutes."

Lainie turned in surprise. "Bob does? Why?"

Her mind instantly went into panic mode, flicking back over the past week. With the exception of touching His Majesty's sacred arm for about two seconds—and she wouldn't put it past Richard to lay a complaint about that—she couldn't think of any reason for a summons to the stage manager's office. As a rule, Robert Carson viewed his actors as so many figureheads. They were useful for pulling out at cocktail parties and generating social media buzz, but operated beneath his general notice unless they did something wrong. Bob preferred to concentrate on the bottom line, and the bottom line in question was located at the end of his bank statement.

Margaret shrugged. "He didn't say. He's been in a bad mood all day, though," she warned, and Lainie sighed.

"I could have been in bed right now," she mused wistfully. "With a cream cheese bagel and a completely trashy book. Bloody Will."

On the flip side, she could also still have been in bed *with* Will, enjoying the taste of his morning breath and a lecture on her questionable tastes in literature. From the man who still thought *To Kill a Mockingbird* was a nonfiction guide for the huntin', shootin' and fishin' set.

Life could really only improve.

On that cheering thought, she made her way out of the wings and backstage into the rabbit's warren of tunnelling hallways that led to the staff offices. The floors and walls creaked as she went, as if the theatre were quietly grumbling under its breath. Despite the occasional sticking door handle and an insidious smell of damp, she liked the decrepit old lady. The Metronome was one of the oldest theatres in the West End. They might not have decent seating and fancy automated loos, but they had history. Legendary actors had walked these halls.

"And Edmund Kean probably thought the place was an absolute dump as well" had been Meghan's opinion on that subject.

Historical opinion was divided on the original seventeenth-century use of the Metronome. Debate raged in textbooks as to whether it had been a parliamentary annex or a high-class brothel. Lainie couldn't see that it really mattered. It would likely have been frequented by the same men in either instance.

Personally, she voted for the brothel. It would add a bit of spice to the inevitable haunting rumours. Much more interesting to have a randy ghost who had succumbed midcoitus than an overworked civil servant who had died of boredom midpaperwork.

Aware that Bob's idea of "in ten minutes" could be loosely translated as "right now," she headed straight for his office, which was one of the few rooms at the front of the theatre and had a view looking out over the busy road. Her memories of the room were associated with foot shuffling, mild sweating and a fervent wish to be outside amid an anonymous throng of shoppers and tourists heading for Oxford Street.

"Enter," called a voice at her knock, and she took the opportunity to roll her eyes before she opened the door. Her most convincing fake smile was firmly in place by the time she walked inside, but it faltered when she saw the two women standing with Bob.

"Good. Elaine," Bob said briskly. He was wearing his usual incorrectly buttoned shirt. Every day it was a different button. Same shirt, apparently, but different button. He *had* to be doing it on purpose. "You remember Lynette Stern and Patricia Bligh."

Naturally, Lainie remembered Lynette and Pat. She saw them every week, usually from a safe distance. An uneasy prickling sensation was beginning to uncurl at the base of her neck. She greeted Pat with a mild unconcern she didn't feel, and returned Lynette's nod. She couldn't imagine why the tall sharp-nosed blonde was here for this obviously less-than-impromptu meeting. She would have thought her more likely to be passed out in a mental health spa. Or just sobbing in a remote corner. Lynette Stern was Richard Troy's agent, and she had Lainie's sincere sympathies. Every time she saw the woman, there was a new line on her forehead.

It was Pat Bligh's presence that gave Lainie serious pause. Pat was the Metronome's PR manager. She ruled over their collective public image with an iron hand and very little sense of humour. And woe betide anyone who was trending for unfortunate reasons on Twitter.

What the hell had she done?

She was biting on her thumbnail. It was a habit she had successfully kicked at school, and she forced herself to stop now, clasping her hands tightly together. She had been in a running panic this morning to get to the Tube on time, and now she wished she'd taken time to check her Google alerts.

Nude photos? Not unless someone had wired her

shower. Even as an infant, she had disliked being naked. She usually broke speed records in changing her clothes.

She blanched. *Unless Will had taken…*

In which case she was going to hit the stage and make short work of borrowing Richard's sword, and Will was going to find himself minus two of his favourite accessories.

"Sit down, Elaine," Bob said, his expression unreadable. Reluctantly, she obeyed the order—Bob didn't do invitations—and chose the most uncomfortable chair in the room, as if in a preemptive admittance of guilt.

Get a grip.

"I'll come right to the point." Bob sat on the edge of the wide mahogany desk and gestured the other women to sit down with an impatient wiggle of his index finger. Reaching for the iPad on his blotter, he flipped it open and keyed in the password. "I presume you've seen this."

He held the iPad in front of Lainie's face and she blinked, trying to bring the screen into focus. She could feel the heavy pulse of her heartbeat, but dread dwindled into confusion when she saw the news item. *London Celebrity* had struck again, but she wasn't the latest offering for the sacrificial pit after all.

It appeared that Richard had dined out last night. The fact that he'd entered into a shouting match with a notable chef and decided to launch a full-scale offensive on the tableware seemed about right. She took a closer look at the lead photograph. Of *course* his paparazzi shots were that flattering. No piggy-looking eyes and double chins for Richard Troy. He probably didn't *have* a bad angle.

God, he was irritating.

She shrugged, and three sets of pursed lips tightened. "Well," she said hastily, trying to recover her ground, "it's unfortunate, but…"

"But Richard does this kind of shit all the time" was probably not the answer they were looking for.

And what exactly did this have to do with her? Surely they weren't expecting her to cough up for his damages bill. The spoon in baby Richard Troy's mouth had been diamond-encrusted platinum. He was old family money, a millionaire multiple times over. He could pay for his own damn broken Meissen. If he had a propensity for throwing public temper tantrums and hurling objects about the room, his management team should have restricted him to eating at McDonald's. There was only so much damage he could do with paper wrappers and plastic forks.

"It's getting to be more than *unfortunate*," Lynette said, in such an ominous tone that Lainie decided to keep her opinions to herself on that score.

Pat at last broke her simmering silence. "There have been eight separate incidents in this month alone." Three strands of blond hair had come loose from her exquisitely arranged chignon. For most women, that would be a barely noticeable dishevelment. Lainie's own hair tended to collapse with a resigned sigh the moment she turned away from the mirror. For Pat, three unpinned locks was a shocking state of disarray. "It's only the second week of October."

Lainie thought that even Richard should fear that particular tone of voice from this woman. She flinched on his behalf.

"Any publicity is good publicity. Isn't that the idea?" She glanced warily from one mutinous face to the next.

It was an identical expression, replicated thrice over. A sort of incredulous outrage, as if the whole class were being punished for the sins of one naughty child.

Apt, really. If one considered the personalities involved.

"To a point." Bob's nostrils flared. She couldn't help noticing that a trim wouldn't go astray there. "Which Troy has now exceeded." He gave her a filthy look that suggested she was personally responsible for Richard's behaviour. God forbid.

"Men in particular," he went on, stating the loathsome truth, "are given a fair amount of leeway in the public eye. A certain reputation for devilry, a habit of thumbing one's nose at the establishment, sowing one's wild oats…" He paused, looking hard at her, and Lainie hoped that her facial expression read "listening." As opposed to "nauseated." He sounded like a 1950s summary of the ideal man's man. Which had been despicably sexist sixty years ago and had not improved since.

"However," Bob continued, and the word came down like a sledgehammer, "there is a line at which a likable bad boy becomes a nasty entitled bastard whom the public would rather see hung out to dry in the street than pay to watch prance about a stage in his bloomers. And when somebody starts abusing their fans, making an absolute arse of themselves in public places, and alienating the people who paid for their bloody Ferrari, they may consider that line *crossed*."

Lainie wondered if an actual "Hallelujah" chorus had appeared in the doorway, or if it was just the sound of her own glee.

She still had no idea why she was the privileged audience to this character assassination, but she warmly appreciated it. Surely, though, they weren't…

"Are you *firing* him?" Her voice squeaked as if she had uttered the most outrageous profanity. Voiced the great unspoken. The mere suggestion of firing Richard Troy was the theatrical equivalent of hollering "Voldemort!" in the halls of Hogwarts. He-Who-Shall-Not-Be-Missed.

Still…

She wondered if it would be mean-spirited to cross her fingers.

Bob's return look was disappointingly exasperated. "Of course we're not firing him. It would cost an absolute bloody fortune to break his contract."

"And I suggest you don't attempt it." Lynette sounded steely.

"Besides," Bob said grudgingly, "nobody is denying that he's a decent actor, when he confines his histrionics to the script."

That was a typical Bob-ism. Pure understatement. Richard Troy had made the cover of *Time* magazine the previous year. The extravagantly handsome headshot had been accompanied by an article lauding him as a talent surpassing Olivier, and only two critics had been appalled.

"And if he conducted his outbursts with a bit of discretion," Bob said, as if they were discussing a string of irregular liaisons, "then we wouldn't be having this discussion. But Troy's deplorable public image is beginning to affect ticket sales. The management is not pleased."

Lainie couldn't match his awe of a bunch of walking wallets in suits, but she echoed the general feeling of dismay. If the management weren't pleased, Bob would make everyone else's life an utter misery until their mood improved.

"I'm not sure what this has to do with me," she said warily.

"If ticket sales are down, it's everybody's problem," Lynette said pompously, and Pat looked at her impatiently.

"We need some good publicity for Richard." She folded her arms and subjected Lainie to an intense scrutiny, which wavered into scepticism. "The general consensus is so overwhelmingly negative that he's in danger of falling victim to a hate campaign in the press. People might flock to see a subject of scandal, but they won't fork over hard-earned cash to watch someone they wholeheartedly despise. Not in this competitive market. At least not since it became socially unacceptable to heave rotten vegetables at the stage," she added with a brief, taut smile.

Lainie allowed herself three seconds to fantasize about that.

"How badly have sales dropped?" she asked, wondering if she ought to be contacting her agent. She had a third audition lined up for a period drama that was due to begin shooting early next year, but if there was a chance the play might actually fold…

An internationally acclaimed West End production, brought down by Richard Troy's foot-stamping sulks. Unbelievable.

"We're down fourteen percent on last month," Bob said, and she bit her lip. "We're not going bust." He sounded a bit put out at having to lessen his grievance. "It would take a pipe bomb as well as Richard's presence onstage before there was any real threat of that. But we've had to paper the house four nights running this month, and we opened to a six-week waiting list. This play has another four months to run, and we want to end on a high. Not in a damp fizzle of insulted fans and critics."

Lainie was silent for a moment. It was news to her that management were giving out free tickets in order to fill empty seats. "Well, excuse the stupidity, but I'm still not sure what you expect me to do about it. Ask him nicely to be a good boy and pull up his socks? Three guesses as to the outcome."

The tension zapped back into her spine when Bob and Pat exchanged a glance.

Pat seemed to be debating her approach. Eventually, she commented almost casually, "Ticket sales at the Palladium have gone up ten percent in the last three months."

Lainie snorted. "I know. Since Jack Trenton lost his last remaining brain cell after rehab and hooked up with Sadie Foster."

Or, as she was affectionately known in the world of musical theatre, the She-Devil of Soho. Lainie had known Sadie since they were in their late teens. They had been at drama school together. She had been short-listed against her for a role in a community theatre production of *42nd Street*, and had found shards of broken glass in the toes of her tap shoes. Fortunately before she'd put them on.

She was so preoccupied with a short-lived trip down a murky memory lane that she missed the implication.

"Quite." Pat's left eyebrow rose behind the lens of her glasses. She was now leaning on the edge of Bob's desk, her blunt, fuchsia-painted nails tapping a jaunty little medley on the surface. "And the only genuine buzz of excitement Richard has generated in the past month was when *London Celebrity* printed photos of the two of you attending the Bollinger party together." She again stared at Lainie, as if she was examining her limb by limb in an attempt to discover her appeal, and was coming up short.

The penny had dropped. With the clattering, appalling clamour of an anvil.

Don't miss ACT LIKE IT by Lucy Parker. Available now wherever Carina Press e-books are sold.

www.CarinaPress.com

Author's Note

Like several of the West End theaters in this book, Elisabetta Canali and her alter ego Edmund Cane are fictional. You won't find the Canali necklace among London's jewel collections—which might be fortunate!

Acknowledgments

To my editor, Deborah Nemeth, and the whole team at Carina Press: thank you so much for your support, patience and hard work.

To Hallie Sweet and Jennifer Margaret Holmes, the real-life speech therapists who put together a treatment plan for a fictional character: thank you for your time and expertise, and for taking on a fairly unusual brief without hesitation!

To my friends, whether I've known you for years or I've gotten to know you online: I'm surrounded by talent and humor and kindness, and you make everything better.

To my family: you're always my strongest source of support and you get me through the tough times. I love you and I can't thank you enough.

And to everyone who reads this book: thank you. It means more than I can say.

About the Author

Lucy Parker lives in the gorgeous Central Otago region of New Zealand, where she feels lucky every day to look out at mountains, lakes and vineyards. She has a degree in art history, loves museums and art galleries, and doodles unrecognizable flowers when she has writer's block.

When she's not writing, working or sleeping, she happily tackles the towering pile of to-be-read books that never gets any smaller. Thankfully, there's always another story waiting.

Her interest in romantic fiction began with a preteen viewing of *Pride and Prejudice* (Firth-style), which prompted her to read the book, as well. A family friend introduced her to Georgette Heyer, and the rest was history.

She loves to talk to other readers and writers, and you can find her on Twitter, @_lucyparker, or on her website, www.lucyparkerfiction.com.

Get 2 Free Books,
Plus 2 Free Gifts –
just for trying the **Reader Service!**

STRS17R

Get 2 Free Books,
Plus 2 Free Gifts—
just for trying the
Reader Service!

Get 2 Free Books,
Plus 2 Free Gifts—
just for trying the *Reader Service!*

Get 2 Free Books,
Plus **2** Free Gifts—
just for trying the Reader Service!

❋ HARLEQUIN *Desire*

Get 2 Free Books,

Plus 2 Free Gifts—

just for trying the

Reader Service!

HARLEQUIN

SPECIAL EDITION

H5E17R2